MW01531917

RENEGADE

The Warrior

C. L. Rossman

Bloomington, IN

Milton Keynes, UK

AuthorHouse™
1663 Liberty Drive, Suite 200
Bloomington, IN 47403
www.authorhouse.com
Phone: 1-800-839-8640

AuthorHouse™ UK Ltd.
500 Avebury Boulevard
Central Milton Keynes, MK9 2BE
www.authorhouse.co.uk
Phone: 08001974150

This book is a work of fiction. People, places, events, and situations are the product of the author's imagination. Any resemblance to actual persons, living or dead, or historical events, is purely coincidental.

First published by AuthorHouse 7/5/2006

ISBN: 1-4259-1784-4 (sc)

Printed in the United States of America
Bloomington, Indiana

This book is printed on acid-free paper.

Dedicated to my husband, Gary, for continually encouraging me, to my son John, who first enjoyed "the Renegade stories," And to my parents: my father, Stanley Choskey for believing in me, and to my mother Marcella Choskey, for being my best promoter, along with my brother, Cornel.

PROLOGUE

The beast fled through its mountain caves and the hunter pursued it. Sometimes he had room to run upright; sometimes he had to crawl on hands and knees through narrow tunnels where the rock tore at him. And he knew, he always knew, that even though the Beast fled now, it could turn at any moment and charge him. It was bigger and stronger and faster than the young hunter; and if he couldn't stop it, it would slaughter everyone who lived on this lonely world.

Suddenly the cave opened out into a huge hollow room with a series of rough stone ledges descending to its center. As Renegade straightened and stood, he could not see the beast anywhere. But then, no-one could. Its light-shifting coat concealed it from the eye.

All he had in his arsenal was knowledge, and little of that. He knew the beast's name: It Gets Behind You.

And from that he fashioned his defense.

As he descended into the pit, he felt something watching him from behind. He felt it loom—and he fired.

Three blue-white bolts hissed through the darkness. A terrible howl rose at his back. Three solid hits—from the laser mounted ***backwards*** *on his shoulder.*

The Gets Behind You fell, knocking Renegade to the ground as it died.

***

Later, back at the freehold, bombarded by praise and adulation and honor, Renegade felt relieved it was over. He had come here not knowing what he would face; but he had faced it, challenged it and done what he had to do. He had survived his Master Hunt, triumphant; and because of it, he'd won his rite of passage, his lifelong title of Esteemed Hunter, and the respect of his people.

None of this mattered to him now. Later, he might ponder it.

But now all he could think of was his two friends, undergoing their own ordeal on separate worlds. And he could only hope they would make it out alive.

He trusted them to do it. He believed in them. But Chance always haunted your foot-trace, ready to throw you down. On this hunt, Chance had intervened as the Nine Systems Hunt Council, who were jealous of the young hunters' clan-raised teacher Broken Spear, and who had given his three students terrible hunts against mighty beasts which had defeated even experienced adult hunters.

Just let us succeed, Renegade prayed, so we can blunt our enemies' lance and they won't trouble us any more.

The Warrior

In the end, it is more important to live with honor than to die for it.

---Dreamseeker's Journal

Strike hard, strike fast, strike home.

---'The Way of the Warrior,"
By Gracean d'ilde,
10th Century Marsh Clan

Expect no honor from the prey.

--- Hunt Law

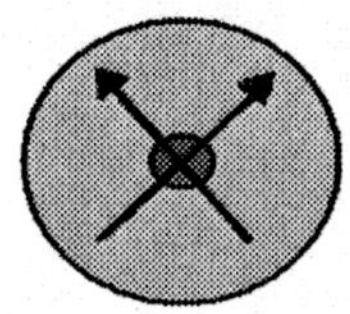

One...Messages

"HO! RENEGADE! Anything on the requests today?" Rampage came into the study from the baths, his long smoke-gray mane hanging wet and glistening down his back. He'd been growing it longer for the past year.

"No, nothing." Renegade was sitting at the comset, flicking through the messages onscreen. He was trying to find a near-port starship which might be bound for new worlds this winter, and which might have an open berth or two. "Just the standard traders and freighters – and the Hunt Council hasn't done much about our applications for berths, either."

"Well, you know their 'unbiased' director has ignored everything we've sent out. He would rather we fade away into our little freehold here." Rampage gave a bitter laugh.

"No trouble," Renegade reassured him; "Broken Spear says if we can't find anything, we'll take the school ship out this winter any-route, and cruise around the star systems looking for adventure."

"He does? Prime!" Rampage enthused. Since his Master Hunt, he'd remained at the school. He and Renegade helped Broken Spear teach a record enrollment of new students, for the first time male *and* female, while the two plotted the course of their own lives. There had been no opposition from Rampage's parents when he announced he was going to live at the hall: they had two other sons to rear, after all. Sometimes in his worst moments, Rampage believed they were glad to be rid of him...

Didn't matter, he told himself. He'd rather be *here* than anywhere else.

Renegade was responding to their conversation, though, not his thoughts, so Rampage listened:

His friend chuckled. "Grandfather says he'd rather not spend another winter on this benighted world if he can get away instead; so we may as well go hunting in warmer climates. *Krr*...and there's a message here from Dasrylion, too."

"On-stat. How's our Cold Tracker doing? Does he think he'll make it back in time for winter and our hunting trip?"

Dasrylion was the first break in their triad: since their Master Hunt ceremony, his father had put him to work watching the local herds, and immersed him in the day-to-day tedium that preceded the excitement of the Autumn Drives. Dasrylion did it, but without enthusiasm. It was not his path in life and he had no passion for it. He'd rather be with his friends. Then Broken Spear spoke to Rydderrak Clan on Homeworld about giving his star tracker a throw at rainforest beasts, and Dasrylion sprang at the chance to visit and do some trapping there.

"I don't know if he'll turn his trail in time or not," Renegade replied. "He says he'll try. But he was so happy to get away from herd-duty and off to Homeworld that he might make an expedition of it till spring – our spring," he corrected.

"I'll miss him – I miss the days when we were all together," Rampage said rather wistfully. It was a new quality of his, this ability to be open, at least with his friends, which he had learned while with the Dinosaur Clan. He'd been injured there in his Master Hunt; and they had saved him.

"I do too," Renegade said. "Sometimes I wonder if there isn't some way we could all be together, keeping our pack together for the rest of our lives... Still, he's doing what he wants to, while we can't seem to take the trail."

"Oh, I have *my* life on the right path, Esteemed Warrior," Rampage drawled. "It's my aim to cover myself in glory – and major trophies – for the next four years, then go back to the Dinosaur Clan and lay them all at K'orrynia's feet."(The young shaman he'd met during his healing.)

"T'chak!" his friend retorted. "How could I forget? You've only been telling me this all year, every chance you had. Still, after all this trophy-laying, what are you going to do next? Stay here? Move there? Bring her with you? If her father allows her to leave, that is."

"We'll choose the path when we come to it," Rampage said serenely.

"Truly spoken like a *tautsche* in love!" Renegade snorted at him, then pulled back. "Ah, I'm sorry, brother. I act as if I'm jealous; and I'm not, really, not of your happiness...I'm just..."

"At knives' point yourself," Rampage finished for him. "Bad Chance you weren't old enough for that huntress – what's her name---?"

"Kyva. Yes."

"Kyva. On your Master Hunt world. It'll be on-stat. You'll find someone else." Rampage had become impulsively kinder, at least to his friends, as he became impulsively less angry. He could offer comfort now.

Renegade's two best friends knew about his *ashe-kvar,* giving the warrior's gift of a child to Kyva and her new husband Stands Fast after he'd saved their people from a terrible beast. Unable to keep such a momentous secret from his close-chosen, Renegade had ended up telling them. Expecting gibes, he was blessedly surprised to receive expressions of awe and wonder instead. Now, before Renegade could protest that he didn't *want* anyone else, Rampage hurried on to add,

"Wasn't her baby due about a tenday ago? Have you heard anything yet?"

The gold-and-grey hunter rubbed his jaw line reflectively. "Nothing yet. I suppose even hyperlight communication takes a little time."

"Have you *sent* them a message lately?" Rampage pressed him.

"Rrr—ah, no; I – I've been busy…I didn't think of it." He looked rueful.

"So there you are. Missed your throw. Do it, brother. We still have time to get a message back before we shut down for the winter and head outbound. I'll even sit here and watch you until you do." Rampage parked himself across from the console and fixed Renegade with a mock glare.

His friend laughed. "Yes, Elder. Right away, sir…oh, and why don't I send a second one while I'm on the track, to your light-o-love, and tell her how you're long in the jaw for h –" and ducked, laughing, as a wet fur cloth came sailing at him….

***

"WE WILL FLY to these two newer systems first, at 55 and 60 lightyears. They have three worlds suitable for our hunt: a so-called 'temperate' one similar to Arvien 4, a larger, more humid one like Homeworld, and a rather small arid one, like the desert, only cooler, with thinner air."

Broken Spear showed them a three-dimensional star map on his wide-screen monitor. "They were found on survey, and then passed by for livelier planets on the galactic arm itself."

He glanced up at the two young men. "In the other direction, we find the Dinosaur World *here,* and the P'taal system *here,* both part of the original Nine Systems. We may visit them after we swing by and pick up Dasrylion from Homeworld. That will give each of you time to see to some personal matters." He smiled and leaned back.

"Good!" cried Rampage; "I can see K—uh, the clan hunter Flashing Sky. I have some more furs for him in exchange for that spear."

"And see K'orrynia," smiled Broken Spear, making Rampage blush.

"*Churr-urr,* K'orrynia too," he admitted.

"That spear must be repaid ten times over," Renegade said. "Haven't you shipped about half of everything you hunted or trapped last winter out to Dinosaur Clan and K'or—rrr, Flashing Sky?" Renegade was not above teasing Rampage himself.

"Well, yes," Rampage replied with great dignity; "But he says he can get me some nice trades going with the excess. And did you tell Broken Spear you heard from P'taal 5 – or should I call it 'Renegade Freehold' now?" Rampage neatly deflected the questioning with an expression too sweet to be real.

"T'churr! No. Elder, the baby's been in the world a tenday now…" and his mentor looked up in delight.

"Stands Fast and Kyva say it's a little boy," Renegade went on, his eyes shining, "and he's marked on the back like them – like me, too – Marsh Clan and Cloud Forest.. But down the throat line and sternum he has one black stripe like me, and black spots on the chest. They're going to try and send a holopix soon…and they're calling him Blackstripe, till he earns his one true name."

"So maybe our Esteemed Warrior would like to divert and see to *his* 'personal matter' as well, *churr?"* Rampage put in wickedly.

"Rampage –"

"Esteemed Hunters," their teacher cut in. "I would address you as 'boys' but you have outgrown all of this; so I will tell you merely that anything further will earn you both two extra *tare'* of combat exercises."

They sobered up. "Yes, Elder," and "Yes, sir," came back all innocence, and Broken Spear had to turn away to keep a straight face.

***

THEY STOPPED at Nine Systems' space station to pick up extra supplies. Rampage could at last afford his coveted golden armor. It had been made to order. He would make final payment and pick it up today.

The station had grown during the five years they had been visiting it. Distant colonies had grown, others had sprung up; and new products and trade items became available. Two new "satellites" had been constructed in near-space. One housed a gigantic research complex. The old research lab had been moved out of the hospital and expanded to process more data and specimens from the out-worlds. The House of Healing would take over

The young hunters looked bewildered.

"Keep doing what, honored trader?" Renegade asked him.

"He means how you can keep hunting and trapping animals without driving them out of existence, do you not, good trader?" Broken Spear put in.

At his chinlift, the old warrior explained, "What most of our Starborn folk don't realize is that hunters are not indiscriminate killers. We learned some hard lessons on Homeworld and now we apply them to our new worlds. We watch the populations of different species carefully, and take only the surplus animals that are usually the spring-issue. In other seasons, we take only unwary males and barren females. If a species is diminishing, we do not hunt it until its population grows again."

"And we have game reserves, too," Renegade added, "where no hunting of any kind is allowed; so all the animals have a safe haven."

"*Chak,*" his teacher agreed, "At the same time, our own outworld populations are limited, as you probably know, He-walks-lightly. For example, Arvien 4's total allowable population is set at 250 million. That is determined by the Hunt Council as the safest upper limit which the planet can comfortably support, which the prey there can sustain. And our present population there is – Renegade? Rampage?"

"Twenty million, in six large habitats," Renegade said promptly; "and that's giving every single family or holder there four to five *kri-veh*[*] of personal hunting territory and a homesite of their own."

"While the rest is set aside as reserves and public hunting land. We get the large herds for our winter meat from public land; and trophy hunters can use the same land to hunt without trespassing on somebody's holding," Rampage chipped in.

He-walks-lightly looked impressed. "You certainly know your profession. I am not much more than a sport hunter, myself, and not even that, any more…" he gave an almost inaudible sigh. "I rely on hunters to bring me meat, like the rest of the station."

"For which you supply them with some fitted clothing, finished leathers, and cloth, I believe," Broken Spear put in, "as well as run this shop as a personal sideline offering manufactured goods."

"Yes; yes in truth, Great Warrior. We put in our hideshare along with the rest of the shop owners. A complex system, yet it works," the trader agreed. "But I stand here cloud-talking – let me get on to the valuation."

---

[*] One *kri-veh* is equal to about two miles or 3 K. clr

While he figured out a fair exchange rate for the furs, Broken Spear asked for information:

"We are outbound to the Ar'raked'dikan and R'shba systems on our far-hunt, good trader; and I wonder if you have heard anything of them recently?"

"A *veren-tautsch*?" The trader's eyes lit up. "Now there's an adventure for you! Let me remember…

"Yes, *tyr rakash,* I have heard something. There was a settlers' ship of 150 souls outbound for R'shba 3 recently – perhaps one year ago, star-time – but nothing seems to have been heard from them since. In truth, I believe the Six Systems Hunt Council made tie at this station not one quarter ago, asking for a Hunt Ship to investigate. I don't know how much of a pack they put together or when it was set to breaktie, Elder. But there may have been some trouble there."

Suddenly he had the entire interest of all three hunters focused on him; and the trader shivered slightly under the weight of that triple stare.

"We will talk further to the stationmaster then," Broken Spear remarked, his tone quite level and calm, though his eyes smoldered "Perhaps they can use our help as well."

More to defuse that terrible attention than anything else, the trader swallowed and said, "And, ah, I have good news, too." He turned aside to take something from a low cabinet.

"Your friend Cold Tracker sent these," he said. "I just received them yesterday, with the message: *Give my friends greetings along with this gift*," he smiled, "*and let them know I am enjoying myself.*"

Renegade laughed. "Good old Dasryl!" and the other two smiled with him, their intensity broken.

The opened bundle revealed a pile of brilliantly-colored –

"Feathers! Birdskins!" Rampage cried in delight. "And look at the colors!" A quick glance at He-walks-lightly gave him permission to touch, and he stroked them gently.

Broken Spear bent to look. "Ah. There are many bright-feathered birds on Homeworld. They thrive in the rainforest; and some of my clan even keep them as pets, for they can mimic our speech."

"They can talk?" Renegade asked.

"Yes; but we think they do not understand what they say…still, no one really knows."

To the Plains hunter he said, "Rampage, these may make a fine gift."

"Gift? Chak!" Rampage got the message. "He-walks-lightly, can these be made into a…" he hesitated…

"Perhaps a half-cape," his teacher suggested, "for a young huntress."

"Ah, a young huntress! On-course, *vr'*hunter." The trader seemed relieved at the more normal subject. "About her: how tall would you say she is? And what are her clan designations, if any?"

While Rampage was occupied with that, Renegade had an idea.

"Grandfather, would it be out-of-track if I sent a present to the baby?"

"A birth-gift? No, I think it would be most appropriate and welcome," his elder reassured him.

So the young masters ended up trading some of their smaller furs and one Sloth-bear hide for two special gifts: a hand-stitched half cape of gold, white and copper feathers, cinched with a gold chain at the neck; and a baby slumber-bag with hood, made of white thermo-lite, that excellent winter cloth, to be hand-decorated in green, gray, black and gold designs If He-walks-lightly thought they matched Renegade's own colors, he did not mention it.

"There," he said, after writing up the description and bills of lading and shipping; "We should have these ready and sent out by the end of a fiveday, honored ones, so you don't have to come back for them yourselves."

"Good throw!" they told him; and Renegade resolved that after this he would send as many gifts to his unseen son as he could. White winter furs and even well-tanned leathers might be appreciated.

"I'm sorry I can't leave the other Sloth-bear hides," Rampage said, "but I need them as the last payment on something at the weapons store."

"No trouble, Esteemed Hunter," the trader replied. "I will get enough on the one to pay for all my costs, and a profit besides. Your patronage means a great deal to me, you know."

They thanked him rather self-consciously and left the shop, making their way on through the corridor.

Rampage strode eagerly toward the weapons shop and armory, but Renegade dropped back to talk to Broken Spear:

"He-walks-lightly is sometimes a little awed and a little –cautious– of us, isn't he?" He didn't want to say "afraid." The trader was a friend.

"You've hit a favorite target of mine, Renegade," his elder replied. "Each one of us is a carnivore, a born hunter; yet some *tautschen* deny their own natures. They don't even know they sublimate the instinct under the guise of 'a sharp trade' or as 'the pursuit of knowledge,' but it is still hunting.

"We need to deal with who we are. That is why I advocate the true hunting skills, and actual hunting, for everyone. It's done in the clans; and whatever their faults, the clans have produced fine hunters and warriors with a code of moral conduct and honor for generations.

"No," he continued, "He-walks-lightly must someday come to terms with his true nature – with who he really is – in a non-lethal way, I hope. He is a good man. But here is Rampage in his new finery. Look."

"Look at this! Isn't it prime?" Rampage crowed as they came up. He'd made the last payment on his golden armor and immediately put it on. He had a full breast plate, a central backplate, thigh guards, and an unusual kind of face shield. He had equally gold over-boots to go with it. The armor was made in segments and flexed freely with his movements.

"Ho, brother, you look good," Renegade complimented. "Are those new boots, too?'

"Well, they're sort of shin-shield and arch cover demi-boots so I can still get a clawhold," and he wiggled his toes to demonstrate. Slit openings in the covering leather allowed his toeclaws to protrude. "This armor is really hi-tech, but the color and look are modeled after spearhorn, on Homeworld."

"Haa—aah." Broken Spear was somewhat skeptical of things masquerading as what they were not, but he withheld any criticism. "You look resplendent, Rampage; you traded a clan leader's share of your catches for this…and what of the facemask? Is that a laser built in?"

"A *double* laser mount," Rampage pointed out, "on either side of the head – you don't have to aim the center mount on this, Elder – just look and shoot."

"Just sight and fire…it would make the shot nearly instant; and thus one should be doubly sure of his target," the old warrior murmured. But he didn't want to lessen Rampage's moment. "You do look splendid, son. You have earned your new armor."

"I'm honored," Rampage remembered to say. He preened a little more before he conceded it was Renegade's turn:

His friend traded a small-bear skin and skull and a large swamp dweller's colorful beaded hide for a laser with greater power and range, and some wrist-rockets. Rampage urged the shop owner to throw in a pair of studded part-gloves too.

"You ought to get some tougher body-armor," he told his friend. "Even Dasrylion has that, and he's just running a trap line."

"There is merit in what he says, son." Broken Spear unexpectedly sided with Rampage.

"I know, I know," Renegade confessed, "but I can't move freely with the heavy armor on; it's too stiff. And on short-throw I can't afford the ultralight." (There are no naturally-armored large beasts on Arvien 4, except the swamp dweller; and Renegade had only the one hide.)

"Well, maybe we'll bring back some real prizes from our expedition, then you can buy some," Rampage concluded.

Renegade allowed that he might.

***

THEY SPENT three full days at the space station, longer than they ever had before. But now they were outfitting a serious hunt, and they must make certain they had everything they needed. They slept aboard the school ship after the first day and returned to the station for the second, where Broken Spear planned to talk to the stationmaster and some star-captains he knew.

The stationmaster confirmed that no contact had been made with the R'shba freeholders for more than a year.

"We encourage the settlements to call in at least twice during their new world's year even if they don't need supplies," he told the hunters. "But after 500 days, we decided it ran long past reason to expect a half-year report – perhaps even a full-year report. So the new Six Systems Council came here to enlist aid from Nine, since their own population is still low.

"They raised twenty of the best trophy hunters they could find on short-throw," he continued, "and broke tie here a full tenday ago, Homeworld time. I expect they are just making planetide, Elder; they are supposed to call us from orbit above R'shba 3."

"I see," said Broken Spear. "Perhaps you could tell them we will be in their quadrant when they do call. We will visit the Ar'raked'dikan system first. It may be a shipboard accident or just an oversight at R'shba, *t'd'faal*."

"True," the stationmaster replied; "We've had a number of those over the years, by the Nine! I'm honored by your concern, Great Warrior. I'll relay your message."

The small company thanked him, and Broken Spear led them next to the Pilots' Berth, a hearth-type room where the star-captains and crew lingered during short planetides. Here they could sit and talk in quiet comfort, with a glass or two of citrus or berry wine.

"A lot of them know him, don't they?" Rampage whispered to his friend, as the old warrior was greeted by captain after captain.

"Somehow I'm not surprised," Renegade smiled.

The two young hunters stood in for their share of welcome, though. And this time Renegade *was* surprised, for several of the captains seemed to know about them and about him in particular:

"Where have you been keeping these fine new Master Hunters, T'akaion, and one already a warrior, too? Are they the New Hunters? Well-met, lads; we have berths available, and stars to sail," one faded yellow and brown veteran said heartily. "Come adventuring with us!"

While the young men exchanged startled glances, their teacher said with some asperity, "They would have be pleased to sail with you – any of you – but our requests have gone unheard; so we mounted an expedition ourselves."

"Unheard? Not by us! By the Hunt Council?"

"Unthinkable! And yet from what I heard…"

"How your three were set against the worst of untried beasts in their Master Hunts, and yet they succeeded…"

"And some extraordinary trail-talk about their ceremony."

"—one who calls himself the Director *and* a hunter, yet can do *this*. Time for a change, I say!"

"Aroh!"

They might have had an insurrection right there and then, if the old warrior had not calmed them and told them they could call his station direct on Arvien 4 next time they needed a hunt crew.

Here are non-hunters who have a code of honor, Renegade thought; *if I weren't what I am, I would be a star captain instead.* He took an immediate liking to them, from grizzled veteran to eager young pilot. He felt a kinship to them.

He saw a new clan here today, a blend of blue on green, or green-blue over yellow. Although the star captains obviously came from many clans and mixes, this pattern dominated.

They seemed just as interested in him and Rampage as he was in them; and the game hunters spent a few *tare'* with the star-hunters, exchanging stories.

Rampage never failed to be thrilled by the attention his rank and accomplishments brought him; but the admiration and respect which his double title earned Renegade always seemed to amaze him. It had been a hard hunt to him, nothing more; though he was beginning to realize just what he had done for the people of P'taal 5, and to wonder how he could possibly live up to it in the future.

As they talked, flights were called; a ship loaded here and there; others arrived; and their gathering began to dissolve. Cordially and with respect, they bid each other not "good hunting," but "safe harbor," and "safe home."

The three hunters left the Pilots' Berth.

"So; we have learned something else here," Broken Spear told his former students. "That your requests were never passed along by the head of Nine Systems' Hunt Council. The director's bias against me is one thing, but to deliberately break all ethical law against you, just for being my students!" The length of his great strides increased and his eyes turned to fire.

The Hunt Council Director, the two youngsters felt, had better tremble.

By the time they reached the dining area, Broken Spear had his rage under control and managed not to brood about it over main-meat. He deflected his anger into thinking about how different it might be if the planetary Hunt Councils had more autonomy in working with the space bases.

To distract him as much as anything, Renegade and Rampage talked about trivial things.

"Let's see what you bought at the information shop," Rampage asked his friend.

"*Krr—rr…*a book, an old one. Here," Renegade pulled it out of his pack.

It was an actual bound volume, not an electronic one, and Rampage turned it over, looking for the title. "*Compendium of the Clans:* I didn't know you were interested in this, Renegade."

"Nor did I," Broken Spear said. "Your parents had the opposite view, you know. They came to Arvien 4 to make what they felt was a life free of clan restrictions."

"I know, Grandfather," Renegade said, feeling he had to apologize; "But I've never seen anyone who looks so much like me until I went to P'taal 5; and now there are those star captains today: the light blue and green colors look like some sort of clan."

"They are. Sea Clan. More of our ocean voyagers became star voyagers than perhaps any other clan." Broken Spear told him. "Only hybrids outnumber them. As for P'taal 5, that would be both your father's former tribe, the Marsh Clan, and your mother's, the Cloud Forest Clan."

"I'm sorry, Grandfather; I crave pardon. I should have asked you first."

Broken Spear waived it. "I take no offense, son. I never knew you were interested in your own background. You did not ask about it before; and I thought I was following your parents' wishes."

I've been a fool, Renegade thought. *Here is the best source on clan history I could have, and I never asked him.* "I still crave your pardon, Elder."

"Please, Renegade, I am not insulted and I am not angry – and that is a book I would be interested in, myself, after you finish it."

So after-meat evolved into a pleasant lesson for the young hunters. Renegade learned that the Marsh Clan, his father's people, first lived in the great freshwater swamplands on Homeworld, later following the major rivers down to the brackish marshes near the sea and adapting their lifestyle there.

As for his mother, he noticed that Broken Spear spoke of Kr'ra'klv'tt with genuine affection and regret. He himself remembered without pain now how she had run with him to class that last day, and how the old hunter had asked her to critique his students. Then both his parents died in a hunting accident.

"The Clan of the Cloud Forest, the tropical high mountain forest, is hers," his mentor said. "The members have that beautiful reticulated or 'clouded' pattern on their backs, which becomes the spots, stripes and dapples of the Plains People further north. You saw the old star captain who first spoke to you? He has that heritage. It comes out as the round black spots and the stripe on your chest, Renegade, while the gold and grey comes from your father's Marsh coloring.

"The fact that so many clans share similar patterns teaches us that not only are we one People, from one stock, but also that our separation in different habitats occurred not long ago in geologic time," he said.

Despite himself, Rampage began to be interested. "What about me, Elder?"

"Ser'rk'saa-na or Plains is your Homeworld clan," Broken Spear told him. "No. you're not a hybrid, Rampage; you just didn't inherit the patterns you might have...black, brown, white, and tan, overlain with stripes, dapples or rosettes. Some families are so striking, their subclan is known as the Dappled Grass."

"And I turned out so plain," Rampage said miserably.

"I would say you turned out to be someone *new*." Broken Spear corrected him. "You were born on a new world, after all. You are tall and thin and fast on your feet, like all your kin, but with a single-shade coloring. You are unique, Rampage. Perhaps you represent Arvien's future."

And morose as he was about his plainness, Rampage felt a little heartened by that.

As they relaxed after eating, Broken Spear told them that Flashing Sky, Dinosaur Clan's Chief Hunter, came from the People of the Shadowed Forest, or Shadow Clan, as they called themselves.

"A clan with an excellent night hunting tradition," he said, "they live in the deepest parts of the coniferous forest, hunting beasts which are some of the best furbearers on Homeworld. Most clan members, like Flashing Sky, are deep ebony with an overlay of stripes, splashes and dapples of silver and white, more rarely copper and gold. Their eyes and manes also stand out in contrast to their base color. They are as beautiful as High Sun's people, and they have suffered no similar tragedy."

Other diners were arriving, filling the alcoves, and Renegade had time for only one more question:

"How many clans are there, Grandfather?"

"On Homeworld, sixteen major ones plus a few groups claiming that title, and a number of subclans within the larger ones, such as Riverbank in mine," he answered. "But I have no doubt that thanks to our outward movement, in future we shall see many more on the different worlds as we adapt to them."

Finally they gave the old warrior some peace, and left their alcove for their bunks in the school ship. But Renegade found that the brief description only whetted his appetite for more. He skimmed through his book before sleeping that night…

***

TO THE HUNT---Nineteen *tare'* later, the school ship left safe harbor for the stars beyond. She still carried only a crew of three – Dasrylion sent a message that he had injured his foot on Homeworld and would not be able to join them after all, much to their disappointment. But Broken Spear kept them busy so they wouldn't dwell on it.: Renegade had to fix a course for the Ar'raked'dikan system and Rampage would pilot the ship out of its berth at the station.

"Time to put learning to life," he told them; "Next planetide, you change places."

Two....Star Hunters

THE SHIP popped out of hyperspace within laser-shot of a sere and beautiful world. A deep ruddy color, the planet had three large moons and a ring of glowing light around it. The huge curve of its horizon nearly filled the viewscreen.

"Well-thrown, honored crew!" their mentor teased them. "A little closer and you could have practiced your emergency landing techniques! Now, Renegade, calculate a higher orbit for us: find the system's center of gravity; and Rampage, you put us there."

They ascended to a higher orbit and Broken Spear asked them for input.

"That's ferrous dust down there," Renegade said; "iron oxide. This world is rich in minerals, and not too generous with oxygen. I read that the Six Systems Hunt Council once considered it for an ore-smelting site."

"Except for – Rampage?"

"Except for its few species of life," Rampage answered. He never liked being called on to recite, but you had to do it with Broken Spear. "Some creatures live just under the soil here. A few of them are some kind of floating gasbags, even in this thin air."

"Very good. Esteemed Hunters, to your gear."

***

NOT ONLY did they have to use their masks to collect more oxygen to breathe, but they found that the lower gravity lent them unexpected buoyancy.

"Natural power jumps," Renegade laughed, bounding past Rampage like someone in slow motion, like swimming underwater.

"Remember to account for that when you are walking about or tracking prey," their mentor warned. "It will be faster but weaker than you are, here."

They left the school ship sealed and shuttered atop its flat rock mesa ("On sand, seek hard ground," Broken Spear told them) and got aboard the Scout to look around.

"Now," the old warrior said after they closed the Scout's canopy and re-pressurized, "we'll do a slow air-search. Renegade, take the helm."

He did, and the little ship lifted smoothly in a slow arc over red sands and purple mesas.

"It might be a desert, but it's beautiful," Renegade said.

"Beautiful but dead-looking," Rampage remarked. "It looks as barren as an asteroid."

"Recall: the main lifeforms are underground," Broken Spear said. "If this were a standard trophy hunt, you would each go off by yourself to roam this world. But it's been a long time between voyages for me; so I believe I shall go sight-seeking with you."

They soon found something interesting.

"Look there," Renegade pointed. The edge of rusty sand stopped suddenly, and a vast round hollow yawned below.

"A…valley?" Rampage asked. "Odd shape."

"Maybe an old meteor crater," Renegade guessed; "*Br-rt*! Look at the floor!"

The almost flat floor seemed to be webbed with a series of fine cracks or lines.

"Ground water – or moisture, any-route," Renegade said. "Remember the desert?"

"How could I forget? This is even more barren," Rampage said. "The books says there's game down there, Elder, but how are we going to get at it – dig a hole?"

Their mentor smiled mysteriously. "Perhaps…and perhaps not;" which didn't satisfy Rampage.

Renegade was flying the Scout along the cliff faces which etched the crater's sides. He thought he'd check the perimeter first, then dissect the bowl itself at a lower altitude.

Something burst from the cliffs like a flight of dry leaves.

"What's that?" Rampage cried out. "There they go! Chase 'em, Renegade!"

His friend banked the ship hard and dived. But it was like trying to catch leaves blown by a hurricane. He cut in; they zipped under. He dove; they whipped high. He wasn't helped by Rampage's excited, "No! Left, left! -- Dive, no, *there* they go! You missed them!"

"Mind the cliff!" Broken Spear roared – and Renegade heeled the Scout up and over, then braked sharply. His companions hit the restraining straps.

"Vascht! Sorry, your pardon, Elder, Rampage," he said, flustered. He'd forgotten one of the primal rules: *Watch,* and almost rammed them into the rocks.

When Broken Spear felt his stomach settle, he remarked, *"That, vr'*hunters, is the prize trophy creature of this planet, the main reason this world is not an ore foundry. Do you know its name?"

"The starbeast!" they both exclaimed at once, Renegade adding, "It flies by air jet, has five or six 'points' and looks like an artist's drawing. And I'd like to see the trophy hunter get close enough on foot to catch one of those."

"It was first photographed with a long-range lens from low-flying starships, not satellites." Broken Spear stirred restively. "Now if you will be so kind as to set this ship down on that flattop dell, I believe I shall wear my coldsuit and camouflage, and watch your hunt from there…No, no more apologies, Renegade; we are all still alive and healthy. On any-path, this is a young man's hunt; you need to maneuver sharply, and *that* will be too much for an old man's stomach. You two are on your own. Remember, take only one animal apiece. That is the Law."

So they left the old hunter on a perch of crimson cliff, wearing his thermal suit, air filter, camo, and shoulder weapon. He bid them "Good hunting," and sat down to watch.

I am growing too old for a young man's hunt, he mused to himself, *especially a thrilling one. This is the beast they should have had for their Master Hunt, testing their skill without being lethal.*

Renegade flew the Scout sedately back to cruise the crater rim.

"That was a stupid thing I did," he admitted, "flying straight at it like that. Let's see if I can do better this time."

Rampage shrugged. "Don't scratch yourself for it. You don't hunt that way alone, do you? Any-route, do you want me to pilot?"

Renegade laughed. "Oh no you don't. I'll finish my run—"

"—Or slam us into the cliff—"

"Or slam us into the cliff. But it'll be a quick death, *churr?* And after that you can take your throw. Why don't you fly 'catcher' this time,

Rampage" – referring to the capture equipment on the outside of the ship...*if we ever see another one of those starbeasts,* he thought.

Rampage took Second Seat willingly, locating the levers to extend the capture jaws on the ship's bow. While he practiced with them, he heard Renegade muttering to himself:

"Starbeast? What do we know? That it isn't really dangerous, but very fast and elusive... that it hangs from the cliffs in daytime...ah, that's it."

"What's it?"

"It hangs from *sunlit* cliffs in daytime, to help its central heating organs. So we can look for it on the sun-side of the crater." And he banked them in the opposite direction. They passed Broken Spear's outpost again, but the old hunter was invisible now, camouflaged.

"What else?" Renegade said as he banked the Scout on edge, its clear dome toward the cliffside. "They fly by a kind of ramjet propulsion; and they *spin* on their central axis, with air-jets out of each arm's point. That's why they can turn so fast."

"What do they eat?" Rampage asked. "Don't they catch their food on the fly?"

"Churr; they have sharpened knobs on the arms and they knock other creatures out of – There!"

A flight of starbeasts – perhaps the same one – broke from the cliff. Renegade skewed the agile little craft between them and cover, and this time tried to drive them out over open ground.

It took every *t'mearn* of skill and reaction time he had, because as soon as the creatures realized they were being herded, they dove, veered or dodged around him and back towards shelter. Rampage forgot himself and began yelling directions again to the straining pilot. The Scout ship plunged, lifted, zigzagged in high-speed pursuit.

It was a wild ride.

Broken Spear watched the little craft skittering madly across the sky like a bug on a pond, and roared with laughter. Sometimes he winced. But mostly he laughed, enjoying the chase with them.

"Go, lads! Live life!" he saluted them from his rock. "Feast and celebrate."

The Scout was changing its tactics. The capture bars slid forward. Their metal jaws opened.

Broken Spear wiped a tearing eye under his mask. "Oho lads, not that way! Ah well, you'll learn." And he leaned forward, chuckling to himself.

Now the Scout ship lowered *under* the starbeast flight. Once in position, it shot up straight at them, and the startled creatures broke to either side – except for one. The capture jaws closed.

"Well-shot. Too bad..." Broken Spear praised them even as he shook out his mane, laughing helplessly.

For just as the jaws closed on it, the starbeast collapsed on itself, and oozed out of the trap like a deflated bladder.

"H'vack-hah!" Rampage screamed in disbelief, "Look at that – just *look,* Renegade!"

"I see it." Renegade stared at the empty trap and reacted by tilting the ship down, seeking the beast.

The flat sack falling to the ground would have been hard to see by anyone else's eyes; but Renegade homed in and dived for it.

Suddenly – puff! – it filled again and sailed away along the crater floor.

"No you don't!" Renegade cried out. "Rampage! Take the helm!"

"Why? What for? Even if we get close to it – "

"Don't argue, just do it!" Renegade was out of his seat and Rampage into it before he could blink. "I've got an idea." And he fell into Second Seat, hauled in the capture jaws, and began pulling at something on his left arm.

"Whatever you say," Rampage answered sweetly. He'd rather do this any-route; he was *sure* he could outfly the thing.

"Cut it off! Don't let it regroup!" Renegade shouted at him – not without a smile – *talon on the other toe now, churr?*

"I can – *do* – it," Rampage grunted, cutting hard right, then left. "Oh, sorry, brother."

Renegade had left his seat and been thrown to the floor.

"No trouble. Just keep flying." Renegade was crawling along the floor toward the belly bay hatch. He began unbolting it.

In that moment, Rampage managed to clear the starbeast and drive it away from the wall. He lost track of what Renegade was doing, and the ship's wild jogging and looping kept him busy. He did register the hiss and clank of the hatch being opened, though.

"What's going on? Blast! Get back there!" he shouted as he snarked the machine into some impossible turn, and a whoosh of air whistled through the bay. No answer. "Fine."

Presently: "On-stat, Rampage. Get in close for a catch." There was a creak as Renegade bounced back into his seat.

"I'll get you there; you catch him," Rampage promised. "Jaws first?"

"Yes. Reach for him."

"On-course. Going to be *close"* – and the Scout flipped edgewise, dome toward the cliff, the jaws toward the beast. The starbeast was slightly faster and it was angling in toward the rock. "Make it quick, brother."

"Go!" Renegade shot the jaws out. Something lay between them...

"A net! You got it!" Rampage shouted as he saw the capture net stretched between the skids billow out and snap down over the star.

"We got it. Watch the wall!"

"Yes, Elder." Rampage couldn't resist teasing even as he edged away from the crater rim, narrowly avoiding an outthrust butte. He slowed and floated the Scout over the top.

In the net, the starbeast collapsed again; but this time it couldn't escape.

Rampage whooped, "It's ours!" and extended the Scout's landing gear. Red dust rose in billows around them.

"Nice flying," Renegade complimented.

"Nice *thinking,*" his friend returned.

After carefully inspecting their surroundings, they turned their camo-suits on and dismounted to examine their catch.

The starbeast couldn't keep itself deflated for long. It swelled up again and rattled the heavy net; but it couldn't even spin, much less fly.

It seemed pitiable somehow and Renegade felt for it. "Let's finish this," he said, turning his camouflage off. "It wants to fly. You want it, Rampage?"

Rampage also re-appeared, and made a negative motion. "No; you did most of the hunting. It's yours."

Renegade nodded. He clenched his fist and the knives sprang out. "No real brain or heart – just a central nerve ganglion, right—" his hand poised above the red-loop central markings ... *"—there!"* and stabbed down.

The beast heaved, like a great sigh, rattled the net once more, and went still. Air leaked from it.

"Flat as a scallop," Rampage said, looking down. "You don't like this part much, do you?"

"Not unless I'm hungry, or something's trying to kill me," Renegade admitted. "The chase is more fun." He paused to offer a silent prayer for its spirit.

He unwrapped one corner of the net and jabbed lightly at the beast. Not a quiver. "Dead. Not poisonous, the texts say... it has a little lightweight flexible skeleton, spokes and center of a wheel. We'll have to be careful skinning it." He spoke flatly, which meant he wanted no more prying into his emotions.

That was on-stat with Rampage. He liked uncomplicated moments. He didn't understand his friend's attitude sometimes, but he respected it.

Just then they heard, "Hunters! Bring your catch here!" And there was Broken Spear, visible now, waving at them from his perch not far away. "You are losing daylight; and you need one more!"

"On target we do," Rampage muttered; while Renegade waved back and shouted, "Coming!"

They flew to the high flat butte and landed. Renegade detached the net from the Scout's prongs, and deposited his catch at the old warrior's feet.

"Well thrown," he congratulated them. "A grand chase, is it not? These creatures live in every large crater on the planet. The skinning will keep a while. I believe the flight you were chasing has come to roost *there*, on the dividing line between day and night"—*sunlight and shadow,* he almost said, but bit it back in time. It had been Renegade's mother's name.

"Thank you, Grandfather. I'm sure Rampage wants a trophy too," Renegade said, and they left him.

Since Rampage also wanted more flight time, they kept the same positions as before. The starbeasts were still there, but despite several passes close to them, they refused to bolt.

In frustration, Rampage hovered the Scout directly in front of them and had Renegade extend and retract the capture jaws quickly.

That did it. The starbeasts burst from their holdfast and sprayed around them. This time Rampage took a different tack: he sheered off after one part of the flight and split them again.

"Two in front!" he yelled. He let the smaller one slip by and went after the larger.

And the whole wild ride began again.

Broken Spear watched them maneuver as the shadows lengthened and the deep-blue sky turned violet. If the starbeast was tired, it didn't show it.

Finally the hunters snared the second creature up against the failing sky and flew back with it. Rampage gaffed it, and they skinned both quickly in the failing light. As they had learned as students, the big inflatable star was mostly a gasbag with a delicate radial skeleton; the knobby skin itself was tough and elastic – "a prize worth mounting or trading," Broken Spear remarked.

"Now clean and disinfect it thoroughly," he went on. "We can put the bones in preservative and reconstruct the skeleton later."

Once back in the Scout ship, the three underwent the standard personal cleansing under steam and "above blue" light. They again disinfected themselves, their gear, and the entire Scout, not only to kill any foreign microorganisms (almost none transfer infection to alien hosts), but also to keep the planet's surface as free of introduced bacteria as possible. Wherever they can, the Hunters try to retain original conditions on the planets they visit. Even as they take life, they respect it.

When the hunters finally boarded the school ship and placed their gear in steamer racks, utter blackness pressed against the viewscreen from outside.

"We'll spend the night in orbit," Broken Spear declared. "There is nothing more for us here: the underground animals are dull and slow. Did you enjoy the hunt? Was it enough of a challenge for you?" and he smiled at the way their eyes were shining.

He moved to the master console. "Get seated and strapped-in, please, I need some exercise, so I will do the breaktie myself."

And the two secured themselves while the old hunter began firing up the Bank of Lights, or main control panel. They were a little tired by this time, and happy to let him do the work.

Once underway, Broken Spear dimmed the cabin lights down, letting the planet's moons light their viewscreen. He tipped the ship's nose toward the planet and gave them a stunning overview of white moonlight illuminating dark red mesas and making the sands glow blood. The world's rings could be seen as a faint shimmer near the horizon.

They were so drawn to the sight that at first they didn't notice the red comset light blinking on the console. Broken Spear noticed it first and said, "It seems we have a message."

He reached for the comset controls: "It may be from the colony or the expedition ship..." and *at once* the dire cold of warning fell upon him –

It took all he could do to suppress a groan of real pain, and open the channel. *It's back, and it's bad.*

Rampage looked over to see what was causing the delay, and was stunned to see both the old warrior *and Renegade* staring at the comset "like it was a poisonous snake."

"What? What's the matter?" he asked, puzzled.

"I don't know, but something's wrong," was all Renegade could tell him.

Broken Spear merely sighed, and acknowledged the call: "Hunt Ship 1707, First Sector, receiving your signal. Are you in distress, caller?"

Back came a crackle of static and space noise, scattered with faint words: "...Hunt Ship...this...out... Six Systems...reply."

"Speak again, caller, your signal is broken," the old warrior answered.

"This...1441 out of...Systems...distress...reply..."

Broken Spear stabbed buttons and twisted knobs, to no avail.

"Caller," he said louder, "stand by to receive subspace digital set. Sending..." and he reset the signal.

He leaned back, watching the com. "There. The laser signal is extremely powerful. If they're anywhere nearby, they will be able to fix our position, and may be able to tell us theirs."

They waited. Communication at the speed of light in deep space takes as long as light does to reach anything. The other ship would have to be very close indeed.

Several *kt'tare* stretched into a full *tare'* and still they waited. Broken Spear had the boys help him go over the star system's maps and a long-range 'cast while they waited. He was about to switch back to hyperlight and hope for the best when the computer woke up and began a rapid printout.

"Renegade, can you get that?"

"I have it, Elder. It repeats 'distress' and gives their location…hold, that can't be far from here. Rampage, can you bring up the other planet's position, the habitable one?"

"On-stat. Here it comes." The message and the interpretation flashed across the screen together. It coincided with the second planet of the system, Ar'raked'dikan 2.

"They're in orbit above it," Renegade said. "And no sign of a settlement ship, just the Hunt Ship…"

"Maybe it landed on the wrong planet, here instead of at R'shba; and they just found out," Rampage suggested.

"In another *system?* That doesn't make sense. And this doesn't feel right." Renegade looked at his guardian.

"I agree," Broken Spear said. "Therefore we will observe caution. Rampage, plot us a course to the second planet, but triangulate it with that ship's position. I want you to place us just over the planet's horizon from them until we can find out exactly who they are."

"Yes, Elder," Rampage became as respectful as Renegade.

Their ship coasted out into the night sky. It began a slow spiral outward from the desert world, while Rampage calculated their next jump –

Broken Spear did an unprecedented thing: he armed the ship's laser cannons, set their entries to SEARCH and LOCK.

Then he left his seat to collect and distribute their personal weapons – and one more thing.

The two young hunters looked at him, speechless, when he gave them the ship-detonating triggers, the ones other hunters call the Final Surrender – to be used only in utter defeat – and mortal danger.

"I pray we do not need to use these, but I do not know what waits for us out there," he told them.

***

THE RUSTY desert planet vanished from their screens and was replaced by a silvery-blue globe, as if a picture had been flipped over, front to back, red to silver.

Their computations placed the other ship just over this new planet's 'shoulder.'

"Good," Broken Spear said; "Now let us open the channel, and listen." They could pick up the other ship's signal more easily now.

This time they heard: "Come in, Hunt Ship, come in. This is 1441 out of Six Systems broadcasting…where are you?" and "…I lost them."

It sounded quite ordinary except for the note of despair.

"We shall answer," Broken Spear said. "Watch our flanks, hunters. Be ready to maneuver should this be a trick…Hunt Ship 1441, this is 1707. We stand within moments of you, 1441. Can you transmit your location in subspace, and give us interior visual?"

"Thank the Spirit! Yes. Hold to receive signal."

Renegade and Rampage exchanged a look: that uncharacteristic outburst on 1441's part could only mean deep trouble. The Hunting People are passionate and open with those they know well, but reserved and ritually courteous with strangers.

"So. I shall fly it from here, hunters," Broken Spear told them. "Renegade, Rampage, stand watch over the telemetry system. We will flank Hunt Ship 1441 until we know more about this."

The young men's soft, "Yes, Elder," came taut and ready.

They rounded the planet's curve. And there was the other ship, bright with heat, right where it had promised.

"A standard cruiser," Broken Spear remarked as he positioned them a little above, and nose to broadside, of the other ship.

"Hunt Ship 1441 – this is 1707 – we have arrived. Now let us have the interior visual."

"Ah, we see you. Visual, yes. On-course," the other sounded relieved, even grateful.

"Stand fast," the old hunter murmured to his crew. His own hands rested lightly near both the comset and the weapons' controls.

What they saw on visual shocked their hands away from any touch of weapons.

Inside the other Hunt Ship chaos sprawled. Behind the man at the comset they saw fire-blackened hulls, seating torn and ripped apart and equipment strewn about.

Broken Spear half-rose from his chair. "Great Spirit! What *happened* in there?"

The other hunter glanced behind himself, then turned back to the screen. He had injuries, his right arm and shoulder swathed in wrappings. "We were attacked, *vr'tautsche,* aboard our own ship, by a beast of prey..."

"What manner of beast does this?" asked the old warrior. His Boding weighed on him.

"A new creature, one that apparently destroyed – and devoured – our brothers and sisters on the colony ship we were sent to track. One which has spread itself over an entire world, devouring every living being in its path."

The injured hunter drew a deep breath. "I...we...had to detonate the settlers' ship, all 150 souls aboard – dead to us." (A strange way to put it.)

"*T'chak!*" the old warrior exclaimed. Words left him.

"Even so," the other continued. He sounded very weary. "Several of the creatures got aboard our ship somehow. We left planetide fighting for our lives and they struck us after we were spacebourne."

"And now?"

Pain filled the other hunter's face. "There were five left. We killed two and repulsed the others at great cost. I have six good hunters lying in the healing alcove, unable to move. I and two others remain standing." He indicated right and left at unseen companions. "None escaped injury."

"That's all – nine of 20 experienced hunters survive?' Broken Spear was astonished; the two young men aghast. "You say you *repelled* three of these beasts? Where? How?"

"Another tragedy, honored one. We forced them into one of the Scouts at flame point, not risking lasers or projectiles. We intended to blow off the shuttle and explode it once we were clear, but two of our people were trapped in there with them. They sprang the Scout free, but it did not explode. We tracked it to freefall, down to the planet – *there.*"

Ar'raked'dikan 2, the world below them.

The other hunter made an effort to keep talking. He was on the verge of collapse. "That's why we hoped to raise you, or anyone...Spirit be thanked you came here. Our other shuttle is inoperative. Forgive my discourtesy; but can you aid us?"

"Say no more; we are on the trail," Broken Spear told him. Suddenly he was up and moving. "Renegade, help me with medical supplies and prepare our Scout for launch. Rampage, you stay here – no argument, son; I need your reflexes on Chance we run into trouble aboard that ship. Tell others what we've found here, and *keep* sending it, to Nine Systems

Station and to Six Systems. Let them know everything. Here, Renegade, pack this… Rampage, you set a course one-quarter lightyear outbound of this system, with an auto-stop in deep space. Rig for the Final Surrender. This is something we *don't* want to bring home."

Just as he and Renegade lowered themselves into the Scout, the old warrior gave one last order: "Rampage, wear your best armor and full facemask even here; and if we don't come back, you must – I repeat *must* – get away yourself to warn our people. After the auto-stop, and if you are clear of any 'riders,' you must go on. Rampage, as your elder and teacher, I *order* you to do it. Understand?"

Rampage's lower jaw trembled but he set his teeth and lifted his chin. "I understand, Elder…and…good hunting." He exchanged an anguished look with Renegade.

"Ah, yes!" Broken Spear thundered. "May we have good hunting in truth!"

Moments later, the Scout dropped into space and they were gone.

***

HUNTED AND HUNTER--- Renegade's heart was pounding and his blood racing when they clamped their Scout to the other ship's bay hatch. This vessel was nearly twice the size of their school ship, and they fit to its belly like a fluke to a fish.

"Seal the ship, including pressure hatches and air exchange vents. We want nothing else slipping aboard," Broken Spear ordered. "Are your weapons set? Good." Then, "Son, I don't know what could kill eleven master hunters in a fight, but be prepared for anything. I will exit first."

And he did, in one fluid leap through the double hatches. When his instincts were roused, Broken Spear moved with the agility and ferocity of the great sabretooth itself.

Renegade did his best to imitate him, clearing the opening in a bound. Under his elder's watchful eye, he sealed first the Scout ship's hatch, then the starship's.

The three relatively whole survivors of the massacre waited to meet them. Their speaker, a brown, yellow and gray-splotched hunter, was still standing, if barely. He looked pale and faint from his wounds. His two hunt-mates were not much better off: one was a Shadow Clan hunter, jet-black basal color with silvery broken dashes and spots as an over-pattern, gleaming red-gold mane, and green eyes. The other was a red-over buff hunter reminiscent of Broken Spear's clan. They said their names were Starseeker and Signal Fire.

These two did not seem as badly hurt as the speaker: Starseeker had one thigh bandaged above the knee; Signal Fire had spots of antiseptic and patch-bandages in a peculiar splash pattern on his upper body.

The speaker took one look at Broken Spear and tried to greet him properly: "Great Warrior, I know of you. You and your hunt-mates are welcome here."

Broken Spear, his eyes still scanning the room, introduced his pack in turn. "This is the warrior and Master Hunter Renegade of Arvien 4. Aboard ship is the Master Hunter Rampage. What we lack in numbers we make up for in skill. Esteemed Hunter…?" ending on a question.

"So few, yet another…warrior? Good throw. I – I am called…Singing Spear – of …" and he collapsed into his companions' arms.

"Here, brothers, I'll take him," Broken Spear turned instantly to gentleness and concern, as only he could, and gathered up the fallen hunter.

"Lead us to the healing alcove," he directed the others. "You may explain on the way. No, honored hunter" (to Singing Spear) "rest a span; your fight is ours, now." He gave a quick glance at Renegade, who nodded and brought up the rear flank, medi-kit in hand.

The rest of the Hunt Ship looked as ravaged as its control room. They wove their way through the rubble, between fire-scorched walls, and into a large healing alcove…

Renegade's throat constricted: here were six other strong hunters lying helpless on the tables, their vital signs monitored, all of them swathed in gauze wrappings, a few breathing harshly.

"Great Spirit guide us," he heard Broken Spear whisper as they passed.

"Here, sir," one of the walking wounded told him, and the old warrior placed Singing Spear down on an empty cot.

Two more badly hurt, and this place will be filled, Renegade thought uneasily. He went to the newest victim without being asked and helped Broken Spear carefully peel the arm and shoulder wrappings off.

"You may rest now, also," the warrior told the two other hunters, who hovered nearby; "Rest and talk, while we tend your hunt leader. We need to know what you know."

The dressings on Singing Spear pulled back to reveal ugly seared patches all along his arm. "What are these, burns?" Broken Spear said in surprise. "Antiseptic please, Renegade."

"No, *tyr rakash* – well, of a sort," the Shadow Clan hunter Starseeker told him. "These creatures, they *spew* a strong corrosive. Glands in the mouth are full of it—they spit it out and try to blind and burn you."

"Chak, face one with a vai-ator, knife, or a spear, and its spittle will rot your flesh, like this..." Signal Fire added. He plucked one of his scattered patches off, to reveal another ugly scorch. "Flame is your best weapon."

Broken Spear stiffened. "Tell me more," he demanded, while he held the bandages apart so Renegade could spray antiseptic into the wounds. Singing Spear flinched, but did not cry out.

And he and Renegade learned about a new and deadly enemy:

"Like this," the Shadow hunter pulled a hand-drawn sketch out of his pack and showed it to them. "That's a warrior beast. It fights relentlessly, and it does not retreat."

"It looks like a rack of bones!" Renegade exclaimed, leaning over the picture, "Like a beast made all of bones. And the skin—is it shrunken between the bones?"

"Churr," Starseeker agreed; "We've been calling it a 'bone beast,' but there really is skin stretched tight between those bones, and all of it tough as armor. Ordinary steel does not penetrate it. The corrosive is packed inside the head and jaw and usually spat from the mouth. And see the spiked, shield-shaped head? Beware the long stabbing tongue which comes from that – three *kri* it can shoot out and jab you with a paralyzing -poison different from the other fluid. It's meant to immobilize prey. There is a stinger in the tail, too."

The bone-beast looked all knobbed and armored, with peculiar holes in the skull. A series of flat jet eyes were hooded there; and it stood a tall Hunter's height above the ground. "It can open that rack of ribs once it's stung you, and...carry you off..."

That wasn't the worst thing. The worst was, these creatures used that paralyzing poison to immobilize their prey, and then implanted their living embryos within your body. The embryos developed swiftly inside a paralyzed but still conscious host, and when they were ready to emerge –

"They eat their way out of the still-living host, and feed upon its flesh."

Renegade gasped and Broken Spear nearly did so.

"But surely the different blood chemistries don't mix," the young hunter protested.

"The embryo is protected by a tough but permeable membrane," Signal Fire said. "They can transmute *whatever* species' blood chemistry they foster in so long as it breathes oxygen."

"We discovered this to our sorrow," Starseeker added, his voice heavy. He seemed remote and withdrawn.

Singing Spear roused long enough to say, "They are insatiable, and hermaphrodite. Our settlers ran into a huge den of them on R'shba 3, and we—tracked down what was left of the settlers." A shiver raced down his back. He fell silent.

"We think these creatures have overrun R'shba Three now. They came from nowhere, from blind space, to overtake the planet's native animals," Signal Fire added, "between our first survey of the planet and the settlers' approach…the beast wasn't there ten years ago."

"At that speed..." Renegade began.

"It could subvert the entire galaxy within a few centuries, if allowed to spread," Broken Spear said. Few things awed the old warrior, but the loss of every living creature save one, the loss of all diversity among species, stunned him.

"And you say another Scout ship with three creatures in it, plus your two hunters, crashed onto the world below?"

"Yes; wait, warrior," Singing Spear caught his wrist. "If the beasts—prevailed—they will stack the bodies—possibly in the ship. Time is short, warrior. Leave us, take my hunters, and find them."

"We shall, *vr'*hunter," Broken Spear said crisply, and the other man's hand dropped. Carefully the old hunter replaced the wrappings on his wounds. "I will leave this medi-kit with you. Stand sentinel over the others, if you can; and wait for us: we will send a continuous signal. If our signal fails, detonate the ground ship and head back home. Take our school ship as well."

"I am honored, noble warrior," Singing Spear almost whispered as he sank back down. "I will rise shortly. If not – key a detonator to your wrist set, will you?"

"I will. Rest now," Broken Spear touched his forearm and went to look at the other wounded to see if they were comfortable before he strode out of the room, the three smaller hunters in tow.

Renegade had noticed that Starseeker seemed especially anxious to get moving. His biting teeth were grit, and while he did not panic, desperation shone in his eyes.

They all boarded the Scout and broke-tie to fly to the school ship first. Broken Spear contacted Rampage, telling him to get ready to join them, and rig a detonator signal to both the school and the Scout ships. They could hear the young man's shock through the comset.

Broken Spear explained: "By splitting you two, I had hoped to keep at least one of you alive, if we fail. But if there are three of those beasts to fight, we will need every hunter." He looked long and deep into Renegade's serious green eyes. "Son, I – "

But it was Renegade who reached out, Renegade who said, "Grandfather, don't despair. Our Master Hunts faced us against the worst beasts known, and we prevailed. That will help us against the worst of the unknown, now." He touched his beloved elder's upper arm, and gave the old, old salutation reserved for a near-hopeless fight: "Let fall Chance!"

Broken Spear pressed his wrist hard. "Let fall Chance, Renegade. Great Spirit guide us all."

The hunters behind them murmured it in turn.

In this atmosphere, Rampage came aboard. He grabbed Renegade fiercely, as if he had never expected to see him again, then hastily resumed control when he saw the two strangers present. Renegade filled him in; and the now-somber young hunter exchanged wrist-clasps with the two new hunters and a quick, fierce shoulder clasp with his mentor.

Then they descended.

Three...Victory or Death

MOUNTAINS AND FORESTS unrolled beneath them; rivers and lakes flashed the sun's spear back at them. Except for the grayish-green cast of this world's vegetation, it could have been Arvien 4.

Did all worlds look something like his own if their size and atmosphere were similar? Renegade wondered. He watched as they coursed over the continents, homing in on the lost Scout's signal. What of Broken Spear? How much did the loss of a world like R'shba 3, so like Homeworld, mean to him? Now this one stood on knife-point as well...

The Shadow Clan hunter Starseeker brooded over other questions.

"Life is so thin a sinew, so easily snapped," he murmured, his eyes fixed to the viewscreen, his agitation mounting. He controlled it well, but it was there.

He glanced at Renegade as if he recognized a kindred soul, "You, young warrior and you, *vr'* hunter" (to Rampage) "on this hunt we shall discover who will prevail – the Hunter or the Beast."

Renegade gave him a slow chinlift of agreement.

A silence grew. Then –

"There it is. I read a ship by that waterfall, near the top," Broken Spear said, so very calm now. He arced the Scout down. "Hunters, prepare. The game awaits us."

He touched down about 100 *kri* farther along the embankment, on a clear patch of stony ground. No moving life-forms showed anywhere.

"Secure all hatches and vents as we leave," the old hunter ordered. "Internal security on. Detonator field signal fixed. Follow after me, two by two;" and he swung down from the bay hatch, then stood aside to guard them as they followed.

Starseeker and Signal Fire jumped down next, moved fluidly aside into defensive positions; then came Rampage and Renegade, quick and strong. Their gazes touched once – *Good hunting, brothers* -- and moved away.

With the smallest of head and chin motions, Broken Spear fanned his pack apart on the bank, and they advanced on the crash site. No rock or tree or blade of grass went unnoticed, and Signal Fire watched the rear flank.

The weather wasn't good for tracking. Dark purple clouds rolled over the sky, threatening rain. The cold grim feeling in Broken Spear's heart increased.

The river they had landed near rushed past them on their level. Then the ground stopped and the surprised river fell over it with a roar and a protest of foam.

The crashed Scout lay broken-backed on the high embankment, just where the water fell.

Stop, the old warrior signaled; and they formed an irregular semi-circle around one side of the wreck.

"...Hull's been ruptured," Signal Fire muttered.

Broken Spear said nothing, but pointed down at the grass and indicated what looked like parallel lines, withered brown, leading away from the ship.

"One lives, at least," the old hunter murmured. "Backtrail me." With a single smooth leap, he reached the ruptured hull and pulled the sheet metal plating off like paper. He sprang lithely to the top of a fin and shone his laser sight into the breach.

The two trophy hunters exchanged awed glances. Starseeker and Signal Fire had never seen Broken Spear in action before.

"Two bodies in here, losing heat, perhaps one is still alive," the warrior announced. "Renegade, Rampage, to me. You others, watch our flanks!" sharply this time, since they seemed frozen by the news, Starseeker especially...

As meekly as disciplined children, the two master hunters obeyed him.

Broken Spear gestured his two youngsters forward. "Follow me in; then each of you take someone out. They are both *tautschen*." He crouched under the metal overhang to go first. They followed.

The ship was not dark and not large, but the old hunter searched it as if it were a savage beast's lair. *As it might be,* Renegade thought.

The young hunter nearly missed the first body. It lay partially buried under rubble. He bent to clear the debris, and exposed a man's upper body:

he was a handsome cream scratch-stripe over a dark red base – *some clan, I remember. Ah, Burning Forest...* and when Renegade knelt alongside, he saw that the hunter's throat had been torn out-- *in one massive bite.* Darkening blood pooled all around, and he shuddered.

"Too late for this hunter," he said softly.

"It's on-stat, Renegade; I'll take him," Rampage said, lifting the fallen man under the shoulders, as carefully as if he still breathed.

"Another lies near the First Seat, Renegade," Broken Spear told him. He ranged up and down, examining some substance on the inner hull. "I do not think these two were infected by the beasts. It was a hard fight; they were killed, instead."

The young warrior stood and went to the pilot's chair. This victim had died in furious self-defense, half-fallen from his chair. He lay on his right side, back to Renegade, one arm extended, holding a –

"*Flame gun,*" Renegade recognized it. "*With a barrel and tank, both empty.*"

The hunter's back was an even medium gray in color, lighter than Dasrylion's, but "snowflaked," or as they call it, "egg-speckled" with tiny rounded white dots – a handsome pattern.

Maybe Tracker or Silver Marsh subclan, Renegade thought, trying to keep his reactions neutral. He slid one arm under the head and shoulders to turn the body over.

It fell back softly against him, as if it were boneless. Renegade found himself staring at chemical-burned armor twisted across the chest. Life heat still fled from it; and he wondered how long ago this brave soul had died.

Gently he pushed the charred armor aside, and touched something soft underneath. He turned back the leathers – and exposed a delicate breast, soft gray stippled with white.

"*Rrr—arh!*" Renegade gasped. He winced in pain. A huntress. "Kkt!" came his involuntary distress call; and very gently, as if she were still able to feel, he eased her legs and lower body off the pilot's chair and held her, his eyes filling.

"Son?" Broken Spear was there, suddenly. "*Aaah...*" He knelt beside Renegade, looked at the corpse, and said, "This is – unexpected. And difficult for you. I did not know... She looks only a few years older than you."

Carefully he reached down and used his thumb-tip, not his nails, to close her mist-blue eyes. "I will take her, Renegade."

"No," Renegade said abruptly. "I'll do it." He rose with the slimly-muscular body in his arms, to take her outside.

He laid her gently on the grass beside the male hunter, and pulled her mangled leathers back into place as best he could. As he did, he heard one of the other hunters gasp out, then give a high-pitched keening noise, as if his heart were ripped from his chest. *Starseeker,* he knew without looking.

The wail choked off, and the hunter's packmate spoke to him softly.

Renegade stood and backed away.

"*Hunters.*" Not a shout, not a roar, but it carried the force of command. Broken Spear had emerged from the Scout ship. "There were only two *tautschen* left aboard. The three bone-beasts are gone. We must follow their trail before the rain comes. They have doubtless gone to seek live prey."

He glanced up, then across to the men. "Signal Fire, come with me. Starseeker...?"

The Shadow hunter visibly tightened himself. "I will hunt them, *tyr rakash,"* he said, flat.

"Good," Broken Spear approved. He glanced toward his two young hunters. "Rampage, Renegade, stay here. Use your suits. Guard our backtrail on Chance the creatures return."

Rebellion flared in the young men's eyes. The old warrior quelled it with, "Find concealment and watch our ship and this one. These beasts may be more cunning than we think. I know you want vengeance for this slaughter; and I know you are excellent hunters..."

He gestured the two adult hunters forward; and when they moved off, addressed his young men once more: "If you will not stay willingly for *them"* -- gesturing toward the bodies, "Then do it..." more softly, "...for an old man who loves you." And he turned and strode away.

They watched the hunting pack disappear through the tall grass and scrub. Then Rampage adjusted his facemask and remarked, "That settles *us.* Let's get to it, Renegade."

"Which stand do you want?'

"What if I watch our ship...?"

Renegade looked quizzical, so Rampage explained, "I won't leave you here if you don't want me to." An unusually sensitive reading from him. He would never have said it if anyone else had been there.

Renegade gave a chinlift of assent. "I'll stay here;" and Rampage accepted that. They switched on their camo-suits and separated.

Renegade decided his best vantage point lay on top of the crashed ship. Camouflaged or not, he fitted himself along the dorsal curve, trying to put some of its darkness between him and the sky...not that the sky was much lighter. Its scudding clouds ran from dark gray to purple, and the rising wind lashed him.

A greenish-yellow lightning fork jabbed the western sky without a sound. *Too far away yet to hear thunder,* he thought; *but when the rains begin, forget the camo-suits.*

He could see most of the embankment and part of their Scout ship from here, but his attention kept wandering to the two bodies on the ground. The Hunters believe in the cleansing power of nature, especially fire, to dispose of their dead. Thus they are returned to the land and the Circle.

To Renegade, these two lost *tautschen*, with much of their armor being ripped away, looked somehow more vulnerable and helpless than his People should ever look. They lay face up; and the thought of their being exposed to a drenching downpour and lying in the mud made him uneasy.

I should cover their faces, least-route, he decided. *Maybe there's something in the ship.* He opened his wrist-com briefly and whispered into it, "Rampage, I'm going inside the ship. Be back on the nock."

His friend replied, "On-stat," and Renegade slipped down soundlessly and lowered himself through the ruptured hull.

He found nothing inside except a capture net. Folded and laid over them, it might be adequate. He removed it and went outside, being cautious and watchful even as he knelt beside the fallen. But he'd lost sight of the embankment and Rampage's outpost for a few moments...and they were crucial.

He heard the short scream just as he remounted the hull.

"Rampage!" he cried and leaped to the top.

He saw a struggle by the other ship. Something big and raw-boned and gaunt reared up –dark, shining, armored – the creature from the drawing! A horror like a cross between a skeleton and a machine, like black bones jointed together, it rose with spiked tail flailing. It stood upright and had clawed "hands;" and the long jaw gaped and glistened...

Something flashed and spun toward it – the *vai-ator* – "No, Rampage! The laser!" Renegade shouted, too late, and the sawblade disc met the thing's bony chest, *hung there,* and finally clove deep. The beast spat a deadly stream. It fell.

Smoky yellow liquid spewed from its mouth and struck something in mid-air.

Another flash, a hoarse scream, and Rampage became visible. His golden armor flashed against the darkened sky. He flung up a hand and fell back.

Renegade could see the burst of sulfuric venom, could hear the hiss of it striking...*"The poison,"* he moaned. He braced himself to spring down and help his friend when he saw the *second* bone-beast come over the top of the Scout ship.

Already hurt, Rampage would surely die.

Renegade dropped to one knee and aimed his laser – a long shot, but he had the range.

He fired; and something hit him *hard* in the back and knocked him forward.

The blow shoved him frontward off the ship's hull, and the motion saved his life. Another hard jolt hit his shoulder, high, and he felt the laser tear free of its padding and pull away.

Even as he fell, Renegade twisted to land on his feet, then ducked and rolled away from the spiky thing falling on him. Something lashed his ribs even as he rolled, and nearly cost him his balance.

The tail, he thought; *keep away from the stinger.* He prayed his shot for Rampage had flown true, because he could not help him now.

The suit is no good. It knows where I am. And it was as big as Broken Spear, bigger than Renegade himself. He rose to face it.

It studied him, a black many-holed skull with four shrunken dead eyes, waiting. It was gauging its next move. *It's had practice – on us,* Renegade thought. Slowly his arm came up to aim his wrist-dart.

The beast gave a sibilant *hssss,* and shot its speared tongue out.

Renegade fired on the recoil, barely got his hand away. The dart thunked into the beast's chest, shoved it backwards – and *fell out.*

Too late the warrior regretted he had not updated his weapons...

The beast whipsawed away from him. *The tail* – he leaped high to clear it, but the prehensile lash scored his ankle and whipped away, spinning him.

Renegade crashed onto one shoulder, got his legs up, and fended off first the stabbing tail's end, then the rest of the bone-and-barb beast with a heave. It was tossed away, not far enough, and reached its feet when he did.

Renegade went cold. He was fighting for his life and he knew it. He felt a quick flash of gratitude for Broken Spear's lessons in unarmed combat. If he had tried to fumble for his laser, he would be dead now.

The bone-beast sprang at him, jagged jaws thrusting and snapping. Saliva sprayed out; it spat, he dodged, and Renegade heard the hiss of hot venom as a few drops spattered on his leathers. He ducked under it again, but not fast enough to dodge the tail, and it struck him, knocking his facemask free. The poison tip barely skinned by his eye.

"Uhh!" he grunted, locked his wrists and smashed the spiky head as it swung towards him. The blow, given with all his considerable strength, knocked the beast sideways – and did no damage.

For the first time in his life, Renegade felt fear for himself. How could he defeat this thing? It was bigger than he was and probably just as fast. His dart-points could not penetrate its armored hide; and his laser lay trampled underfoot somewhere. That left his wristknives, close work for a poison biter and tail-stinger. And it seemed relentless.

The thing circled to his left. Renegade moved away from the ship's bow. It leaped and whirled, again left. The tail tip scored his shinguards as he dodged, missing a telling strike by a few *kli.*

It was driving him toward the cliff, like the *tautschen* sometimes drove game herds. *So that's your play,* he thought; *let's see who falls first.* Renegade clenched his fist and the wristknives sprang out. He feinted right, between beast and embankment. When it lunged, he wheeled and struck at the head. The carapace was both holed and slick: the knives nicked a protrusion and angled off, their force skewed.

But the creature stumbled forward, and Renegade followed up with a one-legged kick at its spine. The blow would have smashed a brick wall. Here, it just sent the creature rolling.

Renegade landed like a dancer and went airborne again, for a two-footed kick given with all his strength.

The bone-thing hissed, claws up, and the tail whipped him *in the back,* between the shoulders.

He fell forward into the outstretched claws.

At the last nock, he put his hands out in front of him, clutched the bone-thing's hands in a grotesque parody of greeting. With immense effort, he snapped his legs straight up overhead, and for a micro-flash stood on his hands in the thing's grasp

He flipped himself forward and down, using his full weight and momentum to spin the bone-beast up over his head.

Renegade came down on his feet in a crouch, at the lip of the gorge, and barreled the thing out over the edge. He thrust the creature's "hands" away from him, and felt a flash of triumph when it went flying out over the waterfall.

The tail slashed past his waist and caught him around the neck. Renegade gasped, fingers prying, and then was jerked off the cliff with the beast.

They bounced off the rocks and hit the waterfall together.

Shock slammed the breath from Renegade's lungs. His head drooped – and water rushed into his nostrils and mouth. He came up spluttering.

He half-lay in shallow water against a hard gravel streambed, his suit fizzled out. At least the tail round his neck was gone…

No sooner did he think that than something hard and bony tightened around his waist.

Renegade had one moment of purblind panic. *This thing never lets up, it never stops – and I can't hurt it at all.*

It began moving, dragging him roughly over the stony bottom. Feigning unconsciousness, Renegade went limp and let himself be dragged. The thing was intent on hauling him back to its nest site aboard the broken Scout, where it would sting him and…

Slowly his hand crept toward his left wrist and the Final Surrender button. He had to do it, even though he didn't want to die...

A sharp yank, and his legs sank into deeper water. The beast had stopped. He risked peering around at it.

In trying to haul him out of the water, it had turned to avoid a pile of rocks and stepped into a pothole. Now it stood chest-deep in cold water, and twisted its head back and forth, hissing. It started to expand its ribcage, halted, and closed it again. *The water's too deep.* And that gave Renegade an idea.

Before it could make up whatever passed for its mind, Renegade turned over, pried a rock off the pile with both hands – and smashed it down on the tail.

The beast squalled and its tail stiffened out. The hunter wrenched himself free and flung the rock at its head.

Solid hit! The thing teetered. Renegade got his hips grounded on the shallow side and launched a mighty kick with both legs.

And it fell.

Wristknives out, Renegade spun around, ripped another rock off the pile, and jumped in on top of the beast as it splashed to the surface.

His feet drove its midsection under water, and he smashed down on its snout hard enough to pulverize the rock. The head dropped back under.

"Now let's see you breathe water!" he screamed at it. Knees on the knobbed ribcage, he bent and straight-armed the short neck stem with his killing-knives.

The points stabbed down on either side of the neck, and Renegade drove them deep into the streambed. Into stone. He gripped his right arm with his left hand to fortify it, and braced one bare foot on the bottom to keep his knee in place on the beast's midsection.

The creature recovered and began to thrash. Savagely Renegade bore down. Pinned, the ghastly head could not rise. Nor could the body.

"Stay down!" he roared at it. His muscles were stretched to their limit; his eyes were on fire. He dripped water and sweat and held on for his life.

The tail – *vascht! The tail!* – went whipping over him, trying to find a place to sting. He kept his head low, chin touching his chest, and bowed his back with the effort. He felt the hard ridges of the tail beat and thrash him, the point slide past his shoulder, scoring it.

But the beast's arms and legs were at the wrong angle for fighting: they clawed and kicked uselessly. The barbed tail kept seeking him. It slashed him and he snarled at it. The creature's hard body bucked and heaved under him.

"*Die, rot you, die*!" he roared at it, his fangs bared. It kept twisting and writhing under him – it was like holding down a huge snake ... *What's taking so long? What if it can breathe under water, too?* How did the bone-beast breathe anyway – through its mouth, through those extra holes in its skull? Or through the great gap between its ribs? He held and held and held, and the tail beat and flayed him from behind. He could feel every stroke, his cuts filled with fire...*Come on, hold on...I can't... You can. You must.*

Movement slowed beneath him. The body stopped heaving; the head relaxed at the neck; a few slow-motion waves rippled from the beast. Then it lay still.

The tail was the last to go. It gave one more great spurt of lashing, its poison barb extended and oozing. Then it stiffened, shook along its length, and sank beneath the stream.

Even now Renegade did not let go. He half-knelt there, pressing down, making *sure* it wouldn't resurrect itself, for another full *kt-tare'.*

Finally he gave a kind of sob, raised one shaking arm to his face, and shivered. *Was it really dead?*

Time to find out. He tried to pull the wristknives up. They stuck fast, embedded in stone. Renegade inhaled deeply and ripped them free.

His hand flew up, overbalancing him. He slipped backward and sideways off the beast, and fell into the pothole with a splash.

Water surged into his mouth. He coughed, closed his larynx, and flailed himself upright. His legs quivered under him. His jaw ached where he had clenched his teeth in concentration; and he rubbed a hand along it absently.

The hard-boned creature's body began to drift upward as the current took it, light for all its size and strength.

"No you don't," he told it, seizing the tail... his turn to drag the thing through water and in to shore. "How do you like it?" he muttered. "Have to make sure you're dead, though. Didn't see the life-force leave; but then I was a little busy..." and he broke off the poison tail-barb to make sure, shielding his hand inside his gauntlet.

It must be dead. When he pulled it ashore, it lay in a glistening dark heap and didn't move.

To make certain, he grabbed the skulled head and standing with one foot on the upper body, gave it a hard twist. The neck snapped with crisp wet shock of breaking bone.

Renegade stood. Spirit, but he was tired! Standing safe on that spit of pebbly sand and jumbled rocks, the young warrior took time to catch his breath and stare upward at the embankment above him.

It rose tall and steep, and mostly stone.

"Ah, *good,*" he growled. "Faster coming down, wasn't it? Well and *good …*"

Then he remembered Rampage, and the thought that there was *another* bone-thing up there, waiting for him. He couldn't desert his friend.

He still had his detonator. And a plan. He wrapped the dead thing's tail around his waist now that the stinger was gone and tucked the end through his belt – he still had on belt and loincloth even if most of his armor was gone.

Plotting his course on a series of rocky step-ledges up the embankment, he began to climb. To make his hunt complete, it began to rain. It came down in fat heavy droplets at first, then the clouds tore along their undersides and deluged him.

A grueling climb. He made it dragging his long tall burden, his back scored with fire, the rain pelting onto his face, and his strength at low ebb. And he quailed at the thought of reaching the top just to find his friend dead.

He steeled himself. If so, if Rampage were dead, then the murdering creature that killed him would die, too. Renegade planned to use this beast's body as a disguise – to come in low behind it, once on the crest, and then – and then what? Pin the other to the ground and bash its head in with a rock, if necessary.

Sever the spine, and the game is yours. The thought came to him in his mentor's voice.

Ah yes, that's it, he agreed mutely. I can do that. Break its *vrakking* neck.

The last few *kri* of rock went almost straight up. Pinpoints of light danced in his brain; every breath was labored. His body ached in a hundred separate hurts.

He drew up just below the edge and hung there, panting. When he recovered enough to pay attention, he tried to listen, to hear something, anything, to give him a clue as to what was up there.

Nothing. Even the rain had softened to a low drone.

"On-course,' he mumbled, letting go the ledge with one hand and reaching down to haul the beast up by its tail.

But the creature was bulky and clumsy to lift, and the body spikes kept catching on the rocks. "*T'chrrt!*" he snapped, pulling hard.

And lost his grip with the other hand.

He fell, grabbed, scraped, struck his jaw, and yelped with pain. *Fine. There goes surprise.*

Sure as sunlight, he heard (or maybe felt) a movement on the bank above him. Vibrations shivered through the stone.

A great weariness overcame him. He clutched the rock firmly with his left hand, brought his right over to his left wrist. He flipped up the gauntlet's cover, took a deep breath, and then, through blurring eyes, began to press the detonation sequence.

"Renegade, stop! Renegade!"

The voice… he looked up. Someone leaned over the edge, looking at him.

"Grandfather?" he whispered.

"Oh Great Spirit – yes, son, yes. Stop what you're doing. Stop it now."

Renegade stayed his hand. He blinked through tears. "What -- about Rampage?"

Another shape appeared, bearing another voice: "Here, brother, a little damaged but – what have you got there?"

"Never trouble over that now," Broken Spear said. He leaned over the embankment, reaching – *another cliff, another time…* "Hold on, son."

Renegade felt a light touch. Then something seized his wrist like iron, and began to pull. Renegade tried to help, but collapsed into it instead – he had no strength left – docilely letting his mentor lift him one-handed over the edge to safety.

Once on top, he was stretched along the grass, his unwieldy burden bumping along after him.

Exclamations rose around him: "The third beast!"

"Dead; he killed it!"

"It's unmarked – how did he – great galaxy! – with *his hands*?"

But Renegade was aware of only two people around him: Broken Spear, his great hands disconnecting the wrist band, stripping it off, then running over him, searching the back wounds "Renegade, it's on-stat. Lie still and rest."

And Rampage, Rampage *alive,* kneeling close, holding his friend's shoulder, saying, "You're here; you're alive.You saved me with that shot. And Broken Spear doubled back; and the armor stopped most of the chemical, but not all – see this arm? Brother, how in bloody battle did you do it?"

Renegade closed his eyes gratefully. "Brothers...they can't...breathe... under...*water*." he said, and consciousness left him.

***

HE CAME TO inside the school ship's healing alcove.

"He's awake." Starseeker sat nearby, leaning over him.

"I'm coming," Rampage made sure of the autopilot and hurried over.

Renegade, lying on his stomach with his head turned to one side, blinked up at him. Rampage wore gauze patches dotted over his right arm and partly on his chest like the others had. His new armor was pitted on the right side.

Rampage followed his gaze. "Wouldn't you know, just paid for and dinged up already...?" His voice was shaky. "Now I guess we'll have matching scars in back, too" – referring to the raptor claw gouge from his Master Hunt, which had healed to a narrow crevice, shiny white.

Renegade smiled. "Yours will still be deeper; I'll just have more." He stirred, but felt Starseeker's hand on him.

"Rest, great warrior," the trophy hunter said; "You deserve rest."

"*Rrrhurr*," muttered Renegade, as the pain of at least a thousand cuts and bruises assailed him. "No argument, *vr'*hunter. And I'm not a – I'm just me."

Starseeker and Rampage exchanged looks, the equivalent of a wink.

Renegade missed it. He kept trying to resettle so it didn't hurt so much. "What else happened?" he asked to get his mind off it. "Before and after?"

"Broken Spear's piloting the other ship back," Rampage said. "Singing Spear is still recovering; and our leader says he can use his healing arts and navigation skills aboard their ship. Signal Fire went with him to help. All the wounded hunters are doing better, too."

"—While I have some piloting skills myself, and can stay here with both of you," Starseeker added.

"The bone-beasts – are they all dead?"

"The five we had on board with us are, yes, but the one planet, R'shba 3, is over-run; and we had a – short Leavetaking – of our dead," Starseeker answered, his voice dropping near the end; and Renegade remembered who gave the death-keen for the fallen huntress.

"I'm sorry, Starseeker; I mourn with you," he told the Shadow Clan hunter, who sheathed his eyes once.

Rampage took a seat next to the healing bed (gingerly, Renegade noticed) and filled him in on the fight he'd missed. After the Plains hunter had slain the first beast, and been splashed with corrosive which injured his throwing arm and immobilized his laser, he'd fallen back and watched, helpless, as the second creature came over the Scout at him. Then "out of the sky" a laser bolt struck it, shearing off a leg...

"I'm glad I hit it. The third one jumped me, threw off my aim," Renegade explained, apologetic.

"A leg was enough." Rampage assured him. "I crawled away under our ship and it hobbled after me; so we played hunt-and-find around the Scout for oh, an eternity or thereabouts. I couldn't throw, but *it* couldn't run, either.'

"How did you kill it?"

"I finally opened up enough ground to unlimber my spear from my pack, and decided to make a stand near the waterfall. If I couldn't penetrate its armor, I thought I could least-route pitch it over the waterfall...more company for you, brother, as it tracked out."

"One beast was enough, thank you," Renegade said dryly.

His friend grinned and continued, "I was standing there, ready, when another laser bolt seared past, and tore that critter's head right off." Broken Spear had returned. "He said the further he got from the scene, the worse he felt; so he left the other two hunters on the trail and doubled back."

"And later the tracks confirmed that the beasts had backtrailed," Starseeker put in. "By good Chance he left on his impulse. He has the *vrei-chee,* the Far-seeing Eye, we call it."

I know what that is, Renegade thought.

"You should have seen him in action," Rampage enthused. "He really *is* a Great Warrior, like his title. He made that shot *running*, and then jumped clear over the thing, spearing its ribcage to the ground as he sprang. The spear point went in and *through,* brother. Then he landed in front of me, spun around and had his laser sighted and aimed before it stopped moving. But the first shot did for it."

Renegade smiled.

Very softly Starseeker said, "He is not the only Great Warrior here."

Renegade shifted restlessly. To change the subject, he asked, "But what about R'shba 3? It was a world of normal life forms when it was surveyed a few years ago. Where did those things come from?"

Rampage shook out his mane. "They're going to look into that. Singing Spear is a member of the Six Systems Hunt Council. He's going to call for a grand conclave of them all; and they'll decide what to do about R'shba 3. I'd like to be there. I'd like to tell them what to do with the frosted beasts!"

"And I too," said the trophy hunter.

"I'd like to see those things exterminated," said Renegade. "I'll go with you."

Four...Recovery

AS IT TRACKED OUT, the only place he went for a few days, along with Rampage and the other wounded, was to the nearest space station and into its House of Healing.

Broken Spear went in and out, visiting them. One day he arrived with a solemn group of people, males and females, who were dressed basically in hunt-fashion, but who also wore cloaks and insignia of office. Dignified and austere, they asked the two Arvien hunters for their stories.

Renegade told his simple and plain, Rampage more flamboyantly; but the Hunt Council heard them both out with equal seriousness, thanked them gravely, and left.

"What's going on?" Rampage asked Broken Spear, who had lingered behind.

"Something unprecedented," he told them, settling between their beds. "A survey ship found evidence that the creatures are not native to that world. It seemed they were introduced there, willingly or not, by another starship."

"Another starship!" Renegade exclaimed. "You mean there's someone *else* riding around the galaxy besides us? And they bring these things with them?"

"Yes; it may be an accident, though, such as what happened to the Hunt and settlers' ships. We found no survivors." Broken Spear rubbed his cupped hands along his broken tooth. He did that only when he was worried or deeply thoughtful. "More will be revealed at the Conclave, no doubt."

"The Conclave? When is it? Can we go?" they asked in unison, making the old warrior laugh.

"Sometimes you still *sound* like the little *chk-kiy-teh* I taught," he teased them. "But yes, if you are well healed in about a tenday, you may go. As shall I."

The old hunter visited with them for a while longer, asking after their healing, before he finally rose to leave, telling them, "So; I must go back to our own system, to Arvien and Homeworld, and prepare for this Conclave. But I shall return for you on the nock. Until then, Rampage, Renegade, I will leave you to recover and – enjoy yourselves here. The station and the people of Six Systems are prepared to be very cordial to you." He embraced them both and turned to leave.

"Grandfather, is there anything we can do for you here? To help?" Renegade asked him.

Broken Spear stood in his tracks. He gave them one of his most heartfelt smiles.

"*Do* for me, Renegade? The two of you have already done so much more than your old teacher ever thought – you have both made me so proud. I am honored, my sons." And he left them.

***

WHEN THEIR MENTOR said the station personnel were prepared to be "very cordial" to them, he wasn't exaggerating. If anything, he had made an understatement.

The two found themselves swamped with visitor requests – all very respectful of their privacy, but all very concerned about their health. When the two young hunters politely declined any visits from strangers, the stationmaster himself came to convey his respects, and relay a number of offers…outright gifts made to them on behalf of the station and Six Systems' inhabited worlds.

"Can we *accept* these?" Rampage quizzed, his eyes gleaming with desire. There were new sets of ultralight body armor for both of them, custom-designed by the local armorer; solvent-proof newmetal spears and wristknives which would pierce armor plating; computer discs and videos from the electronics outlet; rare furs and hides from the furriers'; an offer to repair free of charge their own weapons and armor; and even a small auto-cam and disc with the delicately-worded request that they "tell their own story for the People's benefit, and keep the equipment afterward," from the local documentarians.

"Maybe we'd better ask someone. How about Starseeker?" Renegade suggested. "He's still here with the others from the Hunt Ship."

They did; and the Shadow Clan hunter took one look at the horde and laughed. "What, no proposals of marriage yet?"

Renegade held up a folder stuffed with notes, printouts, and parchment-thin writing- skins: "I'm afraid to look."

Starseeker roared with laughter. "Well, if there are," he choked out finally, "you *don't* need to accept any of those!" Then he laughed until he could not catch his breath.

"Oh young warriors, your pardon," he gasped. "We have had our due, but these! And yes, you may accept the gifts. And you should politely acknowledge them, at least by computer message. There is a protocol to it, you see: they all want to glimpse you in person. But that isn't necessary. Expect more of the same."

They looked so apprehensive that he made a suggestion: "Why don't you come down the corridor and visit my huntmates? We can help you with the proper tone for your thanks – and reduce the mountain of it – and then we can trade hunting stories. Singing Spear and Signal Fire keep asking after you; and my other packmates would like to meet you as well.

"And…*krr…*" he started chuckling again, "in a space station, there is *no way* to avoid your public."

***

IN A FEW DAYS, when they managed to clear the last of the thank-you hurdles, they dared venture out into the station itself.

"Better go in day-camo – simple disguise," Starseeker offered cheerfully; then took pity on them and said, "Everyone may know you're here, but almost no one knows what you look like, least-route until that news-disc is edited and released." (He and his cronies had seen to that, filming the young men unobtrusively while they told their stories.) "Leave your rank insignia in your room, and go out simply as young hunters, which you are."

That seemed to be working.

"Good," said Renegade, "now if we don't cross trails with the stationmaster or any of our healers, we should have a little time to scout around."

"Since a few people already know where we're quartered, I figure we have about a half-day, best, until that documentary shows," Rampage said. He had mixed feelings about fame. One part of him needed and relished it; the other part shied from all the physical bodies it brought near – the feeling of being surrounded, those crowds!

"Or less than that," Renegade added. "Remember how even those hunters from the other ship acted?"

When the young men had taken Starseeker's advice and gone to see the other survivors, they had been treated with the deference normally according an esteemed elder or even a clan leader. They were astounded; but the others seemed to be doing it quite naturally, not at all as if they were playing a joke, or had been told to…

Even Starseeker, who'd come to know the young hunters best, agreed, "Honor among the *tautschen* is not based solely on age, but on merit too. I and my huntmates have been through the fire; most of us were murdered. To meet warriors such as you…!" Which had been no help at all.

The two took their freedom where they found it. Strolling down the corridor of shops, they noticed a crowd gathered at the far end, standing around a small recess or alcove of some kind.

"*H'vack,* not around our own threshold!" Rampage joked in mock-dismay.

"No, nowhere near," Renegade answered him seriously. "They're looking at something off to the side –in one of the shops, maybe?"

Curious, the two friends went to investigate. The crowd stood three deep, an unusual closeness for *tautschen*, and they had to weave their way in slowly, with many a "your pardon" to get by.

It was a trophy display, set aside in a wall alcove. There, lighted from within and mounted on spike-stands, were two skulls and one complete exoskeleton of –

"Bone beasts!" Rampage exclaimed.

"They put them *here,"* Renegade echoed. "I thought they were going to be turned over for study."

"No, young hunter," said one well-fed-looking trader. "The Hunt Council said there were *five* such beasts. Two were killed in a firefight with an entire *shipload* of hunters, but these – *these* were bested by individual warriors."

"Mighty warriors from Homeworld, we hear," a woman standing behind him put in. She was dressed as a station-keeper, in cream-color service coveralls.

"Arvien," Rampage muttered in his friend's ear, ticked by the mistake.

"Just read the inscriptions, young hunters," their first informant said.

The two bent to read the metal plates mounted beside each specimen.

Under one head: "Slain in single combat by Master Hunter Rampage of the Nine Systems, with a simple vai-ator."

"Still not Arvien," Renegade whispered to Rampage, seized by a sudden playful impulse.

And under the other head: "Jointly slain by T'akaion, Great Warrior of Nine Systems, and Clan Rydderrak, Homeworld, and the Warrior Renegade of the Home systems, who drew first blood."

"Arvien *Four,*" Rampage said defiantly, drawing stares. They read further, under the skeleton of the whole creature:

"Deadly Unknown Beast, extremely venomous, SLAIN IN SINGLE UNARMED COMBAT, by the Esteemed Master Hunter and Warrior Renegade of Arvien System."

"Got that mostly right, I see," came from Rampage. His friend nudged him.

"Unarmed?" Renegade asked, all innocence.

"What's that, young man?" The trader, distracted, didn't quite overhear; but their whispers had drawn others' attention. "Never mind. Gaze at them well, for they leave for their slayers' trophy halls soon."

"Their slayers?" Renegade teased out more line.

The trader beamed. "In truth, yes. We are honored to have these mighty warriors as our guests in the station, where they are being treated for wounds suffered in this combat."

Aaah, went the crowd.

"Really? They're *here?"* came from Rampage, eyes widened and voice hushed.

"Uh!" He felt a sharp jab from Renegade's toeclaw.

"T'churr, brother, don't you think we should move on and give others a chance to see these trophies?" *Jab.*

"Uff! Yes, yes I do, brother," Rampage enthused. "Many thanks, honored trader, for telling us." A number of eyes were on them now, including those of a few shrewd-looking older hunters; and the two quickly excused themselves, nearly bursting with concealed laughter.

"A privilege, young hunters!" the trader called after them. "Perhaps someday when you are older and stronger, you may aspire to such trophies as these!"

The two bolted around the curve of the hall and dived into an alcove between shops, where they leaned on the walls and gasped with laughter.

"Wh-When we get o-o-older and s-strong-er! Uh!" Rampage wheezed, holding his sides.

"Perhaps! Just perhaps, brother! We might be a-able to hunt that way!" Renegade pressed back against a column of imported stone and howled. "What bad spirit took you, Rampage?"

"Me? What bad spirit took *me*?" Rampage gasped through snorts of glee. And they both laughed outrageously, until they could finally collect themselves and slink into cover. It was the most fun they'd had in days.

Five....Conclave

THE CONCLAVE was held in an immense amphitheatre, far larger than the one at Broken Spear's hall. Usually a clear dome stretched over it. Today it lay open to the sky...and the hot, humid air of Homeworld.

"Already some of our freeholders are not comfortable here," Broken Spear remarked to his former students. "They are used to cooler climes and drier air." He looked at them with sympathy and amusement, for clearly the Three were in that category.

They looked a little too warm and a little too damp, but they were together again. Dasrylion had been there at planetide to greet his friends, and he was limping, one foot wrapped and padded.

"I stepped on something poisonous," he told them, "in the jungle. Broken Spear's old clan has been helping me out. With their shaman's potions I should be better in a quick-throw. But you two walked into something more than a beast-bite, I hear."

"You hear correctly. It was the beast itself," Renegade informed him; "and you'll probably hear more when we have to tell it all over again to the Conclave." He nodded toward the vast gathering: "Look at them. There must be nearly ten thousand *tautschen* here!"

"Yes; each huntpack is seated in their own section," the old warrior supplied. "Each section is wedge-shaped...Look again, vr'hunters, what else – or *who* else – do you see?"

"*Krrr,* it's – that looks like some Dinosaur Clan members there!" Rampage exclaimed.

"And there's the leader of Rydderrak Clan, too," came from Dasrylion. "I met him, Broken Spear. I didn't know that clan leaders were members of planetary Hunt Councils."

"They usually are not. Look again; there are others."

Renegade frowned by tightening his thin lips against his teeth. "I see some people with my two parents' markings – one section each of them – some other individuals in other sections, with the freeholds...Grandfather, are there *clans* at this meeting too?"

"Indeed there are. You have good eyes, Esteemed Hunters, for not only are the Hunt Councils of all nine worlds and this entire system represented, plus Six Systems, but so are fourteen of the 16 Clans of Homeworld. Even the public sections are full."

They looked at him in awe. "This is very important, then," Renegade remarked.

"Vital. The fate of a species and of a world – perhaps many worlds – will be decided today," their mentor agreed. "Now, if you will, v'hunters, let us take seats in the lower center portion of the bowl – the Chairs of Witness. Dasrylion, you may accompany us if you like, though you will not be asked to speak. Come."

As they walked across that long, long amphitheatre floor, its upper levels astir with more of the People than the Three had ever seen together in their lives, the old hunter remembered something:

"Ah. Renegade, this was in your receiving box at the hall. A trade ship and runner special-delivered it for you;" and he handed a small cube to the young man, adding, "Rampage, you have a note from your friend the Chief Hunter of Dinosaur Clan. It came in hyperlight, via satellite relay."

"Flashing Sky says he forwarded the best of my furs and hides to K'orrynia...and here's her note of thanks!" Rampage crowed. "And she says she especially likes the birdfeather cape!" Even as he waved the notes around to show everyone, he scanned the seats where Dinosaur Clan was...he *thought* he could see Flashing Sky's dark-and-silver pattern among the golden. He would seek him out, after.

"Good for you, brother," Renegade smiled absently as he turned the cube he'd received over in his hands. On it, or rather inside it, were holopixes of three people, two adults and a baby. Stands Fast and Kyva smiled back at him in three dimensions. He turned it around, looking intently into every facet. The baby looked out at him with two big dark amber eyes full of wonder: the little one bore his frontal color, pale gold, with the round black spots and the black stripe down his heartline. He looked striking.

His mother's eyes, my marks, Renegade thought. From the back, the baby had his father's pale grey over-color, phasing into gold in the front; and short, slightly waved black locks grew from his scalp.

The inscription under the holopix read: "To Renegade with our love: Kyva, Stands Fast and little Blackstripe."

They look very happy; they make a nice family, he thought. With a pang, he realized, *I didn't get there after all.*

Then he and his friends reached their posts and he placed the cube on the short wooden stand before him.

They sat down.

The huge convention started promptly. The Six Systems Hunt Council Director led it, since his pack had called for the meeting.

As melodic chimes announced the opening, each person present could see and hear everything on the small screens set in the tables before them, or on the large screen-in-the-round above them.

"Will we have to stand center-circle and speak?" Rampage asked, suddenly nervous. He'd soaked up the adulation back at the space base; but this had the aspects of a test, set before a huge crowd; and the Hunting People prefer to avoid large crowds when they can.

"Yes," Broken Spear whispered in response. *"You will have to stand out a little way, so the cameras can pick you up; but you may speak directly into your console– on the desk, here...take the headset forward with you."*

The Six Systems Director began by explaining why they had called the meeting. Then he introduced Singing Spear to tell the story of their hunt for the settlement ship.

"When will we be up, Elder?" Rampage fretted in place.

"After the Hunt Ship members speak, then I, then you two. Your testimony may take some time. Besides hearing you, the Conclave members will want to ask questions."

"All of them?"

"No doubt, but only a small number will be permitted, perhaps one from each delegation."

That's at least fourteen from the clans, and from the Hunt Councils, Spirit knows how many, Renegade added up. He noticed that drinking water had been provided for the witnesses; he at least would need it.

Broken Spear continued, "Most importantly, you will be asked your opinions of this creature, and how we should treat it. I would urge you to speak freely. Every major judicial body of the People is here today. You *will* be heard, and you *will* make a difference."

He was correct, as usual. After depositions from the trophy hunters, the Conclave called upon the rescue pack one at a time.

Broken Spear went first. Renegade noticed that they treated him with the utmost deference and respect, and they didn't even blink when he suggested the alien species be annihilated.

"I know this is not our way," he boomed out at them. "Traditionally we leave a dangerous species alone, and add it to our list of trophy animals. But what I saw there...our brave hunters and warriors lying there with their throats and abdomens ripped open – the utter destructiveness of this creature toward all other living things, its relentless takeover of another world... I ask that we show it no quarter. Either we destroy it, or it will destroy *us* – and it will come *here* to do so."

A rumble of concern ran round them. Broken Spear stood for questions, but none came; and he was released with the stipulation that he might be recalled later.

Then came the young hunters' turn.

Rampage went first, and found it unsettling.

Being the focus of thousands of watchful eyes is an unnerving experience for any species; but the carnivores' intensity pushes the feeling beyond mere stage fright into terror, since they are born to watch and stalk, and they can fix you with a soul-burning concentration, and do it in utter silence.

Rampage's color drained away until he was almost beige; and his story lost much of its flamboyance. This time he gave it swiftly and directly, and was ready to leave when he finished. They held him there, though, asking him in particular about the *vai-ator's* use against the creatures, and whether the fluid produced had burned him just on his exposed skin surfaces, or gone through his armor too.

He impressed them with the creature's speed, strength and sheer determination, stressing that it came after him even with one leg shot away.

Then they asked him the key question, "In your opinion, Esteemed Hunter, does this species pose a threat to our people as a whole, or may it be treated as a trophy animal?"

Rampage's answer was unusually thoughtful, for him: "If it tracks out – if research into its habits proves it can travel through space somehow, planet to planet – and use a lot of different creatures for its hosts, then *yes,* I would say it does pose a threat to our people as a whole, and to all the worlds of life as we know it."

That earned him some *t'churrs* of astonishment – and a reprieve. He was allowed to sit down.

Renegade's turn. He stood away from his chair as the others had, and the monitor followed him.

--When something dropped down from the center of the amphitheatre, from the sky, and landed in front of him

A bone-beast, poised to attack.

Renegade gave a noticeable start and dropped into a combat stance. His heat-colors ran cold in his veins…until he realized this was a mockup, a dummy, not the real thing.

They had all seen his reaction, of course. Behind him, Renegade could hear Broken Spear's low rumble of anger…

"Forgive us, noble warrior." It was Singing Spear, standing, a tiny figure among the thousands above him. "We wish to apologize for doing this to you. Others in this assembly thought it would be 'instructive' to watch your reaction to the creature, without warning. We did not know what would be done until this moment. This is just a model, as you now know: its joints and mouth-parts have been designed to move as the live beast does…We wondered if you would please demonstrate them as you tell us of your hunt."

"On-course, *vr'*hunter." Renegade felt a fireburst of anger, though he kept his voice neutral. *Was it necessary to frighten me out of my wits and dishonor me before the whole Conclave?*

Singing Spear apologized again. Clearly he hadn't been part of this. Renegade thought he knew who had. But you can't mend a broken branch on the trail, so he began.

As the young warrior spoke and had to touch the dummy, to manipulate it, he began to go through all the emotions he'd had in the fight – shock, fear, anger, resolve, exhaustion, and finally – relief.

"And then the *tyr rakash* stopped me from using the detonator, because the beasts were all dead, and he pulled me up over the embankment, where I lost consciousness and – that was all." He was shaking a little, overcome by the emotional display. *I hope you got a bellyful, Director,* he thought bitterly.

"Thank you Esteemed Warrior, Renegade of Arvien – yes, Great Warrior, now you may speak."

Renegade just vaguely heard Broken Spear's deep and angry tone. He was spent.

"I strongly protest this outrageous and discourteous invasion of this honored warrior's privacy, and demand those involved make reparations to him!" The full Conclave could hear him without the speakers.

"I, too rise to register the protests of myself and my surviving huntmates of Ship 1441. The young warrior and his companions did what twenty of us couldn't. For that they deserve our honor and our gratitude," came a new voice from the witness chairs behind them. *Starseeker,* Renegade thought; *thank you.*

Singing Spear's Council Director rose, looking quite unhappy. "Again, we are deeply, deeply sorry it was done this way…not to shame him, for fear walks with the bravest hunter, but rather some members of other councils desired to see the depth of this confrontation. I think the warrior handled himself with exemplary courage and heart."

He looked directly at Renegade, still standing there, and said. "Esteemed Hunter and Warrior, we hold you and your companions in the highest regard. To demonstrate our sincerity the Six Systems Hunt Council had resolved to make a presentation, as is our right under Code, even if we are not *your* Hunt Council.

"*Vr'*Renegade, please stand a moment longer. Honored hunters and warriors Rampage and Broken Spear, will you join him there?"

They came forward, and Renegade was no longer alone. Rampage flashed him a quick smile, and he felt the warm weight of Broken Spear's approval and regard. He straightened his spine.

The Conclave had at last floated the mockup bone-beast away. Now they were going to do something else.

The Six Systems Director himself came forward, and in a ringing voice decreed, "We hereby do all honor to our defenders, to the protectors of the People, by acknowledging their prowess with these new insignia of rank." And he withdrew some glittering medallions from his cloak and brought them forward.

He began with the lowest-ranked of the three before him: "Rampage, Master Hunter of Arvien 4, we now proclaim you an Esteemed Warrior and protector of the People!" and the youngster accepted his new honor with flashing eyes.

Renegade stood in stunned disbelief as the director approached him next, lifted a medallion and its intricate chain above his head, and lowered it around his neck.

"Noble warrior Renegade, proven in battle beyond all expectation, we award you the highest honor that the *tautschen* can bestow. Henceforth, you shall be among the youngest and most illustrious few to be recognized by this title, O Great Warrior and Defender of Worlds!"

And the director smiled kindly at the young man's obvious shock. This ranked him with an elite few, such as Broken Spear.

The elder Great Warrior was next. The director stood opposite the old hunter, had to look up to meet his eyes. He looked into that burning gaze, then lowered his head to honor him, saying, "O Great Warrior, few indeed have stood on the pinnacle where you stand today. Protector of your people, defender of worlds, man of honor, we have exhausted our list of accolades to salute you; so we have had to create a new ranking, and strike a special medallion for this ceremony. Please allow us to award you this simple insignia – it is only a token, a small thing to contain such love and respect as we hold for you. T'akaion, elder, hunter, warrior, please accept this from us to you, as the Champion of our race, the Hunting People."

And he raised his arms to lay on the medallion. He had to reach up, so Broken Spear saved him embarrassment by bowing his head to receive it. The director returned this with an even lower head incline of greater honor, and the Conclave lost its silence in tumultuous roars, which did not end for some *kt-tare'*.

When the three honorees were finally allowed to sit down, the surviving Hunt Ship pack members were brought up, including Singing Spear and Starseeker, and raised to the rank of warrior. The ovation thundered forth again.

"Now *that,* my sons, is a proper honors ceremony!" Broken Spear told them. He was almost over his outrage.

"And you should have seen *our* Hunt Council director, from Nine Systems. I saw him," Dasrylion whispered to them. "He was *hackled!"*

"Good," Rampage grit through his teeth.

Renegade mirrored his response and asked, "Will they keep me here for questions, Grandfather?"

"Not now," the old warrior assured him. "They will break until the evening session. They may recall us tomorrow."

The Conclave *did* break then, till the cool of evening. The delegates were invited to visit the university, which owned this amphitheatre.

The Three decided to look for their friends among the delegates. Broken Spear encouraged them to go, since he wished to speak to his former clan leader before they left. They parted company for the moment.

***

THE CONCLAVE was after all able to conduct its business is just three days. The delegates had a number of issues to deal with and they didn't waste any heat going after them.

The Three heard some shocking revelations.

The afternoon session saw the university's researchers discussing their findings about the bone-beasts. These were not heartening: apparently the embryos could survive in *any* living creature with a good size range, warm-blood or cold. They could survive in many types of atmospheres, so long as there was oxygen available, synthesizing their chemical reactions from a spectrum of different gases –except under a thick fluid, water – which meant Renegade was more Chance-favored than he knew.

The newborn beasts could adapt to take advantage of a wide range of habitat – "though we *think* we can rule out nearly airless worlds, or very hot surfaces," one researcher said. "But if there is any kind of carbon-based life on a world, these can parasitize it."

The research ship, which had been swiftly sent back to R'shba 3, had observed (while safely in orbit) that almost none of the original animal species still remained. Every species above the size of a small rodent had been made into bone-beast hatcheries – and even those smaller species were being rapidly devoured as food. The researchers thought that once the native species disappeared, different nests or tribes of the bone-beasts would then begin preying on each other: "a process which can go on almost indefinitely, the way these creatures breed."

That shocked the Conclave. So did the next finding:

By clever use of multi-wave sounding techniques and satellite surveillance, the research team had been able to analyze the ruins of the ship which brought the beasts with it.

"It *had* been by accident: for a few skeletons of alien beings – *not* bone-beasts – showed that these bodies had been ravaged by the parasites, too. They had been overcome in flight and crashed on R'shba 3."

"Great Spirit! That means the entire galaxy might be over-run, but for us!" Broken Spear exclaimed. "Have you attempted to backtrail that ship?"

"We are running the numbers even as we speak here today, *vr'Champion,"* a researcher told him.

Renegade felt excited as well as appalled by the news. That meant there was at least one more civilized race out there, which had left its planet and made a run for the stars. Where had it come from? What did its members look like?

That concluded the first day's agenda. Overnight, various clans offered hospitality to the delegates; and they were offered rooms at University as well.

"My clan has a small encampment nearby," Broken Spear said; "not their main gathering, for the university is on public grounds once donated by Rydderrak and others. But my clan leader says he would be honored to have us stay there."

They accepted, and found an aircar waiting for them.

Renegade felt very tired, emotionally exhausted, and afterward had only a dim memory of the trip… something like going back in time, from starships to aircars to hide tents set amid tall and flaring torches in the dark. Another warrior met them, of powerful build, as big as Broken Spear; and the young hunter barely had the presence of mind to incline his head and murmur,

"We are honored by your hospitality, Esteemed Clan Leader…"

-- And hear a deep but half-amused voice reply: "My guests do honor to my hearth. Esteemed Warriors, perhaps we shall save the storytelling and feasting for another night. Come into the tent, honored guests, and sleep."

Inside the spacious tent, the young hunters found soft thick sleeping mats stuffed with feathers and dried grass, along with the most delicate *teveh* skin-covered cushions and blankets, light as down, and very welcoming.

"Ah—*aaahrr*," Renegade heard Rampage groan in pure contentment as he lay down. Then his own head and body touched the soft padding, and he lost himself in sleep.

***

THE SECOND MORNING saw them eating a meal made of a rare treat: fresh cooked eggs.

"Tropical birds lay several times during the year. Rydderrak encourages them with nesting sites," Broken Spear explained. "Take your ease, young warriors," he added as he noted their enjoyment; "the clan members decided to let you sleep past the sun, so they departed early and left the eggs for us."

They took an aircar back to the Conclave – the same or a different flier, they didn't know; but they were not eager to rejoin the fray.

Today saw both Renegade and Broken Spear recalled for questioning; and this time, Renegade gave his opinion, siding with the other survivors and adding,

"I think it would be a good trail to use our classic alliance with the star captains to form large hunting packs when we go back to these worlds, and when we explore new ones," he said. "We could equip even the starliners and settlement ships with more firepower…use them to survey the world thoroughly from orbit, before we send the hunters down." (Hunters are the traditional first landers to touch a new world) "If we can trace that crashed alien ship back to its original planet, perhaps we can learn the truth about that species."

When Broken Spear rose to take questions, he had a new proposal for them: "I would recommend we re-evaluate any other intelligent technological species we know or meet as potential allies."

A collective gasp exploded through them.

"*Respected* Champion, we know of only one other," the Nine Systems Director put in with the suggestion of a sneer, "and if I recall, you *wholeheartedly* agreed to place them at trophy status some years ago."

"That is true," Broken Spear said mildly. "I still do not believe them capable of honor. And we have tested ourselves against them for many years now, I agree; so we should be familiar with their nature and abilities. But I *now* believe it is a mistake to hunt them. They are not totally beasts, however we may rationalize it. They may prove to be more valuable as allies against this foe."

Excited hisses and rattling all around.

"But they are a major trophy species!" the director protested.

"What can we hunt in their place?" someone else cried out.

"*V'chaien*! Come to order!" roared the Conclave leader – and they did, with an expectant air.

"As to that, *honored* hunter," Broken Spear could put an edge in his voice, too; "if this new species we call bone-beasts proves as virulent as it looks, I suggest we may have a near endless trophy hunt to eradicate it. For the others: I do not advise contact at this time; but I think a re-evaluation is in order, particularly if that species survives its pre-stellar era."

"Point well shot, *vr'*Champion," said the Six Systems Director, re-taking control. "If there are any more *relevant* questions – I do not include protests and expressions of temper" (forcefully) "let the meeting continue."

During the second evening session, they opened the floor to more delegates' suggestions, and progressed to framing final resolutions, which would become part of Hunt Law.

These would be debated on the third day, with some input from the general public; and after a short break, they would push on to voting in the afternoon. And the course of *Tautschen* history would be set for the foreseeable future, unless or until something else as extraordinary happened to make them call a Conclave again.

***

THE CLAN AT NIGHT---Broken Spear came back to Rydderrak late that night, looking a little dusty but extremely satisfied. He sat down without comment.

But the clan leader, who had been keeping the youngsters company, looked up and grinned. "Is honor satisfied, brother?"

Broken Spear shifted on his hip. "It is. And now the council may choose a new leader, *d'faal*."

"What? What!" His Three leaned in close, agog with questions.

But for once, the old warrior would not answer them, not even Renegade's; and he waved them back to their meal.

Burning Spear covered his tracks: "Honored warriors! How are you tonight? Not so tired? Although, by sky and water, politics tires *me!* And how did you enjoy the eggs this morning?"

"Very much, Esteemed Leader," Renegade answered, and the others piped up after him. *This is a younger clan leader than High Sun,* Renegade thought, *and he doesn't take himself as seriously.*

"Good! Excellent! And you may forget my title in private; we are surely huntmates here. Two of you outrank me, in truth," he smiled at them. "My earned name is Burning Spear. Please call me so. Your friend Dasrylion already does."

"Yes, hon—uh, Burning Spear," Renegade said. .

The leader went on, "And do you, good warriors, feel rested enough to tell us your stories tonight?"

One look at their apprehensive faces, and he roared with laughter again. Even Broken Spear chuckled.

"No matter!" Burning Spear boomed at them. "My Elders and I heard them told to the Conclave; that will be enough for now. Such misery! A fine hunting tale should be told with joy. Let us make up for your ordeal by a good feast tomorrow, and a round of *other* stories, *churr,* my brother?" to Broken Spear, who nodded.

Burning Spear felt their unspoken question, and enlightened them. "Your noble teacher is my half-brother *and* my Elder – and was my teacher as well."

"I am indeed," Broken Spear said with dry good humor. "And I had hoped the clan leadership would have settled you down, Burning Spear. But I hoped in vain, I see."

That set the other man off again. He laughed and gripped the old warrior's shoulder. "My good older brother and friend! To you I will always be the *little* brother, I see. Remember that, young warriors" – to the Three.

"Ah. I suspect they already know," said Broken Spear, and the Three grinned.

"So they do. Better hunting tonight, young warriors. Here, help yourselves to the spiced roast; feed up for tomorrow," the Clan Leader urged them. "Perhaps after the Conclave our Great Warrior and Champion would like to go home with us and see his grandchildren."

"I would," the old hunter said. "I would indeed like that…" and their talk drifted off into the night.

***

RENEGADE
The Warrior

THE THIRD DAY of the Conclave saw every topic thrown open to debate—and a few people missing who had been there, K'vash in particular, Renegade noticed. He'd probably never hear about *that* Challenge...

Today *everyone* had something to say, it seemed, and Renegade wondered how they could reach any conclusions in a year, let alone a day.

But they surprised him. In the early evening, debate was shut down, delegates recalled to their seats, and votes taken. They had some unexpected issues and unpredicted results:

* They placed R'shba 3 under quarantine until they could determine whether any native species survived above the insect level. If not, the planet would be scoured of its alien parasites. (This alone was a wrenching decision for the Hunters.)

"We decide this with great regret," said the Six Systems Director. "We have never deliberately caused widespread species' death and extinction before, never in our spacefaring history. However, in this case we think it justified, or the entire Galaxy will wear one face, and diversity will be lost. And the People might be, also."

* A Hunt Ship would retrieve a flight computer, if any, from the alien ship on R'shba 3, and attempt to retrace its course. A cautious observation of that technological species would be made to see if they had generated of the bone-beasts or were their victims. All members of the *tautschen* pack would wear the detonator device.

* Broken Spear's recommendation to re-evaluate the Divided World with its hostile intelligence would be carried out. No one really expected that situation to change, but "in a few years, with a well-protected research and hunt team, it shall be done," the Six Systems Director promised.

* And finally, a watch bulletin would go out to all starships, which act under Hunt Council auspices, to be on guard against the bone-beasts, and to operate only while carrying trained hunters aboard. The custom among traders and passenger ships had been falling off lately; and the Conclave re-established it.

These were the major decisions. There were a few minor ones.

"I don't like letting the R'shba system wait," Broken Spear told his half-brother. "If only I had been able to convince them to attack the beast at once!"

"You did your share and more," the clan leader soothed him. "And it will run your way in the end, strong trophy contingent notwithstanding. By-the-path, you won some other important victories in the minor resolutions."

"Other victories? Ah, yes, allowing Hunt schools anywhere among our inhabited starworlds, as long as they are taught by a recognized master hunter, hybrid or no, or a clan hunter of rank...

"And granting more autonomy to planetary Hunt Councils—under the guise of letting them react quickly to a threat—yes, that will take us far, I think."

"And don't forget the concession made for any clan hunters, so long as they are not Chief Hunters, to be allowed to sit on Hunt Councils from now on. A great victory, I call it," Burning Spear added.

"Perhaps...if the freeholders lose their fears that we will take over once there," his old teacher told him.

Burning Spear laughed. "Don't be surprised if *you* receive an invitation to sit on one yourself, brother. And don't be too quick to pass it by either."

"Ah, so you want me to do more work, do you?"

The clan leader slapped him lightly on the shoulder, a familiarity Broken Spear would have permitted few other adults. "Work will keep you young, old warrior. And being young will keep you with us for many more years. Now, where are your Three tonight?"

"Ambushed by delegates from P'taal 5 and the Dinosaur Clan. A friendly ambush. They have bonds there."

Burning Spear nodded. "Why don't you go and see those grandchildren of yours, brother? Your daughter asks after you every night. I'll wait for your Three here, and conduct them myself. Are they also like sons to you?"

A smile. "Oh yes. On-course they are. Now it is I who tremble when they go afield...ah, I am getting too old for this, my brother. A warrior should die in battle, saving his loved ones from harm, not sit by his window and search the night, yearning for them to come home..." he started for the aircar.

"But not die yet, brother," the leader said softly after him; "by the Spirit-of-all, not yet."

***

THE THREE returned after the feasting started. They'd had to politely refuse a number of other invitations for meat-sharing because they were expected here with Rydderrak. Burning Spear waived their apologies for being late, seated them between himself and Broken Spear, and plied them with food.

Their mentor sat near a young couple, perhaps in their late forties or early fifties, and dandled two small children on his lap, who didn't look more than nine or ten years old, themselves.

Renegade wondered how old his "grandfather" had been, when he and his mate had the young woman who was his daughter. He also noticed something else…

He's happy here. He belongs. He has family here. I wonder, is he ever that happy out there on Arvien 4, with us?

But these were questions he could not ask.

Broken Spear's two grandchildren were girl and boy – Ja'shyk and R'tter-dzai – Red Flower and Little Panther – but the girl with her brick red coloring and orange tummy bands looked the most like the old warrior, as did her mother, Antelope Singer, a game caller and master huntress in her own right. The father, G'atian Halfhand, was a former ranked hunter disabled by partial loss of a hand. The clan would send him to University to have his hand restored and to learn the latest methods of game management. When he finished with his studies, he would teach them to the clan's hunters.

The entire clan, Burning Spear told the Three, numbered nearly twenty million souls. "There were once three times that many, before so many of our young people went off to the stars; yet we feel this is a better number, more easily supported by the land. And now we have Rydderrak daughter-clans on some of the starworlds too."

The clan, he told them, traced its origins back to a few families at the dawn of time.

"Relationships within a clan can be incredibly entwined," the leader went on: "You would need a computer or one of our eldest storytellers to keep track of all the half-brothers and sisters, cousins and uncles and aunts…" He noticed Renegade's mouth open a little, showing the points of his biting teeth, and then close, as if he'd thought better of something.

"Yes, Great Warrior, you have a question? Ask, and I'll answer if I can."

"Yes, Es—ah, Burning Spear– and I'm just Renegade, please – I do have a question." Renegade chose his words carefully: "How is it I see aircars and lasers, and hear of computers, being used alongside, ah…tents and spears and cooking fires? I mean no offense, *vr'*Leader," – that last added to make sure his intentions were plain.

"And none is taken, Renegade." The flame-red giant looked at him closely for a moment. Finally he nodded to himself, and said:

"You were brought up on a high technology world, weren't you? Yes, I thought so…

"Well, our original system, our clan system, still exists here on Homeworld and on some of the outworlds because of our beliefs: We believe it is right and natural to live as one with the land as the Great Spirit made us. The land feeds us and in return we cherish the land and its creatures; we do as little as possible to disturb its balance. We build our homes and make our clothes out of natural products. We may kill our food with lasers, but we use it all, from meat and sinew to hoof and bone. What little we do not use is left far from camp for the scavengers to find.

"We live like this because we *choose* to; we feel close to life, at one with all life..."

"The Credo," Renegade said.

Burning Spear's smile turned personal and warm. "Yes, in truth; the Credo gives the words the *tautschen* live by: *'—to the rock and the cloud and the stars of the sea, we are kindred.'* And we may only hope, young warrior, that something of it goes out to the stars with you. Come, have more meat, and then tell us about yourselves, about your worlds and how you live on them."

This unusual request convinced Renegade the young clan leader had real depth to him, that he was more than a jocular Chance-farer in life...

So after they ate, Renegade talked about their life on Arvien 4; and the clan leader and his elders listened intently, along with everyone sitting nearby. His words were passed on by True Speakers, who relay news and stories to all those people who might be seated too far away for even their sharp ears to hear.

Soon Rampage became inspired to put in his part; then Dasrylion, the most reluctant talker of the three. It became a real dialogue between them and Rydderrak Clan, comparing their different yet similar cultures; and to Renegade it was more exciting than his best hunting tale, to learn how a people lived and in what they believed.

The night deepened. The youngest children had been put to bed in the tents when Burning Spear turned to his older brother and said,

"You were correct about the hunt school, my brother, and about your off-world hunters. I am not as concerned as I was, if this is what they learn."

"Thank you, Burning Spear; I am honored. I try to include morality with the training, sometimes to satiation..." and the old hunter smiled at his Three.

Rampage spoke up. "What about hunting here on Homeworld, Clan Leader? Is it good? What's a Master Hunt like?"

"It is good, but hard. The animals grow in great numbers. Our lessened population relieved the pressure on them, and they prosper. But they are very shy, Rampage, very hard to get close to without the camouflage suits. And the Master Hunts mostly go off-world now." He was struck by a sudden thought, and turned to Broken Spear:

"Have you ever told them about your Master Hunt, brother?"

"It is not a story for children," Broken Spear said. His Three made a subdued movement, and he smiled, gently rebuked. "Still, all the children are abed now, aren't they? Even some of the adults" – for the clan was breaking up, seeking tents and slumber; "and since we spoke of that planet in Conclave…."

Yet he hesitated, looking uncomfortable.

"It is time, my brother," the Clan Leader said. His eyes and tone were quite serious. He was not making a suggestion.

The three young men were astounded to see their mentor obey.

"I suppose it is, Esteemed Leader," he said, and began…

Six....The Divided World

T'AKAION'S STORY---Well, young warriors, my Master Hunt took place on what we call the Divided World. It is inhabited by the only other existing technological race we know of...

One that lives in fear and thrives on hatred.

(He paused. Burning Spear signaled to have his waterskin and cup replaced. The youngsters drew in their breaths.)

I was not told everything when I was dropped off, but our good Chief Hunter Devereaux* did tell me to use my new camo-suit and leave the animal-call translator on at all times, to observe for a while before I decided on a trophy beast. And to be very careful.

He was also kind enough to leave me on a sort of scrubby plain, near the only waterhole within many *kri-veh,* where I could conceal myself. He'd come back in a 10-day span, he said, if I did not call sooner.

("He set a day limit?" Burning Spear asked in disbelief.)

He did. I didn't know it then, but it is almost never done...

(Neither did Burning Spear, Renegade thought. He's never heard this story either.)

So. I turned my suit on – they weren't as well-made as they are now, and more prone to distortion and failure – and I moved into the scrubby vegetation at the waterhole.

This world was cooler than mine and its air thinner and drier, I noticed. Not too much cooler, in this region, but *much* drier. Even though it was a warm summer day there, I had to go to water vapor at once.

---

* Pronounced Dev-er-ROW—Some names may use sounds and nuances familiar to the human ear. They are not human.

The waterhole stirred with living creatures. Birds chattered in the small trees; little ground creatures scurried through the brush; and my approach startled a number of four-legged grasseaters, handsomely marked in brown and white, with short blackish horns on their heads. I learned later these were excellent food animals. But their senses were very sharp. They sensed me coming and bolted.

Any-route, I chose a slightly larger tree as my watchtower and camped at its base, since the branches were too thin to hold me. I decided to wait for larger prey.

I watched the rest of that day and through the night, their days being slightly longer than ours. Just before dawn I heard a distant rumbling.

It became louder, and louder still, and the ground began to shake.

I couldn't see anything while sitting in the scrub, so I sprang from my hiding place and ran out into the grass.

The ground shook and shook and the uproar became deafening. What was it, a landbreaker? Or the vibration of some huge and terrible machine?

Then they burst over a nearby ground swell, and I saw them in their thousands: a herd of great shaggy stampeding beasts whose body-heat made the dark land glow, as if a wave of lava swept over it.

I felt a moment of distress: they were charging straight for me, and I was invisible! I thought I would be trampled. I was not sure they could avoid me even if I turned the suit off. I would have to take a stand near the waterhole.

Before I could get there, the vast herd began to slow. They were not stampeding after all, merely coming to water. They slowed to a trot, then a walk, and began fanning out on all sides of the oasis.

They might be able to sense me, as the *teveh* had; but I switched the suit off any-path and stood there while they spread out around me.

These beasts resembled a type of krolf, of stocky build with a pair of stout horns. They were peculiarly furred: a pile of curly dark hair over the shoulder hump and forequarters, very short hair and a skinny tail on the hind. Most were medium-sized, though some were larger, their shoulders just below the height of mine.

While they would not come close enough to touch, they did not seem particularly afraid of me, either. There were some big bulls among them, massive and powerful. My jaw opened in anticipation.

And they came on, number after number of them, snuffling the air, a few drinking at a time, the rest grazing all around me, till they covered the waterhole and surrounding plains. There were almost as many of them as there were blades of grass on the prairie.

And I thought *here* is a prime hunting animal. I would give them peace until dawn, then see if I could get a big bull to challenge me.

I sat a while by my chosen tree and observed them. Clearly this was not the most intelligent beast on this planet, but it might show some spirit in a fight.

That world's light yellowish sun rose in glory. The sky took on fabulous colors and the vast prairie shone and rippled like the sea. It was such a sunrise as I, born on this more tropic world, enclosed by high jungle, had rarely seen; and I simply enjoyed it for a while.

Finally it was time. I had selected my prey: a bull – an old chieftain so experienced in battle that the younger bulls avoided him. But he had passed his prime: his motions were a little stiff, his eyes rheumy. It would not hurt to remove him from the herd.

Still, when I went before him, he stood in his strength and did not run. I had the laser, but this would be better with the spear.

"Hai!" I challenged him, and he rolled his eyes and stared at me. Who was this two-legged upstart to defy him?

I shouted again and shook the spear. His heart lay deep under that heavy fur coat – a neck stab might be called for...

This time he pawed the ground and tossed his massive head. Weighing his choices.

"*Chai'k hai*!" I yelled and made a quick feint at him. That did it. Almost before I could set my spear he charged, bellowing. I stood fast with the lance aimed at his shoulder, below the hump.

He slammed into it with the force of a falling mountain. He must have been two or three times my weight, and all muscle. The tremendous shock lifted me from my feet; and then that horned head was under me, and the bull hooked upward. I twisted on the spear shaft, trying to turn aside.

A short sharp horn came up against my inner thigh, slid along it – and dropped back down. The spear had done its work. The old chieftain died nobly and well.

I came down rather shakily myself and stared at him. When I was sure he was dead, I pulled the spear out and saluted his spirit, thanking him for his courage.

Then I gave a victory roar, which startled the animals nearby, and had a completely unexpected result.

An ululating cry answered mine. I looked around, astonished. It hadn't come from the shaggy beasts.

Then I saw them. A row of figures, twenty in all, stretched along the horizon and nearer, below the crest.

At first I thought they were another kind of animal, a quadruped with a heavy head in front, and some kind of taller, thinner hump in the middle of the back.

Some of them loped forward, and I could see them free of the sun's glare. They were two creatures, the spinal "humps" a species of biped, seated upon the second creature, the four-legged mounts, which bore them willingly. Were they some kind of symbiote?

("Riders!" two of the young listeners burst out, as Broken Spear paused to drink.)

Yes, in truth, riders, lightweight enough to mount and control an animal, which you know we as adults have always been too heavy to do. –Although I know some children who try it from time to time…

("Do they?" the young clan leader put in, all innocence, and everyone burst out laughing. When they subsided, Broken Spear resumed his story.)

So. Here they came, scattering the shaggy beasts before them; and there I stood, in plain sight – for I had forgotten to turn my light-shielding back on.

I could have done it then, I suppose. I had an eyeblink to decide. But I had already scanned their weapons, and all they seemed to have were spears and some sort of longbow. So I remember thinking how foolish I was even as they came thundering down on me.

About 50 *kri* away, they stopped their mounts – which were interesting long-necked and long-tailed animals with single-hoofed feet. Two of the riders stayed there, hands on their bows, while the one in the middle walked his mount forward.

He halved the distance, halted, and leaned over slightly to look at me. I had my facemask on and my translator running; and even though he sat on a tall animal, his head barely topped mine.

But all he said was "Hah!" – no meaning here – and his steed snorted. I thought: *Their faces are different. They have no big biting akai...and look at that long fleshy proboscis running down the middle of their faces. No small neat nose, but more of a snout than we have. But their manes are like ours; they even wear them in a similar way.* This fellow wore his both braided and free.

He studied me for a long time. Then he raised his spear, vertically, not horizontally, not threatening, and shouted something my computer called a greeting.

I decided to imitate him. I raised *my* spear point-up and repeated his words – clumsily, but it seemed to come across: "Greetings!"

I felt encouraged. They were all looking at me, and none showed any hostility yet.

My greeter said something else, a series of words at which my translator could only guess. I decided not to reply verbally, but with slow hand signals showing him I did not understand.

Whether he could interpret them or not, he knew we were not communicating, for he signaled me with an outspread hand, which they use to mean "wait" or "hold," then turned his horse (I learned the name later) and galloped back to the other two riders.

The three of them had a conference. After a while, his two companions turned their mounts and galloped off together. I still stood there with my dead *krolf* and my spear in hand, watching them as they had watched me.

The two companions split again, moving their mounts expertly; and when they drove into a knot of the shaggy beasts and began running them back toward me, I knew what they were doing.

They were going to herd one of the beasts back toward me so I could kill it. In effect, they were saying, "Let's see you do that again!"

I nearly laughed out loud with relief. I stepped away from my kill and onto open ground, hoping they wouldn't send four or five animals to me at once.

They didn't. Smoothly and neatly, they thinned that group down to three running beasts, two adults and a calf.

Coming almost straight at me now, they let one adult and the calf slip away, and drove the last adult directly on.

What a sight it was! Those beings moved like one with their mounts, and they whooped and shouted as much from joy as from the pursuit.

At the last *ktarn,* the lone animal veered to pass around me. It was a female, smaller than the bull, and made for a trickier throw. I would not normally take a female during a hunt unless I knew she was barren, but these beings had offered up a Challenge, and I felt I needed to impress them.

I aimed and threw.

The spear plunged through the cow's brisket, just behind the front legs. Its force sent her down and rolling and I ran over to her before she could recover. She went into shock, her eyes glazing, so I seized her by one horn and cut her throat with the killing-knives – and it was done.

Victory whoops and ululations burst out of my watchers then, as I stood over my second kill. The first rider came up, inspected the cow, said something of approval to me, and made an arm-and-spear signal to the others on the horizon.

This time they all began riding forward among the plains-krolf, whooping and yelling. I stood to admire their technique: they would ride full-tilt at the herd, start small stampedes, then line up with a particular animal and proceed to lance it; or more amazing yet, shoot an arrow into it at a dead run.

The warrior who had greeted me, stayed with me, whether out of curiosity or desire to protect his people, I do not know. But I found myself admiring him and to some degree *trusting* him…I did not think he would attempt to kill me now.

After I watched the hunt a while, telling him how much I admired his people's bravery and skill – which he on-course didn't understand but listened to closely – I knew I had to get busy and dress out my kills or they would spoil.

So I made hand signals and gestures offering to give him the cow I had killed, which would be the proper move if I were hunting on some other clan's territory on Homeworld, to share part of the kill. Thankfully, he seemed to understand and wasn't offended; so I deliberately moved away from it to the slain bull.

I knelt to disembowel it, then skin it and remove the head and horns. Since these people ate the meat, I reasoned I could also, and I butchered the rest as food.

I heard the warrior saying something, and surreptitiously watched as two young females of his kind came up and began to clean the cow. After that, clip-clop, clip-clop, sounded the beat of hooves against the ground, and the warrior rode up to me. He watched what I was doing in utter silence. The Divided World may be a cacophony of jabber now, but in the past, *some* knew the value of silence.

I had grown very impressed with these people; and there was no question in my mind that they *were* people. They had neither offered to attack me nor fled in panic. Certain that I had made an important discovery, I resolved to let Devereaux and our elders know about them when I finished my hunt. I knew others of our People hunted here; but at this point, I had not been told anything about that, or much about the Divided World either.

As the day waned, I prepared the meat and bagged it, rolled up the hide, and made ready to find a camp for the night. I was just wondering if I should abandon the oasis when my first contact rode closer and said something to me.

He gestured; and I saw one of the women leading two riding animals forward. One of these pulled a kind of flat sledge…I had seen other such carrying carts piled with meat and hides, and realized they would use it to carry this meat away, too.

They apparently meant for me to ride the second horse. I was thrilled but dubious: what did they have in mind? Was this a gesture of hospitality or --? And that little animal didn't look as if its back could hold me. The other riders were perhaps a third my weight and smaller overall.

But I was young and on an adventure. I decided to go along.

I loaded my bull onto the waiting sledge and put my hand on the back of the horse. It snorted and danced a little…and it still looked small to me.

Nevertheless I did not want to insult my hosts, so I bent my knees and slung one leg over the animal's back, as I had seen them do. Then I was astride!

And the poor beast buckled. I could feel his hocks collapsing under me. As his hindquarters sank down, I stood up and quickly backed off of him.

A small crowd of two-leggers had gathered round me by this time, and they burst out laughing. It must have been the funniest sight they'd seen in a while.

The horse scrambled to his feet, unhurt, and by then I was laughing, too.

My contact grinned (unlike us, they show the small-spears in a humorous mood; it's unsettling) and he gestured to me to "Come! Come!" The women led the packhorse; I proceeded on foot to their gathering. I found that I could keep up with them at the walk or the trot. I thought sometime I must test my running speed against their horses…

That night they gave me a spare lodge to sleep in and left the buffalo meat outside my tent flap. For most of the night, I set up a smoking-fire, quickly ate a little meat (I was wary of raising my facemask before them. Then our differences would become quite evident) and on invitation went to watch the dancing and celebration of the hunt.

They were naturally curious about me and the gear I wore, but seemed to be restrained from physically touching me; although a number of the bolder children in camp did snatch a quick rub at my legs – light, darting touches to see if the red "paint" I wore would come off.

I turned my camo-suit on that night and slept away from their camp; but it was uncannily like being back in my clan. Small-toothed and strange-looking as they were, these people reminded me of home. Here was someone we could learn about, perhaps even trade and hunt with, I felt.

By the second day among them, I had picked up some of their language, and the computer was doing better with it, too. I learned that the individual who had first ridden over to me was this clan's War Chief, Shaken Lance. His title would be First Warrior here.

I also learned they were torn between regarding me as a man, a god, or perhaps a demon.

("A demon is a kind of bad spirit," Broken Spear took time aside to explain, "which has mystical powers. Unlike our present view of the universe, they see powerful entities of both good and evil—whereas, to us, the universe is basically good.")

Their shaman, I discovered, was awaiting a vision about me, which would tell them how to treat me. Forewarned, I prepared for any turn of the Circle it might bring.

Meanwhile, the successful hunt was still being celebrated. They tested me in various ways: they held spear-throwing and arrow-shooting contests, in which they invited me to take part. They were excellent hunters, for they could cast a spear as accurately as I, though not as forcefully or as far – to be expected from my greater size and strength.

They had some consolation with the bow: I wasn't accustomed to bow hunting and did badly. But the few brave warriors who cared to try me at wrestling were shown a quick defeat (though I took care not to unleash my full strength), and they were mightily impressed. They also had footraces, and some kind of ballgame, which I managed to beg out of.

They were intensely curious about why I always wore the mask and backpack (while awake, least-route) and I could tell it wouldn't be long before they asked to see my face.

On the third day Shaken Lance brought me a message from the shaman: he had had a vision and wished to see me at once.

I went with a sinking heart. Surely I was about to be unmasked; and then I would be forced to fight or flee, and ruin what I was building with these people. I had no wish to harm them, although I would defend myself if it came to that.

The shaman, Raven's Feather, greeted me cordially, and bade me share a smoking instrument with him. In his own tongue, I respectfully told him that if I did, I would have to reveal myself to him; which he smiled and said,

"I have already learned something of you, Great Warrior, in my vision. It says you come from the sky."

I was shocked. Here was a shaman in truth, a wise man of another race, and he too could "dream true!"

"Then I will reveal myself." I raised my hand to my mask; "I am not as you are, but that does not mean I am your enemy, for I am not," and I unsnapped the vapor line and eased the mask off. My entire body tensed.

The old medicine man's eyes widened. He uttered a quick prayer, then sat motionless as stone.

"Here you see me as I am, Raven's Feather," I said. "Know that I indeed come from the sky, but I am a man of my People, not a spirit or demon."

"A man! And not a spirit!" he murmured. And with infinite care, he reached out to me.

I froze. He had no weapons, yet it took all my self-control to sit there and let him touch me – as I imagine it took all of his, to do so.

He touched my face: my breathing came fast and hard. But he wished to sense my difference directly, perhaps to verify what his eyes told him; and he touched my jaw, my enlarged *akai* and even passed lightly over the front of my mouth. Then his hands traveled up to my cheeks even to my eyelids, which I closed briefly, then to my mane.

"This is...hair," he murmured, "bound up and thicker than ours... and you have the teeth of a great mountain-cat – these are larger, like some creature deeper in memory – yet you appear somewhat like a cat, only upright, like a man. Are you truly a mortal being, with a heart that beats?"

I took his hand in mine then, and showed him; let him feel my heart pounding in my chest, since he could not see it or hear it as I did.

"So," he said at last, "now I have touched something of wonder...are all men from the sky like you?"

"I know only of myself and my people, called the *tautschen* – hunters," I told him. "There may be other people in the sky. There are many hunting grounds there, with wonderful beasts upon them, each a world circling those little campfires of the stars."

"And what are you called by your people?"

"I am called Dreamseeker." I rendered it as best I could.

His eyes lit up. "Dreamseeker! A good name! And what do you seek from us?"

"To hunt with you," I told him; "Or, rather, to have your help in finding an animal worthy of my spear. It is my rite of manhood, and I must prove my courage in facing it."

"This I understand," he said. "Replace your mask a moment. I must bring in our war chief."

I went through an agony of waiting while he brought in Shaken Lance. Yet I felt a rush of discovery, also. These people were so like us in their customs, in their sense of honor – what a source of wonder they would be!

Shaken Lance became the only other individual in that clan to see my true face. Even though the shaman prepared him by telling him where I came from and how I looked, he nearly reeled when he saw me unmasked.

After a time he recovered himself enough to make a small joke:

"Now I could be called *Shaking Leaf* if others see me like this!"

He took some reassuring that I meant no harm to his people. Like any good warrior, he was concerned.

I offered to leave his camp that night, but he refused, saying it would be a great discourtesy to drive away an invited guest. Shrewdly, he wanted to know if I did not fight them simply because they were many, and I was only one.

"I have weapons which kill at a distance faster than any arrow flies, and which are as deadly as a wildfire," I said. "Come with me into the plains alone sometime and I will show you."

"I believe you," he answered. "I will not go now, but sometime I will, just to see..."

In the end, he agreed to help me with the hunt. He knew of a beast which might be a match for my strength and size, and agreed to take me to it. For my part, I said that at the end of a tenday, (now whittled to seven) even if I did not have a trophy, I would depart and trouble them no more.

Despite their great honor and courtesy, I think they felt relieved at that.

(Broken Spear stopped for a moment to wet his throat with the fresh cool water. After swallowing, he sat staring into the fire for a few kt-tare' before he resumed...)

Shaken Lance kept his word. The next day he and I set out with a small hunting pack. They rode, but I found I could keep up with their pace easily.

We began with a narrow creek near their camp, and followed it through brushy trees for some distance, and finally into canyon country. They were looking for some sort of creature – the Brother to Man, they called it – almost a sacred animal to them.

Finally we came upon its trail: huge clawed pawmarks sunk into the dust. From their depth, it was plain the creature weighed more than I did; and according to my guides, was armed with both biting teeth and long slashing claws.

"This is a mighty being worthy of you, Dreamseeker," the war chief told me. "We will follow along with you, but not to fight."

"Agreed," I said, and thanked him for his help.

We proceeded. The pugmarks became more and more distinct. At last they showed heat-trace. I got excited. *"He is very near,"* I whispered, *"in that thicket ahead."*

Shaken Lance nodded. "To your fight, then, Dreamseeker. It is a good day to live – and a good day to die!" With that stirring salute, he reined in, and I went forward alone.

The bushes rustled ahead. A heavy grunting sound came out of them, like a giant *kreppa-tsrr* makes when he is angry. I stopped just before the brush and uttered my challenge.

I don't know what I expected – not the hairy mountain that rose from the bush. It stood on its hind legs, its tiny eyes glittered, the forepaws spread claws like killing-knives. And it roared a challenge of its own.

I crouched and set my spear. I would aim upward for the heart. I expected him to walk towards me.

But the great beast fell forward and charged on four feet. My spear glanced useless off its shoulder and it hit me like an avalanche.

I went down in a bad spot, where the foreclaws could rip me and the fanged snout tear at my face. It was the worst mistake I'd made in a long time.

I thrust up into the neck with my knives, but that only seemed to enrage it. It tore off my mask, and desperately I forced the clashing jaws back with my arm.

That brought its savage claws into play along my shoulders and sides. My armor gave me some protection, but it was starting to tear away along the seams, and slashes opened up in my unprotected side.

It took the effort of my young life to bend my knees together under that massive body. Slowly, too slowly, I began forcing the beast's shoulders upward and back, still with my knives fixed in its neck, the jaws foaming at my face.

Finally, finally, I held the great bear poised above me. It went mad to reach me, pawing, slashing, biting. I had to pull the knives out and at the same time straighten my legs and kick that great body upward to expose the heart.

I gave a great wrench, jerked out the knives.

It lifted like a slab of stone. I balanced its enormous body with my feet, saw the heart, then twisted my body around under it and let it fall.

Thank the Great Spirit my thrust was clean. It cleaved the breast and heart and a gush of life-blood plunged over me.

That stopped the beast at last. I struggled to free myself from under that bulk and assess my own injuries…I knew they were there.

Shaken Lance came running. "Dreamseeker! Do you live?" He stared at the mingled fluids carpeting me – mine and the great *vraun's*, and he wasn't sure, either.

"Help me…to the water, brother," I wheezed at him. He tried, and I managed to take some of the burden off him by half-supporting myself. I plunged into cool shallow water and let it wash the gore off me. Its cleansing action wakened the fire of my injuries: they were claw-cuts, and some went deep.

"We thought you had joined the spirits," Shaken Lance told me. "Come, we will make a travois and take you back to the shaman for treatment – *never* have I seen anyone fight and kill so mighty a bear as that one, and with only a knife!"

I convinced him that I should not be moved any great distance; and after dragging myself from the stream, I had his help in getting out my med-kit. He sent the two warriors waiting for him back to camp to fetch the healer, and stayed to help me dress my wounds. I think it hit home again how different I was when he saw the color of my blood – theirs has only the iron-oxygenating base, none of the supplemental ones – but he bore up with great courage until I had sealed the wounds and was somewhat comfortable again.

"There is a small cave upstream where you may lie," he told me. "I think the great bear may not need it anymore…your fire-weapon, you did not use it? Does it not work?"

"Look, Shaken Lance," I sat up, pointed out a boulder, and showed him.

He fell back in astonishment. Finally: "But you did not use it because--?"

"It would make the hunt too easy, and not be a test of my courage otherwise," I explained; and he understood. What a warrior he was!

So. To shorten this tale, I spent the next several days recuperating in that small cave near the stream. Their shaman came and tended me with my own medicines; and their clan even skinned and prepared the hide of the great *vraun* for me. Eventually I would bring it home, body and bones; and its mighty form still stands in the center of my trophy hall today.

(The young hunters looked sharply at each other. Ooh! They knew that beast. Broken Spear smiled slightly and went on)

I took only enough meat for several meals and let them have the rest. All I wanted to do was sleep.

At dawn of the tenth day, I had recovered enough to walk out on my own and return to the waterhole and my original dropoff spot.

I bade Shaken Lance and Raven's Feather a reluctant farewell, for as they themselves told me, "We have traveled a long way in a short time; you have become as one of us;" and they invited me to return should I ever pass their way again.

As it happened, I had the chance.

(Broken Spear was silent for many moments. Finally he spoke, in a voice heavy with emotion: "This...is the worst part for me...")

Devereaux was surprised by my friendship with the people of the Divided World, and by my description of their way of life.

"This would in truth make a difference in how we look at them," he told me. "I have a few more of our young hunters to pick up; then we can return here. Perhaps the humans will speak to me, too?"

"I think they will," I said, supremely confident. The word of a Chief Hunter, especially someone like Devereaux, would carry great importance with the Homeworld clans. We might at last enter into talk and trade with the Divided World.

We had a distance to travel, to pick up the other New Hunters, and didn't succeed in returning for perhaps two tendays. I don't know how long it was in that world's time; but my breath crystallized in the planet's morning air, and the rolling plains were silvered when I stepped from the Scout ship with Devereaux.

"Their camp lies over there," I nodded over a few knolls, "unless they have moved it. Where that smoke rises. I can see it. Let me go in first, Devereaux."

The Chief Hunter frowned. "That's a large smoke cloud. Do they burn so much to keep warm…? Well and good, *vr'*hunter, go ahead."

As soon as I topped the knoll, I knew something was wrong. There *was* too much smoke – and now I could see live flame – their lodges were burning.

I cried out and charged down into the village.

Oh, what a tragedy met me there!

(...the old warrior closed his eyes and put his head back. His voice throbbed...)

They were dead, all dead.

The ground was covered with the slain – men – women – even children. Yes, you may well cry out, brothers and sisters! Even little children, incapable of doing harm…I found among the dead those whose faces I remembered, whose names I knew… I found one infant's body half-lying under his mother's: she had died trying to shield him – but the enemy had murdered him too.

Yes; the enemy. Fire had not done this thing, but a mortal foe. At first I thought it might have been a pack of maddened animals, but Devereaux caught up with me and said, "Look, Dreamseeker, this is no beast's work; this was done by their own kind."

"No!" I cried. "They never – they couldn't –"

For answer, he pointed silently to the northeast. There lay many cold-tracks, footmarks similar to but smaller than our own, and animals' hoofprints... Riding animals had passed through here, carrying other human beings…

"Those elongated tracks are the marks of covered feet that you see," he told me, "not bared feet or sandaled. Manufactured weapons made these wounds..." and he attempted to show me, but I could not look and would not listen…

"The tracks of their enemy! Then I will track *them,* and avenge these people!" I roared and sprang away at a run.

I could hear Devereaux call after me, "No! Hunter, wait!"

But I was blind with tears and rage and I ignored him.

The trail was wide and easy to follow. The raiders made no attempt to disguise it – arrogance on top of murder. I ran along swiftly: at full speed I was as fast as their horses. And the massacre was too recent for them to have gone far.

Three *kri-veh* farther on, I caught them. Ahead of me on the prairie rode a group of strangely-clad beings. They formed a long line, two by two, laughing and bragging about their 'victory'. Even in my rage I noticed that these monsters' weapons differed from my friends': they had long stocks and a firing-barrel, far superior to my friends' arrows and spears. How easy it must have been to slay them…

So, I thought, *let us see if you can fight just one warrior – one who is ready for you.* I switched on my light-shielding, took up my spear in one hand, ejected my wristknives in the other – and ran up on them from behind.

Their hearts were hot, but their bodies soft. I killed the first two in line with incredible ease, as they must have slain my friends. Then I pushed them off their mounts, jumped on in their place, one foot on each horse – and vaulted to the next pair in line.

I killed six of these human monsters before they woke up to the fact that they were dying.

They scattered their mounts in confusion and began shooting – outward, where they imagined an enemy must be. I came on them horse by horse, not harming the steeds but slaying the ones who rode them.

The monsters were so wild to see an enemy somewhere beyond them that they couldn't see one in their midst.

They kept discharging their weapons. By the ricochet sounds, I guessed they fired small projectiles with enough velocity to hurt me – if they found me.

Yet I kept coming, between their horses, beside them, even pulling the steeds aside to get at the beasts who rode them. The humans died in terror, as my poor friends must have died.

Finally, as I pursued one off to the side, a small knot of them broke away and went galloping downhill. I finished my kill and took the remaining horses by the mouth-straps, seeking the creatures that fled.

There was a square wooden building down there in the draw, near the declivity of a little creek, and the four survivors stampeded toward it.

I cursed them and pulled my captured horses close together. Then as quickly and lightly as I could, I straddled two of them. They squealed in panic and made for home – the wooden building itself.

So for the first and only time I rode their steeds and my weight was spread sufficiently for them to bear me.

Ahead the wooden doors started to swing open; they were getting away! I sat up to aim the laser and one of my steeds stumbled and fell, pitching me to the ground.

At that moment, my camo-suit chose to go out.

I leaped up in a fury. I could hear cries and exclamations from the fort as they saw me. Their projectiles zinged and zipped around me – so I quickly located the shooters along the top of the wall.

(Renegade stiffened, remembering P'taal 5.)

I sent them laser-bolts to cook on. Two quick shots – whump! whump! – knocked out the walls' top rails. I launched myself toward the fort again.

Something opened up a wound along my arm. Where from this time? Two watchtowers, on both of the near corners. I dropped, rolled, came up and sent whitefire into those towers. The wooden structures began to burn.

They'd closed the huge wooden doors after the riders, so I made a running leap onto the front walls and began to climb.

Someone shouted above me. I looked up….there was an explosion, white smoke – and searing pain erupted along my jaw. I fell back; I fought through the pain and marked my target. The laser knocked him backwards, his head gone. Then I blew some holes in their wall…

(The young hunters with him almost jumped up with realization.

"The dream! The dream!" they cried.

*"Yes, the dream," he agreed, "the wooden wall, my shattered akai**...* *Fortunately I didn't think of it then – I was lost in a blind rage – I scaled their walls, and went in after them."*

---

* akai – spear (their word for 'tooth')

Broken Spear sighed. He knit his fingers together. "Enough to say there was more killing inside the fort, much more. I killed every two-legged being I found in that bolthole. Least-route they were all males; they had no females and young amongst them...good Chance for them.")

A short time later Devereaux found me sitting in the burning ruins with my head bowed into my hands, weeping.

He touched my shoulder, and I jumped.

He looked at me sadly and said, "Now you see what they are. When you spoke of a clan-living people here, I allowed myself to hope…but it always ends this way, with betrayal and slaughter. Even those whom you visited, even others like them." He made a weary gesture, gazed off into the distance. "We have seen a few peaceable peoples here; but they either learn to kill their own kind – or are killed by them.

"This world is ruled by hatred and fear, young hunter," he told me. "These creatures hate and fear their surroundings and other living creatures; they even hate and fear themselves, with reason. And their ways are too easily adopted – look at what *you* have done here!" and I was ashamed.

He sat down beside me.

"It was…like my vision," I realized at last. "What a terrible thing…if only I had known…I've found the place of my vision, and it is nightmare."

He put an arm around my shoulders.

"I know," he said, "I know." Gently he raised his fingertips to my broken *akai.* "And it has made you into Broken Spear – Dreamseeker no more."

***

HIS TALE was done. As the old warrior's Chief Hunter had done so many years before, his former Clan Leader now gently put an arm about his shoulders.

"It is a hard story, I know, brother," the leader said, "but it is over now, gone these many years. It grieves me to have hurt you by forcing you to tell it. Please forgive that rash command. I had never heard the story; and I thought your young masters should hear it –that's all. I hadn't known…"

Broken Spear raised his head to look at Burning Spear directly. "It does not matter, my brother; you are my Clan Leader; and it was time they knew." He lowered his head again.

Burning Spear backed off. *"I command you no longer,"* he whispered.

Abruptly he stood.

"Come!" he called to his assembled people, "this is too sad a note to end an evening. *R' tch'alai' rrn!* Let us have some music and dancing!"

And his people agreed with him. Soon they threw themselves into more lighthearted recreation, ancient tragedy set aside.

When Broken Spear looked up again, he found his Three gathered around him. *Are you all right?* Their expressions asked what their mouths were too polite to say.

He managed to relax his jaw in a slight smile for them. "I am on stat, my sons. I had many good years after that, and probably will have many more." He reached out, touched each one lightly on forearm or shoulder. "You concern touches me; I am honored."

Then he drew his legs up and stood, saying, "But I think I am too tired for further celebration, and I need to sleep. I bid you night's-rest, my fine young warriors. I will see you at first-light tomorrow."

Burning Spear, distracted at a distance by other business, saw the old hunter retreat to his lodge before he could speak to him again. Regret in his face, the Clan Leader started after him – but a hand on his wrist stopped him.

His wife, Wise Woman.

He turned to her. "Look at him. My cruelty has driven him from us. Unthinkingly I commanded him – *him* – who is higher than a hundred of me put together. I must go after him."

The hand on his wrist remained.

"No," his wife said. "He does not bear you any ill-wish. He understands you are young, and often impetuous. Talk to him tomorrow."

Burning Spear winced.

She continued, "He *accepts* you as clan leader, and obeys you in the old fashion, to show respect; even though one of his rank need obey no-one. It is his memories which make him sad. I am wise woman here; I know."

"But he will leave us tomorrow – and I have so much to tell him!"

"Let him go, my heart. He has not been truly happy here since his beloved K'shara died...Look there..." and she pointed toward the three young out-clan warriors, as one by one they rose to go after their friend. "They are the second and better part of his vision. He still follows his dream: *they* are his family now."

Her husband looked long at her. She was older than he, had been born Sunlit Water, but lost her baby-name very quickly when she showed her gift for healing and prophecy.

At last he asked her, "And will he achieve the rest of his vision, too? Will he live and die fulfilled of his dream, to spread the Credo and the

Code even among the Starborn? You, who can see the future, can you see our brother's as well?"

She closed her eyes and stood silent for a time, until Burning Spear felt she had withdrawn from him and from all the world.

When she opened her eyes again, she was smiling. "He will achieve everything he thought to, and more. The Great Spirit grants this to few. It is granted to him and to those around him. He will even be allowed to choose the time and manner of his own death – as we all do, unconsciously – he will do so consciously. Knowing and willing, he will choose.

"And this," she said softly, looking into a far territory, "is a gift only the greatest among us may have..."

***

"IF THE people of the Divided World are so evil, Grandfather, why do you want them studied?"

The questioner, as usual, was Renegade. He and his friends lay on rush mats in the room adjoining Broken Spear's; and the Elder's restless stirrings had kept them awake until Renegade felt he had to say something.

A rustle came from their mentor's room as the old warrior shifted his weight in response. He answered, "Because there is an enemy out there deadlier than they are, Renegade, one that could destroy all life in our galaxy as it rides the star waves with its prey."

Another rustle and heavy movement, then: "And perhaps because I remember what I found among those people, once, and I wonder if it could be there still, among any of them. It is not a world I ever want to go back to – and I pray you never have to go either, any of you."

"We probably never will, Grandfather," Renegade said in the darkness. But he wondered.

Great Warrior

"The thrown spear cannot be recalled."

---Hunt saying

"Take care what you wish for...or you will find it in your camp."

--- Hunters' saying

Seven....The Stars above Arvien

WHEN THE school ship arrived back on Arvien 4, the young hunters were surprised to learn that a *second* winter was just ending. They'd lost a whole year on their home planet; and Broken Spear had lost nearly as much time with his classes.

He regretted the lost season. "That happens after star travel," he told his little pack. "It used to be a much greater time distortion when the ships were slower, in my youth."

Despite the old warrior's guilt, the freehold hunters had delivered his herd share after the Autumn Drives as usual.

Dasrylion was happy that he'd missed his tedious herd duties. He would stay with his friends as long as he could before going home, about a tenday, while Rampage and Renegade put their own trophies together between chores and got ready for another summer of teaching. The Three would barely have time to set a few traplines and put the school in order before spring officially began. Renegade secretly worried that Dasryl would drift further and further away from them as he shouldered an ever-greater burden of duties at home.

They had just settled into their accustomed routine at the school when Broken Spear called them to his communications center.

"Our mail has backed up," he announced, "and it seems to consist of only two kinds of things: congratulations, and invitations."

"Invitations, Elder?" Dasrylion asked, puzzled.

"To begin with," he said, handing over a printout copy to each of them, "an invitation in the aftermath of the Conclave itself. Member systems are now allowed to fill a number of 'in the field' positions; so we have one opening on our local Hunt Council, and two from Six Systems."

"And they're for us!" Renegade read in astonishment.

"Three should cover all of you nicely," their mentor said; "Dasrylion for the local seat, you and Rampage for Six Systems."

He laughed at their sudden expressions of dismay. "It's a benefit to you. Field officials almost never have to attend a meeting physically – most of them are electronic now – and your vote carries as heavy a gamebag as that of any other delegate. You can make a change, a difference, in our people's society."

"But what about you, Grandfather?" Renegade objected. "One of these should go to you, at least."

"Ah." Broken Spear made a wry motion with his jaw. "It seems that I have been *personally* selected for that honor, and by no less than our Nine Systems Council. The Deputy Director, our old friend Kreh-t'vyk, tells me Arvien 4 is populous enough to deserve more than one regular delegate from our Hunt Council; and the vote went almost unanimously for me. Your father is the other one, Cold Tracker."

"'Almost unanimous'," Renegade said. "I have a heat-trace of who voted against you." K'vash, no longer chief director, still clung to a lower status seat.

"So do I," muttered Rampage.

"It does not matter, young warriors," Broken Spear told them. "I already decided to decline when the Deputy Director sent another message hard on the track of the first. He wanted to tell me the job involved mainly a quarterly review, very few in-person meetings, and that most votes are taken electronically, as I said..

"He also said that K'vash lost much of his credibility because of the way he treated...*kr-rr*...'three genuine heroes of the People'---and, ah, another matter." He smiled. "Perhaps I wouldn't have to see most of my suggestions go down to silence, this way."

"And you *could* make a difference in our society," Renegade put in slyly.

Broken Spear laughed. "Now you do me the honor of quoting me to myself, *t'churr?* Very well, I shall think on it."

"Besides, we'll be here to help with the students," Rampage added

The old hunter gave him a keen look. "Perhaps...and perhaps not. There are other invitations" – and he held out another copy of printouts, a long one.

While Rampage automatically reached out to take it, his two friends craned to see.

"Oh, by – in the name of the Nine!" Dasrylion breathed, reading. "These – these are—"

"Starship schedules. Berths open!" Renegade cried out. "Invitations to sail!"

"Look! Look! Made out to us by name!" from Rampage.

"And to the school," said practical Dasrylion. But his eyes were shining like theirs.

Broken Spear had to smile too. "So; our request has come to term at last. Do you want to take these into the hearthroom and study them before you decide?"

"Chak!" they cried and sprang up to leave the room.

He watched them with amusement and pride. Three strapping Hunters, a little over half-grown*, made far less noise than the trio of little boys they had been, even though they still acted like children at times. And Renegade still had no concept of what the title Great Warrior meant to him. They were seventeen and eighteen now, even allowing for the lapsed time in space – a difficult age – *as aren't they all?*

Again, he underestimated his "adopted" sons, for at the far threshold, first Renegade, then the two others halted and looked back.

"Grandfather," Renegade asked politely, "will you come and help advise us, please?"

Well done, the old hunter thought.

"I would be honored," he said.

***

RAMPAGE TORE OFF pieces of the long list so each of them could have one. After they settled down, they found almost 40 openings for hunters' berths. About a third of them came from other systems... Six Systems, no surprise there...but another, from Four Systems, was.

"Four's one of the older, longer-established systems," Renegade remarked. "They have four colonized worlds, two for hunting only, trophy worlds, two with settlements – and hundreds of factory planets and research stations."

"But those worlds are heavily populated, aren't they?" Dasrylion was thinking of cache-lines as usual. "Not much chance for good hunting or trap-running, there."

So they decided against Four Systems. Outdated flight schedules were added to the pile, too.

---

* At this age, Renegade and Rampage stand over six ft. tall, 3 kri in their measure, while Dasrylion is growing faster and stands half-a-head taller, as befits Tracker Clan. Normal height is between 7 and 8 ft.

Renegade was drawn to a local flight with a planetide at P'taal 5, but it was a factory run; and his two friends vetoed it.

Broken Spear knew what he had in mind: "Why don't you write to your family there, son? Tell them about what you're doing; send them a holopix of yourself – perhaps some pelts, too." *Poor lad, now he sees how easy it is to lose track! I feel for him.*

"That's a good idea; I'll do that after we get done here." Renegade didn't even question the way Broken Spear seemed to read his mind; he was too preoccupied.

"There's nothing for Dinosaur Clan except two incoming flights, so maybe I'll do that, too." Rampage had the same problem as Renegade; and Broken Spear told both of them: "We can send the furs with the next supply ship that leaves Arvien, by way of Dasryl's father."

The Cold Tracker himself put in, "I'm going to trade most of my bird skins to He-Walks-Lightly, and I'd be willing to swap a few with either of you."

"For what, Dasryl? You have at least as many furs as we do this year, and in better condition," Rampage huffed.

"But you two have *Starbeast* skins! Do you know how rare those are? And what I could get for them? You need only the bones, any-path…"and he shut his jaw with a snap, realizing what he'd just said.

Renegade laughed. "If we didn't before, we know now. Thanks for telling us, brother; we'll be sure to drive a sharp bargain if we trade;" and Dasrylion groaned, making them laugh. (They would later decide to keep the skins to stretch over the fragile skeletons, and display them in the Trophy Hall.)

"*Chak, chak,* let's get back to these," Rampage said impatiently, gesturing with a batch of invitations.

Eventually they found something they all liked:

The veteran Dappled Grass star captain had passed through Nine Systems Station a couple of times in their absence, and each time he'd forwarded a list of starship schedules from the station. The hunters scanned the most recent list, and found he had marked four flights as having available berths. On one he had written:

The captain here is a protégé of mine. You haven't met him, but he runs a good ship. This is an exploratory mission, something for your young hunters, T'akaion. I can recommend him.

The expedition would be outfitted at Nine Systems Station, and would make its scheduled departure in late summer of this year. Its estimated total flight time, Galactic, was two years.

"That's more than three years Homeworld," Dasrylion said, "and ah..."

"Four years," said Broken Spear.

"Four years for us here," the young man finished.

"The ship is going along the inner side of our galactic arm," the old warrior continued, "through gas and dust clouds filled with young stars, and presumably younger planets. And they are advertising for two to four qualified hunters, a good fit for the three of you. You could journey together."

They pounced on this one, and hastily composed a message to the captain offering their services as a unit – "and be sure to include *all* your titles," their guardian told them. "Your age may go against you, but your honors will bring you home."

"I'm just a master hunter, a trapper really," Dasrylion pointed out. "I probably don't even belong in this renowned company." He was only half joking.

"Nonsense; no one is ever JUST a master hunter; and it is your skill as a tracker and trapper that will collect the most creatures for them to study," Broken Spear scolded him even before his friends could protest. "On-point, there is a trappers' association on Homeworld. I will reference it with you after this, Dasrylion, and we can send off an application today – enough time for it to appear on your credentials. Everything will be fine."

So it was settled.

***

THEY WON acceptance at once. "Just waiting for us!" Rampage crowed, (though Renegade wondered how much of that was due to their teacher's fame).

Along with the acceptance came a page describing where the expedition was going and what equipment they would need to bring – "though I cannot on-course tell such esteemed warriors and hunters as yourselves what weapons to carry, but" – the captain's lengthy note began...

"But he'll do it any-route," Renegade chuckled. He read from the page: "'Nets and traps for capture of small game, laser or rocket for big game...whatever small-bore weapons you wish for self-defense, and – look at this – wristband detonators, for encounters with invasive prey...' "

"They have been notified then," Broken Spear said. "Good. Although the wristbands are standard issue for new worlds, it has never been so worded before."

"Do you think we'll find those bone-beasts out there too, Elder?" Rampage wanted to know.

Broken Spear frowned. "I don't know, son. No one does. That is one of the dangers – and the glories – of new worlds. Anything may be found there."

He inhaled deeply. "Ah! What a time it is to be alive! To go beyond the farthest charted planet, beyond the bounds of what we know, and on to things we have never seen. *That* is living life to the limit, young warriors!"

His gaze fell on Renegade, who seemed about to speak. Gently he said, "No, son, I cannot go with you this time. I have been keeping you too close here, when I should have set you free to wander the stars and hunt the unknown. This is *your* time, young ones, seize it and be glad!

"Any-path, I'll be training our new students, which I sadly neglected last year, when your ship departs."

His little speech, meant to encourage them, abruptly reminded Renegade of something:

I'm leaving and he'll be alone here, with almost 50 students to teach. He won't even have time to hunt, and I'll be gone three or four winters, all-trace.

Then and there, he resolved to do something about it.

Eight....Winter's End

DASRYLION had to return home to help his father with last-throw winter trapping and to convince his parents that he needed to go on this expedition with his friends. Following his Master Hunt, he was considered proven enough to chart his own course in life; but he didn't expect to do it without an argument.

When he left, Renegade enlisted Rampage in his own campaign.

They began going out before dawn and at twilight every day, setting the traps and hunting, staying out until they came back with a kill. They had all of Broken Spear's, Renegade's and Rampage's parents' land to use; and most of the great northern forest below the mountain was public hunting ground.

In the lowlands, the spring meltoff had already begun. Many of the animals were starting to lose their winter coats; so Renegade had to release more than he liked from the traps. He also released pregnant females, in accordance with Hunt Law. He and Rampage were better hunters than trappers anyway, and they made daily treks through the lower woods and swamp. They began stocking up.

In two tendays, they had killed four barren *kai* does and three young bucks, 15 of the fat little coney-like herbivores they called *h'vatka,* and a large bull trey-horn, which looks like a cross between a moose and a rhino with heavy fur.

Spring's breath warmed the land early. The alpine meadows burst into flower; birds sang and courted and laid their eggs; and fish leaped in the rivers and streams.

Renegade's next order of business was to collect birds' eggs and catch fish. He and Rampage haunted the swamplands for a fiveday where huge colonies of water and wading birds had their nests. By taking only the first few eggs from a clutch, the hunters could induce the birds to keep laying, and then leave them alone to hatch their young for the year. Later in the season, there would be upland game birds and their clutches of 15 or more eggs.

While the hunters collected eggs, they also set fish traps, which they emptied daily, cleaned and filleted the fish, and stored them in Broken Spear's huge freezer rooms.

Rampage hung on loyally for most of this, but after days of gutting, skinning, butchering, scaling, plucking, freezing, smoking and drying, he got tired – he needed a change, he needed a steam bath and a long soak, he needed to practice his weapons, his throw...Renegade finally let him off and went doggedly on himself.

And of course, Rampage was soon swallowed by guilt and returned to help him, complaints and all.

Broken Spear thought the two young men seemed unusually busy getting in a late trapping season, since they'd missed most of the winter. They still had time before the school started up, though. Despite the early warmth, the old hunter did not begin teaching until shortly after the spring equinox, weather permitting.

Hunters living in clans have celebrations at the fall of an antelope, it seems; but the freeholders have only a few: Drive Hunt Days, after the herds are driven and enough meat is stored away for the cold season; and Winter's End, which they use to even out their calendars.

They divide the year into quarters, in periods of "tendays," but planetary mechanics being what they are, the hunters end up with a few odd days every year; so they place them at the end of winter, begin their festival the prescribed number of days before the equinox, and end it on Day One of the New Year, the spring equinox. Winter's End* is a lively, musical, skills-testing and games-playing holiday for a people so publicly reserved and austere.

We'll celebrate Winter's End at Arvien's main trophy hall near the trading center this year, Broken Spear thought. *It will be our last one together for a while; but before that I should dust off the targets and exercise equipment, clean and check the weapons, and...*

He pushed open the folding doors leading to the weapons' storeroom and behold!

---

* On warm planets like Homeworld, it is called the Festival of Light

Everything gleamed. Bows and spears were neatly racked, arrows set with new tips, lasers and rockets and even his proton cannon shone in their places.

"What is *this?*" he wondered, and explored further.

Exercise mats – all sewn and stacked. Leather and metal body armor – cleaned and oiled. Targets hung neatly in rows. Not a speck of dust anywhere.

Broken Spear stood staring for a long moment, then reminded himself, "Close your mouth, old man, or you will look foolish. I think I had better investigate this."

The invisible hands had been everywhere: the training room and trophy room floors had been scoured; the trophies shone. Even the computer disc files had been transferred and shelved into the new study, as he'd been meaning to do last year. And when he finally looked into the food storage area...

The culprits were there. In the preparation room. Filleting fish with a pile of entrails between them. To either side, a vat of brine waited for preserving what they didn't smoke or freeze.

"Renegade? Rampage?"

Two notable starts. Two quite different expressions: Rampage, one of relief; Renegade, one of – was that *guilt?*

Their mentor was thunderstruck. "What--?" he managed, "By the Spirit of sky and water, what have you two been up to lately?"

He followed Renegade's quick, almost furtive glance over-shoulder to the freezer compartment beyond. "You mean there are more surprises for me in there?"

Slight chinlift.

As he strode over to the adjoining freezer storage and pulled open the safety door, he heard Renegade say tentatively, "We were just – *krr* – stocking up a little for the winter...next winter..."

Through the icy billow of cold air, Broken Spear could see more of their work. Besides the eleven leftover krolf carcasses from the autumn hunt, there now hung nearly thirty more – kai, swamp-browser, trey-horn, small-bear, large tree-hangers – not to mention some forty game birds and four huge leather pouches containing 180 shelled and frozen eggs. Two days ago, the youngsters had made him an excellent meal of fresh eggs and kai's liver. Here were the materials for many, many more.

The old hunter was dumbfounded. As he stood there, staring, he was vaguely aware of their urgent background talk: Rampage's "See? I *told* you he'd be angry. At least we can quit now; my fingers are frozen to the bone..."

And Renegade's "I hope you aren't too angry with us, Grandfather. We were very careful to follow Hunt Law in our kills; and since we *are* going away for three or four years, we – I thought – we could fill up your larder so you wouldn't …" and here he hesitated. What he wanted to say verged on insult, and he didn't know how to go around it.

"Starve," Broken Spear murmured after him, his back turned toward them, his hands gripping the door frame. "So I wouldn't *starve*... unbelievable…"

He turned slowly toward them. They could see the heat-colors of some great emotion struggling in his body, but they couldn't tell what it was.

"Boys…" he began, then amended, "No, honored *warriors,* I have never, I never expected…" he put a hand to his broken tooth, his sign of great agitation. "I…I will accept this generous offering…with…in the honor and respect in which it was given"—here his voice strengthened, his hand lowered, "if you will do one more thing for me."

"Elder?" they said in shock. Even Rampage looked worried now.

The old warrior dropped his hand to his side, gasped, or choked, or laughed, and asked them, "We have 14 days until Winter's End; and I would be honored…if you will allow me to hunt with you?"

"Oh yes, Grandfather!" they both cried out at once, grinning like wolves.

***

FOR THE NEXT 14 days, Broken Spear went with them, not as their teacher or superior, or even as their guide, but as their hunting companion – and it was one of the best times they had ever known.

Renegade had planned on hunting the *kreppa-tsrr* next*,* the wild boar-type creatures, and the Sloth-bears emerging from their dens; and his packmates followed him.

The Sloth-bears came first. Their stalkers climbed the mountainsides to check on their dens, the old hunter as nimble and spry as either of his former students. Now Renegade too saw him "in action," moving with a grace and strength marvelous to behold. And his lifelong unconscious skill was as much a lesson to the young hunters as anything he had taught them. Broken Spear never felt the effort he made now; he was on holiday with them, carefree at last.

They teased one Sloth-bear after another out of its den and let most of them go. None of them showed fight.

Finally one old veteran roared out at them, thin and mean from the long winter but still in magnificent coat. *This one,* the signal passed between the hunters, and they fanned out in a semi-circle facing the bear.

The huge creature eyed them for a moment, then snarled and inexplicably charged the biggest of them – Broken Spear.

"He Challenges, this old fighter!" the clan warrior called out, even as he neatly sidestepped the charge.

Sure as sunlight, the Sloth-bear didn't attempt to escape, but wheeled in mid-charge and rose on his hind legs, armed paws extended to seize and slash.

T'akaion forsook his laser and sent his great spear flying with such strength that it plunged into the bear's chest for half its length.

The big beast looked astonished, and then dropped, its eyes glazing. It wasn't even necessary to cut its throat for insurance sake, although the old hunter was *there*, ready, when it fell.

"Go in peace, honored one," Broken Spear told him, and thanked the Spirit-of-All for the noble beast. And the three took home their prize.

The deep forest near the wetlands held their next quarry, the aggressive and dangerous kreppa-tsrr, which traveled in herds, the boars guarding the sows and their new piglets from harm.

It took the hunters an entire day to track down and get close to one sizable herd, always staying downwind.

"It's a big herd," Renegade whispered to his friends as they crouched along tree boughs and peered down at the prey.

"And look at the size of their chieftain!" Rampage hissed, "Three *kri* long and almost two high!"

The others agreed. Lean and muscular, with tusks like cutlasses, the great boar was a fearsome sight.

"He leads them, though, and they have young," Broken Spear murmured. "We must wait for the outriders."

The "outriders" were the younger boars that tagged along in the rear. Kept at a distance by the leader, they stayed nearby, sometimes in smaller herds of their own, the potential heirs to the kingdom, the first to guard, and often the first to fall as prey.

The herd moved along slowly under the trees, snuffling and rooting. Old sows guarded the flanks, while the bull moved restlessly back and forth among them. He had a big responsibility: there were 35 adults in the pack, and numerous young.

Finally the main herd drifted by, and the bachelor bands came into view.

"A lot here too," hissed Rampage. They counted thirteen young males in the largest group, many of them almost as big as the old boar. The other two hunters nodded, and by unspoken agreement, each selected a target.

Whoosh! whoosh! whoosh!—laser fire this time; three fell; the rest scattered squealing in disarray.

Three hunters leaped down like leopards, spears and vai-ators in hand.

Most of the outriders dashed after the main herd in full retreat, but four by chance ran back onto the killing-ground. They saw their enemies and charged.

Rampage's vai-ator took one in a superb low-ground throw. Renegade leaped over his, the spear thrust down through its ribcage. Both young hunters pivoted, alert for the third and fourth.

But their companion had that well in hand. He'd shot one with his laser, triggering from the shoulder, then crouched and met the other one with his spearpoint as it came for him, shoving the blade between neck and shoulder with a grunt, fending off the beast's weight with the shaft.

"Well-thrust, hunter!" Renegade saluted him, and, "And well-shot, Rampage!"

"And good hunting, brothers," Broken Spear returned. And his praise and his naming them as equals meant more to them than the accolade of crowds.

***

IN A FEW more days, their hunting was done. They brought in their traps for the season, cleaned weapons and carcasses for the last time.

On the last night, they dined on roast *kreppa-tsrr* with cooked eggs and a wild berry garnish, sweetbreads to the side.

They spent the next three days at the Winter's End festival, toting a whole wild boar carcass as their contribution. They met Dasrylion there with his family, and celebrated the coming of spring.

Nine....Breaktie

CASTING AWAY --- "There it is, Expedition Ship 3145," said Renegade.

"Attached to a dock. They must be boarding already; we'd better hurry" – from Rampage, of course.

"Plenty of time," said Dasrylion, calm as always. "The schedule says they're not leaving for two days, station-time."

They stood on an observation deck, looking down at the ship as it waited in a docking tube. Their belongings lay piled about their feet.

A chain of cargo-crawlers edged slowly up the ramp to the ship's underbay.

"They're all going in, not out..." Rampage grumbled. He caught the others' flicker of amusement and muttered, "Oh, on-stat, on-stat," not altogether mollified.

"Your trouble is," Dasrylion drawled, "you want to be everywhere in a hurry. No sooner do you get there, then you want to be gone – and so on, and so on."

Rampage glared at him.

"*Krr-rr,* let's go down and find the captain," Renegade suggested. "Maybe we can get our gear stowed." He hoped he wouldn't have to play peacekeeper the whole voyage: Dasryl felt a little jealous of the extra time he and Rampage had spent together.

Probably not, he decided. They usually only reverted when they were especially nervous or excited – probably about this flight.

He burred and began slinging carry-straps over his shoulder, wedging things under his arms, and wondering even now if he'd brought enough to last for several years aboard ship.

Broken Spear watched them silently. He'd left his new students on Arvien 4, hopefully for only a few days. But he'd given them plenty to do; and he was not thinking of them now.

At Renegade's "Grandfather, will you come down with us?" he almost started, and made a negative head motion, saying,

"Not unless you need help with your gear. I will go to the Pilot's Berth and wait for you there. Departure is still two days' away…" *if I can bear it even then,* he thought, turning and walking away so he wouldn't see the hurt in their eyes.

Renegade stood staring after him until he received two separate pulls: an elbow-tug from Rampage, and a gentler nudge at his shoulder from Dasrylion: "Come along, brother, let's introduce ourselves."

"This way!" Rampage hurried on, bounding down the ramp.

They reached Bay 17 through double pressurized doors which led into a wide cargo room, orange-lit red, a little dim to their New World eyes.

People and power sleds were everywhere, directing and loading still more cargo crawlers with containers to be offloaded into the ship. To the young hunters' first glance, it seemed like chaos.

Finally Renegade noticed a smallish spotted *tautsche* stationed near the entrance of the docking tube. He held a hand-computer, working busily, and he jerked his head around almost continuously, making his loose-hung brown mane fly.

"That must be the dock steward," Renegade guessed. "He could tell us where to board. Let's go see him."

T'churrn'k (Nervous One, or literally 'not agreeable') became aware of a deep but polite, "Greetings, honored one," which he ignored. Couldn't anyone see he was busy? The greeting was repeated, louder, but still courteous, and he spun around and snapped,

"*T'churrt!* What *is* it you—?" when his jaw fell open at the sight of the trio who had somehow surrounded him, and who towered above him.

"…want. Honored ones," he finished.

The shortest one – who still had several *kli* on him – inclined his head slightly – stars! What a mass of gleaming muscle on him! – What were they wearing? Animal skins? – This one said, "We are the hunters chosen for this voyage. May we board our belongings here?"

"May…here…uhh…" T'churrn'k boggled, and heard the lean brown one in golden armor hiss to his friends,

"*T'chai! Not even polite!*"

But the original questioner waited patiently, his green eyes disturbingly intent.

"Hunting... *krr-uh,* just a moment; I'll get the captain;" and the steward nearly collided with a power sled in his haste to be gone.

The Three exchanged glances. "Nervous little fellow, isn't he?" Dasrylion yawned with a trace of slyness, showing every tooth in his head.

"I think he's moving faster now," Rampage purred.

Renegade crinkled his eye-corners in good humor. "He's a Birdhunter, that Cloud Forest subclan, smallest of them all. I guess we flushed him out of cover."

The "nervous little fellow" returned quickly, drawing someone in his wake. This was a taller individual, dressed in dark red coveralls form-fitted to his body.

He seemed a calmer type. He actually smiled when he saw them.

"That will be all, steward, thank you," he dismissed the clerk, then turned to the three, offering his wrists in welcome.

"Esteemed hunters and warriors," he said, "I am ship's captain Tallevar, originally of Plains Clan, now Shostrak 3. I am honored to welcome you aboard my ship." His manners more than made up for T'churrn'k's lack of them.

The three faced him and Renegade made introductions: "Honored captain, I am Renegade, and these are my companions on the Hunt – the Esteemed Hunter and Warrior Rampage and the Esteemed Hunter and Master Trapper Dasrylion, of Arvien 4."

(*Master Trapper?* Dasrylion withheld a smile)

Renegade continued, "We are honored to be part of this expedition," and he took the captain's wrists in the grip of equals, permitting Tallevar to do the same.

He's young but very courteous, the captain thought, *and that medallion...*"You are the Great Warrior Renegade, are you not?"

"*Chak*, but I don't stand on ceremony. I'm just Renegade, captain. Please call me that."

The captain smiled. "Neither do I, Renegade. Please call me Tallevar. It would be a long voyage otherwise." Next he greeted the others, who told him much the same: the big dark gray hunter as easygoing as his leader, but the thinner one in fancy armor – *Rampage,* he thought as he repeated the name aloud – *this one looks fierce and feral still.*

"Honored ones," Tallevar continued, "you may leave your things here to be loaded on board, or you might like to see your quarters for yourselves, and bring them with you."

When they decided to board themselves, he said, "Please follow me through the passenger airlock in the other gate. I can take you to your lodgings."

"Good. Thank you," said Renegade, re-hefting his gear; and they followed Tallevar.

They got almost as far as the upper entry hatch when another "emergency" called the captain away. He was reluctant to leave. "Most emergencies somehow vanish when the captain arrives," he told them wryly; but Renegade assured him they could follow directions. So Tallevar supplied them and pardoned himself.

The Three walked along the loading tube and into the hatch.

Once inside, Dasrylion murmured, "This is different than a Hunt Ship…and our school ship." (The school ship was actually a scaled-down Hunt Ship.)

"Yes, it is," Renegade agreed. "You don't come out in a big open room but rather another corridor, here. *D'faal,* if we cross over the main bow corridor, which I think this is," he demonstrated, "and face to the left, like this," they came to an inner door, as he expected. He touched it, and it slid back: "This should be the training room."

It was adequate – barely – but it did have exercise equipment, a sealable shooting booth, and a bit of open space.

"Our personal chambers and the bathing area should be just beyond it…" Renegade started across the room, the other two glancing dubiously around.

There was another short hall to the rear. They entered it and found off to the left a tiny room bearing four slide-out beds and scarcely space enough for a micro-desk and chair at one end, where a computer terminal sat. There were latched-panel storage bins above the bed-shelves and to either side. Aft of the bunkroom and opening into it was a small toilet alcove – which didn't seem to give you enough room to turn around in.

Rampage gulped. "Wonderful. I think I'm feeling…trapped."

Dasrylion didn't say a word. He had gone pale.

"Let's try the bathing area," Renegade said hastily, "Maybe there's more room." They squeezed out the bunkroom doorway one after another to arrange themselves single-file in the corridor and face another door in the opposite wall.

Rampage yanked it open; and they faced a ceramic-tiled cubicle with two – "Count 'em, two" – steam shower fixtures, a tiny drying cabinet with a few racks for clothes beyond that – and nothing more.

"Definitely *not* a Hunt Ship," Dasrylion murmured. He and Rampage looked so washed-out that Renegade feared they might be sick.

"Come on, brothers, let's go back and leave our things in the training room" (*and be able to breathe there*) "and we'll figure out something..." He was actually wondering if they could cancel at this *tare'*. The claustrophobic quarters affected him, too.

He strode out the door of the training room and nearly ran into someone coming along the crossover hall.

"—Uh!" A gasp, and Renegade pulled up short, put out a hand to stave off collision ...

And found himself staring into the eyes of a young crew-woman. She was dressed in a thigh-length tunic of crimson with gold trim, with long pants to match, and had surprised cinnamon eyes.

"Milady! Your pardon!" he cried out too, then simmered down. "My apologies. I crave your pardon...I wasn't looking."

She was staring at him, but she didn't seem angry. "It's not a good idea to race down these corridors, you know..." she looked down at his extended arm, raised to fend or brace. He retracted it carefully.

"I ask your pardon," he repeated, trying to explain. "We felt a little closed-in, in there."

Her tiny biting teeth – *like a child's,* he thought, *so delicate* – were re-covered just as carefully by her upper lip. He read her blood –colors: *She doesn't know whether to be angry or what.* There had been something in the way she looked when he burst out of the doorway, shock and... something else. He couldn't get a clawhold on it.

Rampage saved him the problem of apologizing yet again by calling out from behind, "Frost it, Renegade! What's the delay? I'm *suffocating* in here!" despite Dasrylion's effort to hush him.

"One moment, brother," Renegade called back, and turned his attention to the young crew-woman once more.

"You see?" he told her with a self-deprecating smile; "All of us feel too bound up in here, and we were hurrying to get out."

"*Krr...*Oh! You're *hunters!"* she said, as if the word was foreign to her. "Are you the new ship's hunters?'

"Yes, my lady," he became humble with her... a strange contrast to his aura of *maleness,* she thought. *That* was actually frightening.

"I'm...*krr...*holding you back," she began, then, "Wait; you mean you're bunking in those little rooms back there? They're awful, smaller than regular crew members' rooms; and you're so big – I mean – you must be used to the outdoors, all that land and sky..." She could see that: they had that feeling about them of wide and wild places, of endless forests and plains.

Rampage broke her contemplative mood by muttering, "Yes, and we would like to see them again *soon,* if you please!" as he totally ignored Dasrylion's "*Hsst! be quiet*!"

It almost made her smile.

When she raised her eyes to the young hunter still standing in front of her, she noticed that he was almost smiling, too. His bright green eyes managed to look warm and friendly.

"I think I know something else that might fit you," she ventured, barely touching glances with him, flick and away. "Could – could you – would you like me to show you?"

"We would be honored," the hunter replied. No flippancy, no obvious sarcasm there…*an honorable man, a real hunter...and he's not that much taller than me, on second sight – what a stupid thing to notice…am I losing my wits?*

"Ah...*rr*…on-course," she managed out loud, and carefully backed up, to allow all of them out of the room before she led them away. The place she knew of lay beyond them on the other side of this cross-corridor, but she couldn't bring herself to pass them that closely; so she took them by a roundabout way.

A few *kt-tare'* later they were standing in a deep-tone chamber nearly twice the height of the training room and at least the same length, the young female facing the three of them, her back to the open door.

Renegade noticed her cautious manner and couldn't account for it. He had also noted her deep midnight blue-black mane which hung down to her waist and was knotted in a simple twist halfway down. From what he'd seen of her skin – difficult because of the coverings she wore – she had a camo-pattern of brown, beige, gray and umber in back, while her face (and front parts, probably) was the same muted gold as his. He'd taken one glance at the new room and promptly forgotten all about it as he speculated on what kind of hybrid she might be.

Rampage and Dasrylion paid more attention to the chamber, assessing the new space, with Rampage exclaiming, "This is prime!" while Dasrylion breathed deeply and said, "Aaah…this is better, don't you think, Renegade?"

"Yes," his friend replied so absently that Dasrylion gave him a sharp look – then almost smiled.

"Renegade?" he prodded gently.

Renegade snapped back to himself. "On-stat…you say this was a storage room?" he asked the young woman.

"*Churr*," she agreed, "before some other chambers re-divided by moving the inner walls…that's what happened to your quarters, I'm afraid…"

Don't be, Renegade wanted to say, but caught himself in time. "And this chamber isn't needed now?' he resumed his questions.

"*T'chak,*" she said more positively. "You see, with this small door leading in" (the one she was standing before) "it's hard to load very large items; and being near the drive-force, there's a kind of low-grade vibration once we're underway…you might find that irritating to live with…" *Why am I talking so much?* she wondered. "We might store a few medical crates in here, that's all."

"We wouldn't mind that," Renegade assured her. He looked back at his companions. Relief shone on their faces. "The crates or the vibration, that is. Point of fact, we might even find it soothing."

"It's not a mountain meadow, but I guess it's better than that metal *trap* above," Rampage repressed a shudder.

"You've spent most of your lives on-planet, then?" she asked. Then, "Oh, forgive me; my name is K'leura*; I'm a medical technician here."

"A healer? My lady K'leura." There was no other title or designate, so Renegade left it off; "And we are Rampage" – (a chinlift) "Dasrylion" ("Honored, milady") – and myself, Renegade, hunters and warriors from the planet Arvien 4."

"You *are* hunters then! You're not...what I expected…" she started to say, when a sharp rasp went off from the comset on her belt. "Your pardon. Yes? Med-tech K'leura here," she answered it.

The voice broke loud and harsh: "K'leura! Get your pretty little butt up here on the jump! There's a load of medical supplies come in, and we don't know where to put 'em. So get up here *now!*"

Heat rose in her face. "I'm coming." Her eyes downcast, she mumbled, "Y-your pardon, *vr'*hunters; I have to leave. You probably know your way back…"

"Wait."

It was not harsh. Nor loud. But it held urgency and power. She looked up, startled.

The first hunter's sea-green eyes looked straight into hers. The young man's face was very serious, his body very still. Somehow that stillness held unspeakable strength.

"Who speaks to you this way?"

Suddenly she felt very young and small. "It's nothing. It's…he…I'm sorry, I have to go" – and she fled in confusion.

---

* K-LOOR-ah, with a click on the 'K' sound.

Renegade started after her, disturbed by her pain and fear, but Dasrylion grabbed his shoulder and warned him, "Leave it, brother. We don't know the situation here. He might be her mate. Better to keep a hold and find out, first."

Rampage took their leader's part: "Doesn't matter, Dasryl. Couldn't you hear the way – whoever – talked to her?"

"You don't know what's between them. It's still best to wait and find out more. We're on this ship for the long-throw; we don't want to charge into a blind cave. Any-route, Renegade, what did you have in mind doing to this place to make it more livable? It has ports, but they'll be sealed in hyperspace."

That sounded reasonable. They *were* going to spend at least three years in this metal cubicle. Against his intuitive judgment, Renegade let himself be talked down…

"I suppose you're right, Dasryl. A good hunter knows his prey…" and yet he made himself a silent vow: he would track down whomever so embarrassed the young healer in public – and see to it that he knew the difference between public and private matters.

Cold Tracker only thought he had Renegade re-directed when his friend said, "We still have a bundle of furs and leathers to trade, so let's get our gear and see if we can get some things to fix this place up."

Rampage, who didn't have Dasrylion's placid nature, knew a little more about what motivated Renegade; and he too would bide his time. For the present.

***

THE THREE burst out of the ship into open air – even the space station seemed roomy compared to that box trap inside – and went to the Pilots' Berth to collect Broken Spear. Soon they had his wholehearted cooperation in renovating their new quarters.

By day's end, the ship's captain also knew what they'd done to the former storage room. His cargo chief, Stavrof, made it a point to know where K'leura had been and what she had been doing.

"What in thunder?" Tallevar looked around the chamber in amazement. The empty room had been transformed: a huge Sloth-bear rug covered the center of the floor, with smaller kai and other hides to fill the edges. Three cushioned jump seats had been bolted to the floor; while the chamber's far end held a desk with space for a computer screen, terminal, and discs (already transferred from the other room.) The desk's study space had a shiny writing surface, style-boards and styluses in place.

Six large blunt hooks had been bolted into the ceiling, while the bedslings meant to hang from them lay folded neatly on the floor.

The portal wall was coated with faceted milli-foil which filled the chamber with light. This foil could also be darkened at a touch for sleeping comfort. The black wall opposite had been completely covered with a holo-mural – it looked as if you were standing on a mountainside gazing down at a land of rolling meadows and dark forests, under a sunrise pink-and-gold sky.

The captain stood there and took all this in for a long time, hearing but not hearing his cargo chief's gruff complaints beside him.

Finally Tallevar cut him off. "The thing is," he said, "that from the moment they came aboard, those three hunters *owned* a portion of this ship and its cargo. Hunter's share. That's the agreement. It's traditional, Stavrof; you know that. They give us their professional services in exchange for shares on the ship and whatever they help to discover on the journey.

"Now, they can take those shares in any way they wish – I personally think they will remove all of this at journey's end, and take their shares in other things..."

He turned away, smiling. "And frankly, Chief, a man's or woman's living quarters are their own hideshare; and this is an improvement on the old look, in my thinking. We can put the medical supplies in the former hunters' quarters topside. Now let's get some work done, shall we?"

***

STARS TO SAIL --- Renegade was only mortal, and spending his last two days with his beloved Grandfather made K'leura's problem slip to the back of his mind.

Broken Spear took this time to talk to his former students intensely, compassionately, personally. When he finally ran out of advice: "work every day: practice, review, re-learn," he started in with personal reminisces of his own star voyages – which the young hunters found more interesting anyway

He helped them discuss their hopes and dreams and the journey before them. He opened his own life to all of them, as he had to Renegade long ago; and they spent *tare'* talking together after their trading was done.

Finally the time came to depart. And the old warrior grit up his courage – more than he'd ever needed for a hunt – and walked with them to the ship.

He accompanied them to the passenger level, and bidding them "Good journey and good hunting, my sons," embraced them all, Renegade the longest, and let them go.

Bring me back tales of wonder and danger, chk-kiy-teh, he thought, *of places we have never seen...but most of all, bring me back yourselves, safe and whole again.*

And he stood watching until the airlock closed behind them. Then he made his lonely way to planetide and home.

***

AS RENEGADE half-stumbled into the ship, blinded by loss, he never focused on the large blur that appeared in front of him -- Stavrof, waiting to make some jibe about the emotional scene he'd just witnessed, and to warn the young hunter away from K'leura.

But Renegade came at him so abruptly and with such a dire expression on his face that the chief gave ground, startled, even though he was the bigger of the two, and used to forcing others to his way.

This didn't go unnoticed by the crew. The assistant navigator jabbed the pilot with his finger-talon and whispered, "I think he's taken too big a bite this time."

And the pilot chuckled and agreed, "*Chak! This one* won't lie down and surrender without a challenge – mark me on it!"

Then they scattered like chaff when the cargo chief wheeled in their direction.

Ten....Windsinger

THE EXPEDITION SHIP wouldn't make planetide for nearly two tendays, ship-time. Even then it would be a brief re-supply stop at a small way-station at the limits of the known systems. The station was in an area so new it had no factories and only two nearby hunting planets. While there, the starship would undergo a systems' check and supplies' restocking; and the hunters would bring down some game on the trophy planets to help fill the larder.

The three young hunters battled claustrophobia by exercising daily, for two *tare'* at a throw, practicing *tch-won'* and weapons' use in the tiny training room. They also worked off energy by walking and running in place until their muscles ached. Sometimes the ships' corridors were empty enough to trot through, and Renegade did that, mostly.

They really had nothing else to do. They tried to limit their reading and learning to one session a day, to make it last; but it was going to be a long journey.

Renegade jogged down the ship's long corridors during crew changes. Most staff members had regular sleeping periods; and only a third of the 30 crew members stayed awake at any one time.

Renegade enjoyed the corridor jaunts. They made him more familiar with the ship, for one thing; and for another, he hoped to meet K'leura again. That first incident bothered him. Who would speak to her that way? Even a mate, a husband, *no,* he decided, *that was too cruel, to shame her so in public.* He could not imagine treating a loved one like that even in private. It went against his deep moral code.

But he hadn't seen her again, not yet. In fact he saw very few people out in the corridors away from their posts or sleeping alcoves. And those few just acknowledged him with a brief greeting.

K'leura's position in the medical lab, where she served as both a technician and a trainee in microbiology, at least kept her safe from Stavrof's advances while she was on duty; so she didn't stray far from her daily route – sleeping alcove to duty post – with meals taken in her quarters.

The captain here ran a tight ship, unlike the last one, where she'd first encountered Stavrof. She thought Tallevar might at least discipline the bully if he sensed anything wrong; even though her heart shrank from knowing that the cargo chief had followed her here. Least-path, she thought, Stavrof stayed near the holds for most of the day, far out of her circuit.

But as most hunters are taught, even the safest haven has more than one trail in…and distance did not keep the cargo chief and his prey apart for long.

Shortly after break-tie, the lab had taken blood and genetic samples from everyone on board, so the techs might make duplicate supplies of blood and tissue in case of injuries. Many of the samples came in randomly and at odd times; until one sleep-period, K'leura found herself wide awake and working late. The chief healer and second assistant were off duty.

She was absorbed in her work tonight, but she couldn't miss the slow, heavy tread coming up behind her. She petrified in place, listening. Then…

"Well, well, little Windsinger. Working late, I see."

Him. In horror she sprang away from her seat. Too late: a massive arm curled around her, a hand clamped pain-tight around her right wrist.

She raised her left hand, claws arched. He vised it easily, using his great strength to wrench her arm around her back.

"No, no, little bird, mustn't fight your kindly lover…" with both hands behind her back now, "or he might *hurt* you" and she was slammed against the counter's edge, her long mane pulled back hard and wrapped around a cabinet handle.

She was sobbing for breath, out of fear, out of pain, when a powerful hand reached round her front, squeezed her breast hard, claw-gripped her belly, then found the hem of her pants, ripped them down and returned to force her tunic up.

No, no not again! She screamed in silence, and struggled desperately. But she was like a toy to him or a small soft prey, and her hopeless resistance only inflamed him.

Stavrof was that rarest of the Hunters' breed, a sociopath, an amoral brute whose size and strength had always gotten him what he wanted. He was a living example of why the old warrior Broken Spear wanted Hunt training given to everyone, Starborn or not, so such twisted traits could be detected in time – and removed.

Stavrof's arm crushed K'leura harder, forcing her to gasp for breath. Suddenly his hand clamped on her genitals, the hard clawed fingers gouging in, hurting her.

K'leura screamed and flung herself sideways into the lab counter, taking Stavrof with her. She struck some glass vials and they shattered on the floor.

And then – blessed sound from silence! – a voice came from outside the door: "What's that? Who's there?"

"Rot you! See what you've done!" Stavrof cursed her in a hiss and flung her aside. He lunged away through the far door and was gone.

Blind with terror, K'leura sprang to her feet and out the near door, knowing only that she had to get away, anywhere.

So she threw herself into the corridor – and straight into Renegade.

He braced and caught her, recognizing her even as she crashed into him. She began to struggle again, and heard, "K'leura! K'leura, stop! It's me. I won't hurt you. It's me – Renegade."

She looked up out of a wild and tear-stained face, and then collapsed sobbing in his arms. At the height of her terror, she chose to trust the hunter; she could not have said why.

She became vaguely aware that he had picked her up off the floor and was carrying her – *carrying* her – along the corridor, all the while talking and soothing and reassuring her, "Please, my lady K'leura, let me help you; there is no harm in my heart. You're safe with me. Tell me what's wrong, talk to me."

Between her sobs he could hear, "Renegade…take me away from here…"

"On-course, milady, I will," he answered; "Come, I'll take you somewhere safe."

And he took her to the only haven he was certain of, the hunters' training room.

He found an exercise bench and sat down, still holding her. As she curled into a small miserable ball against his chest; she inhaled his clean, spicy scent, felt his body heat warming her, and gradually began to relax, even if he were a male, and a hunter.

He was very gentle and very concerned. He noticed her tunic had ridden up, revealing her; but he was still too innocent to think this had been done deliberately; and to save her privacy, he eased the garment back down.

Not that he thought it was wrong to look honestly at a woman; and in fact the Hunters can see much of what is hidden to lesser eyes. But she had come to him in trouble, and he had no right to reveal what she normally kept private.

So he waited, and held her, pity large in his heart, until they both heard, "Renegade? What's going on up here? What – Spirit save us! What happened?'

It was Rampage, come up from their sleeping quarters below, Dasrylion right behind him.

Renegade looked up.

"Only my friends," he murmured to the young woman. To them he explained, "Brothers, it's K'leura, from the healing alcove. She's in some kind of trouble, but I don't know what...Can you get her some water or something?'

"On-stat, brother," and they were on their way.

While they were gone, he stroked the tears from her face, asking, "Honored healer? Can you tell me what happened? If there is anything I can do, I will. My word on it."

For an instant she had a poignant high hope. Then she looked closely at him, at the youth in his face, at his medium size. He was muscular – oh yes – but smaller overall than Stavrof and much gentler (so she thought) and if she told him the truth, he'd go after the chief and be torn apart. She gave a low moan: Renegade started.

"I'm sorry, Renegade...but I...can't," she breathed, lowering her eyes.

"You *can't?"* in disbelief....

She had been going to tell him she'd had an accident in the lab; but she found she couldn't lie to him: "Please – I'm sorry – it's... I can't – it's personal." (How could she tell him about *that?*)

Miraculously, he didn't draw away. Instead he replied, "I understand. I won't pursue this, milady – only, may I help you now, tonight?"

"Just...I can't go back there yet."

"I know; on-path, I know. Stay here with us. Stay as long as you like," he bent his head to look into her eyes – his eyes somber, a penetrating green, and quite sincere. "You're safe with us."

A shadow moved next to them: Rampage, the fiery-eyed one, as gentle as Renegade now. He knelt beside them, handed her a fluted cup of water from which she drank, shakily.

Then the third, Dasrylion, came up with something – a wrap? – and draped it over her. Renegade tucked it round her shoulders: real fur, soft and warming. And they all stayed there in tableau, watching over her.

K'leura, who normally would have been terrified to be so close to a male, any male, felt completely trusting in the presence of three of them, all allegedly ferocious hunters, at that. --Something she felt too tired to ponder, just yet.

They began to talk softly among themselves, including her but not demanding of her. She listened at first, but soon found herself drifting away to their soft hearth-talk:

"…message to Dinosaur Clan yet?" – something – "done."

"…keeping a journal…last chance…send to Broken Spear…station."

"—clean those traps one more time…need a hobby…"

The talk got cloudier and cloudier, and presently someone asked,

"Asleep?"

"Almost…just drifting."

Suddenly fear returned and she fought to wake, lifting cement-heavy eyelids.

"No I'm not," she declared and struggled to sit up.

As soon as she did, Renegade relaxed his hold. K'leura found herself upright on the exercise bench beside him, his arm lightly balancing her in back. She looked dazed but defiant. What was she thinking?

Yet they hadn't touched her, except for Renegade's supporting hold. Of that she felt sure. Still…

"I have to go back to my quarters,' she said urgently. *And hide in my room and lock the door.*

"On-course," he agreed mildly. "Are you feeling better, honored healer?"

Not honored, never again, she thought, and tears crept into her eyes. "I…yes, I'm fine now. Thank you." Then because that sounded short, and rude, she looked around at all of them, lingered at Renegade, and said, "Thank you for helping me. I mean that."

"I know," he said softly. "Let us at least walk back to your quarters with you. We can keep watch as we go."

Visions of Stavrof lurking around corners in far corridors, perhaps even by her room, brought her quick assent. "Oh *chak;* that would be helpful. Thank you."

She drank some more water and managed to stand, shivering and tugging at her tunic.

"You had best keep the fur," Dasrylion told her, and she thanked him too.

They left the training room in a group and went out into the dim halls.

They had an order of march, she discovered: Rampage went in front about ten paces, his quick eyes scaling and assessing walls, thresholds, connecting corridors; while Renegade walked beside her, his step light but on the verge of action; and the big one they called Dasrylion came along guarding the rear, scanning about much as Rampage did, and with the same intensity. He had startled her at first, the big Tracker – he resembled Stavrof somewhat – but oh, what a contrast in his manners!

Enclosed by them, protected by them, these unknown male hunters, K'leura strangely felt safe, as safe as she ever had in her recent past; and she let tiredness take her closer to Renegade. When he put an arm around her shoulders to steady her, she did not draw away.

After they reached her small room, they didn't just leave her there, even though the door was locked. While the other two hunters watched the corridor, Renegade asked her to wait a moment after she unlocked it, and he slid into the room like a shadow, and searched it swiftly and completely, putting the lights on as he did so.

It was small, and he was quickly done. When he motioned to her, she came in.

He moved aside, not threatening her. Yet he lingered.

"K'leura," he began, and her throat tightened. *No, not him, too!*

He went on, "I wonder if...you've seen our training room – where we just came from?" At her nod, he explained, "*Churr-rr.* All three of us are experts in natural combat, and we can teach you, too. To learn self-defense, that is, if you ...ah... ever need to use it..." he carefully explored the edges of her fear, trying for an inroad: "If you agree to let us teach you, on-path. Will you?"

Her rising heartbeat ebbed; her eyes grew bright – not even so much for the proffered lessons as for the chance to see him again, this gentle hunter.

"Yes," she heard herself say, "I would like that."

His smile softened his fierce intensity. "Good. We can start as soon as you would like: tomorrow, or – when you next have time. Just call us first. I, or any of us, can come and escort you to the training room. ..." he ran out of reasons to delay, and straightened his spine. "We should go now..." although he sounded as if he would rather stay; and his two friends exchanged a quick glance behind him. "Night's rest to you, my lady… and be sure to seal your door."

And the three hovered outside her room until they heard the lock seal tight. Then, after a swift reconnaissance up-hall, they left her alone.

***

THE YOUNG HUNTERS didn't talk about the incident until they had reached their own sleeping quarters. *"Speak of what is private, in private,"* Hunt Law says, and they held their speech.

Finally they broke their silence.

"I don't like it," Rampage said, "and she won't talk about it."

"That's her choice," Renegade answered. "She said it was 'personal,' whatever that includes. I don't like leaving her alone back there."

"Neither do I," said Rampage. "Do you suppose she was attacked by one of those bone-beasts?" He was revved, ready to tear the ship apart in search of it.

"No, Rampage, I suspect we can scratch that one out," Dasrylion put in. "Think, brothers. Remember that voice over the comset? How it talked to her?"

Realization dawned on their faces, followed by disgust. "You mean it's a ...person – one of the *tautschen*? Bothering her? The same one?"

Renegade thought of something else. "She's clearly not married. Remember what Broken Spear told us once, when he was telling us how to act around huntresses?"

At their blank stares, he explained. "He said when courtship is performed between members of the same clan; it's usually a match of equals: men and women are about the same height and strength, and a huntress who doesn't want to be courted could make her wishes known – by force, if necessary – except that it's rarely necessary?"

They both chinlifted in understanding.

"*Chak*," Dasrylion said, "it would be a foolish hunter who incurred a huntress's wrath."

Renegade went on: "But different clans have people of different heights – Cloud Forest is smaller on average than Rydderrak, for example. And when they keep company with each other, you can get two people of very different heights and strengths."

Dasrylion jerked his chin up, his eyes bright with comprehension; but Rampage just prodded, "What's the *point,* Renegade? Get to the sharp end of the spear, will you?"

"He means," Dasrylion broke in, since Renegade seemed to be faltering at what was a delicate subject for him; "He *means,* hot-blood, that if you have a bigger male who wants to court a smaller female, and she isn't trained on how to discourage him, and *he* isn't raised to the Code – there could be trouble."

"Takka-hai!" Rampage exclaimed, "And a male would *do* that, without her consent? That's revolting!"

"That's exactly what I was trying to say," Renegade shot a grateful glance at Dasrylion. "That might be what's happening to K'leura. Few of the Spaceborn are trained in *tch-won'*, or even Hunt Law."

"And you think someone is trying to force his courtship on her? *Vrakking* animal!" Rampage snapped. The others felt the same way. Such behavior was unthinkable.

"It's obvious she doesn't like this – whoever – so we have to help her," Renegade said. "As hunters and warriors, we're here to protect people."

"Sight on it, we will!" Rampage cut in. "To do something like that…*I* couldn't…I mean it wouldn't even have come to me, with or without Hunt training."

"Nor to any normal person, maybe. So this one, this male, might not be normal," Dasrylion added. "Throw in my hideshare too, Renegade. We'll be her clan, and keep her unwanted suitor at bay. We won't let it get any worse, and we'll keep the Code aboard this ship."

"Pact," said Renegade.

And in their innocence, none of them could imagine how much worse it might already be.

***

OVER THE next tenday, they developed a plan and ran a pattern. Whenever she anticipated a slow workday, K'leura would call one of the Three on her comset, usually Renegade. And he would be there at the appointed time to escort her to the training room and back again later. It also gave him a chance to study her superviser, just on chance he was the one.

But the ship's healer was a kindly and compassionate male, raised as an herbalist in Homeworld's Sea Clan, and trained as a physician at the university. He soon earned Renegade's respect for the professional and patient way he treated K'leura and his other assistant. Also, she didn't seem to be afraid of him.

The young *tautsche* woman came to the hunters' training room in growing confidence, for they never made an ill-meant move or remark toward her.

Although she was trim and thought of herself as being in good physical condition, K'leura discovered she was woefully deficient in strength and stamina compared to the three hunters.

Renegade set her first on endurance-building exercises: walking, jogging, and range-of-motion activities, including use of an endless-road machine*.

Even though he gave her a routine which would barely try a seven-year-old in Hunt training, she felt drenched and exhausted after the first few sessions – and extremely disappointed in herself.

"Patience, you'll get there," Renegade said cheerfully; and the hunters let her use their tiny steam-shower in private, afterward.

She soon learned that wearing full ship's uniform was much too warm for these exercises – no wonder they dressed in so little, she thought. But she had nothing else, and she wasn't about to strip down to the loin-and-breechclouts which they wore. She grit her teeth and bore it, sweaty or not.

All three young men often did their exercise routines at the same time; and surreptitiously at first, then more openly, she began to watch them. They had an agility and grace which she had never dreamed possible, and their unarmed combat moves were conducted at a frightening speed.

She forgot herself once, watching Renegade and Rampage in a mock combat in the circle, staring raptly at the throws, locks, drops, spins and blunted kicks as they moved faster and faster, like some kind of wonderful dance. When they called a mutual halt by no agreement she could see, K'leura unthinkingly exclaimed, "Oh, that was wonderful!" then snapped her mouth shut, heated.

"Did you think so?" Rampage asked, grinning at her; and, "Thank you, milady," came from Renegade as they stepped over to her, drying their gleaming bodies with fur cloths.

She was flooded with confusion… they had such male *presence*...

"I – I think it was beautiful – is that on-stat to say? – like a dance," she stammered.

Renegade looked at her with peculiar intensity. "Many clans call it 'the Dance of Death,'" he remarked, "but we use Rydderrak's name for it,

---

* Like a treadmill.

the *tch-won'*. And when you're doing it properly, it does feel like a kind of dance..." his voice trailed off, but he kept a smile for her.

"I don't think I would ever be able to do anything like that," she demurred.

The light changed in Renegade's eyes; though all he said was, "You're getting better, K'leura. Next time I think we can start a few movements from the *tch-won',* even while we keep working on your strength and stamina." He smiled and left her to her work.

And she marveled again at how well in control they were.

Eleven...The Challenge

NONE OF THIS passed unnoticed by Stavrof. Every time he tried to get near the girl, one or another of those *vrakking* hunters stood in the way, mostly the shorter one. He thought he might be able to take that one; though he hesitated, having heard of the rigorous training they endured.

If not directly, he could take him by surprise...

Rumors of the cargo chief's discontent soon floated to the captain's hearing. Tallevar didn't know the cause of the unrest; he just felt a greater tension aboard ship, an atmosphere charged with unease.

"Blast it, what's going on aboard my ship?" the captain asked his second-in-command. "Systems are all functioning smoothly, supplies are good; but morale is – morale has gone to ground, T'saar'k. And when I try to find the source, I feel like I'm chasing a comet's tail. What's going on, Sub-chief? Have you got any clue?"

"Well, sir, there is a whole flight of rumors in the air; and they seem to center on the cargo chief..."

"Stavrof! A bad bargain, him...a bad inheritance, I should say."

"...and the new Hunt contingent," T'saar'k finished.

Tallevar was genuinely surprised. "Those three? But they keep to themselves; they're courteous when spoken to...I haven't had a chip of trouble out of them. Why, just the other day, I had them up for a conference about those bone-beast creatures they fought. It seems they—"

The Second waited until his captain had vented some smoke, then said, "Yes, sir. Everyone else seems to agree with you. Except Stavrof and his packmates."

"*Tsck!* And what is that malcontent's problem?"

"Well, captain, to put it delicately, he's complaining that the young *tyr-rakash* – Renegade, is it? – is monopolizing his female."

"*His* female! Since when does he admit to being interested in only one?"

"It's the young single *tautsche*, sir, the med-tech. It seems she's visiting the hunters in their...uh…quarters, sir, nearly every day."

"And?" Tallevar indicated he'd have to do better than this.

"And we – uh, don't know what goes on there. Stavrof claims she's betrothed to him."

"Betrothed! This is the first I've heard of it." He sighed. "Now I suppose I'll have to look into it personally. Blast and burn! Let me know when she visits them again, T'saar'k. I'll have to risk disrupting the ship even further to investigate."

***

HARD TO TELL who felt more surprise when Capt. Tallevar showed up in the training room two days later.

The hunters were surprised, but pleasantly, since no one else ever visited or inquired after them except K'leura.

While Tallevar was astonished to see the young med-tech apparently doing a slow dance-step to music as she watched one of the hunters do the same.

They noticed him immediately. Two of the Three greeted him with "Day's-light, Captain," heard what he had to say, and then called Renegade over. Slowly, K'leura grew still, watching, listening.

"And this is all that goes on here?" Tallevar was saying.

Renegade looked annoyed; Dasrylion wore an "I-knew-it!" expression, and Rampage's simmer began coming to a boil.

"Why don't you ask the lady herself, captain?" Renegade said.

"It's on-stat, Renegade; I'm here," she said, wiping her face. "Capt. Tallevar, the honored hunters are teaching me *tch-won'*."

"What?"

"It's an ancient system of self-defense based on learned combat movement, often taught to music," Renegade explained.

"Self-defense? Why do you even need that, med-tech?" Tallevar asked K'leura. He felt completely lost now.

When she didn't reply, Renegade glanced over and said, "She was – harassed – at her post about a tenday ago." His eyes never left her face. "Forgive me, K'leura, but you were too upset, more than upset, that night. It's time your commander knew."

"Harassed? *H'vack-hah?*[*] Why didn't you come to me, med-tech?" Tallevar burst in.

The young woman's eyes filled. She lowered her head. "I—couldn't." No one must know the true extent of her shame.

"Great stars beyond!" Tallevar shouted, startling her further. Then he noticed the defensive circle they had drawn around her, and calmed himself.

"Captain, your pardon," Renegade said; "I – she ran into me in the corridor. I brought her here to be safe, until she felt less frightened."

"You didn't see! You couldn't know!" burst from the Plains warrior.

"Rampage," Renegade cautioned.

Tallevar was no fool. He began to put actions and words together, and he didn't like what he came up with. "So you say she was threatened in some way?"

"Chak!" came from all three.

Tallevar lowered his chin and shook out his mane. "I came here only because of a complaint. One of my crew members claims she is his betrothed."

"KKT!" two of them exploded.

But Renegade fixed him with a hard stare and said very slowly, "Which. One?"

The captain met his stare, "Esteemed Warrior, I cannot allow," he began, when Renegade snapped around to the right and called out,

"K'leura, wait! Come back!" And he shot out the door after her..

Tallevar whirled; the other two hunters moved faster.

They found Renegade out in the corridor, blocking K'leura's flight, his hands held out palms up, but not touching her. He was urging her, "You *must* speak out. You must tell us what's wrong!"

"No, I can't...Renega-ade..." she sobbed, drawing his name out in a wail of despair; "He – he says I *belong* to him! You can't fight that!" And she dodged around him and fled down the hall.

Renegade let her go, watching. His shoulders slumped.

"That's enough!" snapped Tallevar. "I'll not have this disruption aboard my ship!"

Renegade turned slowly. His eyes burned. For a moment, the captain thought he was going to be challenged or attacked, and almost gave ground. Then Renegade quelled himself with an effort.

"Yes, on-course," he said wearily. "Captain, I will ask you one thing: does that look like the reaction of a happily-Betrothed woman?"

[*] "H'vack-hah" or "h'vack" used variously for "What's that?" or "What is it?"

Tallevar held up his hands in a warding gesture. "I know. I realize that, *tyr-rakash,*" he admitted; and he *felt* the other two hunters relax. "And I intend to look into it. But I think it would be best if *just for now*, my medical technician doesn't come here for a while."

"Can you safeguard her?" Renegade shot back. "*We* are here to defend the people aboard this ship, from whatever menaces them, within or without. We were doing that."

Stubborn so-and-so... Tallevar rankled, "Still, Renegade, I want peace aboard my vessel; and as long as the accusation's been made, I want time to investigate it."

The warrior conceded. "I understand that. May we know the results of your investigation, when it is completed?"

"Yes, certainly. Now, good day, honored warriors," and he strode off, before the situation deteriorated again.

Rampage glared after him. "Investigation. A complaint – about *us? Vascht,* but that's a knife twist. "

"And it will continue to lie against us as long as she doesn't speak out," Renegade said, downcast.

"Hold your throw, brother," Dasrylion advised him. "You're too close to this. Let Rampage and me scout this particular trail…maybe we can find a name behind this."

Renegade nodded. He had no other choice.

***

THE CAPTAIN informed K'leura that she had to stay at close-quarters until the matter was settled: "Just go to your assigned post and come back here to your room after the shift, med-tech."

Then, partly to offset her obvious misery, he added, "I should have this cleared up by the time we reach the way-station. Unless you have anything to say right now…"

But she answered, "No, captain," in a dead voice, and stared at the walls of her room.

Frustrated, Tallevar left her.

***

RENEGADE held his peace for one entire day, during which he paced like a captive panther and burned up energy on the machines.

"He's beginning to scare even me," Rampage told Dasrylion. "Anything yet?"

"Nothing," his friend replied. "Some odd expressions in the crew's lounge, but everyone's sealed up tight as a stretched skin. They're all very courteous, but won't give a breath of information."

Rampage glanced at their seething huntmate. "Let's keep trying," he said.

***

LATER, after his two companions lay asleep, Renegade slipped out of his hammock and glided soundlessly from the room. Using his trained and natural talents, he eased down the ship's corridors, avoiding the occasional crew member on duty.

If K'leura could not come to him, then he would go to her. *That* had not been forbidden. Somehow he must convince her to give up the name of this alleged "suitor." During her visits to the training area, he had seen her start to bloom, to become more confident and self-reliant, only to be destroyed in a single stroke. Somehow he must convince her she should be free to choose. *Fear is not our natural state,* he thought.

He moved, a phantom among shadows, toward her room.

***

K'leura lay on her bunk. She had been deeply depressed since she'd learned of Stavrof's lie. His Betrothed! And the captain believed him! At that moment, she knew she was lost. No one, not the captain, not the gallant hunter, no one could save her. There remained only one option.

She could not live with honor, so she must die with it.

She lay with a borrowed surgical knife in her hand, resting it against her breast. She began the deep-breathing exercises she had just been learning that would bring her body and mind to the proper pitch.

"K'leura?" The whisper jolted her upright.

"Renegade?" her voice trembled.

"It's me. Open;" in the same hoarse whisper.

Oh noble warrior, just one moment more -- she leaped off the bunk, dropping the knife, and rushed to the door, unlocking it.

"Ren"—she started to say.

When the towering bulk of Stavrof forced itself into the room and took her by the throat.

"Ah my little Windsinger," he sneered, "who did you think it was, your noble hunter?" He forced her backwards. She churned and writhed and choked in his grasp.

"*T-T'chak*," she lied.

"Oh *yes,* little songbird; and for *that* lapse of welcome, you have earned yourself "– backing her against the bed shelf – "a *stroke!"* and he swung with all the power of his arm. The blow lifted her off her feet. He had released her throat and she was knocked across the bed and into the hull.

The knife – where was --?

The next blow slammed into her face, then her lower body was lifted and dumped onto the bed lengthwise with the rest of her. She lay stunned.

Then came jerking, ripping motions as Stavrof tore her clothes from her. A feeble kick earned her another smash – until at last she just lay there, her life drained to a point.

His hands clawed over her. Suddenly her lower body was pierced and she seared inside.

"Now how do you like your Betrothed, little bird?" he was gasping; "Now what do you" –

When his weight was yanked off her and he tore out of her and flew backwards.

And Renegade was *there.*

He hauled Stavrof up and slammed him again and again into the far wall, and there came a terrible roaring without words – rage was loose in the room. Renegade bent every muscle and sinew into pounding his enemy to a pulp, as K'leura lay panting and sobbing, barely aware of the violence around her.

"How – do – *you* – like this – *carrion*!" the warrior thundered. "Or *this?"* and he dragged Stavrof off the wall by his neck, then lashed him with a knife's-edge hand, and Stavrof fell choking to the floor.

Renegade sprang on him, claws arched, ready to deal death – when his two friends burst into the room and tackled him.

"Brother, stop! Stop, you'll kill him!" Dasrylion screamed. "Stop! It means death for you, Renegade!"

"Spirit's sake – hold him!"

Three of them were on him now, Tallevar with them, and they were barely enough to restrain the foaming flame-eyed being who raged between them. Stavrof pointed a shaking finger-talon "Keep – keep him there," he coughed. "He's insane! Attacked my betrothed and –"

"LIAR!" with a bellow, Renegade rose up under his captors, shaking them off. He straightened, and seemed to grow in height until he towered above them.

Stavrof cringed back.

Renegade put his left hand to his right wrist and opened his gauntlet. Between his teeth, he snarled:

"It should be no wrong to kill you. We kill beasts, and *beasts* have no *honor.* Therefore you do not deserve...*this."* Gauntlet off, hand and forearm bare, he slashed out and struck the other in the face. Once. It snapped Stavrof's head back and left four bleeding lines across his face, cheek to jowl.

Then Renegade said in a tone as savage and chill as any his friends had ever heard: "I *challenge* you, less-than-a-man, to a contest of honor, in the place where honor demands, within the day. Deny me this, and I will hunt you down like the beast you are." He stood there, breath and anger heaving his chest.

The captain recovered enough to say, "Take the chief back to his quarters, *v'*hunters, and lock him in. I'll be there in a moment." He stepped aside as Rampage and Dasrylion grabbed the cargo chief and wrestled him out the door.

Renegade went to K'leura's bedside. He looked down at her – at her face, for which she would always be grateful, then he bent and lifted her fur blanket from the floor and carefully placed it over her. Gently he rested his hand alongside her bruised cheek. *"Oh, my lady, I am so sorry..."* he breathed.

He tossed a command back over his shoulder, easily, as if he'd been doing it all his life. "She needs a healer. At once."

Tallevar was halfway down the hall before he realized he was obeying an order. He hesitated, remembered Renegade in the grip of rage; and resumed his walk, coding in his beltset as he went.

Back in the room, K'leura tried to speak, could not, and turned her head away so she would not have to meet Renegade's eyes.

He understood. He lowered his head and pressed his own cheek very lightly against her unbruised side.

"The past is a dry bone, and dust," he murmured; "and I shall free you from him forever."

And he stayed with her, even through the healer's visit, as if he expected danger from every corner and everyone.

The old man nearly wept as he examined her and packed her wounds. "Help me to take her into the surgery, warrior," he said. "We must reduce the swelling and bleeding inside. She may even need some tissue-reconstruction surgery."

And bearing her as easily as he had the first time, Renegade did as he was asked.

***

RENEGADE'S friends found him outside the surgery alcove.

"How is she?" died in Rampage's throat: one look at his friend's face told him. The young hunter had seen the damaged areas as clearly as the healer had, including those glowing beneath the skin.

Finally the healer returned. "She is not in danger," he announced with satisfaction. "Fortunately she is young and strong. Her vital organs are still growing. There should be no permanent harm."

He swept them with a glance. "*One* of you may go in and see her, but not for long. She needs rest."

It was a foregone conclusion that Renegade should be that one, and he slipped into the alcove.

How bruised and tired she looks, he thought. He scooted down by the low healing table and took her hands, mindful of the tube-feed line taped to one wrist.

"K'leura, my lady," he began, low. She opened her swollen eyes.

"*Lady...still?*" she whispered, her eyes filling. Her face was bruised and swollen, even around her small canines.

"Oh yes," Renegade told her. "To me, always." He brought her hand up and placed it against his heart.

"*...Renegade...*" she managed, sleep pulling at her.

"Yes, dear one? I'm here."

"You will …fight him?"

"Tomorrow. Then it will be over."

She fought to keep her eyes open. "Be…careful. He …will…trick… you," said with great anxiety now. *Willing* him to understand.

He did. "In Hunt Law we have a saying: 'Expect no honor from the prey.' And this is how I will treat him, my lady, as an amoral beast that might do anything."

She seemed to hear him. She let her eyes sheathe again, and her hands ebb limply from his. She slept.

He rejoined his friends. "Come on, brothers," he told them; "Let's go back to our quarters. I have to get ready for the Challenge."

***

EXPECT NO HONOR --- The training room was well-lit and utterly silent, despite the nearly twenty *tautschen* who waited there. News of yesterday's events had flashed through the ship; and any crew members not on active duty gathered here, including the captain.

Tallevar wasn't pleased with this challenge. Stavrof's guilt had been established by medical science, and he would have as soon banished him to be judged by the nearest Hunt Council or its equivalent aboard the space station, as to follow some archaic custom like this. But once issued, Renegade's challenge could not be denied. It too was the Law.

The warrior in question limbered up in one corner of the room. He seemed unconcerned…no, that wasn't right – he seemed *concentrated:* every fluid movement heightened his mental state.

Not so his friends. Rampage paced about in full armor, restless as a hunting cat, while the big gray Tracker haunted room edges and machine fittings, looking for hidden traps.

A little stir among the watchers announced Stavrof's arrival. Four husky crew members brought him in; although he wasn't chained as Rampage thought he should be. Like Renegade, he had stripped down to a breechclout and plain leather gauntlets and shinguards, which Dasrylion insisted be checked for hidden snares.

"What are you *afraid* of?" Stavrof began to sneer, but lost his speech under the trapper's hot-eyed glare.

Rampage joined Renegade.. "You see him?" he murmured to his friend.

"I do. He's big but he's soft," Renegade commented quietly. "A few hard kicks to that gut will settle him. Not that I want to hurry."

Rampage ranged up and down before him. "No, shorten it, brother. I don't trust him."

"Neither do I," said Renegade, stopping his warm-up; "but this is our room. His packmates shouldn't have had time to do anything to it."

He wiped his face and arms off with a cured skin; rubbed grit into his palms. "Come on, Rampage, the sooner begun, the sooner done. And the game is running."

He walked over to face his antagonist, where Rampage had to leave him.

The two stood with the captain between them, who proclaimed the rules:

"This is to be an unarmed combat to full Surrender. There will be no weapons, natural *or* unnatural, allowed. Claws and talons will be fitted with these"—and he produced a double handful of felt caps and passed them to each fighter with the warning, "I want no maiming or disemboweling from this challenge. If you do not put them on, they will be put on for you."

After each man silently fitted the felt caps to talons and toeclaws, the captain resumed. "Chief Stavrof, since you are the challenged on this occasion, you are allowed to choose the exact placing of the Circle, so long as it is in this room. No weapons will be allowed."

'Why captain, sir, how generous of you – all of that!" the massive cargo chief sneered at him.

Tallevar said nothing. His distaste showed in his eyes.

Renegade studied his opponent. *He's more confident than he should be. Maybe he's got something planned – but what? Or maybe it's the size difference...*Stavrof was a head taller than and half again as wide as the young Arvien warrior.

But a lot of his opponents had been bigger than Renegade: sloth-bears, the Gets-Behind-You, the bone-beasts—and one by one he had overcome them all.

"On-stat, then," the chief finally decided. He pointed, "I choose *there*, inside the target-range; and half the normal size will be fine." He seemed almost negligent in his choice, but arrogant enough as he strode over to the spot and said, "Well, let's get on with it, shall we? Or is our 'noble' hunter not ready yet?"

Renegade put a hand to Rampage's shoulder, to stop his impetuous lunge. "I'm ready," he said; then aside to his friend, "Just watch the crowd for me, Rampage. Keep them honest."

"I don't like this!" Rampage snapped. "Take him out fast, brother."

"-do my best," and Renegade gave his shoulder a light slap and walked away.

He first got that odd warning tingle when he stepped inside the target zone. It poured out full-bore when the clear laser-proof walls rose around him.

"What! What's this?" Rampage snarled outside, barely audible. "It's a trap!"

The clear walls cut off almost all sound; they were as smooth as ice and ended very close to the ceiling. Renegade crouched in reflex.

"Just a little insurance, 'honored' hunter," Stavrof told him, snickering. "On Chance your quick-trigger friend there decided to end this fight his way."

"He wouldn't, but I don't expect you to know that," Renegade said flatly. *That's not his reason – what is?*

Outside the box, Rampage wheeled for the automatic controls, but Dasrylion was already there, pounding on them.

"Locked!" he snapped. "He's locked up the mechanism somehow!"

Capt. Tallevar was livid. "At the main terminal, no doubt. Quick, T'saar'k, go to Systems at the Bank of Lights and find the operator," he ordered his Second.

"I'm going too," Dasrylion declared, and raced off with him. "Rampage! Watch them!"

"I'll do more than that, brother." Rampage called his *vai-ator* to hand and tensed to throw.

"Do that and the hunter forfeits!" someone yelled from the crowd.

Rampage held his throw and scanned the crowd. Stavrof had perhaps four or five backers there, he estimated. He watched the fighters for one wrong move. His eyes glowed in fury.

Stavrof lost no heat and no edge from the surprise. He threw himself at Renegade immediately, a bull's rush which the warrior easily evaded.

Stavrof skidded to a stop. "What's the matter, *little* hunter?" he mocked Renegade. "Afraid to stand your ground?"

Renegade knew this must be a trick of some kind, but he also knew he had to make this a total victory. Unquestioned. Final.

He moved in.

Stavrof bellowed and fell on him – only to have his elusive quarry roll onto his back and pull him down too, legs braced against him – then flip him with his own momentum.

The bigger man crashed to the floor, breathless. He lurched up to face the nimble shadow dancing in – and got a kick in the jaw for his haste.

"Uh!" His head snapped back. He had never seen fighting like this; he was a brawler, not an artist, and he was in real danger of losing the match before he could launch his next surprise. This time he lunged to his feet and charged, head down, arms widespread.

Renegade used his outspread arms as a vaulting-beam, boosting himself up and over before landing feet first on the broad back.

Stavrof went down with a grunt. He began to roll, and Renegade chopped him smartly on the back of the neck – not quite enough to knock him out.

Thick neck, Renegade thought.

Stavrof made a wild grab at those lightly-moving legs, closed on air, and got a side heel thunked into his ribs.

Renegade was winning. With style.

Stavrof rolled himself like a barrel. Renegade sprang over him, then paused as his enemy rolled up against a corner.

"Let me up!" Stavrof wheezed. "Or did you forget *honor*, stripling?"

Stung, Renegade backed off and waited.

Stavrof made a great show of slowly finding his feet. Now his back was to Renegade as he pulled himself up by a few air holes in the plastic shield.

The warrior's eyes narrowed. Something was wrong here...

Stavrof puffed as he turned back around.

"See if *this* fits you!" he said suddenly as he threw something at Renegade.

A weapon. Renegade lost a vital fraction. *A net!* He dropped, tried to skid under it – and the capture-net caught his upper body and pinned him to the floor.

He was completely vulnerable, caught under his chin to just below his waist, one arm partly up-flung, the other outstretched and useless. Only his legs were free as the net's spikes drove into the floor. He was helpless.

And Stavrof fell on him. His weight knocked the breath from Renegade's lungs, and his hands vised around the warrior's throat.

Renegade gasped and tried to breathe. In an attitude of complete surrender, his fight should have ended here. But his enemy could kill the helpless, even other *tautschen* – and Renegade knew he was going to die.

Stavrof's friends had somehow hidden the net in one of the air holes in that corner; or maybe he had seen it there previously. No matter: the end was the same.

Renegade thrashed helplessly as his thoughts went to violet, as his lungs seared, trying to think before his world turned black.

"Stop the fight!" Rampage screamed outside the walls. The crowd was in tumult, outrage roared through them at this betrayal of the law. Even the chief's friends shrank back, afraid of the sudden change in the crowd.

But Stavrof was in a fortress, immune.

One look at the captain's equally desperate plunging about, and Rampage acted. *Forget the laser* – he launched an assault disc at the top of the wall, and himself right after.

Under Stavrof, the smaller hunter's struggles were growing weaker. The chief grunted with effort, leaned into it, knuckling the net fabric aside to get at the throat better.

Sliding to black, Renegade was dimly aware of the knuckles now pressing against his lower jaw, against his teeth. If only…

Something hit the wall high up. There came a grinding sound; then it stopped. Next the crash of a heavier body struck the same place.

Stavrof, startled, let up for just a fraction, as he looked up to see Rampage on the wall with his *vai-ator* grinding through it.

Renegade tipped his head slightly, opened his mouth as wide as he could, and part of Stavrof's finger slipped inside his lower jaw. It was enough. Rule of Law was broken. Survival prevailed.

Renegade bit down.

Even though he rarely uses his teeth and claws to bring down prey anymore, a Hunter can use his sharp-toothed bite to shear down at more than two thousand pounds of pressure per centimeter. And he never forgets those teeth and talons are there.

Blood spurted as Renegade bit the finger to the bone, then broke the bone. Below Stavrof his knees tensed.

Stavrof screamed and jerked backward – a natural reaction. He tore the bitten hand from Renegade's failing strength and reared up and back – to bang against his legs, which Renegade slung straight up with his last gasp of strength. One leg bent and slipped over Stavrof's head to catch his throat, and both ankles locked around it.

Renegade, heaving for breath, his blackened world starred with pain-bright sparks, put everything he had into the hold. If he failed, he would never get up again.

Pressing, pressing…*wrench,* and Stavrof's weight began to lift off him backwards. The chief tried clawing at the leghold, but the agony of a near-severed finger distracted him.

He toppled even as Rampage's blade-disc cut through the wall completely to let him in. The lithe brown warrior dropped into the fray, was at the combatants' sides in a leap, disc raised to tear flesh. Then he saw that Renegade was alive – *alive* – and paused, astounded.

Through ragged breaths, Renegade rasped at him, "Thanks…brother… my fight…cut me loose."

"Great Spirit, Renegade, I thought I got here only to avenge you," Rampage said as he knelt and slashed through the metal net to free him.

Renegade forced himself to sit up, gave one more twist of his legs to keep Stavrof down. Now there would be no question of right or wrong. He had never felt more like killing.

Just then the walls slid down.

"Good old Dasryl," Rampage said. He caught Renegade by the shoulders as the crowd poured in. "Easy, brother, easy now…"

Renegade felt Stavrof torn from his grip, and as he tried to draw his legs up against his body, the world spun, and he leaned against Rampage.

"Hold hard; we'll have you to a healer in no time," the Plains warrior told him.

Finally the captain and Dasrylion came running up, forcing their way through the raging crowd.

"Were we on the nock? Oh, praise the Great Spirit!" Dasrylion cried, kneeling by Renegade's other side. "Let's get him out of here."

Renegade choked: "…Stavrof…"

The captain glanced at the crowd and turned away again. They had become a pack, and blood flamed from tooth and claw.

"Justice has been served," Tallevar said quietly.

Renegade lapsed into his friends' arms and let them handle it.

***

AFTERMATH---Renegade spent the next few days in the healing chambers, with K'leura near enough to talk to – not that he could do much talking with his throat packed in ice and recovering from delicate laser surgery. *Nearly lost that one,* he thought; *if my friends hadn't been there...*

He tried to convey this to Rampage, who was sitting at his bedside: "Good thing…I fought you…long ago."

His friend laughed. "Who could have known then? Let fall Chance, *t'churr?* And here we are."

More seriously he added, "I only regret I didn't get a piece of that coward's hide before the pack finished him. I wanted to do it myself."

"You did…enough…saved…mine," Renegade told him haltingly. He was thinking that this was the only time Hunt Law allowed a person's life to be taken, when he had killed or tried to kill another:

"Who takes a life of the People shall forfeit his own."

Otherwise the Credo and the Code, not to mention instinctual Surrender, prevented it. In this way, murderers had been removed from the Hunters' society through the centuries. It was a classic piece of clan justice, if only this Starborn crowd had known it.

He wondered whether Stavrof would have been spared if he *had* surrendered: *Would that have stopped them? Would it have stopped me?*

He was so lost in thought that he barely felt Rampage's friendly shoulder-squeeze, and his parting, "Get your rest, brother. The healer's chasing me out and Dasrylion wants a turn. We're two days out of the way station and it'll be on to new worlds after that." He paused at the threshold long enough to crease one eyelid in humorous afterthought: "Besides, that means *you'll* have to explain this little incident to Broken Spear when you send to him."

And Renegade groaned.

Twelve...The Hunter Overtaken

EXPEDITION SHIP 3145 stood off the clouded planet M'rra'kr'ryal 4. Heavy atmosphere swirled over the world's surface in red, purple, and bronze. Three ringed moons floated beyond, two of them large enough to have their atmospheres.

"Nock up another habitable planet," Rampage told Tallevar as the three hunters re-entered the ship from their Scout. "A little bigger, a little heavier than Homeworld, but any of the clans ought to be comfortable here."

The captain nodded. "And the animal life?" he asked Dasrylion, who was disembarking with a full trapline's catch.

"Swimmers, a few flyers, some floaters," the trapper replied; "land creatures somewhat squat and strong – and on the small side, nothing large there. Still, we caught enough in this trapline run to keep your research team busy for a tenday. And so far, nothing has been willing to attack *us.*"

"Very good. And what is your estimation, Great Warrior? When might we send down the research team in person – under your guidance, on-course?" (After atmospheric surveys by satellite, and samplings of microbial life by automated probes, hunters are the real investigators of new planets. They make landing first, and bear the brunt of the new world's compatibility or hostility. They have the most dangerous job.)

Renegade was the last to emerge from the Scout ship. He looked measured and steady, at full strength and health. He had gone down to the surface with his friends at every one of the last nine planetides, hadn't missed one.

His mask hid a grimace at the "Great Warrior" title. He was hearing it from everyone now, including the entire crew. "The Legend of Renegade continues," as Rampage put it, much to the legend's dismay...

"I think you could send your researchers down there shortly after this next microbiologist's report and our own analyses, Captain," he said. "We've mapped out a good landing site. The gravity may tire Starborn legs a little" – a quick smile – "it did ours – but the beasts there are small, nonpoisonous, and more curious than hostile. The plant life is abundant. We have plenty of recordings from our ten days on the surface."

He paused before following his companions aft to the lab, as he considered something: "This makes what? Eight habitable worlds in as many systems? No: *nine* planets, eight systems – two worlds in the life zone at Ar'rky'vul – and we had no trouble at any of them. They're close together here."

"That would be because of the gas and dust cloud these systems have passed through, and the abundance of younger stars, I imagine," the captain told him.

"It's strange, though," Renegade was thinking aloud, "how on several of these worlds there were *so few* large species, so many habitat niches unfilled, except for a few like that last one, Darashena, where life abounds The others at least have some larger game species on land and in the sea, but not as many as you would expect. And here there are none, and empty niches everywhere."

The captain shrugged, a gesture involving head tilt and closure of the nictating membrane in one eye. "Perhaps because the planets are young yet."

"Perhaps," Renegade said. "Yet I'm going to recommend full-scale satellite surveillance on each of the nine and their larger moons, too. Maybe we're missing something. And our report will include a caution for any settlers coming here to M'rra'kr'ryal 4. The planet needs to be re-stocked." He stood there, pulling off his studded half-gloves and facemask. "Well. Any-route, what's next on our trail, honored captain?" – the honorific deliberately added.

"We've almost finished this stellar group, Great – ah, Renegade. Eight systems in little over a year, setting a new record of habitable planets found in close conjunction. Next we're going to swing a little 'north' of the Galactic plane and take in two 'straggler suns' which weren't part of the original cloud, but which seem to have fallen in with the herd. After that we'll breaktie for home."

That's more than two years, Homeworld time, Renegade thought, *nearly three for Arvien. I wonder how he's doing?*

He thanked Tallevar and went deeper into the ship.

On his way to the lab with his specimens, Renegade politely acknowledged more greetings of "Day's-light, Great Warrior," and "Good hunting, Great Warrior," from his fellow shipmates, his face impassive and his thoughts racing:

Earlier on, they'd had messages waiting for them at the way station before entering this territory, and their last chance to leave a few of their own – his friends did it for him, since he was still recovering.

One of the most damaging bites of news came from Broken Spear himself. He said the crashed alien ship on R'shba 3 had been traced to its home planet, and a tragedy there.

Hunt ships had found no other living beings there above the size of an insect, save one. They found a stripped planet, barren of all larger lifeforms except the bone-beasts. It held the ruins of a technological civilization, eaten down to the marrow. The bone-beasts roamed everywhere, making their dens in the ruins.

Not one of the builders remained.

"Because of this," the old warrior's message went on, "the Conclave's decision is being carried out: R'shba 3 back in Six Systems will be scoured of all animal life, something we unfortunately know how to do. If we can snap up a few healthy live specimens, we will, but the outlook is grim.

"After making the Circle of Death over the planet, the extermination teams will go in and burn any viable underground den which may remain. R'shba 3 will have to be totally re-stocked with life; but trophy hunters can still fill their gamebags with the bone-beasts on that newly-discovered world, and doubtless others to come.

"Our quarantine regulations are even tighter now, as they should be; but I wonder, my sons, whether there is anything or anyone left in all the Galaxy for us to discover, except these creatures."

***

RENEGADE reached the healing chambers and med-lab, his strides lengthening the closer he came to it. Dasrylion and Rampage were already there, talking to K'leura; but when she heard Renegade's step, she spun and almost ran to him.

"Renegade!" she took him by the upper arms, then blended into a full-frontal embrace.

The other two young hunters exchanged knowing glances.

This is a match, mimed Dasrylion, and when the couple parted, Rampage sang out, *"Arah! Tyr-rakash!"* and howled with laughter when Renegade glared at him.

K'leura distracted him by saying, "Another clean bug report...micro-bugs, that is," she added merrily, ignoring the teasing. "Nothing down there to infect us. We'll develop antibodies as always—though the biting bugs seem to be an annoyance....and when are you going to let me go on-planet with you, Renegade? The other researchers have already been down to the last worlds we visited."

He pondered, his hands still resting on her shoulders. "*Krrr*--- let's see how well you do in practice before our next planetide," he ventured.

***

OVER THE next several ship-days, K'leura underwent rigorous *tch-won'* and weapons' testing; until finally Renegade had to admit, "You're ready—at least with weapons and basic *tch-won'*." He had been doing something unusual with her training: he had been teaching her the killing moves first.

And K'leura had thrown herself into the combat arts with a zeal he saw in only the best, like Rampage. Her confidence had grown alongside her skill, until her self-image became one of independence and power. If she had a personal credo, he suspected it was: *"Never again."*

That seemed to apply to further intimacy as well. She would greet him warmly, even tenderly, and allow his physical closeness. But if the embrace went on even a *ktarn* longer than what she felt safe with, she would stiffen and pull herself back. Then she'd look hurt and apologetic, as if she couldn't help her body's reaction.

Renegade understood that. He was patient. He could wait.

***

THE LAST PLANET---The two "straggler stars" were almost twins, 28 degrees Galactic north of the main dust cloud, about four lightyears away from the nearest other habitable system, and only 2.5 lightyears apart.

The expedition chose to investigate the one which seemed to have more planets, one pair a double.

"A double planet!" K'leura exclaimed as they hove to around the common center of gravity. Two great blue-green globes wheeled about each other, almost perfectly matched, and fertile with life.

"We'll make planetide at that one with the large continent shaped like a double diamond – see?" Renegade said as they broke away in one of the Scouts. "It's between Homeworld and Arvien 4 in size and gravity; the oceans modify the climate; and its atmosphere is pretty near perfect."

Two vast blue "moons" filled the Scout ship's dome view, taking the explorers' breath away.

Then, "Ready, set, let fall Chance!" Rampage sang out and the ship rushed in to meet the blue.

***

SURVEYED FIRST by autoprobe, land masses mapped and bodies of water charted, the two worlds soon advanced to the next stage – physical contact. The Hunters like to feel new worlds beneath their feet. They say no robot probe can substitute for a trained observer. And the hunter's eye is keen to see and his brain to interpret what a machine may or may not record.

This first planet made up for all the others in its richness. Armed with sensors, sample kits, lasers, traps and curiosity, the hunting pack spent a tenday on its surface in their first foray alone. Here were wonders enough for everyone:

* A three hundred *kri-veh* long canyon where seasonal winds could whip up to hurricane force. They had a wild rocket-ride through it in the Scout ship, laughing with joy;

* A huge gloomy freshwater swamp crowded with ancient trees 100 *kri* tall, whose vast canopy spread perpetual twilight below, and which the young explorers promptly named "the Caverns of Gloom." Here they shot treecat-sized chameleons that clung to those boles, and watched iridescent pebble-skinned carnivores swim underwater;

* A rolling savannah-land lush with galloping, bounding and hopping herds, and the whip-thin, panther-size predators swift enough to catch them;

* Plants with gaudy-colored leaves; plants with slotted leaves that crooned in the wind;

* Giant spiny mammals big as bears that peacefully chewed vegetation in the northern forests, and had no real enemies except a large weasel-like *hstae,* that tunneled under them to reach the soft underbelly. (The sight of the *hstaen* gave Dasrylion a few bad moments);

And one day in their northern camp, the three male warriors awoke to see K'leura standing in the field outside the sensors, holding out handfuls of grass to a herd of magnificent herbivores, their shoulders as high as hers, a single spirally-twisted horn on their foreheads, male and female, with glossy coats that shimmered in copper, bronze, jet and alabaster.

"Look at them," Renegade breathed, "and she's right in among them... No, brothers, don't shoot...don't you see what she can do?"

"She's *calling* them to her," Dasrylion said in awe. "She's a game-caller, and never knew it."

"Chak; and she'll never forgive us if we kill 'her' creatures." Renegade glided forward. "Easy now."

They were able to approach the great animals almost as closely as K'leura had.

"Pick some grass or green buds," she ordered them; "and offer it like I'm doing."

Slowly their hands went out. Renegade, who had never approached an animal without wondering if it would try to kill him, felt the velvet softness of the creature's muzzle lipping at the grass in his hand. When that tuft was done, he pulled another, and carefully lifted his other hand to touch the creature's neck.

It *whuffed* through its nostrils, tossed that splendid horn and its long neck-hairs.

"You see," K'leura said quietly, "you don't have to kill them..."

"I'm glad of that," Renegade said. Their eyes met under the animal's long curved neck.

"Churr, this is...different," Rampage commented. "It's like leaving the fur on, right, Dasryl?"

He chuckled and the hoofed beasts grew uneasy.

"We're scaring them. Let's leave...slowly," K'leura suggested.

"Yes, milady," Rampage said meekly; and they walked off. The herd drifted in the other direction.

Dasrylion looked after them, admiring, "Still, brother, that splendid coat, that horn..."

"Dasrylion!" K'leura cried, outraged – until she heard the sly "Yes, milady," in imitation of his friend; and she gave the trapper an indignant "*T'chrrt!"*

"Say, Renegade, you remember that hot springs pool we found, up near the big river?" Dasrylion changed the subject.

"On-path."

"Isn't it just a short walk from here?"

"Yes. Just above the river where it comes through the rocks, west of here. Why?"

"Krr-rr... after all those steam-chambers aboard ship..."

"After *years* of steam-chambers..." Rampage picked up.

"Ah. I see. You mean what about a real bath, *t'churr?"* and Renegade broke into a jog, winking at K'leura, who joined him. "Last one in has to scrub with lava rock!"

"KKT! Unfair – wait!" and Rampage was off after them, Dasrylion at his heels.

Rampage won, of course; Renegade and K'leura loped up in stride with Dasrylion close behind.

"Hai!" called Rampage, jumping into knee-deep water.

"Hold your throw, warrior," Renegade told him, pulling off his own backpack and mask. "You don't bathe with your gear on, or without setting..." he produced a small black cube with a flourish and plunked it down on a nearby rock "—your alarm sensors."

"Oh frost," Rampage said. He stuck a cube on a flat north-side rock (the hot spring pool was entirely rock-rimmed) and began stripping off gear and leathers as he stood there.

"Carrion-trick, Rampage; I think you should forfeit," scoffed the Cold Tracker, placing his cube on the piled rocks at the far end. "Put those things up *here* and I'll dunk them for you." He skinned out of his own gear neatly. Naked except for the wristknives, which they always wore on-planet; he plunged in after Rampage, who struggled to flee through the water carrying his bundle.

"—see you try!" came back defiantly.

And they were off. Rampage won the race for the opposite shore, but Dasrylion dunked him on the rebound.

Renegade laughed. "Ignore them, K'leura. Something about warm water makes them revert to childhood."

He removed his own things with an easy natural grace, leaving on only the wrist-weapons, and prepared to slide into the water – when the two miscreants re-surfaced, grabbed his legs, and hauled him in. He made a satisfying splash and came up spluttering

He shook them off, raised his arms invitingly and said, "Come on in, K'leura. I'll see to these tricksters!" Then he turned and went after them.

K'leura had placed her alarm sensor at the near side of the pool (the only place left vacant) and stood there in shock as she realized that all three of them were naked now, and didn't seem to care. Granted, they didn't wear much clothing anyway, and her heat vision was almost as good as theirs; but it was like being presented with the fact of their sexuality as starkly as when she had been mauled by Stavrof.

So she hesitated, watching them; but they were so natural, so easy with their condition, and the water looked so *good*, that she wound up her courage, undid her pack and tunic, and let them both fall to the ground. Suddenly chilly and shy, she lowered herself in.

Warmth circled her knees. She waded deeper. Near the center of the pool the water rose to her chest.

"Aah," she breathed.

"Feels good, doesn't it?" Rampage called to her from near the opposite shore. He was sitting down, in water to his waist, and unbraiding his long and complicated hair-tail. He was the only one who seemed to take any notice of her.

"Yes it does!" she called back, "And that's a good idea, too." She undid the knot that held her own waist-length blue-black mane, and let it slide free. With half its length in water, her hair made a misty black cloud around her.

Renegade paddled up. His black mane, already unbound, fanned out behind him. He sloshed upright at her side, the water a little lower on him. "Steam just can't compare with this," he remarked. "You remember our bathing pool at the hall, brothers?"

"Indeed I do," Dasrylion sighed, "and how Broken Spear would tell us we might spend days in mud and blood, so to be glad of a bath when we found it?"

"Well, that's become a fact of life, hasn't it?" Rampage put in.

"He taught us well," Renegade said, with a shade of wistfulness.

"You had a bathing-room? In a hall? At school?" K'leura hazarded. She had been raised quite differently, and the images puzzled her.

"At our Hunt training school," Renegade said, and he drifted closer to the poolside, K'leura following, to sit near Rampage, while he told her about their Hunt training and their teacher. K'leura was fascinated: she'd had some teaching in the Credo and Code, but none in the Hunt.

Dasrylion soon joined them, his fiery mane in sharp contrast to his glistening dark-gray body. He'd seemed to grow daily on this voyage, and was now bigger and more muscular than both his companions.

By the time Renegade had explained about hunting school to K'leura, they each had half-a-hundred reminiscences to talk about, lolling at ease in the water. This was perfect bathwater: it never got cold or ran dry. The little stone-scooped pool lay at the bottom of a series of stacked, flat rock ledges, and the hot springs trickled down from above.

K'leura soon forgot her nudity. The Three acted as friendly and natural in this setting as they did aboard ship. More so, perhaps, since they were free and outdoors again. What she looked like didn't seem to bother them. She had forgotten that the splendid Hunter darksight told them about her body and organs even under clothing – although it did not reveal the normal reflective colors of her skin as daylight did.

They could have also told her that most freehold or clan huntresses wore almost as little clothing as the men did, except in cold climates or on a hunt. Breast-wraps or armored cup-shields served to protect the mammary glands, while a light wrap or embroidered cloth sheathed the hips.

But K'leura was Starborn, and had spent much of her young life aboard ships or in a high-tech environment. Starship service required that crew members wear uniforms; and each ship tended to have its own colors and designs, depending on which clan or freehold sponsored it. She was accustomed to a coverall type of clothing which the hunters privately thought masked the crews' true emotions, and made them harder to read. It seemed like a form of lying to them. And while the sight of a female's uncovered body stirred them, the discipline they had learned during hunt training enabled them to keep it in check.

So they talked, and swam or drifted, dove under the shallow water and got thoroughly wet…the kind of cleansing that the hunters, at least, had missed for a long, long time.

The afternoon passed in luxury. Wetting eventually led to sunning, and one after another, Dasrylion and Rampage left the water to stretch out on the flat rocks ringing the pool.

"Be sure you move those sensors out with you, brothers. We still need a perimeter," Renegade reminded them. "And one of you stays awake on watch."

Their chorus of "Yes, Elder," brought K'leura's laughter bubbling up, and a smile to Renegade.

"Do you want to sun yourself a little?" he asked her gently.

Her throat constricted. She glanced over at the other two young men stretched out on the rocks.

Renegade read her correctly. "They would never harm you either; they simply think you beautiful, as I do. But let's look for a more private ledge." And he stood and took her hand to lead her through the deeper water.

Her heart began to pound so loud she was sure he could hear it. But he said nothing, just angled for the far end of the pool, where the water ran down from the rocks.

"Here we are, almost private." They stood near the flat rocks which jutted out at the far end, and she could see the water dribble down in tiny streams at several places along the edges.

"Sort of a divided waterfall," he called it, "with warm sun on the south side. I'd better put these up…" He was holding two more alarm sensors which she hadn't even seen him pick up on the way.

He let go her hand and balanced himself on some piled rocks to get out of the water and into the dry space behind the several little falls. His shining muscular body emerged dripping, and it was all she could do not to gasp aloud. His grey-and-gold coloring seemed to glow, like alternating clouds and sun, and he too was beautiful in her eyes.

Renegade placed the motion sensors carefully; one aimed outward, the other scanning up over the rocks above the waterfalls. The river running alongside them dropped suddenly at the pool, and was too far below to give them any unwanted company. In this little hollow beneath the falls, they were backed and bedded by stone, and no animal they had yet found could burrow through that.

Renegade padded back to the poolside and knelt, reaching out a hand for her. "Careful; it's slippery climbing out."

She rose gracefully; and he moved to the side to give her space – even though his heart skipped a beat when he saw her full-length, body and light-colors unmasked by water. Even as she must be able to see him.

When she drew away as usual, he bowed his head to the inevitable. He must give up his feelings for her; their match would never be. She had been too badly hurt to accept his courtship. He had waited nearly a year, and she still shied away from him.

"I'll find a place nearby," he said, low, "to keep watch."

She hear the change of tone, looked at him quickly, saw the dullness to his blood-colors and how he bowed his head. And suddenly she ached for him – he had fought for her, protected her, selflessly taught her to defend herself. This so-called "primitive" hunter-warrior had been the most *civilized* member of the entire crew.

She found her voice.

"Renegade."

He'd placed one foot on a stepping-stone to go down into the water again. He stopped. And when he turned to her, it was very slowly. His eyes met hers. She took a deep breath.

"You don't have to leave."

And his eyes and mouth widened. Life unfolded in him again. He rose from the step-stone and approached her. Unconsciously, she steeled herself.

Even then he didn't do the expected. Rather, he took her hands and leading the way, sank down to a sitting position with her, then eased them both into a reclining one, lying side by side facing each other, with a little distance between them. He knew she would be uneasy; he knew he must be slow.

Letting her lean on one arm, he brought her other hand to his face, touched her fingers to his cheek, then to his throat, and released her hand.

"Here," he said gently, "There will be no more than you wish and only *when* you wish. I will lie still, and await you."

Then astoundingly, unbelievably, his head turned toward her, he lay flat on his back, put his arms to his sides and took the Surrender posture, with the front of his body and his throat exposed.

Her breath caught. *"Oh!"* she cried out softly. And using her free hand, hesitant at first, she began to touch him – his face, his eyelids, which he closed, the long thick black length of his mane. Blood-heat rose and fell in his face, but he held still.

She traced the smooth strength of his underjaw, to the curve of his still-boyish biting teeth*…he's young, younger than I thought…yet he acts much older sometimes.*

…Down along his throat, mended now, no scars visible, to his chest, the broad muscles gleaming there, to his attractive pattern: the narrow black stripe down his sternum was actually composed of many tiny black dots, she saw now, with the larger round black spots scattered over his breast of gleaming gold. One black spot covered a nipple; while his other nipple shone pale gold, lost in the background color. They erected at her touch…she could feel her own rising in sympathy.

She felt like an explorer of more than new worlds, of new life forms, able to contact directly what she had been afraid to touch before. She continued down his flat muscular belly; his breathing quickened. Now she was near the dreaded organ – his phallus. More black speckling from his lower abdomen drew a line to it – and the organ itself pulled up taut against his belly. The organ of her torture in another man, here offered, controlled, *given* by this one, so she might not fear it anymore. Gingerly she touched it, felt it was warm flesh like every other part of his body – and he uttered a low moan.

Renegade felt as if he were on fire. He moaned, and that drew her attention and her touch back to his face.

"*Renegade,"* he heard her whisper: "*I – could…I want—*"

He controlled himself with every ounce of discipline he possessed.

"Not yet," he murmured, and slipping his left arm under her head and shoulders, he raised himself up on one elbow and turned toward her. Then as she had, he touched her all along the length of her body, long, gentle strokes, not at all hesitant, but not hurried, either. He stroked along her face and neck until she closed her eyes in bliss; then his hand circled and smoothed over her breasts. The two proud little nipples rose to him. Her

body temperature was rising. She, who had never felt a micron of desire, who had never had a season, was being stroked into one by this gentle lover.

He slid his hand along the smooth incurve of her waist, admiring the camouflage splashes of many colors that flowed along her flank. Next he put his palm to her belly, making circles over it, lower, lower…

The smaller mound now, at the juncture of her thighs. She was trembling. But she did not want him to stop. And then his deft, gentle fingers slid inside the lower folds, rubbing softly, his finger talons pointed away.

He drew her closer, lay his head against hers, at the temple. She held him tightly around the shoulders. The slow stroking continued, until he suddenly felt her grow wet.

A spasm seemed to pass through her body; her legs rolled apart. Renegade remembered Kyva, on P'taal 5, and blessed her for this insight, so he could give joy to K'leura now.

She pressed to him, shaking, her hips open. He slipped his exploring hand under her inner thigh, and raised her leg over his own hip. His phallus tipped her inner opening, yet he held back. He had one more thing to tell her.

"K'leura," he murmured, "it will be different with me. This is our bond; it seals us to a lifetime together. My lady…do you want that too?"

She had time to breathe *"Oh yes, Renegade!"* before the long smooth pole of flesh slid into her.

***

OUTSIDE, farther away on the pool's rimrock, Dasrylion woke Rampage for his turn at watch. The young warrior shook the grogginess from his head, then sat up and began re-dressing himself.

He had slipped on laser and shinguards when he became aware of the strange sounds.

"Do you hear that?" he asked Dasrylion. "It sounds like someone in pain…no, different…where's Renegade?" he demanded sharply. "And K'leura?"

"Hvaah-haah," his friend soothed. He slid closer to Rampage, touched his shoulder. "No one's in pain. That *is* Renegade and K'leura." He nodded toward the far end of the pool.

Behind several thin streams of warm water falling from a rock ledge, Rampage could just make out two figures' heat-shapes, so close together they looked like one.

"Renegade and K'leura?" he asked, surprised. "You mean they're finally…?"

"—joining, yes. Here! Don't watch; it's not polite."

"But I've never seen it done," Rampage protested with little-boy innocence.

"Well, I have. You can't live in a big family without stumbling into places you don't belong now and then; and believe me, it's a very private act between the two individuals, not for display."

Rampage felt hurt. "But we're his friends! And any-route, he's done it twice now; he even has a *child* – and when I marry K'orrynia, I won't even know what to do!"

Dasrylion sighed and wrapped his arms around his knees. "Spirit of sky and water, Rampage! You sound petulant, you know that?"

He glanced at his friend; saw the pain on his face. "*Krr*; your pardon, brother. I'm not thinking." Another huge sigh. "Ah well. If I *tell* you what you have to do, will that be good enough? Will you let them alone, and let me catch a nap, and stay on watch without—?"

"—watching them. *Chak, chak, chak,* brother," Rampage finished for him. A long wild cry came from the far edge, and he jumped. "Only get *on* with it, will you?"

***

BECAUSE they would have no secrets from each other, Renegade told K'leura about his *ashe-kvar* son being raised by other parents.

"He'll be about three years old now, and I've never seen him in person," he said glumly. "Broken Spear was right: you lose track, and they grow up not knowing you. It won't be that way with us, K'leura. We'll announce our bonding at once, and have the captain read the rites over us, and if we've started a child, make a home for him or her."

"I know, dear Renegade," she said, placing a hand on his chest. "I will be of bearing age in about two quarters, not fertile until then. That's why... that…beast…didn't..."

He held her close to stop her thoughts.

***

WHEN THE PAIR emerged from their nuptial bed, freshly-dressed, their skin damp and glowing, the first people they told were Renegade's two friends – who already knew, but followed custom and pretended they didn't.

Dasrylion and Rampage both congratulated them; only Rampage looked them over discretely to see if this made them "different" in any way. He noticed they gave off a faint scent, like warm saltwater, different than their normal individual scents, and they both seemed vibrant with heat-colors, as if their blood was exceptionally aerated, vitally alive.

I wonder if K'orrynia and I will look like that, after, he thought. *I have to go back to her soon.* And despite his joy in this great adventure, a small urgency took root and began to grow.

As if he read his friend's mind, Renegade said, "It'll soon be time for you to return to the Dinosaur Clan, Rampage. It's been about three years now, I think."

"I'm going as soon as this expedition is over," Rampage declared. "What about you, Dasryl?"

Their Cold Tracker shook his mane. "I haven't really looked around or given it much thought yet. You two are early to table*; I'll wait a little longer. I don't even know any huntresses yet."

"Each to his own trail, brother," Renegade said affably. "Come on. Let's return to camp."

***

THE SHIP'S CAPTAIN read the wedding rites over them with what Renegade felt was relief, as one major problem settled. He had a few others: first about the short crew his ship was carrying since he'd dropped Stavrof's co-conspirators off at the way station for punishment (not the death sentence in their case); and secondly, the ship's instruments had detected another promising sphere circling the second star. Finding this many good worlds in such a small space was a great prize, and he wanted to bring news of their discoveries home soon.

Renegade persuaded him to finish researching the double planet, and suggested that only one or two hunters could take the smaller survey ship to look at the world in the other system, leaving the Scouts here. After all, the farther planet might not be suitable. A quick inspection would tell them.

Since he'd suggested it, he found himself in charge of the next mission. "On-course, I'll make the jump. And be back quick enough." *Then we can go home.*

He hit a cross trail when K'leura wanted to go with him.

---

* More usual marriage years come after full maturity, in their 30's and 40's. For convenience' sake, all Hunters are considered full grown by age 32. clr

"You're good at the exercises, but you haven't been tried in the hunt yet," Renegade protested. "You haven't made a kill, or had to survive on your own. It would be too dangerous for you."

Those were the wrong words, he discovered. They first made her angry, then sad, then so imploring that it tore at him. But he remained firm. This mission called for a trained hunter at the least, a proven warrior at best.

It made him wonder about the marriage: would he always be torn like this? Star-sailing was wonderful; he could do that with her at his side; but trophy hunting was not for him anymore. Just as well; he wouldn't miss it. What he had to do now was to think of something they could both be happy doing. He put the need at the back of his mind. It would percolate and come up with something in due time.

It did, almost immediately.

"K'leura," he said to her before he left, "you know we're entitled to shares of a new world, you and me and anyone else aboard this ship. And the hunters can have prime game territory as well, first pick. Would you like to settle here someday with me? We'll go back to Nine Systems first."

Her eyes lit up. "Settle? Have a home, and a beautiful new world of our own? These are such extraordinary planets…yes, Renegade, I think I would."

"Good. Then, while the main ship is still here at the Twin Worlds, you could choose some good land, with plenty of game and fresh water. Dasrylion and Rampage can help you pick it out and maybe…" a new idea, just a hint in the proper place… "they might like to choose something here too. That way we could all be together." (*Yes, that was it; that way he could keep his friends around him)*

"That would be wonderful; and I'll tell you what, my hunter…"

"What's that, my heart?"

"It's going to include that stone pool of ours."

And he laughed with her, glad to see her happiness restored.

***

RENEGADE had not expected trouble from his friends either; but they turned out to be as insistent as K'leura. They wouldn't think of letting him go off by himself to survey an entire planet; and if he was going to take any of them, he would have to take them both.

"I'll do all of it from space, with satellites and probes," he argued, "just to see if it's worth bringing the expedition ship over. You're both needed here. We know that the other twin world is fertile; and beside-the-path, I need you to watch over the people here, to guard them."

"You mean watch over K'leura in particular, don't you?" Rampage said shrewdly.

Renegade flushed. "You know what I mean, brother. She's safer with both of you, and on this ship, now, than she would be with me alone."

In the end he talked them down. He would go alone.

How did everyone get so dependent on me? he wondered. Why do they all think they have to guard me? At least Rampage will give me an argument now and then. Who chose me leader anyhow?

Yet he realized it had been that way for years, from the beginning. He just hadn't felt the full weight of it till now.

Duty digs a deep burrow in the heart, he thought wryly, quoting Hunt Law to himself. At last he knew what that meant. Taking responsibility for even one other life seemed an enormous challenge; now he had three.

He hoped he could be equal to it. He prayed for it.

And he finished packing his supplies lost in thought.

Thirteen...Dark Passage

THE WORLD lay below him, its surface a ruin of cinders and ash. Below-ground, it seethed like a volcanic cauldron. The probes confirmed it: a nuclear wasteland.

"Another dead world," Renegade murmured. A civilization had been here once; there were still traces of it which had not been burned beyond recognition. Then it had gone to dust – radioactive dust. The destruction was so great that in some places fires still burned underground to the roots of the soil…as they must have burned for a thousand years.

His friends shouldn't have worried. It wouldn't be possible to set foot here.

The creatures that had lived here must have destroyed themselves before they could reach a neighboring star, and kept their havoc at home; though it was impossible to tell, now. *Whatever our own People's faults,* Renegade thought, *our Credo and our Code have kept us together to reach the stars.* Honor and the Hunt. He wondered if anyone else had found the successful combination.

Ah. Well. Call in the probes and get tracking for home.

The survey ship was like the expedition ship in miniature. It had a small lab to analyze samples, robot probes and satellites which could be launched to scan a planet. It had everything except another Scout ship smaller than itself.

Renegade stayed in orbit until he had a chance to look at the latest series of live images: there seemed to be an anomalous moon here, very distant from its primary. He should track that down…

It wasn't a moon.

"Not a natural satellite, no; an artificial one…no, bigger than that…a *space station*," he muttered to himself. "Old…centuries old, pitted…but no serious radiation. Let's have a look…maybe they left a trace of who they were." *Of themselves and their destruction.*

He did the math and adjusted his trajectory to intersect the unknown's.

The abandoned space station was huge, several times bigger than the Hunters' expedition ship. Old and battered as it looked, the hull was still intact. Incredibly, he detected traces of atmosphere within. Air pressure, too. He could explore it wearing only his facemask and light armor, with the air-exchange cylinder mounted on his back – for he was already planning to go inside.

It turned out to be rather tricky. The station was spherical with two large bays, one at the north and another at the south "poles." These were closed, of course; nor was he capable of opening them from the outside with anything short of a laser cannon. And he felt reluctant to destroy anything.

He did find a number of entrance "funnels" along the equator like the more familiar docking tubes of the People's space stations; and he could see what looked like a small airlock inside each one. One tube still held the remains of a ship, stillborn these many centuries.

The funnels were narrower than expected – they had been built by a different species, *t'd'faal* – so he had to back in and maneuver carefully to align the survey ship's flexible pressure tube to the airlock.

He got it reconfigured and fastened down, donned his equipment including weapons, and cautiously made his way in.

The hatch door took some prying, and he didn't relish having to unlock it again later; but he obeyed his long training and re-closed all the hatches, his own and the aliens', behind him.

Inside, the space station was dark and dead. He shone the twin headlamps mounted on his mask around its cracks and crannies.

-- Old equipment, damaged equipment, a scene of disarray in here. Things thrown about, things lying on the floor to trip him. It shouldn't be this messy if the outer hull bore no damage.

Where had he seen something like this before?

Then he remembered, and he froze.

The rescued Hunt ship.

The disorder left after a deadly firefight. The shiver that passed through him sent the light beams dancing.

"Stop it!" he snarled at himself. "These are the remains of some other trouble, that's all. It doesn't mean that *they* were here."

Yet once he thought of it, he couldn't shake the feeling that the bone-beasts lurked somewhere near.

He had to get information, and quickly. Where was the computer system? Were there terminals and screens? And would they be any good after all these years?

He found some likely-looking panels and opened them: just ancient wiring. He found something that looked like a console and pried around, searching for an intelligible keyboard or power source. There were no recording tapes, crystals or discs, no printed circuits – nothing that he recognized any-route. Or else centuries of bad air had eaten them away. A prolonged search in the dark and cold yielded him nothing.

But there had to be some major power source: the station was warmer than the deep cold of space, warm enough for him to walk around here.

Finally he remembered the docking tubes, and the ship still lodged there. That ship might have an onboard computer, flight recorder, or other storage system more durable than these.

The station seemed to have three levels on its equator. The docking tubes were on this one, with him. He made his way haltingly along the corridor. His memory placed the docked ship at the fourth or fifth tube over.

Upright narrow doors lined the corridor, like the one he'd entered. These people had walked erect, apparently, but been shorter and narrower than the average Hunter.

At the fourth door, he stopped and tried the seal, glad he'd remembered another old saying: "*Mark your backtrail: the land looks different coming back*." Except that here everything inside the station looked so much alike.

The rusted airlock yielded, cracking open with a *whoosh.* Renegade looked down sharply, to see if it would lose more air. It didn't. Both ends were sealed. He walked the few steps to the far end and un-visored the small window – no ship there.

To the next one, then. Renegade re-sealed everything behind him as he re-entered the station.

On the way he bumped against something on the floor. When he shone his mask-lights on it, it took the distinctive shape of a long weapon. He picked it up.

Something fragile and pale crumbled away from one end of it: he glanced down and saw bone fragments – and a distinctive bulky shape nearby, lying under a cabinet. Renegade had done too much hunting and cleaning of trophies not to know a skull when he saw one, even a partial, alien one. So someone had used this weapon – and died with it in hand.

He studied the weapon. It had a manual trigger and two hollow tubes where the force or projectile discharged. It most resembled a simple flame gun.

Fire – the safest weapon to use aboard ship when you didn't want to puncture the hull. This might say something useful about its makers. He clipped it to his belt to take with him.

The fifth lock. He cranked it open and stared inside – and the *feeling* came over him – the gut-deep warning of doom.

It's down there, the cause of this destruction, down there in the ship. Whatever killed them is still here.

He set his laser to short-range bolts, just on chance he could use it, but it was the spear and the wristknives he held out before him as he descended to the ship. The end hatch's view-port was blackened as if by fire; he couldn't see out. Yet he knew the Other was there, he could feel it, a floating weight on his consciousness. He cracked open the lock. *Too bad the flame gun's useless.*

This lock fed directly into the abandoned ship, and a gush of atmosphere rushed out. More air, better pressure, even more heat…the ship must be fueled-up and ready to go, an ancient carrier, awaiting a dead pilot's hand.

Don't stand here, he told himself. *Move. Attack is the best surprise.* He sprang down into the ship and spun full-circle, ready to fight.

Nothing attacked him. Instead he noticed something out of the corner of his eye: after his twin lamps sped over an area, they left a strange residual glow.

He switched the headlamps off. With his special sight, anything giving off body heat would show up superbly on this cold dark ship.

There. Eerie blue-violet glows all along the walls of this narrow tube of a ship. A memory stirred in his mind – he knew – he knew –

He knew nothing.

Walk up to one of those inset bays and look, mighty warrior, he chided himself. They were set in some kind of berth or alcove, recessed all along the ship's inner hull. When he approached the nearest, the toe of his boot touched the pale glow and a greenish light-spear arced through the air. He pulled his foot back.

An alarm. Some kind of alarm.

But nothing happened except that the blue-violet lights brightened. He waited, spear at the ready. When several *ktarn* ticked by without another sign, he moved up to look into the long shallow berth again.

Some kind of translucent jelly covered a mass of the strangest things he had ever seen. He studied it for a while before he realized he was looking at: bodies, stacks and stacks of wasted animal bodies of all sorts, mostly medium-size, but with their flesh so wasted away it was like looking through a glass wall. He could see their bones clearly—and even these were shrunken and small.

Yet their abdomens were bloated, swollen out of all proportion to their size; and within them he could see the coiled embryos, waiting. Were they pregnant? They were of many different species, he could see. He bent closer.

Alive. The embryos were alive. He could see the hearts, the blood-pumps beat, with extreme slowness, and as he leaned closer, the nearest one opened its eyes.

Now he knew.

When the bone-beast juvenile ripped free of its host, the Arvien warrior was ready. His spear took it in mid-air, spun it over his head, and rammed it back against the ship's hull.

Writhing and leaking, it died there.

Renegade expected its virulent corrosive spew to eat through the hull as the beast threshed and bit at him. But except for a few curls of smoke, it didn't. Even as he was shaking the thing off his newmetal spear and backing up for another attack, his mind filed that information, and worked furiously.

When the beast finally died, his theory was served ready-cooked to him, and he knew what this ship was:

A nursery for the bone-things' young, where they were birthed, protected, and grown to adulthood. Deliberately. The entire inner hull of the ship thrummed with working engines which ran nutrient fluid to the embryos when the original host animals' bodies were completely consumed. How long had they been here? Years? Centuries? The ship was old…

He backed up against the far wall, away from the birth-chamber, away from the thing he'd just killed, one arm bent before his eyes as if he would shield himself from the very sight of them. Horror coursed through his veins. *They raised these things here. They nurtured them. And I would lay a clan leader's hideshare that they loosed them on that planet below.*

It sickened him even to think of one race of sapient beings doing that to another. They had been enemies, these creatures above and those below. Those above had loosed the beasts against that world, and in a terrible act of self-defense, the survivors had wrought their own nuclear night. What a sickness festered here, among the indifferent stars!

"This isn't a ship," he said to himself, "It's a missile. Whoever put those creatures aboard *meant* to use them against the planet. And they did, because all the launch tubes are empty, except this one. But something went wrong. Some of the embryos escaped – and killed everyone aboard."

No more than they deserved, his mind told him.

Whether these same beings had followed up with nuclear weapons, or whether the beings down there had used them in a desperate attempt to stop the beasts, he didn't know. Nor did it matter.

Because the attack succeeded, but the Hunt was lost. The bone-beasts had turned on their creators and devoured them; hence the chaos aboard this space station – not a station at all but some huge battleship. Genocide on a scale which would have appalled his People…they had been reluctant even to clean one planet of the rapacious horde.

His thoughts were racing and he felt ill, but his senses worked as well as ever. He noticed a movement from the partial ceiling wall *inside* the birth chamber…

…and was already leaping backward keying in his laser when the ceiling shattered into blue-glass ice and something huge, dark and rattling fell from it…*kri* after *kri* of dark glistening bones, preceded by an enormous mantled and pincered head.

The giant nest guardian crashed to the floor, half in the nutrient stew, slopping it over the side, and half into the corridor outside it. It was too big for its confines. It cluttered up berth and hall – and that gave Renegade his fraction to react.

It gathered itself on its many legs and swung that wide head at him, the pincers gaped wide – and Renegade fired into the gap, fired the laser, once, twice, again.

The spear flew from his hand as he dived to the floor and went rolling to avoid the great beast's armored head. It smashed into the hull where he had been.

The ship itself groaned under the blow.

Renegade snap-rolled again, bounced to his feet, and re-sighted the laser. *Burn it and seal it. No poison must escape.*

The dripping mass of bones did not move. Renegade watched, a man caught in nightmare, as the smoke of its life-heat arose and dissipated along the hull. He saw no spirit.

His aim had been true. It was dead.

He let out the breath he'd been holding in a long rasping hiss. *Get out of here,* his good sense told him, and he obeyed.

Renegade moved at a fast walk through the missile-ship, tensed for action, his mind racing. He must find some clue to the guidance system before he destroyed this ship. There had been a lot of missiles launched, he knew, and not all of them hit their target. Some of them had missed and passed on through the stars, rumbling along at sublight speed, their deadly cargoes in stasis, asleep for centuries.

But ready to wake at the touch of a living being, *any* living being, including those on an unnamed world, whose inhabitants later spread them to R'shba 3. And where the bone-beasts wakened, worlds died.

Where had those other ships gone?

He strode through the ship, avoiding the eerily-lighted bays down its length. He went forward, to the nose, where he found the guidance system encased in a protective box, and pried at it until a little printed square popped out. A notched metallic square, which had outworn centuries of neglect.

"Good enough," he said, slipping it inside a wrist gauntlet. "Now for the rest."

The craft had a primitive nuclear engine. Renegade had studied all sorts of propulsion systems as part of his technical training. In these, you had only to remove some of the radiation absorbing devices, dump the extra fuel in there, if any, and the fission would create a chain reaction in short order.

It still had enough fuel to make the reaction possible. When it blew, the embryos, the missile, and the huge space base itself would be vaporized.

He mastered the project, set his own timer, slapped down levers and buttons, and ran.

--Back to the entry hatch, *shut* the hatch, through the short tunnel into the bigger station, slam that door too, and up over the aisle debris toward his ship.

He was almost there when he tripped over the computer terminal lying on the floor: its monitor screen was cracked, but – he shook the terminal – three *kt-tare'* remaining – something was inside. *Take the whole thing...* tucking the computer under his arm, fumbling at the hatch to his docking tube, where *his* ship was waiting…

Open it. Get out. Run. Two *kt-tare'* left. Outer lock. Open. Quick check inside. No beasts…*I hope.*

One *kt-tare'.*

Down to the pilot's cabin. Start the retro-impulse engines. Warm up the main ones. Begin easing out of the docking tube.

One-half to go.

Slowly, slowly, gliding out. Bump the wall and it's over, the records gone with him. One quarter left. *Where's that blasted hole?*

Mere *ktarn* now.

And then he was counting: Ten. Nine. Eight…black space and stars ahead of him…seven, six…firing up the main engine…five, four, steady, steady…three, two – *hit it.* One.

The survey ship blasted hyperlight as the station went nuclear behind it, outrunning the bomb and the light-blast too.

Renegade huffed out a breath, slumped in his seat. Made it. And not an eye-blink to spare. He throttled down.

He'd lost a quarter lightyear blowing out that way, but he made it up on the return trip, out-sprinting light and nightmares all the way home.

***

AFTER SCOURING the survey ship to make sure it was clean, and depositing his find with Captain Tallevar, Renegade skated it down to the second of the twin worlds, which they had taken to calling Blue Two, to collect his friends.

They were easy to find. A surface hunting pack usually left a radio beacon on nearby to let the expedition ship know of its whereabouts. Renegade followed it down.

A crimson sunset bled into the sky as he landed near the camp. The alarm sensors placed outside its circle screamed at his approach.

Nobody home. He waited, noting that the camp itself was properly placed under heavy cover.

Twilight pearled one side of the sky while a nightwing of darkness swept up the other by the time a little Scout ship banked and touched down just inside the camp circle. Two of its riders jumped out and exclaimed over seeing the bigger vessel on site.

Renegade came out of the brush and they called to each other. All three were out of the Scout now, and they put down a long heavy object they were dragging and went to meet him: Rampage, Dasrylion, K'leura.

After a long embrace, K'leura told him. "You should see what I got, Renegade. I shot it myself!"

"Shot it? Shot what?"

"Got her first solo kill, that's what," Rampage said, as proud as if it had been his own. "She's a real huntress now." He bent to the long object they'd dropped, which looked like a rolled canvas with iridescent scales. "Here; let's show it to him."

They hauled it over and unrolled it.

It turned out to be three spectacular-looking skins. They stretched as long as small sauropods, with knife-toothed snouts and horned and carbuncled heads and long flanged tails. Covered with shining scales of deep red, copper and silver-green, each its own color, the hides looked like a cross between a dinosaur and a giant swamp lurker.

"I've never seen anything like these," Renegade admitted, kneeling to finger them. "Are they from warm-blooded creatures?"

"*Krr*, maybe. They act it," Rampage said. "But they're found only in a few places in the southern latitudes – volcanic islands and sea cliffs rising out of the ocean. Now, look at these!" And from either side of a single skin, he began unraveling a large membrane. When both were fully stretched out, Renegade could see they were a pair of

"Wings," he murmured. "Full size wings. Are they functional?"

The other three exchanged glances.

"Are they *functional?*" Rampage chortled. "Brother, can these things *fly!* Hollow bones, like a bird, but very flexible too…lots of power in all four legs…they're big, fast, and hungry, and they make one *krst* of a trophy!"

"And we saw them flying below us, fishing from the sea," Dasrylion explained; "so we went down on one of those volcanic islands to investigate, and found some of their nests in the sea caves…the adults are bigger than this."

"The *adults? These are juveniles?"*

The trio laughed outrageously.

"That's what *we* said," K'leura told him. "They're incredible creatures. These are about half-grown."

"*Krr-rr*, when we came upon one nest, or lair, if you like," Rampage went on, "Momma was away, but *six* of the babies attacked."

"Six!" Renegade was really concerned now. He'd told them to keep K'leura out of danger, and they…

"Rampage and Dasrylion killed the first two, and drove the rest away," K'leura put in hastily, guessing his thoughts. "I was farther down the mountain, away from the caves, when one of them – this one, the coppery gold – came scooting down at me and nearly knocked me over. I just fired the laser on instinct."

"And *tauw!* Knocked him right down. Straight through the eye! By the time we got back to her, it was all over." Rampage unwittingly dug himself in deeper.

Renegade had developed a terrific pain in the head. He rubbed the space between his eyes. "So I leave you two behind to keep my new bride safe, and the first thing you do is go off hunting real live dragons…"

The three exchanged guilty looks.

"Now that's bitten it," muttered Dasrylion.

"It wasn't deliberate," Rampage protested. "They *did* attack us."

And, "Don't you think it was a good kill?" came from K'leura, with innocent wistfulness.

"Don't I think --?" *Now I know exactly what Broken Spear must have gone through with us.* Renegade clenched down on his temper with an effort. Despite his worry and pain, he forced out a compliment:

"Well and good. It *was* a good kill, K'leura. The past is a dry bone, and dust, as our old teacher used to say. I think we should recommend you for regular hunter status, milady, if the Council agrees – and you three had a far better adventure than I did."

With his approval the trio relaxed and grew happy again.

Renegade bent down and stretched one beast's near wing to full length. "It's a tremendous trophy. Did you keep the bones, too?"

"On-stat, brother. All cleaned and shined," came from Rampage.

"Then let's load them up. I think we'll breaktie soon, and return to Nine Systems."

"We will?" Disbelief.

Renegade chinlifted. "I'll tell you about it back at the ship," he said.

***

DEATH TRAIN---"The second record you retrieved, the actual memory bank, is the more helpful of the two," Capt. Tallevar told the three male hunters in confidence the next day. "The missile's guidance system memory shows that that one in particular was definitely aimed at the dead planet. The other chip shows the detailed number of missiles aboard the larger ship, and their destinations."

He paused, choosing his words, then continued, "There were 36 of them, every one aimed at exterminating whoever lived on the world below."

His face drawn and serious, he said, "You were correct, *vr'*Renegade, not all of those missiles met their target. Twenty-two of them did, but 14 others went astray somehow, probably during the on-board firefight..."

The Three leaned toward him, intense.

The captain continued, "One of these never left its firing tube – the one you examined, *tyr rakash.* The other thirteen were cast loose in the Galaxy."

"Thirteen!" said Rampage. "Where did they go? Can you tell?"

"Yes, Esteemed Warrior. We were able to trace their trajectories for the most part, barring further accidents like meteor strikes."

He took a deeper breath. "Of these thirteen, seven are headed in-Galaxy toward the Hub and the stars around it. They may never connect to a planet…or they may. Or other beings may find them and unwittingly spread them to other worlds."

"And the last six?' Renegade asked, his voice flat.

"The last six, Great Warrior, are coming in a slow train toward our systems."

A resonant *kkt!* went round the table. Then,

"One of them came down on that nameless planet our Hunt ships backtrailed from R'shba 3," Renegade said. "The inhabitants must have involuntarily taken the creatures with them to R'shba recently, since that world is – was – still alive when we first discovered it. They may have been trying to escape there."

"Yes; but the others," Dasrylion said, "Are they coming down now?"

"If not now, then they're close," the captain told them. "The fact is, we can intercept them, or our Hunt ships can."

"Then we have to go back at once," Renegade said.

"With one important tie-over at the way station," Tallevar corrected. "We can relay the information from there. It will reach Nine Systems' Hunt Council faster than we can."

Rampage sprang up. "Then why are we sitting here? Let's breaktie and go!"

For once, no one disagreed with him.

Fourteen...Back Home

DAZZLING blue-white snow covered the slopes and the roof of the great hall; mounds of it piled against the windows and doors.

The Three dismounted their borrowed aircar and stood knee-deep in cold. Their unprotected breath frosted in air.

The hall was empty. It looked as if it had been abandoned for a hundred years.

Renegade felt disappointed even though they had known Broken Spear might be away. This was the second winter of their absence from Arvien 4, and deep cold. The old warrior had left a message at Nine Systems Station saying that he would probably be taking his students out to hunt the starworlds. He'd gone even before they sent their emergency message home.

Still, Renegade longed to see the old man again. To him, his "grandfather" was the one who made this planet home.

Dasrylion coughed behind him, and Rampage stamped. Despite their all-weather gear, the bitter cold seared their lungs as they stood there.

Renegade stiffened his spine.

"Well," he said, "he's still away, then. Let's go inside and warm ourselves – unless your father needs that aircar back right away, Dasrylion?"

"No; he says we can keep it for a few days...are you going to shelter it?"

"Yes, in here." Renegade found the old digital coder and used it to open the landing bay door. The wide door slid smoothly aside, leaving a ice-frame of snow around its edges. Broken Spear's aircar sat inside, and Renegade's heart leaped – until he remembered they also kept the school ship on the grounds, so his guardian wouldn't need to fly to the spaceport.

White stillness and echoing chambers met their footsteps as they walked through the building. Renegade wished K'leura had been able to join him.

But the expedition ship was being deactivated at Nine Systems' space station, and she had to stay with it until all the information had been collated, copied and forwarded to their sponsors on the Hunt Council and Homeworld. She would catch the next ship to Arvien 4 after that.

The Three passed their old training room and their booted footsteps ricocheted from the walls, sounding hollow and forlorn.

"It's so empty here," Rampage remarked softly; and Renegade remembered another, smaller boy, walking through the dark halls and saying, *"It's different with everybody gone. Emptier. Lonelier"* ...about a thousand years ago...

What a dismal homecoming.

They felt a little better when they had ensconced themselves in the hearthroom and started a small cheerful fire. This room felt closer, cozier: it still held some sense of the old hunter's presence. Renegade sank into Broken Spear's favorite handmade chair and leaned back, absorbing the worn spots, the depressions, the feel, and maybe even the faint scent of him. His essence still lingered here.

They talked about their plans. They had originally been hot to go on a search for those alien ships – what a Hunt that would have been! – a Hunt across the sky, chasing a deadly horde to an unknown lair. The stuff of legends, Rampage told them,

But the home systems' Hunt Councils acted faster. By the time the expedition ship reached the local space station, Hunt ships had already been dispatched from every quadrant to pursue the invaders. Hunters and warriors are the guardians of their people. Where danger threatens, they rise to meet it.

So the ships had gone out to intercept the bone-beasts' missiles, and the Arvien Three had come home to an empty house.

They mixed up a bit of broth, sat and talked till they were sleepy. Then Renegade decided to shut up the hall for the evening and check it over, out of habit. His friends went along.

They lit up and examined the trophy room first. It now had an addition, a kind of antechamber dug deeper into the mountain alongside part of the old warrior's display. Here Renegade's and most of Rampage's trophies were displayed. (Rampage's brothers had a problem with their younger sibling's success; and he felt his things were safer here. Dasrylion's family, on the other talon, was proud of his, and kept them at home.)

The young men exchanged wondering glances. Broken Spear must have had the antechamber built to surprise them, and it had, even though the warrior wasn't home. They admired it for a while, then dimmed the lights and headed back out the inner door. Renegade cast one last look at the great bear that reared up in the rotunda's center, retrieved bones, fur and all from a distant world; then he too left the chamber.

From the trophy hall, they went on to Broken Spear's living quarters, which had been left neat, clean and lifeless, and went on to the former study, where the comset and computers were now kept.

"T'chai! There's a message," Rampage remarked on the obvious: a pulsing violet light on the board indicated a hyperlight message had been received and stored.

"Maybe it's from Grandfather," Renegade said hopefully as he opened it..

But it came from Kreh-t'vyk, now Director of the Nine Systems Hunt Council, and it said:

"Great Warrior and Champion, we have urgent news. Please contact us at once. Kreh-t'vyk, Nine Systems Hunt Council."

"Krr, that's probably an old one," Rampage declared. "What's the date on it?"

Renegade frowned. "Not that old. Two days ago – the Hunt ships were sent out nearly two tendays before we arrived."

"I wonder if it's something about the bone-beasts, or about them coming *here,*" Dasrylion worried, "though I doubt it," in a tone which said he didn't doubt it at all.

"I doubt it, too," Renegade said, meaning it. "I'll send a reply and see if he wants to talk to us instead."

He did. During the next few *tare'* in which the Three had bathed (ah, luxury!) and made ready to sleep, their message was received and another sent back. The comset chime sounded just as they were getting into bed. A tired group of warriors dragged themselves into the room to answer the call. Renegade read it off the small screen:

"Honored hunters and warriors, this is Kreh-t'vyk returning your message. I give you greetings from the Nine Systems Hunt Council, and in the absence of your teacher, ask if I may speak to you personally on this matter. I am Director now, and can speak for the Council."

"That's strong enough," Renegade said.

"Director...he's moved up," Rampage muttered; while Renegade said, "He's holding, live. Shall we tell him yes?"

He scanned the faces of his friends, and found grudging acceptance there, along with some doubt.

"It's only a message. We can tell Broken Spear ourselves if we ever find out where he went," Rampage said. He yawned, flanked his sharp teeth with his forearm. "Beside-the-path, this'll only take a few *kt'tare'* if he's standing sentinel, *churr?"*

This time the reply came even faster:

"It is a blunted lance, Great Warrior. I shall be with you in two days and tell you in person. Transmission over."

The Three stared at each other over the silenced comset.

Now what? their expressions asked each other. *What has gone wrong now?*

Fifteen...The Question

"ESTEEMED hunters and warriors, I am honored to see you again," Kreh-t'vyk's broad smile gave warmth to the ritual words as he gripped each set of forearms in turn, Dasrylion at the upper arms, since he had been the Elder on the young man's Master Hunt.

"You have journeyed far, brothers." He certainly didn't sound like the anxious individual responsible for that message.

"We are honored, Esteemed Hunter and Council Director," Renegade took the lead; "Please sit and share meat with us – although your message seemed urgent..."

"Urgent...yes...*krr*...the Council's in a blind trap: we need to come to a decision about one of those alien ships you so promptly warned us about."

"One of them? What about the other five, Director?" Renegade slipped into more vernacular speech. He indicated a chair.

Kreh-t'vyk sat, grew more somber. "Yes, those. We have had some thrilling hunts, and some terrible hunts, close to the bone, but fortunately we prevailed."

"*Had?*" Rampage cut in. "You mean they're over?

Kreh-t'vyk gave an assenting chinlift. "Chak. It went like this:

"Of the six ships, one was disabled by a collision with a small meteor, and we were able to track it down and blow it apart without any trouble. Another plunged into a sun and was destroyed.

"Three of the others landed on inhabited places, two of them our planets with colonies. That was far too often for coincidence. We still don't know how they did it."

Renegade's throat went dry. "Which planets?"

"One was Krt'chr 2 in Four Systems – heavily settled. *That* one we dispatched almost instantly, because our people were alerted. Another was a large planetoid, a factory world where ores and minerals are mined and processed…" His eyes clouded. "That became a pitched battle during which some lives were lost, because few of the machine-tenders had been raised to hunt. We won eventually and exterminated the beasts to the last spawn.

"The third missile struck a new world, its life just forming from primitive compounds. That gave us a hard hunt... the missile broke up and the embryos scattered. We finally found and burned them all. But we don't know what effect all this contamination will have on the planet. We had researchers there hoping to study it untouched."

He turned to Renegade directly. "We took a blow, but we will recover. Not so whoever touches those other seven ships which went beyond our ken…what kind of monsters were these beings, to launch such destruction, Great Warrior?"

"We don't know," Renegade said. "The bombs and the bone beasts eliminated almost all trace of them. We think that the other life-bearing planets we investigated had gaps or holes in their eco-systems because these beings hopped from world to world, stopping only long enough to do some serious damage at each one, before they went on to attack their enemies directly."

"Something else to stand sentinel over, then," the director commented. "We must make sure those settlements that take hold out there are surrounded by armed outposts and ready to defend themselves. *T'chrrt!* Is *no* other race civilized in this Galaxy?'

"A good question, Elder," Renegade said rather sadly. "With these, in their hatred and haste to fight an enemy, they loosed death upon all living worlds."

"Kreh-t'vyk," Dasrylion made an uncharacteristic interruption, "I mean no disrespect by hurrying you…"

"None taken, Dasrylion."

"But what happened to the *sixth* ship, the one you spoke of in coming here?"

Kreh-t'vyk snapped out of his reverie. "The sixth! On-course, *vr'*hunter – that ship did not arrive where expected, near P'taal 5."

Renegade's breath stopped.

"So we had to search all of nearby space for a clue. Apparently it passed quite close to a dense dwarf star and was given a sort of gravity-whip which accelerated it briefly into hyperlight. If it is still intact, it is now more than 500 lightyears beyond the P'taal system…"

Renegade breathed again.

"And heading for the only still-extant technological species we know of, save our own..."

"H'vack-hah?[*] Your pardon, do you mean the one that Broken Spear wanted re-studied?" Renegade burst out.

"That is the one. A pity we've been so involved in other things we never got to it," Kreh-t'vyk said. "We may never know, now."

"But," Renegade sought his friends' eyes, "surely we can intercept *that* ship?"

"Perhaps. But it may already be too late. We may have lost one of our fine trophy worlds...there are no researchers or Hunt ships currently in that area. At any-route, it would merely replace one trophy species with another."

"Yes, but there are more creatures than one living on that world--and if that one really is intelligent..."

"Intelligent, perhaps. Civilized, no, Great Warrior. And very hostile. It may even be interesting to see *which* one of these is the more hostile and aggressive...survive or die, *churr?* That explains part of our indecision about whether to ask T'akaion to investigate or not. He holds the highest rank, you know. And as you say, there are other lives down there – other wild creatures that have evolved naturally to that planet. It would be a shame to lose them. As I mentioned, we are divided on this. That is why I wished to see your noble guardian. That—and for one other reason."

The three looked puzzled. Other reason?

Kreh-t'vyk snorted. "*T'churr!*" with a kind of annoyed good humor. "Another secret? The old *tsh'ombre* is a wonder! Do you know he has recordings of various creatures in his library?"

"Yes, whole series, but we've rarely used them," came from Rampage. "It's always been a 'learn as you go' thing with Broken Spear."

"Or else you get thrown right into the fray," Dasrylion observed dryly, thinking of his Master Hunt.

Kreh-t'vyk scanned them, amused. "Why then you *don't* know, do you? The Champion has the most extensive collection of recordings and translations of that species – the *hew-mahns,* I believe – in existence. I wanted to make copies of them so that their calls will not be lost along with them."

***

[*] What is it? Or, What's that?

"JUST RECONSIDER, brother! You're married now, practically ready to have a family, for Spirit's sake!" Dasrylion implored him. "The Divided World is one of the most dangerous in the known systems."

"Or at least let us go with you, Renegade," pleaded Rampage.

Renegade snapped his laser rifle cylinders together with a loud *thock*. "No, brothers, better me than Broken Spear, you know that. And it's just a reconnaissance, like the other mission. By-the-path, K'leura may be busy for nearly a full quarter with her studies. I could go there and be back before she returns. Now I want to hear no more about it. We've decided this."

"*We?* You mean you did, all on your own. What about us? What about her? Even trophy hunters have never gone there alone..." Rampage's voice became blurred with grief.

Renegade's expression softened. Gently he reached out and took his friend's shoulder. "I know, Rampage; but it's better that K'leura comes back here to stay with you two. If she were here right now, she would only want to go too.

"Just think – chances are good I'll never even have to make planetide. We just need to find out where that alien ship actually *is*...whether it even reached that system or not. And if it is there, I'll be able to destroy it from space, at a safe distance, and the whole trip will be a blunted lance, any-route."

He released Rampage. His eyes were grave and his voice full of emotion. "Suppose that world *can* be saved? And we just stand by and let another life-bearing planet go down to darkness? What are *we* then? Aren't we sworn to preserve the lives we hunt? And you know Broken Spear would have wanted to go there himself, even though he hates the place, never wants to see it again. He would be forced to, as the People's greatest warrior. I have to go there instead."

He cased the rifle, turned away to put it and a block of batteries in the Hunter craft's small storage bay...turned away so he might not se his friends' stricken faces: Dasrylion's mute with abandonment; Rampage's very near to weeping. Those might well have unsettled him and changed his mind.

In truth, he didn't know himself whether this was the right decision. He only knew that if he didn't go, Broken Spear would have to, as soon as the Council located him. So he kept his attention on packing the craft, instead.

The ship was a loan from the Hunt Council, small and fast and well-armed. It had an extra feature lacking from the Hunting People's older spacecraft – light-shielding, like their trail suits. Kreh-t'vyk said it was the least he could do for a fellow hunter on a dangerous quest.

To his credit, the director was as torn about Renegade's decision to volunteer as he was about telling the youngsters in the first place, though he never told them that.

It hadn't taken much to persuade the Hunt Council, though: Renegade was a member-at-large and his title and reputation carried more weight than the young man ever dreamed.

"I'll have plenty of time to learn some of their languages," Renegade was telling his friends as he finished packing. "They have a great number of them, but only three or four widely-used ones…" (He insisted on calling them "languages" rather than "calls") "And I've packed away copies of some of Grandfather's tapes. I can devote my time to that. I'm taking along the most modern translator we have, so I can program the languages into it. If I have to land— no, Rampage, I don't *plan* to – but if I *have* to, I should be able to understand them."

Dead silence. Renegade sighed. Leaned his forearms against the ship's hull and said, "Listen, brothers, you know I wouldn't do this unless I felt strongly about it – and I do. So please, stay at the hall. Wait for Broken Spear; let him see you're on-stat, at least. Please.

"If the game runs well, I should be back in one quarter or less. If not…" he looked off into the distance, then turned back. "I need to stop at Nine Systems station and tell K'leura now. Would you like to come along for the short-throw?'

Of course they would.

***

RENEGADE decided to do the honorable thing and tell K'leura personally. He flew his friends out to the base, where he would leave them; since Kreh-t'vyk told him he would see that they got a berth home. Renegade expected K'leura to be busy for some days yet, but to his surprise, she told him she would be finished in no more than a fiveday, which meant she could come back to Arvien…with him.

It made what he had to say to her harder. While Dasrylion and Rampage went to distract themselves among the shops after main-meat, Renegade retreated with K'leura to a more private alcove, where they had a long, long, discussion – which only made her very unhappy.

Her warrior felt rather miserable himself; and it dampened the little surprise he had for her afterward. They went to the records and news section of the base, and had their names entered as "married" in Nine Systems' database.

Then he took her to a shop; and because he had not given her a single wedding gift (so he said; she said he'd given her the best gift of all), he asked her to pick out the finest neckchain she could find to put her new hunter's medallion on (not *esteemed* hunter, but the medallion many freeholds gave their regular hunters who have never had a Master Hunt.)

He was further surprised when she chose a rather modest one, worked with copper and gold and a few sea-green emeralds – the color of his eyes, she said.

They rendezvoused with Rampage and Dasrylion and all four of them spent the afternoon together--a solemn enough company; since none of them seemed inclined to talk.

That night Renegade rented a separate alcove and spent the sleep period with his new wife, something they hadn't been able to do since returning home. She reached for him hungrily and he responded; and their lovemaking was long and passionate.

But when they finished, she held him close and wept. And that came near to breaking him. He kept her close and wept with her; but he would not break his word to the Hunt Council and call off the journey.

"I don't want you to go," she sobbed; "I'm afraid you'll never come back."

"Beloved, beloved," he whispered. "I'm a hunter and a warrior for our people. There are things I must do. I can't tell you not to worry or guarantee that I'll come back unharmed" – fresh sobbing broke out at that – "what I can do, my heart, is to tell you that I will use every *t'mearn* of my skill and training, and every micron of caution, to come back to you. This I promise, on my Oath," and he stroked her face, taking the tears away, and rubbed his cheek to hers, trying to comfort her.

When she managed to restrain her weeping, though, she pulled back a fraction and looked him in the eye. In a firm voice, she said, "I want more than that from you, Renegade."

He was puzzled but answered, "I'll give it if I can, milady."

Taking hold of his shoulders, her nails digging in, she said with great intensity, "I want you to promise *on your Oath,* warrior, that after this, you will never leave me or go without me again. On the Code, *vr'*hunter!"

Renegade hesitated, but he was trapped. He'd brought this on himself. In fact, many a hunter worked as a pair with his huntress wife – even artisans did – among the *tautschen.*

He said, "I promise, K'leura. On my honor and my Oath." He thought there might come a time when he regretted this; but a hunter's word *is* his honor, according to his Credo and his Code. That's what Renegade promised, when he gave his word.

It seemed to mollify K'leura, give her hope that there *would* be a future together, after this foolish (to her) quest. It didn't stop her sorrow, but it sustained her. In return she snuggled close to him, and they slept in each other's arms, exhausted if not content.

***

RENEGADE LEFT his close-chosen at the observation deck the next day. They had dined lightly together and now his friends and his bride formed a semi-circle around him to bid him good hunting.

Renegade again doubted his decision, just briefly, yet when Rampage asked him,

"Brother, do you have any of your 'bad feelings' about this trip?" he answered "No, none," quite honestly, and knew he would be able to leave them.

K'leura would stay at the Hunt school with Rampage and Dasrylion until Broken Spear returned. Renegade felt she and the old warrior would be good company for each other. He only wished he could have seen his beloved Grandfather before breaktie. But it was not to be.

So Renegade embraced them and left them, his friends and his wife, and rode the sea of space toward an unknown harbor once again.

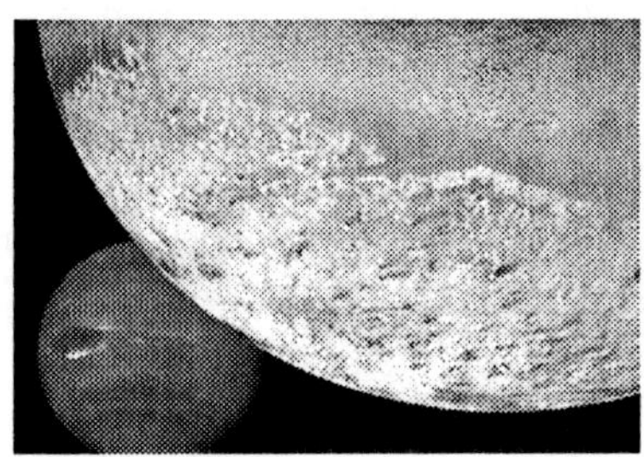

Sixteen....The Divided Planet

THREE DAYS LATER on Arvien 4, the remaining hunters had just finished their morning workout. Rampage was showing K'leura around the trophy room, while Dasrylion once again cleaned his traps for wont of anything else to do, when they caught a flash of sunlight through the windows. Next they heard the unmistakable sound of the landing bay door rolling open.

The three young people glanced at each other.

"Could it be-?" K'leura began.

"Renegade? Maybe he's come back!" Rampage cried out.

Dasrylion stepped over to the big windows and scraped out a clear patch in the frost coating. "*Krr-rr,* that's not the Hunter craft, it's-"

"The school ship!" Rampage yelled right next to him, making him flinch. "Broken Spear is home!"

K'leura strained to see out between them: the biggest Hunter she had ever laid eyes on stood between the open bay door and a Hunt-type starship. He wore a white coverall garment and mask, and had two large fangs protruding down from the upper jaw of the mask...one had been partly snapped off. *Broken Spear...* obvious where he'd got that name. Was he a clan leader too? That *height...* he was even bigger than Dasrylion...or Stavrof.

He saw or sensed his watchers, for he turned toward their window and raised an arm in greeting. Then he indicated the open bay door.

"He's going in there. Come on; let's go meet him," Rampage said; and they were off – the two hunters almost running in their eagerness, the newly-fledged huntress coming more sedately.

They're really glad to see him, she thought. *I wonder if he will be glad to see me, as well. I wish Renegade was here.*

They caught up with Broken Spear and his latest students just as they offloaded into the bay and were closing the door.

The youngsters with him were astounded to see their dignified elder boom out "Rampage! Dasrylion!" and leave everything behind in his haste to meet them.

--and to see two very professional-looking and well-grown hunters fling themselves into his arms and cry out, "Grandfather!" in joyous reunion

He hugged them fiercely. "*V'*hunters and warriors! My sons, and..." he glanced up as K'leura entered behind them, his first surprise..."milady huntress." His face held a courteous but quizzical look. "Introduce us please, Dasrylion, Rampage. And where is Renegade?"

"Your pardon, Grandfather," Dasrylion stepped back. "This is the healer and huntress K'leura, formerly of Expedition Ship 3145..."

"...and she's Renegade's wife," Rampage burst in, to his friend's annoyance.

That stunned the old warrior. "*H'vack-hah!*" he gasped, then, "Your pardon, *chai* K'leura, but I – you are Renegade's *wife?* Ah...aah...I *am* pleased – if shocked, milady." He recovered his courtliness, holding out both forearms to her, which she stepped forward to grasp.

Big, but very gentle, and very kind, she thought. She found no need to be afraid of him.

Greetings completed, the old warrior remarked to his grown hunters, "You Three can still surprise me, it seems. Now, where is Renegade?"

"He's off on a *veren-tautsch*[*], Elder," Dasrylion cut Rampage off with a look.

"Ah, I see. And you wish to tell me about it in private. Well, let me get my students settled in and myself a quick hot bath, and I will meet you in the hearth room. Could you find me something hot to drink, *v'*hunters? The students have already eaten."

"On-course, Elder," and Dasrylion firmly steered Rampage from the room, K'leura following.

***

THE HUNTER SHIP was very fast but also very small. Within its cramped confines, Renegade could do little except listen to the educational programs he'd brought with him, and learn about the languages of the Divided World as much as he could. He could get out of his seat (barely)

---

[*] Far-hunt

and do some limited *tch-won',* but he'd spend most of his time on his back. And he hated to feel helpless.

He was grateful that the journey would take mere days instead of many tendays, as it used to; and he resolved to spend most that time occupying his mind with learning languages, and even sleeping, so he would not have to think about his decision and those he had left behind. It would give him less time to mourn…

***

BY THE FIRE---"He's gone *where?* To do *what?"* The big warrior's voice thundered in the small room. K'leura cringed back even though it wasn't directed at her. Rampage and Dasrylion almost did.

"We couldn't stop him, Elder," Rampage said at last. "He was set to the trail."

Broken Spear's outrage fell away. "Oh Great Spirit," he moaned, his hand to his jaw, clenching the broken tooth. "Such an errand, and alone…" More sharply, "How long ago did he leave?"

"Barely three days ago, Elder." Rampage was the only one with a voice. His friend Dasrylion looked too cowed to answer.

The old warrior put his hands down, looked at K'leura. "And he married you, and left all the same."

She nodded, her eyes brimming.

Broken Spear held out a hand to her, and impulsively she grasped it with both of her own.

He spoke more softly. "I know that world, as he does not. I know he thought to spare me the journey, but this time he was wrong. This is something only I can do. I must go to help him. He will need me there."

Their eyes lit up. The two male hunters chorused, "*Chak!*"

"We're going with you," Rampage declared; and Dasrylion gave a deep rumble in his chest, agreeing.

K'leura's eyes never left the old warrior's. They changed from sorrow to joy, and then to steel.

"And so am I," she said.

To the others' shock, Broken Spear agreed with her:

"Provided there is no child, and you can fire a weapon, that is as it should be. Good. We will share-meat and rest overnight. Then while you, Rampage and Dasrylion, outfit the school ship, I shall return the students to their homes at first light.

"Then we leave for the Divided Planet."

***

HE HID behind the world's giant moon. *A little bigger and this would have been a planet too,* he mused.

The difference between a dead world and an inhabited one became clear when his fast little Hunter ship popped into this solar system. This space was alive with radio noise. More noise chattered from here than from Homeworld even, in a continuous, confusing jabber of short and medium length signals, heat echoes, and simple sonar. All of it sub-light, though.

"They're a noisy lot, always chattering, usually about nothing, just to hear themselves talk," Kreh-t'vyk had told him. Indeed they were. Renegade concluded that the best way to find out what was happening was to monitor their transmissions and try to siphon out any pertinent reports.

So he'd crouched back here for four days on their big moon's far side, near its north pole, and intercepted everything he could run through his translators. He'd put in every single language he could find on Broken Spear's recordings, more than 100 of them, hoping to decipher a "fallen meteor" or a "monster report" amid the babble. He wondered how these *hew-mahns* could possibly communicate with each other in so many different speech patterns.

Evidently they didn't.

That's part of their problem, he concluded, *many clans and many tongues* – for he also monitored the imaged light pictures sent out: "T-V" they called it.

And the violence there appalled him. Not just the man-against-beast type of film or adventure story Renegade was familiar with, but almost every report seemed to be about these creatures attacking *each other*, singly or in packs; bringing down death upon their own heads in wonderfully ingenious ways, many of them so dishonorable and immoral that his people would have scorned to use them on prey.

Again he felt he might be wrong in coming here. These creatures didn't seem worthy of living. Their ways were deceitful and violent; their "Challenges" continuous and pointless; their prospects dim.

Still, once in a while he caught a glimpse of something else, something more…he'd seen an animated video program directed at young *hew-mahns* where the main characters seemed to have a sense of honor and the desire to fight well. And more rarely, on documentaries, he saw what might be construed as individual heroism in action – some of these beings selflessly risking their own lives to save their fellows.

The thing was, he just couldn't be sure. He understood his Grandfather's dilemma better now. Were they or weren't they capable of honor? He was missing some of the broadcasts, too, by hiding back here with this moon for a tree stand. So he resolved to try a different tactic.

Time to test the Hunter's lightshielding.

This small craft was special, a prototype really, for not only did it have camouflage, it also had the speed of the newest Hunt ships, like the Broken Spear's top-of-the-mark school ship. It was also heavily armed. It was in fact considered so special that it had its own name, Wings upon the Wind, rare among the People's spacecraft.

Renegade already felt very fond of the ship. He particularly liked the camouflage feature; he could see how useful it would be approaching an enemy in deep space, supposing they ever found a race like the one that had destroyed the Dead Planet…

--or like his situation here.

Renegade composed and sent one short-burst signal hyperlight to Homeworld and Nine Systems Station about what he was doing; then he floated the ship free of this satellite and engaged the lightshield. With hardly a ripple against the stars, the little craft vanished from view…

…and stalked closer to its goal, the blue-and-silver globe.

Lying just above the ionosphere, Renegade could pick up almost every transmission made from the surface or the swarms of artificial satellites, and listen in.

He'd preset the computer to net-out reports of fallen meteorites, sudden mass disappearances, odd reports of strange beasts or monsters, and the like. While the computer sieved through the hubbub, he continued with his language lessons.

He'd chosen two different and quite difficult languages which had little in the way of clicks, hisses, or rolling consonants. But they did have a fair number of vowel sounds, which also form a large part of Hunter speech. Once he got the track of it, his pronunciation became almost flawless.

It was like learning to call game, only with many more nuances and tonal shades.

The best data he had from Nine Systems' experts was that the alien missile would come into the near-space of this world.

Whether it would actually impact or not – well, Chance would take the throw in that.

He settled Wings upon the Wind into a hovering orbit nightside of the planet, near its equator, and let the sparkling constellations of its many gatherings roll by beneath him.

This went on for more than a day, their planet-time. Already he'd been here for a fiveday; and at the end of Sixday, if he heard nothing; he planned to breaktie for home.

Renegade sifted through his reports. He expected another barren collection.

But tonight he found something.

["There has been no word from the apparent site of the meteorite strike of a few nights ago; so we probably don't have a visitor from outer space near (*name of someplace)*. Now for other local news..."]

That "visitor from outer space" struck Renegade as both ominous and darkly funny...*if only they knew...*

Where was the signal coming from? It had a weak transmission.

Whatever qualms his Elder had about using technology, Renegade found it an excellent tool. He was able to fine-tune the signal to a place on one of the northern continents, and down to within 1.5 *kri-veh* of its origins. He nosed the ship into a long slow dive. The transmission was still running; perhaps the station or whatever kept sending all night.

There, on that oddly-shaped double peninsula, surrounded by four bodies of water – inland seas, perhaps. His readout showed forest cover to within a few *kri-veh* of the source. A good place to narrow his sights.

Now he had to do something more difficult: freefall through their atmosphere without attracting undue attention. He would light up a fire trail whether or not his Hunter was camouflaged. So he could pretend to be a meteor falling, something natural and familiar. Once on the ground, he could pinpoint the source better and think of some way to find out where that "other meteor" might have hit. He doubted he could ask the *hewmahns* without making a target of himself.

Renegade suited up, weapons and leathers. Besides the shoulder laser, he slung an ion rifle over his other shoulder and clipped the spear to his backpack. His heartbeat picked up, but his hands were steady.

Time to go down.

***

WKLL-TV---near Manistee, Michigan:

"Hey, Dorrie!"

She grimaced. She hated her nickname. It made her sound like a fishing boat, and a dinky one at that. *Dorothy, it's Dorothy.*

Aloud: "Yeah, Scott, what is it?"

"You know that meteorite report?"

Like I know my own name... "What about it?" She yanked her coat off the hook viciously.

"Now don't get hostile; I *know* you...Well, there's been another one."

"Another one? Another *what?*" She'd lost track here.

"*Meteor*, darlin'. Close enough to where the first one fell; they could be brothers. Be a good girl and go out now and you could be the first one to film it live – maybe even catch it smokin', babe."

"Don't 'babe' me, you sexist swine...Scott, do you know what *time* it is?" She fumbled with buttons. "Come *on!* I've been here all night, for Chrissake."

"Not quite yet, Dore'. Anyway, it's only one hay-hem; and the boss wants a *first,* beat out Traverse City and Cadillac just once...and besides, where else can you get news from in the boonies, eh? Motown it ain't."

"At least that," she muttered underbreath; and louder, "Scott? I've already got my *coat* on..."

"Good; then you're all set to go. Bill's on camera, and we've got the truck all warmed up for ya, ba—I mean, Dorrie."

She sighed and prepped for the inevitable.

***

THE SCHOOL SHIP had left four days almost to the *tare'* after Renegade. It fell back into its own continuum as Renegade was leaving his lunar orbit for a planetary one. It materialized near the planet Jupiter, and playing hunt-and-find behind the moons, ran squarely into his last message.

"It's him!" Dasrylion said. "He's changing orbit for the Divided World itself...his ship is equipped with – listen to this – a camouflage device; so he's leaving his cover at the big moon and going into orbit around the primary."

"Ours is not so equipped, so we must seek that moon," Broken Spear said. He put the school ship through an in-system jump, and they found themselves at the north pole of the Divided World's huge cratered satellite, lying low near a crater wall.

"Now what?" Rampage asked.

"Now we must wait until he gives us a clue to his whereabouts," the old warrior said. "He will either breaktie or make planetfall; and we should be able to see him as he moves."

What he didn't say was that if Renegade were already on-planet, they had as little chance of finding him as they had of singling out a particular grain of dust on a continent.

But as Broken Spear looked up into the spaceborn K'leura's eyes, he saw understanding.

Understanding and despair.

Sometime later, a huge meteor trail lit up across the night side of that world.

"There!" the old warrior cried. "Not yet, Rampage! Track it; track it all the way down!"

It left a line of heat and light behind it, like an arrow of fire.

***

NIGHT ON EARTH, Manistee National Forest---Renegade swam to shore and emerged, dripping and shivering, from the shallow lake. His camo-suit wasn't functional because of the wetting, so he hid himself in the thick branches of a pine tree until it dried.

What a crowded planet! There was forest here, yes; but the *hewmahns'* camps were crowded through it everywhere. His own people *never* lived so close together, except for the occasional winter camp. They also had trade-circles, not always occupied, and they were small compared to these holdings. *Another one of their problems...*

So many of these beings and so tightly packed—he couldn't chance leaving the ship aboveground, even shielded. He'd finally tucked it on the bottom of this shallow lake, safely sealed up. He could always trace the radio-casts through his personal equipment, or even jog over to the sending station, if need be.

A cold wind blew the dampness from him. He shivered again, yet had to stay hidden until the suit dried off enough to work. Meanwhile he could get a fix on the alleged landing spot.

His thoughts were interrupted by a rumbling, growling noise. Alarmed, he looked down.

A boxy vehicle of some sort trundled along the dirt path around the lake. It came to a stop not far from his tree, and two side doors popped open, followed by a couple of the *hewmahn*s, one out of each door. *Had they tracked him here? Were they coming to attack?* Renegade tensed.

The two met around the vehicle's front and spoke to each other. Renegade switched on the translator in his mask.

They were a male and female, strangely like his folk in some ways, utterly different in others: they had two arms and two legs, a head with eyes, mouth, and hearing organs on it…though he didn't care for the fleshy protuberant ridge down the middle of their faces—was all that really a *nose?* His People's were smaller and more elegant. These human faces seemed incomplete-looking: they had no biting teeth to speak of, only tiny little flat ones set inside the jaw and overhung by that snout – not true carnivores then. Omnivores or scavengers.

He had a sudden insight: *Maybe that's the reason they kill each other so easily, they have no pack carnivore's instinct to stop them.* Not that all carnivores did, either. Perhaps his People's Surrender instinct was rather rare in this man's galaxy.

They looked homely to him, with their pallid slug flesh and strange features; so he made an effort to think of them as normal for their own species, not as sub-normal for his. That helped.

Renegade wished he could just step down and ask them about themselves; but their well-observed hostility kept him in his tree, listening.

They were talking together, and he could understand *that* at least:

"Well, Bill, this is a real wild (bird) chase," the female was saying. "There's no meteorite here. Do you see any smoking heap of stone?"

"Not me, Dore'," he admitted. "If there was a meteor, it probably went into the lake."

The unseen watcher stiffened above them.

The female snorted. "And I'm not *about* to go diving into the lake after it!"

"The boss (*chief*) still wants some kind of coverage, it's a slow night," the male argued. "What say we go to the other site – pretty sure of finding a hole there, anyway…"

"Oh God, not another rehash – listen, the amateur guy's shots were good enough last week."

"Come on, whatever happened to your sense of adventure, of follow-up, of news-worthiness, of-"

"Of *time,* Bill. Do you know what *time* it is? And the sun will be coming up in less than five hours!"

But the cameraman argued they couldn't take back film of "just a pretty lake with a few cottages around it. Besides, what if those scientists who were supposed to arrive there already set up camp, to study the thing, and never let their local news station know?"

'OK, OK, what if?" the woman grumbled. "Serve them right if we dropped in on 'em and woke 'em up at" – she glanced at her wristband, a gesture familiar to Renegade, "one forty-three or so in the morning. How far is that site from here, anyway?"

"Couple of miles," the male said. (*More like twenty,* he thought) "It's out in the boonies. Only thing near it is a trailer park and farmhouse-- National Forest all around *that."*

She sighed. "Alright, but this is *it.* After that I'm going home to *bed."*

(Renegade held back a laugh. She sounded like one of his friends – Rampage, who hated to wake up for an early *anything.* Even as he watched, Renegade's perspective underwent a drastic change: he could *identify* with these people. He didn't understand how any of his folk could possibly fool themselves and claim the *hewmahns* were strictly hostile beasts…though there was that references to "shots.")

And once these two went back inside their vehicle, he carefully eased down the tree to the ground-cart's roof height, his camo-suit flickering on.

Bill ground the van into gear and they bumped along the rough dirt margin slowly, aiming for the paved road. They'd barely started when the van's rear end gave a mighty dip and rebound…

"What's that?" Dorothy asked.

"You know these washboard roads; probably busted a spring," he said, switching on his lights and staring fixedly ahead.

When he heard the sliding and scratching sounds along the news van's roof, he didn't even bother to slow down.

"Goddamn low branches," he grumbled, and drove on.

***

RIDING THE TOP of this blasted ground-cart was like taking a ship through freefall, except it lasted much, much longer. And he was Chance-favored they hadn't paid any heed to all the noise and come rushing out when he'd made that landing and the vehicle dipped alarmingly, causing him to scrabble for a clawhold along its top.

Renegade thought the "paved" road bad enough, until it gave way to a dirt one. By the time the van had bounced over every rough spot, banged into every pothole, and crawled in and out of steep side ruts, Renegade's stomach and ribs had endured a royal bruising. He felt thankful he'd eaten nothing since yesterday, his typical preparation for a hunt.

Now the vehicle was slowing, pulling up outside some kind of rough wooden fence. At least here the trees stood thicker, while the narrow road wound between them.

A brilliant beam of light shot out from the van's left front side, startling him.

From inside came Bill's voice: "Yup. Dis be de place. Eagle's Nest Trailer Park – doesn't *look* burned to the ground, does it?" He played the spotlight over the weather-beaten sign.

"I'll tell you what's burning – *me!"* the female retorted. (Renegade thought her admirably feisty.) "Why don't we just get out of here?"

"Why don't we just look? C'mon, we're here; let's take a look around. I'll shoot some film and then we'll leave."

She sighed. "Let's get it over with. Where are the trailers?"

"Back there. Through the trees."

"Fine, we'll walk. I can't take much more bouncing."

The two got out of vehicle, their feet crunching on the gravel path below.

Renegade slipped down from the van's roof far more quietly than he'd landed on it, and began to follow them.

He found it hard to translate some of the contractions and slang in their speech, but the word "shoot" had come through loud and clear. He followed at a discrete distance, well off the path and to one side, watching them and the forest around them. It was foolish of them to go straight up the middle of the stony path like that...did they even carry weapons? That device the male carried seemed more like a recorder.

He saw the bits of wreckage before they did – chunks of metal strewn here and there, *and still warm, just a few days old.*

The laser went to READY, the rifle slipped neatly from his shoulder to the crook of his arm.

"Bill, what *is* all this junk? Big scraps of metal just lying around out here – yuck! Can't they keep it any neater? Film this, why don't you?"

"Okay, okay. We'll come to the trailers just beyond these trees anyway. You go ahead; I'll get you as you walk up the path." He stopped and filmed her walking forward between low-hanging firs.

Renegade had time to think, *That's not a weapon,* and, *they can't see as well as I do,* when the Dread fell upon him and he froze, watching the alien female walk on...*and it happened again.*

Dorothy started to duck her head and push aside a low-sweeping branch when a nightmare swung down out of the trees at her – a huge dark spiked head, slavering hooked jaws—a monster—a mon-

And a blue bolt exploded into it and knocked the ugly head away.

She fell backwards and heard screaming and it was her own screaming and Bill shouting, "Dorrie!"

And the trees came *alive* with them – rattling bony snapping things, stinger tails whipping, those heads, those jaws –

Then someone pushed her aside and a hoarse voice said, "Get down!" and she was sitting on the hard ground while all hell broke loose around her.

They lunged in from both sides through the trees – at *her*—and *whump!* A firebolt knocked the left one down, a whine and *zap,* the right one lit up like a strobe light and spun flip-flopping away.

Another, from the front. She heard a grunt, felt something bump into her, like someone taking a step back, someone she couldn't see. The tree branches swayed their long fronds above her. Then something flashed in mid-air – *swords,* she thought – and the glistening ugly bone thing spattered fluid, which hissed at her, but stopped, the spatters stopped, in mid-splash.

And someone was there, between her and the monster, a *big* someone. At first he looked like a Masai warrior, but then she realized no, he was different, subtly different than that…despite the height, despite the braided head-hair…his face covered by some sort of fitted shield, along with parts of his body. What she could see of the real *him* gleamed like gold and smoke in the moonlight.

Light and dark together…black spots and a stripe down his front, like a combination leopard and tiger…what a strange costume…

He went on the attack again, clearing a fallen bone-beast with a wonderful leap, pivoting as he came down to fire at the next live one coming; then leap again, spin, twist and *nail* those bastards, one, two!

"Oh my God!" she breathed. She looked at her white-knuckled cameraman trying to keep himself and the lens from juddering in terror. *"Bill, Bill,"* she whispered fiercely, *"he's an alien too! Bill, are you getting this?'*

"Ge—Ge—get—y-yeah—D-Dorrie—"

A lull came in the fighting, and the big fellow wheeled about gracefully – *wow, can he move* – to look back at both of them. Dorothy held her breath. *Are we next?*

Chaos erupted behind him as the still-unseen trailer park boiled over with the gaunt, spiky things. They burst from the shrouding trees in an explosion of skittering nightmares.

The unknown warrior took a brief glance, then was at her side. She felt herself hoisted up under her shoulder like a doll. She was very close to him now and she was petrified. But he bent that almost featureless mask to her face and said in perfect English, "Run! Get back to your vehicle!"

"Ye-yessir," she gasped and then she was free, staggering on her feet. She bolted, pushing Bill ahead of her. He stumbled, almost fell, forgot about film and duty and ran clumsily in her wake.

They reached the van just as more fire-pulses blazed through the woods behind them. Dorothy whipped the rear doors open and shoved the cameraman down on the floor between them.

"I'll drive, you film!" she shrieked at him. Desperately she dug around for the keys, remembered they were probably in the ignition, and scrambled her way around toward the front.

--and another one came over the roof at her.

Dorothy screamed like bloody death and twisted away. The bone-thing's steely jaws gaped and snapped on air…

Frantically she lunged, jumped, crawled to get out of its way. This took her around the back again, where she tripped and fell in the gravel road.

The monster reared above her, talons extended.

A flying shape struck it high in the head and knocked it sideways – the other alien! She just lay there dumbfounded, watching as he landed neatly on his feet and faced the beast.

His laser-fire and the bone-thing's whirling spin coincided…

Even as he knew he'd hit it, Renegade saw that tail whipping round at him and knew its blow would connect too…but he had to be steady, to aim… His bolt killed it; its barbed tail lashed him sideways, smashed him against one of the van's outflung back doors. He lashed out with his right hand, felt his nails hook something – and lost consciousness.

Both newspeople heard his cry of pain, saw his body knock the door off its hinges like a piece of plastic. He fell to earth, his right arm outstretched, finger-talons clutched in the crease of the bumper.

"The hell with this! Let's get out of here!" Bill screamed, dropping the mini-cam and scrambling for shelter.

Dorothy grabbed him. "No, wait! He's caught on the bumper…you'll drag him. We have to help him. Help him, dammit, or I'm not going anywhere!"

Cursing a blue streak, he did. Together they half-lifted, half-dragged 6-foot-8 inches of unconscious Hunter into the van. As they lugged him up over the bumper, his fingertalons released, rather like a cat's when they are pushed forward.

Bill abandoned Dorothy to her fate in the back as he crashed into the driver's seat.

The woods began to break into hulking dark shapes again when the van finally roared to life and bashed through a wooden fence to get away.

But its driver's nerves stalled it about a hundred yards farther down the road.

Dorothy sat in the dark with the alien who had twice saved her life, sat and stared at him, speechless…

The van coughed and shuddered, revved and died, and finally she called out, "Bill, stop; you're just flooding it, and they don't seem to be coming after us…can you come back here a minute?"

"Are you *crazy?"*

"Bill." She made an effort to keep her voice level. "We're sitting on top of the greatest story in the world – right next to a spaceman – I am, anyway; and we've got to find out what's happening. Now come back here and film for me, please. I think he's still alive; and the van's not going anywhere for a while."

Amazingly, he did.

They turned up all the interior lights and began filming Renegade as he lay slumped against one wall of the van; and Dorothy gave a shaky synopsis of the previous events in this incredible story.

She sat within a few feet of him. *God, he's big, and look at those muscles...and the colors on him – what's he wearing, some kind of netting* – she touched the fabric gently, and could see it was like a fine netting of some kind. *He looks a little damp—is he sweating? And what is that faint scent? Yeah, like cinnamon and cloves...kind of nice, really. His body looks mostly like ours, except for the colors and claws...I wonder what his face looks like?*

She was delicately reaching out one hand to his facemask when Renegade awoke.

***

"HE WAS HERE," Dasrylion told them the obvious as they bent to the trail near the lake, "and then this wheeled vehicle came up under the trees, and he left with it."

"Taken captive?" Broken Spear snapped.

"No—ah—I don't know, but the hewmahns' tracks are back here, two sets of them, and they exit and re-enter the vehicle, then Renegade follows it farther along, through the trees—and—I think he jumps – it looks as if he went willingly, that way," he indicated the road.

"And the Hunter ship is still in the lake..." Broken Spear said thoughtfully to the young people standing near him in the dark. All wore armor and were heavily armed; and they stood beside the school ship which poised over them like a bird of prey.

"Willingly..." the old hunter murmured. "Cold Tracker, is the vehicle's trail clear enough to follow from aboard ship?"

"Easily. It leaves a trace on dirt; and see, some liquid drips from it as it goes. Very fresh."

Their leader made up his mind. "Then we will take the ship. Dasrylion tracks; Rampage pilots; K'leura, ready a command frequency for the Hunter ship. We may need to raise it and call it to us..."

"Take the ship? Our ship? With all these settlements around?" Rampage thought his elder had lost his reason.

"Yes; we have no time for subtlety, if you want to see Renegade alive again. Now. Let us fly."

And the hunters' school ship, big as two locomotives, dark except for its side-jets firing, lifted and flew a hundred feet above the road, following a heat-trail and tire-prints too faint for the human eye to see.

***

TRAPPED in the van, Renegade awoke to see the *creature* reaching for him. He jerked up and back – and the red dot of light appeared on the newswoman's blouse.

Her hand retracted fast.

"My God, Dore', that's a *laser* sight!"

--And of all the hunters who could have come here, perhaps it was only Renegade who could have held fire at that moment, seemingly captured and in danger. Only the warrior who as a boy had found the laser too easy to trigger and had it reset deliberately, could have held his shot, and did not fire now.

Hold hard – she's not armed – hold, hold...

The blood-color drained from her face. "I'm not going to hurt you...I just want to...touch"—*no, that's not right; what can I say to him?* She stared straight into the burning gaze in that mask, and said, "Thank you for saving my life."

And the laser sight switched off.

In equal courtesy, appreciating her courage, Renegade said, "I am honored."

A cord of tension loosened in the air.

"You can speak English," she said. Then to her cameraman, "Bill, are you still with us?'

"To my last breath, kiddo."

Carefully Renegade sat up and tucked his long legs under him, waiting for the alien female to make the next move. The situation wasn't as bad as he thought: he was inside the vehicle and no-one had been killed yet. He could see that one of vehicle's back doors was missing – the one he'd been slammed into, no doubt.

"I thank you for my life, as well," he pronounced carefully.

Dorothy thrilled to hear him. What wonderful courtliness he had! "I—you are welcome," she replied, just as carefully.

Then she braced herself. "You – can you tell us what's going on?" she asked.

They heard him sigh, softly yet distinctly.

"The beasts…are dangerous," he began, searching for the words as he spoke. "They breed – in living creatures. Their ship…landed here… not a meteor." His voice was deep and resonant.

"Ship?'

"Yes. A *krych-taundo*—an alien ship" – *that sounds strange to them, I'll lay trace...*"Not one of ours. It was sent … by …another…species…no longer alive...but their…the, *krr..."* he paused frustrated.

"Monsters. Big ugly bony monsters," the male butted in.

That helped. "The creatures, yes, run loose in the galaxy. We are *hunting* them."

There. Enough effort. He paused to catch his breath and loosen his facemask a bit. It felt close in here. And yet…

The little female was bending towards him. "And you? Where do *you* come from? Somewhere else – I mean, not from their planet?"

He thought a moment. Then he lifted one slim-fingered and taloned hand to hers, and put his other hand to his mask. Her small, seemingly fragile hand was almost engulfed in his. Carefully he placed it against his chest, over his own heart, which they could neither hear nor see, apparently.

She gave a little "oh!" cry, but didn't pull away. Her eyes widened – *that* expression was the same in both species – and let him keep her hand in place while she thought:

He's warm, like us. I can feel his heart beating, strong and steady, not excited at all...oh, what's he doing, unsnapping – he's taking off that helmet or mask or whatever...ohmigod. She braced herself.

Renegade told her, "Here, see what you wished to see. It will…explain much…" and lifted the mask from his face.

"Jesus Christ!" the man exploded.

Dorothy took one close look – *He's real, he's flesh and blood—he has fangs*—and felt her senses reel. She toppled.

Renegade caught her. So weak…so frightened…so small… and no discipline… *I can't see why anyone would consider these beings as 'sport' – or why they themselves have a word for 'hunt' in their language.*

But then her eyes flickered open, and shakily, she reached up with he other hand; and he felt the most featherlike touch upon his face, on his cheek, along the lower jaw, and she murmured, stopping, "These are… teeth?"

'Yes; we call them *akai."* His mouth moved much like her own when he spoke; she could see a tongue in there, dark pink. And he did rather remind her of a great cat – if the cat had no hair except on its head and lashes...and startlingly-intelligent eyes…

Despite the impressive biting equipment, he wasn't acting angry – *so he probably won't eat me right away,* she thought wryly.

As he looked down at her thoughtfully, she forced herself to study his eyes: *beautiful green eyes, very normal, and they don't look wild or mad or anything but calm – I hope,* she told herself. They were very intense, though, and after a few moments she had to look away.

On his part, Renegade was thinking, *so weak, yet such great heart. Maybe I do know why they are prized, after all.* Without good natural weapons to protect themselves, though, these beings would tend to lash out in fear with artificial ones at anything they didn't understand. They still had the mentality of prey.

When the alien female stammered an attempt at humor, "Well, I'm glad you're on *our* side," his eye-corners crinkled and he began to laugh: a kind of *prrt, prrt, prrt,* sound in his chest like broken purring, rising into his throat and then a *chrrf! chrrf!* out loud, so recognizable that they both laughed with him.

Seeing Dorothy recovered, Renegade arose carefully and geared up again. He explained about the bone-beasts, and asked the humans "How long?" in various ways until they understood, and told him, "Four days."

That meant the beasts would have had time to grow and breed. They must be stopped *here,* in their den, which from the humans' information must be in some rectangular buildings behind that screen of trees.

Once ready, he indicated he wanted to get out of the van and return to the scene, and the male human made an expostulary sound but nearly fell backwards getting out of his way.

All three of them stepped out onto the road shoulder. The woman glanced toward the unseen trailer park. "Are there…are there *more* of them in there?'

"They are many," he told her.

"But you are only one," she protested. "Shouldn't you – uh – call for help?"

He gave a quick head-twitch, then put it quite flatly: "I am the only… *hunter…*here."

"Well. That tells *us,*" Bill grinned from behind the mini-cam.

Dorothy looked frantically about. "We have to go with him."

"*Wha-at?*" Bill gasped; and even the alien warrior turned toward her sharply…

…and the dark ship descended over them.

They all stared at it, the warrior as surprised as any of them.

It set down about a hundred feet away on the grass across the road. Lower and side hatches slid open and a dark golden light streamed out.

Then the sidelights on the craft blinked several times; though the two humans saw nothing to account for it.

The hunter apparently did, for he stiffened, his body went rigid.

…As *four more* tall figures materialized around them, one an absolute giant. The two humans grabbed each other for support, the camera still running.

"Bill," the newswoman whispered, *"how much film have you got left?"*

He shot her an incredulous look.

The giant strode directly over to them, stared at them hard – *omigod, he's eight feet tall if he's an inch. His hair's white – does that mean he's older, too? And his skin is a dark – red, maybe?* Most impressive were the two much larger fangs curving from his upper jaw – and that one of them appeared to be broken.

Then *their* warrior gave a strange warbling cry and moved in front of them. Not to fight, but –

The huge one reached toward him, rumbled like thunder, and the two grasped each other by first the upper arms, next, fervently, by the shoulders. *He's so big he makes our guy look small...and they know each other!* Trembling, Dorothy let go of her cameraman's arms.

"Grandfather!" Renegade grasped the old warrior's shoulders hard, wanting to embrace him; but with strangers present, it would be unseemly; while Broken Spear boomed out his name, gripped him tight…

"Son." A world of relief and welcome infused that word. He held on to Renegade for a long moment. "Are you harmed?" – meaningfully.

"No, Grandfather, I was just talking to them."

The weight of the old one's gaze fell on the two humans. "Talking?"

"Yes; the bone-things are here, in *that* area. I fought some of them, killed perhaps six or seven; but they were too many…we fell back to here."

"I see. Renegade, there are others here for you. Go to them. I will speak with *these"* – and a quick head-jerk made the white dreadlocks fly.

And while Renegade discovered to his joy – and his shock – that all of his close-chosen had come, even his wife, the old warrior bent his attention to the gawking aliens before him.

Without preamble, in a gravelly voice even deeper than the lone warrior's, he told them, "I greet you. Since you have spared *him,* I will spare you." Ignoring their feeble attempts at gratitude, he went on, "Tell me of where the prey dens. Describe the place."

"Yes, sir," and woozy with terror and wonder, they did.

After a moment, Dorothy let Bill continue without her. Peering around the giant's side, she happened to see Renegade's reception from his friends.

Two he embraced fiercely and called by short-syllabled words which might be their names; the third and last, he took in his arms slowly, deeply, with great tenderness, forgetting that the humans might see him.

That one's more his size, Dorothy noted, *and the shape – why, she must be a female, a woman of his species.* Again the body shape was so similar to a human being's.

"She is his wife," the deep voice informed her, rocking her on her heels. The big fellow was looking down at her, his tone no longer stern, but almost amused.

"That – that's nice," Dorothy faltered. His intuition was spooky, she decided.

She had no more time to think about it, for the big fellow re-directed them: "The place of small dwellings is a den site, as you thought, Renegade" *...Renegade, that must be our guy's name...*"Unfortunately, we are too few to make a flanking movement; so we will have to attack in a wedge shape – yes, Rampage, they can understand *us,* too – I have a speaker on. In a wedge, I repeat, myself in front, K'leura and Renegade behind me; Rampage, Dasrylion, outer edge...the humans well behind."

"They're going to *Hunt* with us?" An outraged protest from the tall thin one in golden armor.

"They are documentarians. They record facts as some of our people do. This will enlighten them about what we are doing here. And these two are responsible for themselves."

Meaning if we get chewed up it's our own fault, Dorothy interpreted.

"Now; let us conceal the ship," and he flicked open some kind of sleeve-thing on his left wrist, pressed recessed buttons with his talons; and the dark ship rose with a soft *hisss,* and floated to a new landing place in a clump of nearby trees.

The big fellow went on: "So. There are some 30 of those dwellings, a larger one at the far side to the east, which may be the local clan leader's."

At Dorothy's puzzled frown, Bill leaned over and whispered, *"Owner's farmhouse..."* and she re-focused on the big warrior:

"...with no cover behind or beside them but this line of trees before. We will drive through this area first, pushing the herd back, then killing them in their dens. It may be enough."

He made some kind of sharp-angled motion with his head, those huge teeth flashing in the dim moonlight. "Form order of attack," he said.

As the smaller hunters did so, something like an artillery cannon automatically raised from where it had been slung along the big one's spine behind his back, its massive barrel poised over his shoulder.

"Migod, a cannon," she whispered. *"Bill, how much film?"*

"Got a spare – hours," he returned; "the old soldier's well-armed, isn't he?" – and he blushed when the "old soldier" threw him a meaningful glance, which somehow wasn't threatening. The translator worked both ways, evidently.

"Suits remain off. Let us begin." And Broken Spear led his oddly-assorted hunting pack into the jaws of hell.

Seventeen....The Burning

THEY MOVED through the trees without incident. But when they got to the double row of trailers screened from the road, the bone-beasts poured out at them. The hunting pack swung into action and lit up the night with fire.

Later, all Dorothy could remember of that endless battle was the spiky monsters coming and coming at them: leaping, running, lunging at them…death in snapping jaws and poison stingers and claws like shined steel…and the bolts of light responding, the quiet autumn night strobed with brilliant flashes, mobile homes there, then gone; her eyes blinded, burned with ghost images, black-on-white, white-on-black, on and off…her sense of the real suspended as she tried to describe above the terrible silent battle the way these alien warriors fought their deadly prey.

Led by the stalwart old warrior, their wedge formation let the hunters protect each other's back and flank, and keep the field of fire open between them – and the woman, K'leura, did her full share of it, Dorothy noticed.

And how they moved! Like dancers in a fatal ballet, like martial artists – shoot, pivot, thrust, throw – and the gaping jaws never overshot them: the bone-beasts loomed above, then fell away at a flash of light; the side guns spouted flame, and the great cannon at the fore thrummed and clove the ranks of their enemies…

Finally, suddenly, there came a lull. No more monsters rushed at them, and the two humans coughed and wheezed on the acid smoke of battle.

"Oh," gasped Dorothy, "the trailers, the trailers are burning!"

The great flame-colored warrior turned to her. “We will look into them, but I do not think any will be still alive. Neither the beasts – nor their prey.”

And when they yanked open door after door, of those which still had doors, she wished she had never asked. People, sprawled on the floor or stacked in hopeless layers like cordwood, their bodies ripped apart, their eyes still open, staring. She and Bill turned away, retching.

Renegade came to them and said quietly, “Take your recordings now. We must burn all of this.”

Bill nodded, choking, and managed to stuff a new tape into the minicam. “Guard this,” he said, pushing the used one at Dorothy. “I think I’ve got an hour or more left; but I just want to make sure.” Then he followed Renegade. He shot a few interiors and put Renegade on voice-over to explain what they saw.

The other warriors switched to flamethrowers, and blasted out whatever wasn’t already burning. If the two humans thought of saving the bodies for proper burial, they didn’t say a word.

Enough of this, Dorothy thought, and trotted back to the news van with the precious film and to get a breath of cool air.

“Whoa, look out, take – *care,”* she said. A mini-van and a pickup truck had pulled onto the road shoulder. As she stowed the film inside the news van and closed it up, she realized that people were piling out of their vehicles; and there was another car stopping…*oh no, oh, no....*

“Hey miss, what’s goin’ on?” one of the guys from the truck called out to her. Out of the minivan came a couple and two little kids, boy and girl; while the third car produced an older man and woman.

“It’s nothing,” Dorothy began, then glanced at the flames springing at the sky and thought *try again:* “Really, folks, it’s a fire at the trailer park. They’re working on it (*never mind who ‘they’ are*) Stay back please.”

“Hey, I’ve got friends in there,” one guy said, and in desperation she rounded on him.

“Stay here! Do you want to get killed? I’ll tell them!” she shrieked. *What do I do when the real fire department shows up?*

He startled backwards, hands raised to placate her.

Then she whirled and ran. She had to warn the warriors.

“I don’t like this, Bo. Somethin’s wrong here,” the second trucker said to the first. He reached inside the cab and pulled out a rifle. “Let’s just *talk* to her.” They began walking toward the fires.

At the same time the couple from the van looked at each other and began backing away.

"Let's go, honey," the husband said.

"Right. Come on, kids," the wife said.

"Kids?" her voice rose to a frightened shrill. "Cody? Jessie? *Where are you?"*

***

RENEGADE and K'leura met the newswoman as she came racing back through the trees. She nearly fell, grabbed Renegade's arm, and rasped at him, "You've got to leave! There're people – other humans – here!"

He and K'leura looked at each other sharply. To Dorothy, Renegade said, "We are almost finished here: Broken Spear is firing down the den in that bigger building – K'leura, are you wearing a speaker too?"

She felt around her mask attachment, did something at her throat level.

"Yes. Here. Can you understand me?" to Dorothy.

"Yes," she panted, "but you have to –"

And the old house in the trees exploded like a bomb.

Renegade shot it a glance. "That's not," he began...

Just as the cameraman came backpedaling into view—

And screams erupted from the humans behind them – and two little children ran squealing from the big fir tree they'd been hiding under...

And Broken Spear came backing toward them followed by—

A bone-beast as long as a lodge pole, as hard as iron, 30 feet of scuttling death. Scythe-sweep jaws clacking, multi-legs burring, it swarmed out of the wreckage.

Renegade shouted, "Elder! Children behind you! K'leura, watch *those*"– meaning the crowd; and he sprang like a lion toward the beast guardian.

One micro-second of frozen tableau, then the end came.

Broken Spear's thunderbolt took the beast in the thorax, as with a single motion he half-turned and swept the toddlers up in one arm.

Renegade reached the triangulation point and his laser poured crossfire into the neck of that armored head swaying above him. The neck, then the nearest legs.

The great beast began to crumple.

K'leura, racing toward the little group of humans, saw one of them fall screaming to her knees, and another one raise and aim – *a weapon, he's got –*

"Stop!" she cried. Not trusting a laser shot into the crowd, she leaped through them to strike the weapon down by hand.

...A micron after it fired...

She ripped the gun away, sent it flipping end over end, until it smashed against the truck. Even as she snatched the human by the throat and flung him after it, screaming, "You fool! We saved you! We *saved* you!" she knew it was too late. *What if he hit Renegade?*

No one else saw Broken Spear stagger as the bullet took him in the throat – in the front, where his great teeth could not protect him. Only the camera saw, and recorded it. The cameraman was past noticing. The old warrior staggered; he did not fall. He came back to the group, holding the children. As the humans shrank away, he knelt and let the children run to their mother.

The pickup's occupants took their chance and ran. The truck roared away.

K'leura, torn between them and the old hunter, saw he was still moving and thought, *Thank the Spirit he's on-stat,* but she barely finished that thought when he turned away from the group, exposing his neck and chest; and she saw all the blood...

And the great warrior fell.

"Elder! No!" she screamed, ran to him, covering the vicious humans with her laser. "Don't move or I'll kill you all myself!" she shouted at them. "Renegade! *Renegade!"*

She knelt by the old warrior's side. She was a healer, she could help... then she saw the extent of the damage and she choked back a sob.

Feebly he reached up to her, tried a smile. "Wind...singer... don't weep. All debts...are paid now."

Her eyes began tearing and she pressed his hand to her cheek.

Even over the heat of battle, Renegade heard his name. He poured one last bolt into the giant beast, thinking, *it's done. This is the last and we've won*...and he glanced back toward the road.

What he saw shook him to the bone.

"Oh no," he whispered, *"not that. Please not that"* – and he began to run like the wind over the grass, faster, faster, racing against death.

Rampage and Dasrylion finished torching the remains of the farmhouse and were circling the fallen beast from the rear when they saw Renegade running, and followed him.

Broken Spear lay there, the proton cannon broken free beside him, his white locks splayed in the dust...

Dorothy turned to follow the warriors, and saw. She plucked at the cameraman's shoulder. "Oh dear God, Bill, look..."

"What have you done? What have you done to him?" Renegade cried out one more soul-wrenching question and slid to his knees beside his beloved guardian. K'leura yielded Broken Spear's hand and slipped away. She trained laser and pulse rifle at the remaining humans and stood watching them. *The killers got away,* her deep grief rebuked her.

"You carrion," she said so softly and intensely that none of them moved. She could kill now, and they knew it.

The human cluster saw the smaller alien drop to his knees beside the larger, saw him clutch the limp hand, lift the fallen one's head on his arm, heard him say brokenly, "...Grandfather..."

The dark eyes opened once more. Between ragged breaths, his mouth moved. "Son...?"

"Stay...with me, Grandfather, please...I'll close the wound..." his other hand was drenched near the throat wound, fumbling to stop it pumping heart's blood..."I'll kill them all – I'll..."

"No...Ren--agade...too late...listen. No *hate,* promise me, no hate..."

Renegade stared blindly. He could not promise.

Broken Spear touched his chosen son's face. The mask came free; he touched flesh. "Listen...son...even if...the past cannot—be erased... sometimes... it can be...atoned..."

Rampage and Dasrylion were there now, kneeling with him, after a fierce glance at the humans – no more had weapons. Broken Spear saw them with an effort; he was dying; but he *must* say one more thing, once for a lifetime...

"Rampage...Dasrylion...all of you...do not regret...remember...I love...and am proud...of you...I am so proud of you all."

His head lapsed back into Renegade's arms. And the Great Warrior, slayer of monsters, renowned throughout the starworlds, Champion of his people for more than two centuries...Broken Spear, Dreamseeker, father to the three in all but blood, passed from this world to the unknown.

'NOOOOOOH!" Renegade flung himself forward, the death-cry bursting from him in one long anguished howl, until his brothers joined in with a rising keen of grief too great to be borne.

The humans watched in awe until K'leura, shaking, sobbing silently for her Renegade as much as for the old hunter she had come to trust and admire, waved her rifle at them and cried, "Go! Get out! You don't belong here with *him.* Run, carrion! Rot you all!"

And they fled, the car doors slamming, engines revving and tires squealing as they tore away.

Dorothy felt the tears streak down her own face as the death-howl ebbed away. She looked at Bill, who shook his head sadly; at Renegade, fallen over the body, sobbing; at his fellow warriors, weeping unashamed.

She faced the camera and tried to say it in words: "So this tragic night ends with one more tragedy. For what they did to save us, for the help they gave to us and the monsters they killed for us, these selfless hunters received treachery and death in return. A bullet has taken the life of their great leader, and his warriors gather around him and mourn. This is how we of Earth have repaid them for their courage, as we repay so many of our own. Looking at them, at their faces, so different from ours, yet their feelings so similar and profound – you have to ask yourself, who is the monster here?"

She bowed her head, lifted it, and said, "That's a wrap, Bill."

He sagged, shut down, set the camera aside." That's a damn dirty shame, Dore'. You'd better tell them to get moving. Those fires will bring some more attention pretty damn soon."

She nodded, but quailed at the thought of approaching Renegade in his grief.

Instead she turned to the female warrior standing nearby. "Ka—Kaloora?"

The featureless mask turned to stare at her, its eye-lenses burning. She tried again: "I – I know you must hate us now, and I don't blame you…but please, I never wanted this to happen."

A curt head movement. Impossible to tell what it meant.

Dorothy plowed on. "Wha—ah, what about your – husband? And his friends? Can you get them out of here before there's more trouble?"

Silence. Then, "Yes, I will call the ship;" and the alien woman tapped her wristband.

The dark ship lifted out of the trees across the road and glided over to settle beside them.

K'leura went to the others. Gently she tried to move them, was able to budge Rampage and Dasrylion. Next she put her arms around Renegade and drew him to his feet.

Looking out of tear-blinded eyes he told her, "It's my fault. I had to come here; so he followed me. I drew him."

"No, no, no," she whispered, stroking his face.

"Brother, he died a warrior's death," Dasryl said. "Come help us move him inside;" and the four of them together managed to lift the body and carry it aboard the ship, the proton cannon riding with its late owner.

Dorothy felt desperate to explain, helpless to act. She wanted to talk to Renegade, to tell him…

After a few moments someone jumped down from the ship's portal. Not Renegade, but the tall thin one in golden armor. He'd taken off his mask and his eyes glowed yellow, fierce as a tiger's. He jogged halfway back to the blazing trailers, stopped at the giant fallen bone-beast, made a quick slashing movement behind the head, then dragged the huge armored head back with him. When he came opposite the two humans, he stopped to glare at them. He looked down at them with unutterable contempt and scorn.

Finally he spoke. "I don't know why he wants me to talk to you, but he does." His voice was livid with hate. The humans shrank back.

Rampage looked at them as if he would scorn to spit on them and added, "*He* says to tell you he knows you two didn't do it – and he says – if it were me, I'd slay you where you stand, and blow this planet to dust – but *he* says to show that file you recorded, and maybe it will change things between us. Personally, I hope you destroy yourselves before you ever see us again, but he's always been better than me--and he gives his word. To *you.*" He almost spat that last out, then spun on his heel, tossed the beast's head into the open bay, and sprang in after it. The hatch sealed and he was gone.

The school ship's lifter jets pushed it skyward. It paused; then blue-white heat shot out of the big engines and it streaked away. Twenty miles distant, another ship arose from its hiding place in the shallow lake and went to meet the first; and they both shot away together, outward bound.

The two newspeople watched them go. Already they could hear the wail of sirens approaching in the distance, but their eyes remained on the sky. Dorothy thought of the young warrior and his lady, of his loyal friends, of the big warrior who had inspired them all and led them…

…and died for his pains.

"Entreat me not to leave thee," she murmured, quoting, "nor to cease from following after thee; for whither thou goest, I will go…

"'And whither thou diest, I will die, and there will I be buried…"

"What? What's that?' the cameraman asked her.

She shook her head. "Nothing. Just…let's get going, Bill. We've got the world's newest story here – and one of the world's oldest, too." She unclipped the mike. "Time to go, Bill."

They climbed back into the van and turned west, driving down the black roadway, passing like a ghost through mist, passing the screaming fire trucks and sheriffs' cars, passing, passing….

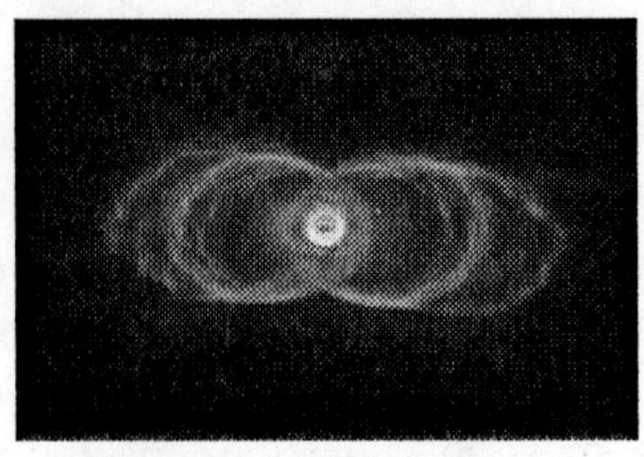

Eighteen....The Eternal Return

A MESSAGE TO P'TAAL 5:

Colony Three
Esteemed Hunter Stands Fast
Esteemed Huntress Kyva
And young Blackstripe

"Once again I have failed to stop and visit with you as I planned. I would have done so on my way back from an out-systems world, but we were struck with great tragedy, through another failure of mine. My dear friend and chosen grandfather is dead, and I have killed him.

"Kyva and Stands Fast, dear friends, please accept all my wishes for your good hunting and long life – may you and your people prosper.

"And when he gets old enough, please tell little Blackstripe that whatever my faults, at least I have loved him."

Renegade

Stands Fast and Kyva stood together outside the Renegade Freehold communications building, their toddler tugging impatiently at his mother's arm. As they read the message, their faces grew long.

"This doesn't sound like our Renegade – what does he mean, he killed his friend?" Kyva demanded.

Stands Fast replied, "This transmission came with another one, made to the whole planet. Remember the Great Warrior who came here after Renegade's Master Hunt?" At her nod, he went on, "Well, they were hunting these bone-beast creatures on some trophy world and the big warrior was killed by hostile aliens after he'd slain the master beast. Not Renegade's fault, according to his friends' messages."

Kyva's sadness and concern matched his. "Then our noble hunter takes blame which is not his – he needs our help."

Stands Fast chinlifted. "If the game will not come to the hunter, then the hunter must follow the game," he quoted. "Except we can't afford such a trip –and you will have another child soon, my lady.'

"We can't afford such a trip *by ourselves*," she said, absently pulling Blackstripe back from playing with the building's automatic door. "But P'taal 5 will send a delegation to the Leavetaking, won't they? And you are close to the Chief Hunter Clouded Sky, aren't you, my husband?"

At her husband's dawning assent, she continued, "Then we must talk to him and be included in that delegation. Who better than we?'

"Who indeed?" Stands Fast agreed.

They made the stop on the way home.

***

HOME IS THE HUNTER---The Scout ship bearing Broken Spear's body rose above the amphitheatre on Homeworld. His corpse had been frozen aboard the school ship and held that way for another tenday, until his whole family and clan, friends and fellow hunters, arrived here.

Now they filled the vast amphitheatre, not only members of his own clan, but many whom he had trained, star captains he had shipped with, and many, many *tautschen* from the worlds he had helped to win.

The Scout was laden with Leavetaking gifts – not all of them, for there were too many to go aboard, and many would have to be burned on the ground. It bore only those from a special few. With Broken Spear rode the gifts of his Clan Leader, the Director of the Nine Systems Hunt Council, his nearest living family and his three best students. One was the head of the giant beast he had killed.

The ship soared above the watching crowd. As the speaker, Burning Spear, finished the Credo, "Let Life prevail--"

--Both the ship and the gifts on the ground blew to whitefire and smoke as the bolts from thirty guns below, and one Hunt ship above, ruptured the air.

And a great warrior was gone, leaving only a drift of ash to filter down upon the land of his birth and the upturned faces of his people.

"A fitting tribute," Burning Spear put his hands on the shoulders of the two tall young warriors standing before him, "for the best among us; honorable death in battle to end an honorable life full of victories." His voice was sorrowful but strong. At some level he had accepted his brother's death. He asked them, "And you, Esteemed Warriors?"

Rampage and Dasrylion looked bleak. "Thank you, Burning Spear," Dasrylion said, "but we will never be able to truly take Leave of him…in our hearts."

"I know. But Life lies all before you now, and soon time will blunt that edge. It is for your young friend I fear…"

They all glanced toward Renegade, who stood apart, head deeply bowed, pale as frost on water. K'leura, renamed K'shara or Warrior Woman* in the Hunt Records, stood by his side, hand to his hand. Shortly, Renegade turned and walked away.

His two friends watched him with a pang.

"It's as if we've lost him, too," Rampage said bitterly. "He was worse on the way home: we had to take his weapons away or he would have joined Broken Spear in death. Even then he might have, if we didn't remind him he's married now and would hurt his wife *and* us if he took the Final Surrender. So instead he spent days and days in mourning by the body. Instead of a Leavetaking gift, we both thought he would throw *himself* on the pyre."

"And we must not lose him," Burning Spear said. "You three are the best of my brother's students. He gave everyone else his knowledge; to you he gave his heart. Dreamseeker said you were the best he'd ever trained"—to their startled glances – "yes, he said it and meant it. Any one of you is too valuable to our people to be lost. Renegade is a Great Warrior in many ways; we must not let him take this blame upon himself. It was Takaion's's choice to go there."

"But what can we *do?"* Rampage beseeched him; while Dasrylion's anguish stared out of his eyes.

"Wait. Bring him to our clan's ancient campground this evening and my wife, who is shaman and Wise Woman, will speak to him there."

"That should be easy to do," Rampage muttered.

"*Chak,*" Dasryl added; "He goes where you take him and he sits where you put him, as if he's lost all his will to live and doesn't care where he is."

"That *is* bad. We should go to him now…look, someone greets him… approach slowly," Burning Spear cautioned.

So unseeing was Renegade that he nearly walked into the people who had come up to him. When he tried to turn aside to avoid them he was stopped by K'leura's touch to his arm.

---

* "K'shara" in the Old Speech, "Rakasha" in the New. But K'leura is used to her old name, and still uses it.

Two people stood in front of him – no, three, one a child carried in his mother's arms.

"Honored warrior," Stands Fast began, but Kyva shook out her mane and made a new start.

"Renegade," she said softly. That brought his eyes to hers.

She held forth her burden, which struggled and squirmed, then stopped and stared wide-eyed at the warrior's bright medals and rainbow-shining cape.

"Trrr, look, Mama! Shiny!" he squealed and reached for them.

In shock Renegade held perfectly still. The child was grey and gold clouded on the back and sides, but pale gold on the front, and a black stripe ran down over his heart...

"Dear Renegade," said Kyva; "will you not welcome your son?"

And Renegade opened his arms.

***

"THE HEALING has begun," Burning Spear said, "though he will need more, I think. Wise Woman will know. But come, we must take him to our hearth..." His stride lengthened, then slowed almost immediately as he had another thought.

"Noble warriors, what are your future plans?"

Dasryl shrugged. "Go back to Broken Spear's trophy hall on Arvien 4 for a while, Esteemed Leader, perhaps long enough to decide what we want to do about the students there. Then we're off to the new planet, the double one we helped explore. We have holdings there. Renegade" – his voice faltered – "Renegade...thought we could all live there."

"And you shall," Burning Spear promised. "We shall reclaim him, on my Oath. And you, young Rampage?"

"First I *have* to get back to the Dinosaur Planet to speak for my bride," Rampage's voice was taut with anxiety. "It's been more than five years there. I've got to get back before something else takes me away."

Burning Spear nodded. He studied them, Dasrylion in particular. "I see. There is one more person I would like you to meet: an outworlder living with our clan, who was part of the Inner Circle at Leavetaking, although I do not see her now..." and he led them forward.

Even as he increased his pace toward the little group surrounding Renegade, he was thinking: *Dear brother and teacher, already I am meddling with their lives; it must track in the family. Let your spirit guide me in this, so I may do no wrong.*

***

WISE WOMAN --- Renegade had started to come around when his son was placed in his arms asking, "You Papa?" as his second-father had taught him. But when he had to give him back to make time for more Leavetaking guests stopping by, he retreated into his stone shell again. He stood with Rampage and Dasrylion and K'leura going through the endless greetings and commiserations, thinking he had no right to be a father. His son would only be ashamed of him when he grew up.

Broken Spear sent Kyva's family on ahead to his clan's rainy season camp. He searched for the woman called Sunrise, but couldn't find her, and assumed she'd gone ahead, too.

When he returned to the three Arvien warriors (Dasrylion now bore that title too) and Renegade's bride, he was alarmed to see they all looked numb from shock, even K'leura, who still loyally stood by her mate.

Enough of this, he thought, and rounded them up. "Esteemed Warriors and Huntress," he growled, "go on to our camp and get meat and drink to refresh yourselves. As a blood relative, I will take your places here." And they found themselves literally herded onto a waiting aircar.

In the wet season, heavy fog fills the valleys and lowlands of Homeworld, even when there is no downpour. Sometimes it puffs to the tops of the low ridges as well. It makes for a climate where heat-sight is necessary, and lurking beats may slink near.

So the Rydderrak Clan had its rainy season quarters along the tops of several high ridges deep in the rainforest, where only the lightest fogs could ascend. The four visitors looked down into a bowl of cloud which smothered the forest below.

Burning Spear's wife, Wise Woman, who was that and also high shaman for the clan, met them near the leader's wooden lodge and sat them down inside with Stands Fast and Kyva.

Renegade showed a spark of interest. "Where's Blackstripe?" he asked.

Kyva smiled. "There." She indicated a group of small children playing with toy spears and balls in a corner of the big hearthroom. "He has lots of little ones to play with here."

"And not in the freehold?" K'leura asked, surprised.

"Not since we moved out of the fort and spread out over the forest and mountains. We have individual holdings now – we're freeholders again. The fort is used mainly for trading days, meetings and winter game storage. And trophy displays, on-course."

Renegade looked up. "No more Gets-Behind-Yous then?"

"No, none," Stands Fast told him. "You gave us a great gift, noble warrior. You gave us life."

His well-intentioned remark went awry. Renegade's face paled, his teeth closed tightly as he thought, *and I took the life of my greatest friend...*

"Your pardon," he choked, and rose to leave.

Stands Fast looked bewildered while his wife hissed in dismay, and K'leura leaped up to follow Renegade.

A strong hand stopped her.

"Let him be, Warrior Woman. He is soul-sick; but you cannot cure him. There is only one who can." The shaman faced her.

"But I'm his *wife!"* the new huntress bristled. "I can help him, I can be with him!"

"But you cannot cure him," Wise Woman went on, still implacable. "For a disease of the spirit, he needs medicine of the spirit."

"Administered by you, no doubt," K'leura was in a fighting mood. Shocked to see it in her, Rampage and Dasrylion half-rose to their feet, while others in the room shifted uneasily.

The big Rydderrak woman, who could have snapped her neck with a single twist, refused to be baited. "I will not take offense because you wish to protect him, huntress. But I alone will go to him after my husband returns here. Your warrior needs a vision quest, and the wisdom to learn from it. You will stay with him tonight as usual. Enough now."

And K'leura simmered down. Dasryl touched her shoulder gently; Kyva gave her a sympathetic look. They understood. K'leura tried to collect herself enough to apologize, but it would be a long time coming.

Wise Woman carried on as if nothing had happened. Rampage, Dasrylion and Stands Fast tried to create some inane small talk, while Kyva went to feed Blackstripe.

Burning Spear walked into this electric tableau when he came home, bringing a young Rydderrak woman with him. She was ruby-red with black spots ringed in gold on her back. She was smaller than the average clan member, and obviously pregnant, a male *chk-kiy* visible inside her abdominal wall.

Burning Spear looked around at the grim company. *Well, here is another shock for them,* he thought, and introduced her.

"Honored guests," he began, "this is Sunrise..."

***

RENEGADE ALONE---The young warrior sat in his assigned sleeping quarters, staring at nothing. A small fire crackled in the hearth, its flames reflected in his wide irises, but he scarcely knew it was there.

His grief felt as deep and as sharp as it had when Broken Spear died. Everything reminded him of his beloved Grandfather: a chance word, a certain quality of light, anything at all seemed to bring him back. Then sorrow would pierce the young hunter like a spear, and pain would overwhelm him.

He shuddered and covered his face with his hands. His ribcage heaved with the effort to restrain his weeping.

"*Vr'*Renegade?"

He sat up, breathless. In a moment he was able to say, "Yes? Who calls me?"

"It is Wise Woman, Burning Spear's mate. May I enter?"

He fought down a brief panic. "…Enter, and be welcome…." He steeled himself to meet yet another unwanted visitor.

The powerful adult woman who entered looked more like a warrior than he did, except she wore a shaman's ceremonial robes. She fixed him with a fiery eye and commanded, "Say nothing, young warrior. I know of thy pain;" and she began taking sachets and small containers from her robes and setting them before the fire.

Some contents she sprinkled into the fire, until a scented smoke filled the room. The smoke went to his head immediately, making him feel dizzy and remote. Apparently it did not affect her at all.

Suddenly she was kneeling before him, taking his hands in hers, studying his face. Renegade felt as if he would weep again, and tried to turn away.

"Chak," she said. Letting his hands go, she anointed him above the eyes and below his nostrils with something that first burned, then cooled.

Renegade felt the room slipping away. She seized his shoulders, forcing his attention. "Listen to me, young warrior, if you wish to live – as you should – tomorrow you must go on a vision quest, to a place of tall standing stones in the valley below. You must not eat or drink, and you must stay there until you see what your grieving heart longs for. Only then will your questions be answered and your spirit find peace.

"Do this, *tyr rakash,* for your wife's sake, for your son's sake, but most of all for your own sake, so that you may be one with the Spirit-of-all again, and take your proper place on the Circle of Life and Death."

She let him go. "Now sleep, Renegade; these herbs will bring you rest for tonight so you may be strong for the vision to follow."

And feeling boneless, he sank down on the straw mat and closed his eyes; while the shaman placed a small pot of smoldering herbs at his head and another at his feet. His eyes closed.

When she rose to leave, Wise Woman spoke to some deeper part of him, which lay beyond waking or sleeping, and said, "Great Warrior, champion of your People even as your teacher was, rest and sleep. Go forth tomorrow and return to us whole again. Your people need you." And she left him.

***

WHEN K'LEURA came in later, she was excited with the revelation they'd had from Sunrise and wanted to tell him right away. But Renegade was sleeping peacefully at last; and she simply lay down beside him, reluctant to disturb his rest.

Nineteen....The Vision

RENEGADE spent the predawn *tare'* in the steam lodge, then bathed in cool running water from a local stream to purify himself. He felt strangely uplifted: the weight still lay on his heart, but now he sensed something different – an anticipation of things to come.

He'd told K'leura where he was going so she wouldn't worry; and no doubt she or Wise Woman would tell the others. Alone, he descended the hillside, weaponless except for his wristknives (carrying them only because he'd sworn not to take his own life) and made his way down.

The Place of Standing Stones lay at the bottom of this valley, she'd told him, the shaman. It was an area the clan patrolled daily to keep clear of brush and wild animals; but she said any other hunters were honor-bound not to disturb him there.

The fog swirled up so thickly around him that he saw no living things, not even a heat-trail, on his descent. The white mist grew denser the lower he got, and it dripped with moisture. Except for the narrow footpath and the inclined slope, he could easily have lost his way.

Something tall and rough loomed out of the fog before him… Too cool to be alive, it revealed a pitted-rock surface damp and massive. One of the standing stones. He was here.

He made a slow circuit to get his bearings – ten great monoliths, upreared in a circle on the valley floor. Nothing in their center-circle; and the air around them was as still as death…as Death.

He sat down with his back to one of the stones, and waited.

The rising sun thinned out some of the mist, enough for him to see the stone sentinels looming all the way around. Nothing more.

He made himself as comfortable as possible. It was going to be a long time, he felt sure, though he did not know what he expected.

As the light changed, he began to see long separate strands of fog, webs and weaves, puffs of mist dancing… For lack of anything better to do, he watched them.

High sun passed, afternoon lengthened. The white mists began to turn gray again. He still saw nothing. As he shifted his cramped muscles, Renegade thought of Dreamseeker's vision quest: *eleven days it took, eleven without food, two without water. I wonder if anyone today could last that long.*

And his mind reared back from the subject like a beast at bay. He tried to force the memories away and the pain with them. If he remembered in detail, the tears would come again, and this time they might never end.

He fought and fought the memories until something gave inside him, and an inner voice told him, *these are good things; do not fight them. Let them come*...and he surrendered.

Come they did – the memories flooding back, pouring into him like remorseless waves of the sea: of his days in the great hall, sitting warm in the midst of a blizzard, listening to the old man's stories; of the games they had played on the mountain, he and Scr'vk trying to find their Elder, who often hid right before them; of the endless, endless patience he had shown, repeating their lessons, re-adjusting Renegade's laser, hunting with them in the hills, that last time…

…and the wild cold night of his parents' death, when Broken Spear had been with him, had saved him from the ledge, and soothed life and sanity back into him again – had *saved* him, over and over and over.

As I could not save him. Renegade's heart gave a great thump, and his feelings opened, and the tears came in a torrent this time while he lay on the ground, sobbing out his soul….

Even the endless must end at last, though; and finally, after an eternity of weeping, Renegade's soul was emptied and he lay there inert, suspended between this world and the unknown, between life and death, and caring naught for either of them.

...Renegade...

He blinked. Did someone speak his name?

There was someone here; he could feel it, and his feelings never lied. He sat up, looked around into a fog turned dense dark gray with the coming night.

He felt the presence again but could not place it.

Then he saw the heat-glimmer, amorphous, faint, yet coming towards him, brightening as it came. The fog shifted and rolled; he could not get a good image.

Suddenly the fog swirled aside, or the figure moved through it, and he recognized the features... Disbelief and joy clove him to his soul. Shaking, he whispered, *"Grandfather?"*

It was he. Glowing with life, radiating the love and kindness he had always felt for the boy, showing it to the man.

Son. The voice was in him and around him all at once. The face was Broken Spear's as he had always known it, humorous and wise. Even the great broken tusk was there.

A question half-formed in Renegade's mind, and his guardian laughed and answered it:

Look, son, he said, touching the broken tooth, sweeping his hand over it--and the cracked fang was whole. *One can be however one wishes, here.* He was smiling.

"Is it really you?" Renegade stammered.

The old warrior laughed, his familiar booming laughter, and the broken tooth reappeared. *Look at me with your eyes and with your heart, and know me.*

Renegade leaned toward him, almost crawled to him. The radiance warmed his face.

His mentor said sadly, *I do not know if you can touch me, dear child; but you can feel my spirit, can you not? I was with you on the voyage, but you were too grieved to sense me. I must hurry and say this now.*

Know that I died as I chose to – a warrior in battle, saving his loved ones, not a feeble old man in bed. Do not forsake your life, Renegade; it is not what I wanted for you, who are my chosen and best-beloved son. Mourn without sacrifice. I want you to live, Renegade; I always have.

The voice was fading, outside or inside his head, Renegade could not tell. He stretched out an arm, imploring, "Grandfather! Don't go!"

And the apparition smiled again and said, *I must, for now. But think of me without pain and I shall be near you always... Two things more...one, on your new world—beware*—fading, ah! fading!*...saltwater...and for me...remember sunrise...*

And he seemed to bend down even as Renegade reached up; and for just one moment, the young man was enfolded in a cloud of light and warmth and love – and he *knew* all was well with him; *Life* was right with him, and the future was his.

You are my life, son. Let Life prevail.

With this thought or whisper, with this cloud or vision, the spirit of Dreamseeker passed through and beyond him, and Renegade fell senseless to the ground.

***

A SMALL BAND of clan hunters, the daily patrol, found him in the morning just as he was waking.

After assuring them he was on-stat – yes, he was! – Renegade left them and jogged uphill to the clan's rainy-season camp. A stiff wind drove the mist away, and in the dark skies, thunder was talking.

The first person he met in camp was little Blackstripe, playing with some Rydderrak children of similar size. Renegade smiled at him and picked him up when the child reached out to him – "Papa?"

"Yes!" the warrior cried, and gave him a playful toss, making him squeal with laughter.

Then K'leura came out of the lodge and saw him, and ran laughing into his arms. The joyful noise roused Kyva and Stands Fast, Dasrylion and Rampage, and they all came to see their leader healed in spirit and whole again.

After their greetings, Renegade went into the lodge to see Wise Woman and Burning Spear, and told everyone about the vision.

Burning Spear laughed in joy, and slapped him on the shoulder; but Wise Woman chinlifted and smiled: "And he released you from blame, as he would. The circle of standing stones, to which I sent you, Renegade, is our Place of the Spirits, where anyone may go to speak with departed loved ones, even without shaman training. They may find peace there. It was a good vision."

"But what I don't understand," Renegade went on, "was his warning – first to beware of saltwater, and next, to remember sunrise."

"Well, of the sea I cannot speak," Burning Spear put in; "but of the other I can."

He indicated the young pregnant huntress standing at the threshold, listening, and he said:

"Great Warrior, *this* is Sunrise...Dreamseeker's wife."

Twenty....Sunrise's Story

AFTER THE initial shock had passed she told them her story:

Sunrise at 26 had already lost one husband. He was a starship pilot, somewhat older than she, and he was bringing a group of colonists over to the frontier world of Sarkasaal 4 when the ship's drive engines malfunctioned and it ruptured in hyperspace. Everyone on board died.

Sunrise had arrived on the planet earlier than her husband, to oversee the construction of their new home. It would be located in a small, new-built trading circle set on a high bluff above the river and plains. The main pack of settlers would come later on her husband's ship.

"So there I was," she said, "the only person in a ghost gathering on Sarkasaal 4, when I heard the terrible news over my comset. And this after I waited and waited, until his ship was overdue and even the builders had gone."

She mourned, for the husband she had never really known, for the life they would never have. More settlers would come eventually, she knew, but "meanwhile I was undecided whether to stay or go back to my Rydderrak relatives in Four Systems; or if I stayed, how was I to survive by myself with the Hunt training I'd had in childhood. It had been ten years since my Master Hunt and little practice after..." So she did nothing, moving about in a benumbed fog.

(Across the circle, Renegade looked up. He understood that state of mind.)

She was still mourning and motionless a few tendays later when the comset chimed again.

Futile with hope, she answered it; and a hunter spoke to her – "A Hunt Leader and teacher actually, bringing his students with him."

(A quick anticipatory glance ran round her listeners' circle.)

"He expected to find a freehold here and seemed stunned when I told him there were no others. 'Then you are alone, milady?' he asked. He seemed very sympathetic and courteous and he addressed me in the Old Style.

"He requested permission to make tie here and hunt..."

She could see no harm in it, and gave him coordinates to make planetide on the river floodplain below the bluff. She even went out to watch the small Hunt ship come down, and saw them – real, living people – unload and set up camp until near dark, when she returned to her home.

"The Hunt Leader was easy to pick out," she said; "he was bigger than any of the students and he moved as if setting up camp was an old trail, many times taken." (And Renegade smiled to himself.)

What Sunrise didn't expect was the light scratching at her main threshold later, just at dusk. She switched on the viewer, and there he stood, the hunter from the camp.

He remained courteous and well-mannered. "Milady, I do not wish to disturb your privacy, but I am puzzled. Would you tell me what happened here? Is there a danger to you?"

She decided to let him come in – he was even more impressive in person – "what my clan calls a *rakash-d'san* (a mighty warrior)," she told them. And a well-trained one, for he was exquisitely polite and soon won her trust. (Now K'leura nodded and smiled)

She invited him to sit by the hearth and share a cup of broth, while she told him her story.

"Ah, I understand," he said at last. The dark brown eyes met hers with great sympathy. "I mourn with you, Huntress Sunrise."

"He was a wonderful person to talk to," she said, her sorrow welling up along with her listeners'.

And it seems he had a plan for her...

"It is customary," he said, "for a visiting Hunt ship to call on the Chief Hunter or Huntress of a settlement to request permission to hunt there, and also to ask their help in locating game."

"Since our colony had no Chief Hunter as yet, and it seemed that I had some hunt training – though I don't know how he could tell that..." Broken Spear proposed that *she* lead them to game, even if only to advise them, for a tracker's portion of the kill.

She lit up. "That would be a fine gift; but I must tell you I am not an active hunter; I had my Master Hunt ten years ago, and haven't done much since."

That didn't bother him. "You have *that,*" he nodded toward her comset computer in the next room, "and better terrain maps than I do. It would be enough."

So they struck a bargain. She would run off some satellite maps and they would pinpoint the herds on them when Broken Spear returned the next morning. "Then hunt with us and have your share," he told her.

And he left her to tend to his students.

Well, she might not feel like going on a hunt tomorrow, but she could certainly earn her share tonight. She ran off three days' worth of satellite photos showing terrain and weather patterns. Then she traced the herd movements over the last three days, filling them, and reduced the map to handy carrying size.

There, that would take the hunt to this evening. If she woke up early next morning, she could get another satellite update and place it on the map, too.

She stepped outside on the roof verandah for one more look at the camp: they had fires burning and sentries set, reminding her of her early childhood in her branch of Rydderrak Clan. Then she went to bed.

***

SHE COULD NOT possibly have gotten up early enough the next morning, since he was at her door two *tare'* before first light; and he had a Scout ship warmed and waiting.

"—Esteemed hunter?" she answered the door groggily.

"Day's-light, Huntress Sunrise! Are my maps ready?"

"Ch-churr—I'll get them," she muttered and turned away, only to have him call cheerfully after,

"Bring them and yourself as well, *vre'chai*! We have a hot meal waiting."

Nor would he hear her objections. She was going with them and *that* was a spear thrown and gone…

Kt-tare' later, she was dressed and riding aboard the Scout ship, map in hand.

There really was hot meat waiting, along with seven 12-to-14-year-olds, busy doing the cooking and cleanup.

Broken Spear had already eaten; so he sat looking at the maps as she finished her food. Sunrise had not been strict about feeding herself lately, and when she exclaimed, "Oh, that was good! Much better than dried rations," the big warrior gave her a sympathetic smile.

"You shall have fresh meat before tomorrow Sunrise," he said, making a gentle pun with her name. She flushed in embarrassment. She hadn't meant to sound so *hungry*.

"I realized he was just being kind," she told her listeners; "he had seen my plight and felt sorry for me, so he was going to fill my larder – and I decided then and there I would work hard for my share, and not be so pitiful. Spirit knows I was feeling sorry enough for myself."

After some perfunctory questions about the map, Broken Spear determined that the nearest large herds were about a half-day's journey away.

So everyone boarded the school ship and broke tie, leaving a perimeter ring of defenses to guard the camp.

Before she could protest, Sunrise found herself equipped with shoulder laser, spear, and wristknives, as well as some spare leather armor. Clearly, the old warrior expected her to take part – or perhaps he was just being cautious.

"Cautious," Rampage put in.

She half-smiled and went on. "Any-route, I had already decided to carry my end of the game pole; and there I stayed, among nearly a ten of young hunters hot for a kill. Broken Spear invited me to take Second Seat at his side, and I felt more comfortable there."

They scouted the herds at the river some distance north and west of the camp. There were two major species: a large heavy one with a curved parrot-like beak and blunted knobs on its head; and a lightly-built, long-legged bounder, swift and alert.

The students challenged a few of the big ones first, but they were dull beasts, mild-tempered and not at all worthy. After two kills, Broken Spear called a halt and tried the second species.

And *these* were magnificent: they had wonderful senses, tremendous speed -- and the first group the hunters tried to drive wheeled on their own tracks and went flying over their pursuers' heads in such superb leaps, they seemed more like birds.

"Splendid. These are our prey," the old hunter told his students. He broke them into several packs and told them to catch their own food.

The first pair of students worked cooperatively, and managed to approach the "dawnfliers" from two sides, narrowly missing a kill.

The second pair bunched up and the graceful creatures never let them come close. The third little pack, three students, managed to flush their chosen prey prematurely and watched it disappear in the distance.

The old warrior was a little disgusted with them. *"Chk-kiy-teh!* Have I not taught you how to *think?* Verain, Clear Talon, go to the rear flank of *that* small herd, and walk them forward – but slowly, very slowly. And watch, all of you.'

And Sunrise as well as the students saw the old master absolutely blend into the tall grass, and approach the beasts downwind. Finally even the other hunters lost trace of him, and the students "working" the small bunch of dawnfliers began to move more impatiently.

The animals slid away from them, bounding in slow motion and stopping, hardly worried – until suddenly the old hunter rose from the grass at their feet and even as the startled animals braked and shied, he brought one down with a powerful spearcast and it was done.

"With a spear!" Sunrise exclaimed, still impressed.

"Out of the grass at their feet!" Renegade and Dasrylion exchanged laughing glances. "Like he used to do with us, remember, brother?" Dasryl said; while Rampage just bounced in place, excited.

Broken Spear walked the few paces to collect his kill and spear, holstered one and slung the other over his shoulder.

"Now," he told the students on his return, "we shall just stay here until you can do *that!"*

(And every male hunter in the lodge roared with laughter.)

"*Vre'*huntress Sunrise," he asked, turning to her, "are these edible?"

"Yes; and the larger ones too."

"Ah." He dropped the dawnflier at her feet. "Then I shall prepare this one and one of the others as your share for today, and my unworthy students may eat the other large beast—and anything else they can catch."

"On-point he was as good as his word," she said, "and after he butchered those two, and the students finally contrived to bring down one of the others, he flew us back to camp. There he instructed his students on making the meal, and helped me load the other meat into my freezer at home.

"We spent a fiveday pursuing the beasts of the plains and honing the students' skills. I helped with the drives and assisted in two more kills, as my former training returned," she said. "When Broken Spear thought we'd had enough, he decided to choose new hunting grounds."

"'The only others in this part of the continent are the marshes to the south,' I said, 'where the river goes to the sea. And no-one knows exactly what lies there: many life forms blend their heat-trace on our maps.'

"So we made another satellite map and set off, a longer trip this time, breaking up the camp and moving it with us."

By now Sunrise felt so much a part of the hunt that she could not have stayed away. She battened down her home on the bluff and went adventuring with the hunters. They lent her a spare tent; and she used the borrowed gear and weapons. She felt good, better than she had in many days.

She had not made a kill for herself yet; she had only assisted with others. But she felt confident that she could do so at any time. Maybe this would be the time... She found herself as eager to please the old warrior as his students were, though he never asked it of her.

***

THE MARSHES covered hundreds of *kri-veh,* for the river widened into a small sea at its mouth, and in this heat and humidity, life flourished.

Broken Spear explored the area for nearly a day before he found a suitable campsite on top of a tall grassy mound which edged the great marsh. He put the camp there, rather than in the marsh itself.

"Too many unknowns below," he said.

In the failing daylight, they set up the tents and the motion-and-heat detectors, and shot a few of the more succulent waterfowl for main-meat. Sunrise briefly exchanged her spear for a dart-bearing gauntlet, and actually knocked down two flying birds, much to her relief. The old hunter's praise made her flush with pride.

When they retired that night, Broken Spear set two students to keep watch. But he felt restless, and before long, Sunrise heard him leave his tent in the dark and wander abroad. Something was bothering him.

"I tried to sleep but it wasn't long before I felt it, too," she admitted; "so I left my tent and moved outside the perimeter, resetting the sensors as I went."

She found herself at the edge of the hill, looking down into the swamp. She saw Broken Spear at the foot, his body heat glowing against the cooler land. He too seemed intent on the swamp.

Quietly she climbed down to join him.

He heard her, of course, and spoke very softly, "So you feel the Boding too, do you, *vre'* huntress? It is a true sense, and one that will never fail you. Come, watch with me."

Together they made their way onto the marshy ground. They spread apart a little at his signal and stayed alert.

All they heard were the numberless night creatures, calling, chirruping, and making stranger noises, none of them threatening.

Finally he approached her and said in a whisper, "Nothing untoward. And yet... there *is* something. I had one student who could feel it too, if he were with us tonight."

(--His friends' eyes focused on Renegade, who thought, *so he was thinking of me even then.*)

Sunrise continued: "We stood there a long time before we heard the first hints of danger. Suddenly the small creatures went silent. Then we heard footsteps, big, splashing footsteps in the water."

"Tell me what you make of that?" Broken Spear asked softly.

I hackled-up. 'Something very large…and it approaches deliberately, from *that* hammock over there,' I pointed.

"Very good," he replied. "About ten *kri* tall, I think. Arm laser. Aim high."

Suddenly the trees of that hummock were pushed aside like reed stems, and a great beast strode out – upright, two-footed, armored like a Homeworld swamp lurker, but with head and teeth like a carnosaur, while a long heavy tail swung behind. It was every *kli* as tall as he'd estimated.

It crashed into open water. There it stopped and stood. And turned toward us. And lowered its head and *charged.*

Both lasers fired. My shot hit him behind the head, in the thick warted neck. Broken Spear's bolt went home, directly into his chest.

The grinning beast shrieked and lunged. I moved like a dawnflier – backwards, but the old master was with me, already in front of me, aiming for the maw.

He didn't need to shoot. The beast fell at our feet, his knived jaws crashing down agape, his rage carrying him within a few *kri* of us.

"That will wake the students," Broken Spear remarked humorously. He took my hand and led me around the beast. "Let us have a look at him."

The creature was as long as a big carnosaur from snout to tail-tip; but his thick armored skin looked different, and he had long workable hands.

By the time we cleared the tail and found our way round to the monster's underbelly, the camp on the rise above us was awake with shouts and alarms.

Broken Spear called up to them, told them where we were, and suggested they change sentries and *stay there.* He'd be right up, he said.

"Now," he told me, "let us get the head off this creature so you may have a suitable trophy."

"I! But it was you—"

"We both killed him. Take the credit you deserve," he said, and splashed through the knee-deep water to its head.

I stayed near the middle, dumbfounded. No use to argue with him; and finally I began high-stepping through muddy water toward him…

--When the second beast charged out of the swamp at me. It lunged head-down and silent, its huge jaws swinging level with my face.

I backed, screamed and fired all at once. I tripped over something behind me and fell, making the laser bolt go high and sear the tip of its snout – good Chance for me.

As I went down, the beast flung up its head, stung.

Another bolt hit it in the side, a third struck the leg; and it staggered, bellowing.

Someone splashed to a halt in front of me as I struggled to get up. Broken Spear.

"Stay down!" he roared, and turned to the beast.

It reached for him with its clawed hands and he hit it *twice* in a single breath: the laser in the throat, the spear in its heart. It fell forward towards us.

It was like a mountain falling. I tried to scramble aside, slipped to one knee; and then the warrior threw himself across me, a living shield.

The huge body crashed down. We were driven into the mud as the fall smashed up water like a fountain. We fell under the beast, Broken Spear pushing his hands and knees into the mud to form a bridge over me, to save me the blow.

(She looked at the people seated around her. *Yes,* they were nodding, *that is what he would do.*

The rain outside the lodge poured down; and after a drink of water to refresh herself, Sunrise went on…)

After a few moments, the two hunters in the swamp realized that even though they were pinned down, they were still breathing, still alive. A tremendous weight lay over them; but the beast had fallen partly on top the first creature's body and that had spared them.

Sunrise could feel the old warrior's body over hers, could feel his every muscle straining as he strove to hold the carcass off her.

She turned over under him, tried to squirm free – and they contacted each other all along their lengths.

For an eyeblink they stilled, her breathing and heartbeat pressed against his.

Then the old warrior collected himself and told her in a strained voice, "Dig, Sunrise, *dig* out from under."

So she plunged into the foul water and sluiced away handfuls of mud until she could wriggle out from under him. He uttered a low groan, but not of pain.

She swallowed water and darkness, and suddenly she tore free, heaving to her feet to gasp in lungfuls of clean air.

He was still down there, sinking lower.

"Broken Spear, hurry!" she called. "Get to the air. I'll help you."

A struggle began under the swamp monster's huge bulk: its mass sank even lower.

Water surged forth; then she bent and pulled on his forearms with a desperate strength, braced her back and bent her knees, putting everything she had into it…

…Until he broke free, and came up gasping for air. Her pull released, she fell backwards, down on her rump in muddy water, her head striking the fallen monster behind her. Broken Spear reached for her, pulled her up by one shoulder. Then they both slumped together against the first beast, hauling for breath.

She had been close to him before, but never touched him save for the ritual greeting. Now she lay against his arm panting, her head against his shoulder, her hand on his chest; and she could feel the great expansion of his lungs, hear his labored breathing against her, feel the pounding of his heart.

They lay like that until they recovered enough to speak.

He spoke first: "Milady, I think I am an old fool."

When she exclaimed and denied it, he shook out his mane, saying, "No, no – I should have thought to check that cover where the first beast came from, just after our kill. I will do that now, then reassure the students, who are getting excited up there." And he stood up, gently resettling her against the dead carnivore.

She would have gone with him into the clump of trees, but he asked her to remove the dead beasts' heads; then together they would take them up to the bluff. So she watched him disappear into the brush, and could not concentrate properly on her work until he emerged again, safe.

By that time, she'd done only one head. He stopped to help her with the second, giving her a long look – and she felt every wet slop of mud and water and swamp brute blood upon her, and how she must look to him.

But the old warrior merely smiled: "Stain from battle is honorable gore, Huntress Sunrise," and when she smiled too, he added, "I think we should return the meat and heads to your holding, milady; and I want to break up camp here and take the students back, at least-path for tonight."

***

SO WE trekked back up the knoll, looking as if we had been through a whole campaign in one night, and he got the students packing.

We both stayed caked with mud and slime all the way home, though the flight was quicker this time.

I suggested he might save his students a few *tare'* of work if he put them up in one of the empty houses in the gathering, and he thanked me and exercised 'wayfarer's privilege' to quarter them in the home nearest mine.

"There," he said, "now I know they are safe enough, although we will keep sentries posted *and* the sensors on. But I regret we cannot turn on the electrical generators..." he looked down at himself and smiled ruefully; "I could use a bath."

"So could I," I said, and offered him the use of my rain- and-steam chamber at home.

"That would be a great favor, thank you, *vre'*huntress," he said, and walked the short distance home with me.

I had enjoyed the hunt, but it felt *so good* to be home! And Broken Spear stepped carefully through my house, as if he was worried about dirtying it. But I told him in his own words, "Battle stain is honorable gore, *vr'*warrior," which made him laugh and relax.

I led him to the bathing chamber and turned on the hot rain-bath for him, then left for a few moments so he could get comfortable. We had only the steam jets to dry in, so I searched for some fur wraps to dry us and keep us warm. When I finally found some and brought them back, I did not see him and thought that he must have finished bathing and stepped out of the room.

The main bathing chamber had a large rain-bath and steam room set off in an alcove to the side. The moisture spread, though, and the entire chamber was filled with white steam and heat when I arrived.

I put the furs down on the drying rack, opened the rain-chamber door, and stepped in. I would feel much better with the dirt washed off, I thought.

As soon as I had, I realized he was still there with the rain-bath running. He turned in surprise, and I started to back away – but I didn't, not quite. Somehow I just stood there and we looked at each other.

"Sunrise," he said gently, "there is plenty of room;" and he reached out and took my hand and drew me under the water with him, and then..."

(She closed her eyes and paused, a long pause, and here is where she deleted some of their most private moments...)

***

...for as the powerful old warrior drew her under the water spray, she had begun to feel her own blood heat rising, warmth spreading outward from the center of her being...

He over-stood her by a head, and his muscular body was many times stronger than hers; yet he was very gentle with her.

She stood before him like a child, feeling the warm water rinse the grime from her.

Then his hands were on her, loosening the knot in her hair (his own white mane already hung free) and next smoothing the cleansing powder all over her, spreading that rising warmth from her center outward.

She leaned forward against his chest, her palms laid flat. Her eyes closed, and she felt the strong hands rub over her

She heard him sigh, "Ah, it has been a long time, milady."

Presently he said, "Now the front," and turned her around. She pressed back against him in perfect trust, knowing he would never attempt to overpower or force her in any way. His wide hands laved her front parts, smoothing over breasts that felt suddenly swollen, a belly that was both taut and stretched...then lower down, and she gasped and pressed back against him.

He was ready, hard against her back; but he did not join with her yet. He held her against himself, his hands still, and said almost humbly, "This...is not just...an incident for me, milady. I am 250 years old, and while I cannot offer you a **long** *marriage..." he turned her carefully to face him; humidity and desire had put tears in her eyes... "I have holdings on two worlds, and you need never be lonely again, Sunrise, or left without hope. And we will be happy while we can. Can you accept that?"*

And she looked straight into his eyes and said, "Yes, I accept that – I accept **you,** *Broken Spear;" and her hands began touching him with a fervor he had not felt for many years; and her smaller teeth and tongue were busy with his proud body, until he inhaled sharply and said, "Hold! Let us be comfortable."*

Turning off the water, he swept her up in his arms and left the chamber. He pulled a wrap about her and carried her over to the bed in the other room.

There he stretched her out and looked at her...she was trembling, aching with desire, and he ran his hands over her again.

To his surprise, her full breasts were swollen, and the nipples leaked milk as he pressed them gently. He touched her lower down, and she moaned and opened to him.

"Oh Sunrise," he murmured, "sweet, sweet Sunrise;" for she had come into season, building toward it all that day and night, and her body was ripe for his entry.

He felt touched.

She felt his hands under her head and buttocks, his warm body lowered very lightly over hers. Then she was pierced, and she cried out. He answered and moved upon her.

His great canines came down on either side of her neck, and even though he was not bearing down, for a moment she felt trapped, and she struggled. But the powerful body held her in place and he moved inside her, making her grasp him around the back, scraping and clawing.

"Yes, little one," he urged her, "scratch, bite, let go, use your strength with me!" and her panic become pungency, and she bucked wildly against him, then pulled him down...

Until they cried out together, as with a mighty roar, the old lion claimed his mate.

***

...Sunrise opened her eyes on the room in present time. She finished her sentence, begun before memories... "And then he bathed me and carried me to bed and made love to me..."

The hands of all the couples there sought each other's: Renegade and K'leura, Kyva and Stands Fast, the clan leader and his wife...

Dasrylion stared at Sunrise as if hypnotized, and Rampage felt short of breath.

***

ONE OF the leader's grown sons brought food in. The day had grown old without being noticed; and Sunrise ended her story quickly:

"Except for leaving me briefly during the night, he stayed with me for all of our time together; and that night, too, the child was made."

A long sigh went around the room.

***

Her private memories brought back the night.

After resting, she aroused again and turned toward him. He smiled and lay back, allowing her to explore him, to touch him as freely as he had her.

After a time he murmured, "Sunrise, there has been a miracle; and one does not question miracles – one accepts them..." and he lifted her onto himself so she could be free to move, and she took them to ecstasy again.

Finally they slept, she half on top of him, he holding her there.

At some point, she felt him slip out from under, murmuring, "I must see that my students are well. But I shall return shortly, beloved Sunrise." What a thrill to hear her name so spoken!

Sleep was overtaking her again when she felt him stretch out beside her and scoop her up to lie against him.

The next morning she woke with him, and nuzzled him affectionately. He returned the greeting, then held her wrists and looked closely at her: she was still in season, her body full and languid with love. The ripeness would pass quickly, but for now…

Thinking of her appearance before the students, he said gently, "You may stay here today if you like, Sunrise;" but she looked at him with shining eyes and declaimed,

"No, my love, I don't care if they see; I'm proud of what happened between us."

"Well-thrown!" he exclaimed, embracing her. "We'll go out together."

***

"THE BONDING set the tenor of our days and nights," she told the little gathering after they finished main-meat. "T'akaion led me before the students the next morning and announced me as his wife before all of them, and not one showed a tooth in protest."

"I should think not," Burning Spear chuckled.

"—and we spent the next several tendays hunting over that planet and others," Sunrise said. She needed to talk now, as she had not talked about him before. "We shared one tent; and I don't *think* it made him any less skilled or distracted him from his teachings. In truth he seemed buoyant and youthful. And I did not know of his fame – not then."

"At least he was happy, and so were you," Renegade said. "Did he know – about the baby – before he left you?"

"Oh yes," she answered, lost in the past; "he said he could see it from the first day, long before I could; and we were together long enough for him to see it grow, and become a child."

"Good," Renegade whispered; *"good."*

"When did you come here?" Rampage asked.

"After about half-a-year of hunting off-planet," she said. "We were read the rites here, and our names set into the clan records."

"Chak," Burning Spear confirmed. "In this instance both the leader and the high shaman read them – I and my wife. We were proud to accept my brother's wife into our care. Broken Spear left Sunrise here when he

flew his students home to Arvien 4. He intended to return in time for the birth, and thought she would be more comfortable here."

Dasrylion leaned forward suddenly, toward Sunrise. "In all of this, esteemed huntress, no one has thought to ask how *you* felt, or what a terrible thing it is to lose two husbands."

"Well-put," muttered Wise Woman; while the others had the grace to look abashed.

Fervently the big trapper leaned toward her, offering his wrists: "Please know that on my and my friends' behalf, we are deeply sorry for your loss. And we mourn with you."

Sunrise's vision blurred. The hands she wrapped around his wrists were trembling. "I – thank you, *vr'*warrior. And all of you." she glanced around quickly. "I – know how you felt about T'akaion, how much you loved him…he often spoke of you three; the best of all his students, he called you, and like sons to him. S-sometime after he left… I – I saw him in a dream, and he told me he – he" – her voice broke, "could not return to me in the flesh anymore. And I must contact you when you came. I don't know why."

Renegade knew. He leaned forward, his eyes intense. "Huntress Sunrise," he said, "Since he mentioned you to me in my vision, you must come with us to Arvien 4, where you could stay at his hall. There are good memories of him there, too."

"I – yes, perhaps that's it," she considered.

"Not until after the child is born," the shaman put in sternly. "Here we have much experience in childbirth, even the University's medicine if we need it. Not like some *frontier* world;" and her husband laughed.

"You would think it an ice-moon out there to hear you talk, Wise Woman," he teased her. "They have medicine and healers on the starworlds too."

She *chuffed* in disbelief, making him laugh again; and shortly after, the group bid each other "night's-rest" and went to their respective rooms in the chief's lodge.

Rampage stopped Renegade and K'leura on their way. To his friends' surprise, he looked a little wild, even desperate.

"Why, brother," Renegade began, but Rampage interrupted him:

"Listen; I *have* to go back to the Dinosaur Planet, Renegade; I have to. It's been at least five years since I was there. I can't waste another day."

"On-course you must go," K'leura said in sympathy; while Renegade took his old friend by the shoulders and told him,

"Go then, brother. I won't delay you any longer. K'leura and Dasrylion and I will go back to Arvien ourselves. Have you thought about how to get there? Do you need the school ship?"

"No," Rampage said. "Kyva and Stands Fast are returning to P'taal 5 with their delegation day after tomorrow. They can drop me on the way; and the starliner can pick me up on its return circuit...and take me and K'orrynia back to Nine Systems Station."

"And we can catch you from there, both of you. Just call us and we'll come," Renegade told him. "Well. We'll miss you, Rampage, but we wish you the best of good hunting for your wedding quest. We'll be waiting at the trophy hall until we hear from you."

"Thanks, Renegade; K'leura." Rampage relaxed a little. "And sweet sleep to both of you tonight;" and he dashed off, as if by rushing through sleep he could leave that much sooner.

"I don't know about sleep, Renegade," K'leura remarked to her husband as they entered their room. "After that story, I think there will be more than one child made, tonight."

"At least one,' Renegade smiled at her, leading her to the bed.

Down the hall, Kyva returned to Stands Fast after checking on little Blackstripe and said, "Do you think we'll disturb his little sister?" and her husband, secure in his heart after seeing Renegade safe again, answered, "No, I don't think we will."

...and in their spacious sleeping chamber, the clan leader was looking at his wife with sparkling eyes and asking, "Might you forget our people just one time, and let this night be ours alone?'

And she purred cheerfully at him, "Come, young panther, and help me to forget!"

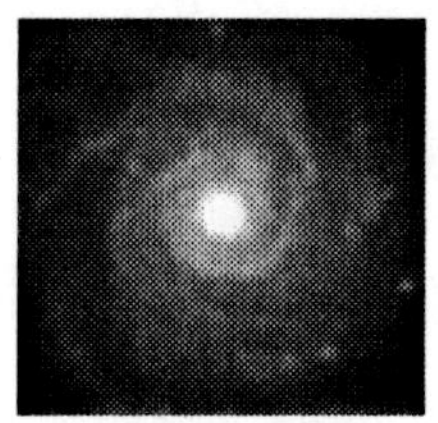

The Star Traveler

A thousand years have I been searching,
And not finding, never found.
A thousand leaves have I been turning,
And still they fall to earth and ground.
A thousand camps have I made and broken,
And left behind me, needing none.
A thousand walls have I been building,
And never yet the one called home.

A thousand stars have I been sailing;
Ten thousand more still glow beyond.
Ten thousand times the sail re-set, then,
And the course...still...outward bound!

"Searching," translated from the works of
Homeworld warrior-poet T'arad-dyr

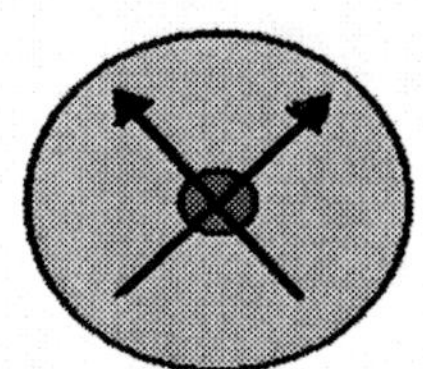

*Twenty-one....*Partings

BUT THE LAST three people did not go home to Arvien 4 as planned. The next declaration came from Dasrylion, who said, "I've decided to stay here with Sunrise until she has her baby. I feel that one of us should stay and bear witness."

Bear witness indeed, Renegade refrained from saying; *I know your reasons.*

Aloud, all he said was, "Whatever you wish, brother. K'leura and I will have to get the school ready for spring; and Burning Spear has promised to look for good Hunt teachers for us." They had decided to keep the school running as a living memorial to Broken Spear, and to find the best teachers they could for it.

Later Renegade confided to his wife, "I just hope we don't lose Dasryl to Rydderrak Clan, however much I like Burning Spear and Wise Woman. He's part of us. He belongs with us."

"Dasrylion belongs wherever he wishes to be, my hunter," she reproved him gently. "But I think he'll come back to us – and Sunrise wants to visit Arvien too, remember? Any-route, we have some work to do here first."

Renegade made a wry jaw movement. "I know. And it isn't going to be easy, leaving Arvien. I'm torn about leaving the school behind. I feel I should be there, carrying on in Broken Spear's name. But I really want to move all of us to the Twin Worlds, Blue One* in particular. Would it be a disservice to our people, leaving here?"

---

* The newly-discovered worlds were dubbed Blue One and Blue Two, at first.

"I don't think so," K'leura said; "you can serve our people from wherever you are, opening a new world as well as staying here. We have time."

"Not as much as we think," he replied, looking down at her fondly. For she was fertile – and pregnant – and Renegade in his newfound happiness discovered that yes, he could tell a baby was there, a fragment of glowing life attached to her uterine wall, that grew slightly every day.

"We should get back to Arvien first," he said; "we have to get the school ready."

So they went; and though the great hall was lonely at first, they soon warmed it with love and laughter: playing in the snow, exercising in the training room, bathing together, cooking all kinds of delectable meats.

With winter ending, Renegade showed her how to set the traplines, and they began collecting furs for a special project he had in mind. They slept in the old warrior's bedroom, and felt welcome there. Renegade sensed him as a spiritual presence in the hall, a good and kindly presence, as the man had been.

Barely two tendays later, they received a hyperlight message from Dasrylion: Sunrise's child had been born, a little delayed by star travel, but perfectly whole and healthy; and he definitely had his father's stamp upon him, though no milkteeth as yet. He had a short curly mane, light brown with touches of gold, like his mother's.

Sunrise had delivered without complications under a tented canopy cleansed by sweet-smoke, and thanks to Wise Woman's herbs, with very little pain.

The next sentence did not surprise Renegade at all:

"We will be with you in the spring," Dasryl wrote, "as soon as the baby can travel, for we are now husband and wife."

Even as they rejoiced over that message, they were anxious to hear from Rampage. But no message came.

Rampage had run into trouble after all.

Twenty-two....Rampage's Journey

DINOSAUR CLAN had changed its quarters, at least temporarily. The planet's lone research station forwarded Rampage some satellite maps and he located their tent gathering about 50 *kri-veh* from the clan's permanent camp. The hide tents were set on a low stony ridge above a forest. Marshy ground rimmed the coniferous trees below.

Rampage landed his borrowed Scout ship on a high flat spot and disembarked. Now that he was actually here, his urgency had given way to hesitation and doubt.

After all, who was he to ask for the clan leader's daughter? And what about K'orrynia? Had she forgotten him, or grown tired of waiting and chosen another?

The camp sentries had seen him, so he shouldered his extra backpack and raised an arm in greeting. The extra pack was full of gifts: a sloth-bear skin for High Sun, an amber bracelet for his wife, and a fancy skinning-knife for Flashing Sky, made of double-edged metal alloy for the blade and a bone handle set with gems.

He had something special for K'orrynia: a neck collar made with polished precious stones linked by a silver-shining chromium alloy. The stones were part of a gift from the Rydderrak Clan Leader to Kyva and her family. Something of a craftswoman, she'd used some of them to make the jewelry as a favor to Rampage on the trip over.

He felt inordinately grateful. He'd had nothing to exchange for it, but she'd smiled and said, "A betrothal gift for your 'Beautiful Girl,' Rampage."

Light-hearted again, he went to meet the clan hunter coming toward him and recognized Flashing Sky.

The Chief Hunter seized him by the upper arms, crying, "Arah! Esteemed Hunter – no, *Warrior* now, I hear. And you have grown, for we are now of a height, I see. Welcome back to our Clan!"

"I'm honored, Chief Hunter," Rampage said. "I've brought gifts – for you, for High Sun, and for"—

"...a certain young lady, I expect," Flashing Sky grinned at him. "Well, you are 'on the nock' for her, Rampage."

Rampage's face fell. The phrase had shadowed meanings. "You mean...I'm too late...?" he faltered.

"No, no, no," the Chief Hunter assured him. "I mean you have come just in time. Let's seek out High Sun. He's arranging the annual drive hunt; and you can speak to him yourself. We can present your gifts and your proposal later. But first we should announce you formally."

He laid an arm across Rampage's shoulders and led him away, saying, "*And* I have some payment saved from the fine furs you gave me to trade for you."

***

THE presentation took place quite a bit later. It had been near sunset when Rampage arrived; it was evening when he finally went before them all outside the clan leader's tent.

High Sun, his wife Golden Bird, the clan's High Shaman D'asault, Flashing Sky and K'orrynia herself waited in a rough semi-circle around the cooking fire.

This was the first time Rampage had seen any of them besides the Chief Hunter and Clan Leader since he'd arrived, but he noticed several good signs: K'orrynia was wearing her shining bird feather cape and she smiled at him. High Sun had an air of tension about him, but he gave the young man a warm glance, which must mean he was glad to see him.

Rampage greeted everyone formally and respectfully, standing before them this time, as befit a master hunter and warrior. Then he handed his gifts around. He hadn't expected to see the shaman, and was grateful to Flashing Sky for warning him and giving him a leather medicine pouch to present his gifts in... he'd scratched together some of the antiseptics and minor surgical tools that were routinely carried aboard the Scout ship (and he'd replace them at the first space station they came to afterward, he vowed to himself.)

The Clan Leader accepted his gift with solemn grace, while the others exclaimed over theirs. As Rampage wondered, *what's wrong? Doesn't he like it?* the leader turned the thick white pelt over in his hands as if examining it.

He wasn't really looking at it, though. He had other concerns, and when he spoke, they became Rampage's concerns too.

"I am honored, Esteemed Warrior Rampage," he told the young man. "When our daughter kept receiving gifts from off-world, we suspected something of your suit." He smiled a little then. "It is an honorable suit, and surely pleasing to our daughter."

Rampage brightened.

"However," High Sun went on, "there is more than one suitor; and this must be decided in some other way."

Rampage's heart sank again. More than one? Some other way?

High Sun glanced at him. Rampage looked stricken. Kindly, the leader said, "There is still hope, *vr'*warrior. Since my daughter seems undecided, I wish to be fair to everyone; so I will discuss the matter with our elders and see what can be done."

Rampage stared at K'orrynia. But for once she avoided his gaze. Her mother did not look happy, either.

High Sun continued: "In the short throw, we will have our annual drive hunt. Will you be pleased to stay and hunt with us, Rampage?'

"I would be honored," Rampage murmured, although he felt neither honored nor wanted. He excused himself from their circle and went out into the night, unaware of their sympathetic glances.

High Sun looked at his Chief Hunter.

"I'll go with him," Flashing Sky said, leaving at once.

He caught up with Rampage: "Young warrior, wait!"

Rampage paused. "Flashing Sky," he said in a toneless voice.

The other man put a hand on his shoulder. "You must not lose heart, Rampage. I know High Sun likes you. The other two suitors are clan members, and no other leader would have even considered your suit."

"Other two? At least-route there aren't twenty," Rampage said, glum. "What do you think they'll have us do – the elders, I mean?'

Flashing Sky shook out his mane. "It varies from clan to clan. Sometimes it's a hunt for the best trophy; sometimes a skill-shooting contest; sometimes a Challenge match, a fight. I don't know, here; it has never come up during my tenure."

To cheer him up, the Chief Hunter continued, "The drive hunt starts tomorrow. It's similar to those the freeholds call autumn drives. But I think you'll find it unlike any drive hunt you've ever seen."

He steered Rampage toward his own tent. "Now come sit by my hearth and tell me and my family about your adventures, Esteemed Warrior. You and your close-chosen are legends across the starworlds, did you know that?'

"We are? And did you say your 'family'?" Rampage perked up. *Hold; I'm beginning to sound like Renegade and all his questions – not that I mind.*

Flashing Sky laughed. "Yes and yes again. Star travel keeps you young, they say; apparently it makes you forgetful as well. Here we are," and he ducked inside the tent flap, Rampage following.

For the first time Rampage met Flashing Sky's betrothed, now his wife, a beautiful clan woman named Dreamspeaker. "She is our interpreter of dreams," her husband explained.

And they had two of the most stunning children Rampage had ever seen: the girl a toddler just learning to walk, the boy a babe in arms. They were a revelation in contrasts – the girl with jet-black skin and ruddy-gold hair, her slender body flashed with copper and gold striping; the boy just the reverse, shining golden-skinned and silver-maned, with narrow black striping from the back of his head down to his calves.

Rampage exclaimed over their beauty, earning a tender look from the mother. The father couldn't resist bantering, "I believe a warm brown mixed with silver and gold would create some outstanding children too."

"Husband!" his wife cried, scandalized yet amused; and even Rampage grinned.

"Come. Ignore him," she told their visitor. "Will you share meat and the hearth with us while you are here?"

And the rest of the evening passed with good food and exciting stories.

***

DINOSAUR DRIVE --- Rampage decided that when Flashing Sky said the hunt would be unlike anything he'd seen before, he'd hit the target dead-on..

They weren't just driving something like trey-horn or kai; they were driving dinosaurs.

They would start a huge herd of sauropods, more than 200 animals, and using every man, woman, and older child in the clan, they would encircle the herd and try to press it toward their permanent camp in the large blind canyon.

"The drivers will use power sleds and what skycycles we have," Flashing Sky told him, "and try to herd them along slowly for several days. The trickiest shot we take will be to stampede them at just the right time and squeeze them into the canyon, where a number can be killed to make a whole season's supply of meat. We will smoke or dry it to preserve it."

"Only *one* tricky part?" Rampage chuckled. "How are you even going to convince them to move in the first place?"

That's when the other hunter told him about the most incredible part…

"Some of the beasts are trained to accept riders."

"Riders!"

"Yes; the clan started working on this particular herd when the present adults were barely out of the egg, about five years ago. We didn't hunt them; we conditioned them to accept our presence in a non-threatening way. Then, as the young grew older, some of our people would get on their backs for a short time, then longer and longer."

"How do they – uh, *steer* them?"

Flashing Sky grunted. "*Chrrt!* They don't steer; not much, any-path. These are big herbivores with very long necks and tiny brains. Their riders have more success slapping them with thorny branches or the flat side of spears, striking them on one side or the other. The creatures barely notice; so the ground herders are still necessary. But the rider's presence accustoms them to having us underfoot. Does this sound interesting to you, Rampage?"

"Does it! I'm going to enjoy this."

The other smiled. "Good, because your fiancé is a dinosaur rider, one of the first, in truth. She almost received the name Dinosaur or Thunder Rider because of it; but her mother bared a tooth at that, and now others hold those names."

That *was* exciting news. Rampage definitely wanted to be in on this Hunt. He even volunteered to use the Scout ship in the drive. But after discussions with his leader and elders, the Chief Hunter decided the ship might cause the herd to stampede too early.

"Hold your throw until the last leg of the drive," he advised. "You'll do more good as a ground driver to begin with, and to help keep carnosaurs away as we go."

So here he was, resigned to his post on a low knoll, waiting for the clan hunters to herd the dinosaurs in his direction where he could help turn them for the box canyon. Once they turned – *if* they did – the drive became more dangerous, Flashing Sky told him, he could use his wristband signal to call his ship and board it for the final run.

K'orrynia a dinosaur rider! What a terrific adventure! What a dangerous one!

Just then he heard it, or rather, he *felt* it, a vibration in the ground. The vibrations got higher and sharper, until the ground actually began to shiver, and a low rumble of sound deepened to become a sky-crowding thunder. Rampage glanced left, toward the forest.

Dust billowed out between the tall trees. A vast dust cloud rolled up the trunks, and they were swaying…but they weren't tree trunks at all; they were separating from the trees, and becoming…

…Long thin necks as tall as the trees, swaying to a mighty drum roll…

They poured out of the forest, vast behemoth bodies with tree-stems for necks and tree trunks for legs, pounding, pounding the land to earthquake and the sky to thunder. A sea of them! A *world* of them!

Rampage stood too awestruck to move.

The gigantic bodies rumbled toward his knoll, and they were just *walking,* Rampage saw.

Now he could see something small on the huge beasts, just at the place where the neck meets the shoulder – figures, riders, *people* on some of those moving mountains.

High Sun was the lead rider, his spear lofted, his voice raised in a roar unheard through the tumult, his gold-and-silver mane streaming out behind him.

And then – was it *her?* Rampage strained forward to see the slim figure seated on another brontosaur further back, a magnificent banner of golden hair flying, spear brandished on high. What a wonder! What a sight – the tiny figures straddling the great beasts, jubilant with the Hunt.

Rampage stood breathtaken.

Suddenly, other figures broke out of the trees to either side of his knoll and ran towards the herd, roaring, whooping, screaming. Spears flashed, rockets hissed upward and exploded in mid-air as the other beaters came charging down.

Rampage woke up. He had to get in there – he couldn't fail his word – he had to be part of this. And he raced down the slope, roaring and yelling with the rest of them. *Turn them, but don't panic them,* the Chief Hunter had said; *although you will have enough trouble just getting them to notice you.*

He shot off his laser, pointed almost straight up, getting the bolts near their heads, hoping they'd notice and swerve. Through the dust cloud he could see a few of the riders futilely beating their mounts' thick skins on the right side – turn, turn.

Rampage was almost among them, a mote they'd never notice stepping on, when he thought of the *vai-ator*. In a flash, he had the golden disc out and the 'caster in his hand.

One toothed wheel shot into the sky, caught the sun like a mirror, and flashed in a dinosaur's eyes. The long neck pulled away, startled, and slowly the body followed.

Rampage let go. He gave everything he had to the challenge, leaping, running, screaming at them, "Chai'k hai! Hai! Hai!" and swooping the bright disc near their eyes, dinosaur after dinosaur.

Until finally under his and the other drivers' efforts, the whole herd began to turn, pressed over from the right side.

"Hai! Hai!" He ran and sprang and threw, glorying in his speed and his power. Not even the landshaking feet could touch him; he was faster and more graceful than any of them…he ran on and on.

"Ho, warrior! Ho, Rampage!" the Chief Hunter shouted. He ran up from the lee of the herd, slapped Rampage on the shoulder, and shouted, "Straight now – keep them straight, Rampage!"

Rampage came out of his hunting trance. He gave himself a shake, and signaled that he understood.

"Good! Well thrown!" the Chief Hunter cried. He fell back to harry the rear. He'd been on his feet since the drive began; the pace was too fast for him up here. But he grinned at the young warrior's. *Here is a worthy spirit, in truth.*

Rampage slowed his wild gyrations to a steady hunting jog, which he found kept up with the dinosaurs quite nicely. He donned his facemask, or the ground dust would have choked him, and settled in to run with the herd until another pack of drivers relieved this one. He might even catch a glimpse of K'orrynia, if he hurried forward a bit. He picked up his pace.

His People have no riding animals; have never ridden any, except for a few playful youngsters sometimes. The grown Hunters are simply too big and heavy for the backs of most creatures which are their natural prey – and those beasts that *are* bigger than they on Homeworld have tempers to match their size.

Except for these, Rampage mused. *Renegade thinks those horn-headed grass eaters on Blue One can carry us; but he really ought to see these dinosaurs. The only steeds we'll ever have that don't even feel our weight!*

Ah. Was that K'orrynia on that grayish-yellow sauropod ahead? He trotted faster. Yes, surely that was her long mane; and the big fellow two dinos ahead – that was High Sun. Rampage stretched out.

"Ho, K'orrynia!" he called as he drew alongside. Look at her, leaning back, spear raised, not deigning to cling to her massive mount, her body held free and proud. *She's magnificent!*

She turned in surprise. She glanced about, up, down, and finally saw the two-legged figure running along in the dust, knee-high to a dinosaur, and recognized the golden armor.

"Rampage!" she cried. She bent towards him and lowered her spear. "Come up!"

Ride a dinosaur? On-stat! He gave a quick glance ahead: less than a *kri-veh* from the next herders' relay. It would be on-stat to relax now. He sheathed his vai-ators one-handed and swung wide for a running jump.

K'orrynia watched him. He'd done an outstanding trophy hunt on her world five years ago; he'd been sending her rare and beautiful gifts ever since…but what she remembered best about him, what had really touched her, was the time she had helped heal him of his terrible wounds, and how he'd lain trustingly under her hands…the look on his face when he opened his eyes. These things mattered more than gifts or even hunting skill. He didn't know she was the clan leader's daughter then; but he'd fallen in love with her any-path.

She knew her other two suitors, had grown up with them. One was especially pleasing to her. But this plain outworlder, this Rampage…there was something about him…

Could he really jump up onto a dinosaur's back? Her father could, and a few of the grown hunters; but she always had to climb on, herself, ever since her dinosaur had grown so big. She smiled down at Rampage to encourage him.

Out on a tangent, Rampage gauged the height, then sprinted in hard.

A tremendous vault – "hunnh!" he grunted, hit the side high, then braced his arms and lifted himself up and astride the spine – *higher than the raptors' anthill,* he thought – and he slid down the curved back *whump* into K'orrynia.

She yelped, and laughed. Balancing, he laughed too. He was pressed against her back, arms spread a little, not knowing where to put his hands. She bent her elbows and he latched onto them gratefully.

She was shouting something.

"H'vack?"

She tipped her head back. Her hair whipped in his face.

"Your mask, take it off!" she shouted. "No dust up here!"

"Oh." He let go one arm, pried his mask off, and the thick soft curls of her mane, fluttered directly onto his face, soft-slapping him.

"*Arah*, K'orrynia!" he laughed. *No dust; lots of hair, though.* He leaned forward, his face nearly overlapping hers. The ground was a long way down.

"How do you like it?" she asked at an almost normal pitch.

"Riding? It's prime!" he enthused. "Like sitting on a really wide log with a moving mountain under you and a tree above."

"Yes, that's exactly it…when is your last turn at relay?"

"Near your regular camp. I'll call the ship there and try to stampede them into the draw."

"So you can stay on till then?"

Rampage felt light of heart. "You know, I can."

The young huntress gave a whoop of delight, and they both leaned into the dinosaur's stride, enjoying their closeness and the ride.

--Unlike the one who watched them with narrowed and envious eyes. He didn't enjoy it at all.

***

CLOSING THE CIRCLE---The hunt ended by mid-afternoon of the second day. They had kept the brontosaurs moving even at night, although more slowly; and Rampage could understand why almost every living soul in the Dinosaur Clan was needed for the hunt. Relays were quickly exhausted and the power sleds kept busy ferrying drivers to the front.

Night was an extra-dangerous time. No one got any sleep; and the riders dared not dismount except for a few moments, and then only for the most necessary functions. During the drive, they ate nothing and drank sparingly from the small water flasks they carried.

Rampage did his best to guide the huge animal when K'orrynia took a short break. The dinosaur actually had a name, she told him: it was Lady Gray.

"And she won't be killed with the food animals; I made sure of that," she said, pointing out a wide ring of yellow paint halfway up the long neck. "The riders will try to move to the extreme front and rear of the herd before the stampede—I couldn't sleep if something were to happen to her…I raised her almost from a hatchling."

So she regarded the huge beast as a pet – an endlessly hungry one at that, Rampage thought. Probably all the riders felt the same way. *You can't kill anyone you've grown to know,* he mused.

When K'orrynia returned from her break that night, Rampage relinquished his ride for a while to help scout outside the herd for prowling carnosaurs – not because he had to, but because he was feeling a little guilty about being away from his duty for so long. A few middling-sized predators approached on his side, but the hunters quickly chased them away.

A more serious attack came from the rear that same night, when a pack of raptors dashed in to hit a lagging young sauropod. Two people were injured; their certain deaths prevented by Flashing Sky's swift counterattack, leading some of his hunters. Still, that cost them the services of the two adults, the shaman needed to treat them, and the power sled that they had to be sent back home on. The baby brontosaur the raptors killed was salvaged and spirited away into the canyon.

Rampage dropped back too late to help combat the raptors, but Flashing Sky kept him there a while to talk.

"Two hurt," the Chief Hunter said; "we are doing better this year... sometimes this Hunt takes lives. What are you using for stamina, young warrior? You seem far fresher than I."

When Rampage told him about the dinosaur ride, he laughed heartily. "O wise suitor, to make work into an opportunity like that! Well, Rampage, I believe we'll need your spaceship tomorrow past high sun; so if you can break away by late morning and bring it to you..."

"I can, *vr'*hunter."

"Well thrown. Then begin your own drive when the herd is about one *kri-veh* from the canyon gate. This is the most dangerous part of the drive. Do it skillfully and you could save lives for us."

That brought him to today, here, a hard run north and west of the herd, which he'd made in his camo-suit to guard against attack by wandering predators; and the Scout descended toward him. The temporary clan camp itself was long gone back there on the ridge. As they'd left, they'd taken down every single tent and packed it aboard one sled or another. The tents were coming home with the drive.

Too bad they can't have the dinos pull the sleds with the tents on them, he mused. *Maybe I can suggest that later.*

Then the ship arrived and he boarded it.

He took the Scout high into the hard brilliant sky, against the sun, and tracked the herd by its vast traveling dust cloud. They were in territory he knew, passing the lake where he'd first seen the hadrosaurs – it was a major obstacle with thirsty animals; some stopped to drink – before moving on through thinning forest to the clan's holding....

He considered how to do this without getting anyone hurt. Visions of K'orrynia's steed tripping and falling under the rush of stampeding monsters tortured him. She and the other riders had already begun their evasive maneuvers—some so simple as to allow their animal to drink at the lake, or browse at a slower pace and fall behind....but they still could get caught in a stampede.

Finally he had a plan and poised there, overhanging the herd until it came close to the box canyon.

Then he dove. If he could split the herd and drive a smaller segment into the canyon, there'd be less risk to everyone. Flashing Sky had told him that even ten prime animals would be a good kill.

As the herd approached, an indentation began to form in that sea of swaying necks: the dinosaurs resisted the small rocky canyon, and were going to pass it on either side.

Rampage selected the right-hand "bulge" in the herd: it was smaller and he could see no riders on the great gray backs. He tilted the ship down toward the borderline animals. He flew at one of those heads, first diving hard at its left side, then skipping up and chivvying it from behind as well.

The sauropod resisted until it almost ran into the rock wall. Rampage swooped behind its head and clicked the Scout's capture jaws in and out. The big animal finally panicked and lurched into the canyon gate.

As Rampage hoped, several other dinosaurs followed it blindly. He gave them a nudge and flew back to peel more animals from the main herd. As he did, he saw he had help: several hunters on skycycles rose up from behind the herd and began to dive at the beasts as he had done.

It was like chasing starbeasts, only a lot slower, he realized, weaving in and out with the creatures, buzzing at their heads like some small angry insect. Slower it might be, but it still took all his skill to bring them home.

He saw ground herders scatter out of the way as the beasts swerved in their direction, and he risked ship and all to fly down in the dust and veer the big creatures away. Heads swung toward him and the dinos trumpeted a blast of sound that jarred him even through the canopy.

Finally he'd sent between 20 and 25 of them into the canyon, and he was able to pull back, praying he'd gotten no-one maimed or killed. *I hope they're shooting them in there,* he thought, rock-hopping his craft away from the herd and around the outer stone walls of the canyon.

At barely hover-speed, he eased the ship over the rim and peered into the bowl.

Pandemonium. Huge dinosaurs racing around in circles, crashing into each other, blinded by fear and herd instinct from finding the narrow way out.

He had to get down there. He parked the ship on somebody's stone roof and leaped out. He ran down the inclined stone path to the level of the dinosaur's heads, snatching up a vai-ator as he went. He surveyed the sea of swaying necks, hollow reeds in a breeze, chose a target, and threw.

The disc cut smoothly through the animal's neck. When it was on its way back, the whole body stumbled on for long moments before it finally came crashing down. Rampage danced along the rocks and swore, but he got no chance at a heart shot and had to let the ghastly dance continue.

Thereafter he would use laser or missiles.

He was picking another dinosaur when he realized the situation wasn't as chaotic as it looked. Bolts of laser-fire and the shriek of rockets came from along the walls – other hunters already stood in position there.

But where was K'orrynia? Or her father, for that 'cast? He'd tried not to herd in any of the ridden animals, but he might have missed one. He couldn't see much in the roiling dust bowl down there.

When it was finally over, eighteen adult sauropods lay stretched in death on the canyon floor. Rampage had accounted for three of them. Several juveniles had been spared and allowed to escape out the gap in the stone.

Rampage came down the wall a bound at a time until he reached he ground. More *tautschen* were entering the canyon now; and another phase of the hunt would begin: butchering mountains of dead dinosaur and packing it on power sleds for the short journey to the smoke-rooms and drying racks deeper inside the walls. Everything would have to be done before the inevitable scavengers gathered. Already he could see pterodons circling overhead, some of them sizable.

He was wondering what he should do next when the rest of the clan members began to arrive. Most were hunters and drivers, some of them now towing sleds. One, however, was a golden giant with two smaller people at his side.

"High Sun!" Rampage called out, running toward him. And the other two people, he saw, were his daughter and his Chief Hunter. They hadn't been in the canyon at all. The riders must have dropped off their mounts outside the walls and let them run on with the main herd.

The clan leader saw Rampage and beckoned. He said something aside to Flashing Sky, who nodded, turned around and looked back. The Chief Hunter raised his arms in an arc, then lowered them.

And two massive tall trees came swinging down sideways to lie across the canyon's entrance. Heavy mesh netting pulled across them had been plugged with brush to make the closure look natural. From the size of the trees, Rampage guessed they could keep out even the largest carnosaurs.

"Honored warrior," High Sun clapped him on both shoulders, nearly staggering him, "that was a noble chase! I did not know you were such an able pilot, too."

Rampage was pleased. "You do me honor, *vr'*Leader. I've never seen a drive like this. It was magnificent!"

The clan leader was in high good humor. "*Chak;* it makes for an epic spectacle, does it not? Perhaps we shall trade for a Scout ship for the next one. On any path, thanks to your skill; we have fewer injuries this year than before. Now, would you be of further help to us?"

"Gladly."

High Sun indicated the rock walls around them. "Then post yourself on this wall, Rampage, and help drive off those flying carrion eaters. They are at best a nuisance, at worst a danger to our children."

"I will, *vr'*Leader."

Before he left, though, Rampage glanced around for K'orrynia. She had not come all the way forward with her father, but fallen behind.

He saw her suddenly, perhaps a sauropod's length away, standing and talking to a young hunter as strikingly marked as she was. He was at least as tall as Rampage, and had much the same lean, wiry build – atypical of Dinosaur Clan.

High Sun followed Rampage's eyes and told him, "That is Dancer of Death, one of your rival suitors." He let the words hang, waiting to see what Rampage would do.

The young Arvien warrior swallowed hard, then gave a chinlift and left in the opposite direction. If he had thought himself to be the only one privileged to hold K'orrynia's attention, he knew differently now. *And he's much better-looking than I am...Dancer of Death, phht!*

He sought his post without another word.

High Sun took this in with a troubled gaze, before other business claimed him.

***

AFTER HE WAS relieved on the wall, Rampage still had energy to spend, so he decided to work with some of the flensers on the butchering crews. He disinfected his wristknives and set to work at the nearest vacancy, where clan members were cutting huge legs into steaks and roasts, barrel-ribbed sides into chops and racks.

To his surprise, everyone including the Chief Hunter and the Clan Leader and their families did the heavy work, cutting and trimming the meat and loading it on the power sleds, which would deliver it to the big smoking and drying chambers hollowed into the rock. There it would be processed for days and later divided among the clan members for their shares.

Rampage wasn't able to get near the carcass which High Sun and his family were working on, so he chose another, and he remarked on the labor to the man standing next to him.

The clan member seemed pleasant enough. "You are the outworlder, are you not, Esteemed Warrior? And this is your first Great Hunt?"

"My first with dinosaurs, honored one." Rampage used the common honorific, hoping the man would give him a clue as to his title.

"On-track then. You see, we must move all this meat indoors sometime tonight," the other went on, glancing up, "or the local predators will be on us in force…and already it is twilight." He tugged at a particularly tough piece of flank; Rampage reached over and incised it neatly with his knives.

The other looked at him, surprised. "Thank you, *vr'*warrior. My own blade is too dull—and my talons not tough enough to skin this."

"Call me Rampage," the Plains warrior offered, taking a sheaf from Renegade's book.

The other man smiled. "And I am Voice of Dawn. I am a Clansinger, as is my mate, here. ..Tsa'lura (Sweet-singer)," he made a head motion at the woman beside him.

She called back cheerfully, "I'm honored, noble Rampage! Voice of Dawn, where are your manners? Greet him properly."

"I *would* greet you properly, Rampage, but my manners are up to their wrists in gore," he glanced ruefully down at his hands.

"No trouble; I greet you, *v'*clansingers," Rampage said graciously, and took the other man's wrists in his hands.

After that, the group around the carcass relaxed and treated him as a friend. Introductions made the rounds. The clansingers' brother was present but their young daughters were under the grandparents' care in their lodge. There was another pair of artisans, stonemasons, working on the sauropod, along with a youth, near to his Master Hunt.

It seemed they all knew about Rampage and his quest for K'orrynia's hand, and were willing to share what they knew.

"There are three of you seeking that privilege. No one knows whom the Lady K'orrynia favors; she keeps it in eclipse," Voice of Dawn said. "We hear it will result in a Challenge match between you, one pair at a time."

Rampage perked up. "A Challenge? A fight, then?"

"Churr – and you have worthy opponents," the man said; "Dancer of Death and White Bull."

"Tschk!" his wife put in. "I don't trust that White Bull, myself; he skims too near the edge of the Code, without actually running over it."

Rampage went taut with attention. He remembered only too vividly seeing Renegade nearly suffocated inside clear, fortress-like walls – *and neither of my friends is with me now,* he thought.

"Your Circle – is it closed?" he asked abruptly.

The clansinger was surprised. "No, warrior, it is an open circle in the dirt, scratched anew each time – though there have been few times it was used in my memory."

He looked at his wife. "T'salura, now you'll have him thinking our hunters are an ignoble lot. You know Dancer of Death is one of our finest young warriors…and I have never *observed* White Bull to be less than honorable."

"Chak, but he ends up on the winning side too near the mark, too often," Sweetsinger grumbled. "I was surprised High Sun even considered an outworlder at first, but we already have an out-clan Chief Hunter, and then, we didn't know *you* were the suitor, Rampage. We remember your trophy hunt."

Rampage felt blood-heat rising in his chest and face, and bent to his work hastily.

Tsa'lura's next words reprieved him: "The Clan Leader would sorrow to lose his daughter off-world, but he thinks highly of you, noble warrior."

He does? News to Rampage.

"…so much so he even had us compose a ballad about your hunt."

"A ballad? About *me?*" Rampage had no clear idea of what clansingers sang about, before. Now he knew.

"Yes," Voice of Dawn put in, "a very fine one. It has everything, from striving and despair to triumph and victory. Would you like to hear it?"

"T'churr, that might seem a little self-serving." Rampage loved praise, but the thought of his initial failure being broadcast over the multitude…

"He's correct, husband. Let us sing, any-path," Tsa'lura remarked. "We have been silent too long."

They chose a song about their clan's voyage here from Homeworld, and the hardships they faced, and the names of those who had died. It began mournfully at first, but finished on a paean of triumph with their survival on the new world.

Soon everyone at the brontosaur except Rampage had joined in; and he was content to listen.

Torches were lit against the darkness in the canyon. The song, sweet and strong and clear, carried across the circle until the rest of the clan picked it up; and their voices, honed by their wonderful ability to mimic and call game, made the sound into a divine choir, and filled the killing field, transforming it to hallowed ground.

After that song came another and another, with Rampage joining in the choruses, and so on to the end of their labors.

Like other clans, like even freehold hunters everywhere, the Dinosaur members used every part of the animal they could: the tough skins would make tents and body leathers; the massive bones were used as building blocks, foundation stones for the large ones, the ribs as tent frames, and the spinal vertebrae stacked to make ancestor poles and religious topiaries. The sinew of course went into thread, ropes and surgical lacings; smaller bones became weapons such as spears, knives and arrows for those who could not afford high-tech weapons. Even the hoof-like toenails were melted down into glue or cut up and boiled for teething babies' chew-toys.

The only parts the people here could not preserve well were the organ meats – the hearts, livers, and sweetbreads went into huge cooking pots the same night, and were tended over relentless fires. The rest of the offal they carted out over the walls and dumped a distance away. There, the scavengers could have it.

The cooking fires burned hot and long that night. Clear white smoke funneled to the sky from the canyon floor and from vents in the walls, where the ovens worked in the stone.

The combination of a hard drive and heavy work mixed with the oxygen-taking fire to make them all dizzy and tired. Rampage had long ago taken off his body armor and was now totally besmirched with blood and grime – *messier than cleaning a hundred Sloth-bear carcasses,* he thought.

Finally they loaded the last power sleds and stood, woozy, around a blood-soaked valley floor, having picked up and burned the last tiny scraps of hide and gristle they could find.

High Sun called a halt then, just a few *tare'* before dawn.

"Enough," he told each crew in turn; "We will bring the sand loads in later today to cover the ground. It is time to rest now."

He came to Rampage's group, and the young hunter was startled by a strong hand falling on his shoulder.

"Enough, good people," the deep voice said. "We have made a season's work in a single night, and your singing has carried us through. Well done."

He smiled at the tired young man before him. "And you, honored guest, have given and earned more than a hunter's portion. We are deeply grateful. Our worthy clansingers can take you to the volcanic pools, where you may bathe before sleeping."

"Hot – baths, leader?" Rampage said, near exhaustion.

High Sun gripped his shoulder more firmly to steady him, and smiled again. "Yes, in truth, *vr'rakash.* We have them inside the stone. Go. You have earned it. –Flashing Sky?" to the Chief Hunter close at his heels.

"Yes, High Sun?" The big Shadow hunter sounded even wearier than before.

"Your hunt-packs too deserve a rest. Bring them down from the walls and the butchering, and let them bathe, then sleep. We will put some of our elders on the walls tonight."

"Thank *you, vr'*Leader," the Chief Hunter breathed; then said to Rampage, "If I do not see you in the baths, young warrior, remember to come to our lodge afterward, where a comfortable bed awaits you."

"I will. I'm honored, Chief Hunter."

"Until later then," and he and the leader's family moved on to the next group. Rampage was so tired he hadn't even noticed if K'orrynia was with them.

***

THE VOLCANIC POOLS consisted of more than a few scattered basins inside the stone; they were a whole series of hotwater ponds, grottos and one large underground lake, where you could bathe as publicly or as privately as you liked. This complex, in the easily-defended box canyon, was why thc clan lived here.

"We can pipe the hot water straight through our homes on chilly days," Voice of Dawn told Rampage. "No nuclear power, some solar power, and only a little wood burning for our hearthfires now and then supply our energy for us."

"It's a great system," Rampage enthused, then submerged entirely and came out gasping, "Roah! I think the entire comfort of civilized life depends on its supply of hot water."

The other man laughed. "A good thought – many share it tonight." The lake and its offset pools were crowded. It looked like almost all of High Sun's 1800 clan members were soaking here.

"What magnificent hair!" Sweetsinger admired as Rampage unbound the full length of his smoke grey hair-tail and let it hang. "I know most hunters prefer to wear their manes long, but yours is exceptional."

"You honor me, milady," he replied. "Most do; I just wanted mine to be distinctive. Would anyone object if I rinsed off under one of those little waterfalls?"

They assured him no one would; and he waded over to one of the tiny falls, backed in, and let the heated water pour over his scalp and down his long trailing mane. He tilted his head so the water ran from front to back, reversed it, and finally sank to his knees to let it rinse down his spine.

While kneeling, eyes closed in enjoyment, he heard a deep shouting from the lake edge beyond. He opened his eyes ...definitely a loud, deep voice talking, booming over the softer sounds of people bathing.

The moment he saw him, Rampage knew who it was:

An albino giant, white skin so pale you could see greenish-blue veins running beneath it...Rampage didn't need to hear someone call him by name to know that this was –

"White Bull! Ho! What did you do in the Hunt?"

The albino thundered, "Do? Why I chased scavengers, shot carnosaurs, and took down two of the pine-eaters with my own gun!" He shrugged out of his armor and loincloth, and lowered himself into the simmering pool.

Someone added slyly, "They say your 'Dinosaur Rider' spent a day teamed with the outworlder," and Rampage's throat tightened.

The giant gave a bellowing laugh – *he's nearly as big as High Sun, as big as Broken Spear was* – and rumbled, "What do I care what he does now? Let him spend a few *kt-tare'* in the circle with *me,* and she won't see him again!" And his cronies echoed his mocking laughter.

Rampage's body called on his reserves, his muscles swelled, his eyes went laser-hot, and he began to raise himself from the water...

"Warrior." The tone was quiet but commanding. Rampage jumped and whirled, sloshing water. He faced Flashing Sky – and his rage was checked.

The Chief Hunter touched his upper arm. "Not now, Rampage; you will have your chance later. I like him no more than you do. His size and strength make him a braggart and a bully. But for you to act now, while you're tired..."

"He must be tired, too," Rampage said, low. His intensity made the Chief Hunter pause.

Then Flashing Sky nodded toward the group of youths rough-housing in the water.

"Look at him. Does he *look* tired? Is he covered with the soil of honest labor, as you were? No. What he says is true, as far as you can draw a short string: however, he hung back at the rear, to shoot his carnosaur – only one – from a power sled. He walked little; and he shot so recklessly from the walls of the canyon that his two 'kills' were only maimed, and had to be finished off by other hunters. He is fit, yes, and muscular too; but he is lazy, and a thorn in my foot, and I have constant discipline problems with him."

The Chief Hunter let go his arm and sighed, "Forgive me for speaking so harshly of another, Rampage; but in a fair fight I think you will have no trouble defeating him."

"—And in an unfair one?"

"We will all be there – High Sun, the shaman, the Clan Elders, and I – to ensure that it *is* a fair fight." He shook water droplets from his mane and bowed his head. His weariness returned. "In future I may have to Challenge him myself; who can say? Let fall Chance, and the Great Spirit guide us all."

Rampage felt repentant. "My behavior was improper, Chief Hunter; I ask your pardon."

"No…I take no offense, Esteemed Warrior. Come; let's go to my lodge. Dreamspeaker has gone ahead of us –and I for one could use some sleep."

So Rampage damped down his anger and followed Flashing Sky home.

His late energy-boost had sapped him more than he knew. No sooner had he eased down into the soft-padded hammock in his private alcove than he was asleep, all his cares forgotten. He did not even know if he dreamed.

***

DINOSAUR CLAN lay in a stupor most of the next day, leaving only a few mothers, elders and juveniles to stand watch or tend fires.

The clan members began rising from their beds near sunset, and the first thing they did, other than care for infants, was to gather round the communal cooking fires to eat the long-simmering stew.

The stew was hot, tasty, spiced with herbs and filled with well-done chunks of organ meat which had been sliced in the night before. Rampage sat with the Chief Hunter's family and devoured his portion.

"Have more, have *enough,*" Dreamspeaker urged him, and he gave in to her, replenishing his bowl every time the main trencher passed by, until he'd had three bowls full.

Their meal over, a happy lull settled over the Dinosaur Clan. They had worked hard; they had fed well; they were content.

Finally High Sun arose from his place on the circle.

"People of the Hunt," he began, his great voice filling the stillness. "I would speak to you."

Rampage felt a thrill run along his back and arms. *Here it comes...*

"First as your leader, I congratulate you, every one whose bravery and endurance, whose willingness to serve, made our hunt so successful this year. Eighteen prime animals were taken. They will bring us enough meat to last through the dry season and the season beyond. No one will be hungry this year."

A roar arose. He waited it out.

"A few days following our great work, we usually have our Hunt Supper, with meat, music, dancing and song enough to please everyone. This year, the Hunt Supper will be the occasion for an even greater feast..." he paused, and it seemed to Rampage that the chieftain was struggling with emotion. "For at that same time, my only daughter will be married" – a terrific roar of approval – "to the winner of a series of Challenge matches..." greater uproar..."between three young *tautschen* who wish to wed her."

Another pause, and his burning gaze seemed to pinpoint Rampage:

"The Challengers are: our fine young warrior Dancer of Death" (*huge* uproar) the Master Hunter White Bull" (a noisy contingent of his followers broke out – other support was subdued, Rampage noticed) – "and the Esteemed Hunter and Warrior Rampage, from Arvien 4."

"Aroaah!" came from Flashing Sky, along with a warbling trill of approval from his wife, and loud calls from the crafters' contingent. Rampage flushed with gratitude to them – *more cheers than for White Bull, any-route, even if I'm not the favorite here.* He inclined his head graciously: *I thank you for your kindness, good people, one and all.*

The clan leader continued, "...draw the bones to determine order of battle in the place where honor demands, under the shadow of the spear. One match will take place at a time with the winner of the first to take on the second challenger, fighting unarmed to full Surrender. The ultimate winner shall wed my daughter. So be it. Will the challengers step forward? "

Quietly Rampage rose and went before High Sun. He looked around at his opponents: Dancer of Death was studying *him*, he found, while White Bull merely gave him a contemptuous downward glance, then stood staring haughtily ahead. It occurred to Rampage that the Dancer might be the more competent of the two. At least he was doing what the Arvien warrior would be doing himself: sizing up the competition.

High Sun held up a carved bowl which he said contained two short slivers of bone and one long. Short draws fought each other first; long draw fought the winner of that match. The chieftain passed the bowl before each young man in turn, holding it above eye level.

Rampage and the Dancer drew short bones. White Bull gave a *chak* of satisfaction at the long. He would have time to watch them now, to plot his strategy between matches.

Rampage's immediate opponent surprised him by being the first to turn to him and incline his head, saying, "I shall be honored to Challenge you, noble warrior," quite mildly and politely, no mockery or anger in him.

"And I am honored to accept, Esteemed Warrior," Rampage bowed his head in turn, his tone matching the other's for courtesy. He found no hatred in his heart for this man; and he suddenly felt confident that Dancer of Death would do everything by the rules, and conduct himself with honor.

The clan gave a full-throated roar or approval as the two young hunters spoke so nobly to each other, and parted to let them return to their places.

White Bull had already gone. He could bide his time.

K'orrynia watched them depart. And what was in her heart, no one could tell.

***

RAMPAGE EXPECTED to spend a restless night. But his host family offered him a cup of hot citrus and sat talking at their own hearth until he almost nodded off. Then Flashing Sky ushered him gently to bed, and he had a second peaceful night.

"You favor him, don't you?" the Chief Hunter's wife smiled at her husband.

"Yes," Flashing Sky said, "I suppose I do. I know what it is to be an outsider and adrift in this life."

"Though not any more?" she asked, taking his arm.

"Not any more," he answered; and they went to their own room.

The night ticked by.

Twenty-three....The First Challenge

NEXT MORNING Rampage descended the canyon after bathing, dressed in nothing but the standard loin-and breechcloth, wearing no wristknives or even shinguards to protect himself, and feeling vulnerable and alone. He did something unusual for him, offering up a small prayer to the Spirit-of-all for battle readiness.

"Allow me to fight well, if it is your will," he prayed, "and to acquit myself with honor before my enemies..." And feeling a little less lonely, he went down to the canyon floor.

High Sun was there with his wife and daughter, the old shaman, the clan's elders –and most of Dinosaur Clan. Awake and waiting for him. High Sun greeted him and called for quiet.

The leader began by hurling a spear into the air with all the force of his mighty arm. Rampage watched it as it dwindled...higher...higher...out of the canyon walls of shadow into the morning sky. Finally it poised in space, then slid backwards, the point tumbling as it fell.

It hit the ground at shattering speed not twenty *kri* from where the Clan Leader stood. A rattle of excitement went round the crowd. The spear had driven in for nearly half its length.

Two Elders brought another spear, tied with a long tail of twine, and affixed this string to the shaft of the first spear. One Elder stretched it taut at full length and made a circle in the dirt with the point of the second spear.

It rounded out amazingly close to the size of T'akaion's stone circle, so long ago. *I lost then, but I was hot-headed, and afraid,* Rampage thought, *I won't make those mistakes again.*

The leader called the fighters into the circle, had them each touch the central spear shaft and stand an arm's-width apart. Courteously they acknowledged each other. Then they crouched into a fighting stance, their heads up and they *watched.*

Rampage stared into a level gaze as alert and assessing as his own.

(Flashing Sky had told him that morning, "I cannot divulge too much, Rampage, but Dancer of Death is a far better foe than White Bull. I can only tell you to think of his name, and what it means.")

Think of his name – in the fleeting moments before the call, Rampage looked into the eyes of a young warrior as alert as he, as lean and wiry as he, and knew what that meant…*Dancer…*

A martial artist, as he was…*he might be facing his twin in expertise…*

"Begin."

And the two moved, side-stepped around the pole, two great cats circling, wary, waiting to strike, knowing the first to do so would lose his advantage…

The Dancer feinted. Rampage matched him, then twitched aside as if to lunge, and his foe flicked backward and *came in…*

And Rampage, who had been worried only about White Bull, knew that here was his real opponent, the only one who could beat him in a fair fight – if he let him.

The Dancer made a half-spin snap-kick; Rampage blocked it, countered with a low kick. The other, barely touched, slid away.

The crowd gave an appreciative *churr.* Something special was happening. Something epic. A battle between two champions, and they would witness it.

The Dancer spun back into an arm-chop; Rampage dodged, followed in along the out-thrust arm, and his foot connected. A gasp came from his foe and from the crowd.

Rampage whirled in fast, threw another kick, had his heel blocked, and took a fall. Air *whuffed* from his lungs. But he brought his other foot up fast and kicked his opponent's arms away. Then he snap-rolled to his feet and came in with a blinding series of hand-chops –

-- which the Dancer not only survived, but managed to throw back some of his own.

Rampage was stunned. He had *never* met a fighter of his caliber in the past 13 years. Until now.

The flurry over, they backed off in a fighting crouch, re-appraising each other.

"You're – everything your ballad has you to be," the Dancer told him, surprising him again.

He stared; there was no mockery here. "They'll be writing ballads about *you* someday," he returned, never taking his eyes off the other hunter. *Observation without distraction.*

Outside the fringe the crowd roared its approval.

The fighters circled, circled. Rampage reined himself in. *Wait for him. Wait for him. Wait...*

The Dancer broke first. Slide, side-step, high kick.

Rampage blocked it without much trouble and jerked at the out-flung leg. His opponent tried to grab him and pull him in, got off a quick arm-chop, then lost his footing.

Quick. Stay with him. Like Renegade had years ago, Rampage moved to close. His opponent rolled. Rampage sprang over him, met him at the end of his roll, fell on him.

The Dancer exploded into a whirlwind of bucks, punches and knee-jabs. When Rampage caught his arms and pinned them, the Dancer flexed his knees and shoved him off.

Rampage snapped to his feet, his opponent just a hair slower. *Now.* He wheeled into a two-step, kick and spin.

It barely flicked his opponent's shoulders; he was that fast. He caught Rampage's next kick, then back-spun his leg, bringing the Arvien warrior within his reach.

Neck lock. Bright with danger, Rampage dropped to the ground, reached up, grabbed his opponent and threw him forward, slicking out of the hold. *Too close.*

They both staggered to their feet. Their breaths were whistling now. *Who tires first, loses...* Rampage feinted high, sprang in low. He hit the Dancer waist-high, and they both came down.

To Rampage's shock, the Dancer recovered first and fell on the Plains warrior's back, trying to bend one leg backward while he kneed the ribs down.

A spasm of pain shot through Rampage as he strained to free his leg. *Burn and blast it, same trick as Renegade,* he thought, *only backward. Don't I ever learn?*

"Do you surrender?" the Dancer rasped, pushing and pulling on him.

"Why?" Rampage grunted. He gathered his strength. "The fight's... only *begun..."* and he collapsed under his foe, jerking his unharmed leg up and hooking him under one arm. The Dancer, off-balance, tipped forward, and Rampage jack-knifed under him, got a leg lock, and put his shoulders down.

From the other's shocked expression, Rampage guessed he'd never had this happen to him. Now if only he could keep this hold until he rolled completely over…

Too slow. And speared by pain – *there's something sprained in that leg, I know it,* Rampage thought just as the Dancer writhed out of his grasp. Rampage gave a quick twist, got to his feet, then fell to one knee as the pain stabbed him.

To his amazement, the foe didn't jump right in and pin him. The Dancer was standing half-crouched, breathing hard, and waiting. Rampage stared at him. *Why not?* his expression asked.

The Dancer gave a negative head-motion and said clearly. "I regret… the injury. You are…too noble an opponent… to defeat that way."

Rampage's eyes stung. With care and grace, he rose to his feet. "If I am," he said, "it's because you are, too."

And the two stared at each other in recognition as beyond them the crowd went wild.

They circled again. Rampage's knifepoint muscle pain ebbed. This time he moved faster: the Dancer made a swift arm thrust but with his great speed Rampage caught it, dropped one shoulder, and sent him flying.

He landed hard, but just outside the circle. Rampage had gained a new kind of respect: he waited, and the Dancer slowly got to his feet and re-entered the circle.

"Warrior," his foe whispered, "we must…*finish*…this."

"In the place where honor demands," Rampage answered, his mouth quirked. He waited longer.

Both fighters moved more slowly now. They had almost forgotten what they were fighting about. Each recognized the spirit in the other, and that except for this one issue, they might have been friends…

When the Dancer made another foray of hand-jabs, Rampage took a few blows, then repaid them with a solid punch to the diaphragm. The Dancer gasped and buckled, looking for breath. Rampage got a shoulder under him and pinwheeled him through the air. The other warrior landed hard on his back on the packed dirt. This time he did not get up. He was wheezing, his hand to his chest.

Rampage went to him. His anger was gone. He hoped he had not maimed this noble foe. He knelt by the Dancer's side and reached out to touch him. Though he was heaving for breath, his skin color was good, so he wasn't suffocating, thank the stars. Now what?

Rampage laid a token arm across his throat. He bent over him.

"Dancer, honored warrior?" he asked softly.

The youth's other hand slipped down. His head turned aside. The Surrender.

A shadow fell over them. Rampage looked up.

"This fight is over," High Sun declared.

"I'll stay here a while," Rampage said.

The clan leader nodded. "You have my respect, *vr'*warrior," and he inclined his head once. He moved off.

Rampage became aware of a commotion from the crowd. But his attention lay with his fallen foe. He had long ago removed his arm from over the Dancer's throat. Now he just wanted to be sure the other hunter was all right.

Dancer of Death's breathing gradually slowed. His consciousness returned. Rampage put a hand on his shoulder.

The other's eyes opened. He found himself staring up at Rampage. "The fight…it's…?" he began.

"Over," Rampage said. "It's over."

The Dancer turned his head away, squeezing his eyes shut. His breathing roughened. Rampage felt a pang for him.

Finally from under tear-laden eyelids the other whispered, *"I—love her..."* and his voice broke.

Rampage's throat constricted. His opponent's anguish became his own. Ludicrously, he felt he should apologize. Instead he murmured, "I know, worthy one…so do I."

He sat back to allow the defeated man to get to his feet alone, so he would not be shamed further. He rose at the same time and watched as the Dancer walked to the edge of the ring.

Friends and family were there to receive him. As he let the other hunter go, Rampage felt he had to add something.

"Noble warrior," he said, almost apologizing, "at this time or any other time, I am proud to know you."

The other gave a long, shuddering breath, and with his head down, passed into the arms of his kindred.

To inflame Rampage's guilt still further, one of *them* gave him a sober, "Well-fought, warrior."

Rampage turned away. He ignored the victory cries and the shouts of congratulation, and found a small flat rock to sit on outside the circle. He was dreadfully tired. His thigh muscle once again spasmed with pain. The fight had taken just about everything he had.

Another presence beside him. Another hand to his shoulder. And Flashing Sky said quietly, "Well done, Rampage. Well done and nobly done. You make me proud…"

(I am so proud of you all)

Rampage looked up. "Honored,, Flashing Sky, but I'm glad it's over. He's the best fighter I've ever seen…I don't think I have another move left in me. It took them all."

His friend chinlifted. "You can rest now. The other Challenge will take place tomorrow or the day after, when your leg has had time to heal."

Out in the circle, High Sun was making a similar announcement.

"And so we shall adjourn this contest until" – when someone interrupted him:

"No. I Challenge NOW."

Twenty-four....White Bull

RAMPAGE stiffened. So did the Chief Hunter. A murmur went through the assembled clan.

High Sun's gaze hardened as White Bull stepped forward.

"You do what?" growled the Clan Leader, shaken out of context.

White Bull could almost look him in the eye. "I Challenge *now.* I will fight him immediately."

High Sun reacted as if slapped. His eyes seared the other's, lowering them.

"I protest!" Flashing Sky stood up straight with anger. "The other Challenge has just finished! This warrior is injured; he must have healing."

White Bull slid him a mocking glance. His tone was snide. "You have no grounds, *O Chief Hunter.* Tell me where *in the Law* it says the Challenges must be separated in time."

Dissension. Uproar. Rampage could see K'orrynia on her feet, clutching her mother's arm. She looked beseechingly from mother to father.

"Husband," the wife began.

"High Sun," came from Flashing Sky.

The Clan Leader held up his hands, palms and talons curved out, as if to ward them off. "I am too close to this," he said. "If there is a provision in Hunt Law or our clan custom, our Elders will know it. I will consult with them – go back outside the circle!" A curt command to White Bull, almost a challenge itself.

The albino backed away.

Rampage had a sinking feeling. He *knew* how this would go. Slowly he began to rub the pulled thigh muscle. His arms quivered with weariness.

Flashing Sky muttered, "We'll see about this," and strode off to the conclave.

The debate was heated but short. At its end, Flashing Sky and High Sun both looked in his direction – and their eyes held pity.

I knew it, Rampage thought. He stopped the massage and began taking the slow deep breaths of tch-won'. *To victory or death.*

Both High Sun and his Chief Hunter came to him…

"I know," he told them. "It's gone against me. Thank you for trying, any-route."

High Sun gave him a glance keen with sympathy. "I regret this, *vr'*warrior."

"And so do I," Flashing Sky added. "But the Elders could find nothing specific either way, and they decided it must go on. Now you will have to fight…again."

High Sun left to announce the decision. Flashing Sky sat down next to Rampage and laid an arm across his shoulders. He could see the heat of that pulled muscle quite clearly.

"Rampage," he said, low, "I can't even get you a healing potion from the shaman; it isn't allowed. I can only beg you to remember an old Hunting axiom…"

Despite himself, Rampage smiled. "I know a lot of old Hunting axioms. Which one?"

"The one which bids 'Strike hard, strike fast, strike home.'" Flashing Sky said. "Take him out quickly. Be merciless. Do whatever is needed. The People's every sentiment goes with you…even Dancer of Death speaks for you."

Rampage nodded. Even now a rumble of anger vibrated through the crowd, from all except White Bull's supporters, who thought he was clever. Glancing at them, Rampage said, "I'll try. One thing: Flashing Sky, can you make sure they *search* him? I don't want him carrying any concealed weapons into the circle."

"Good. I'll request that at once," and he left.

Rampage stood, stretched slowly.

In a moment, White Bull was searched in a very public manner by two elders. He glared across at Rampage, furious.

Rampage returned the glare with a haughty glance like the albino's own. *Good – do you like it? Get mad. Get careless too.*

As he expected, White Bull returned the 'favor,' with a similar demand. Two Elders approached Rampage and did the same to him, but less publicly, with many a "forgive us, noble warrior," and "your pardon, esteemed one." Rampage kept his head high and bore it stoically. He let his anger build. He would need its energy.

Then he was called to the circle. High Sun still presided, but everything in his posture spoke of a great rage barricaded within.

As soon as Rampage started to move, the muscle spasm returned with a vengeance. His entire body had stiffened up and was aching after his short rest. He refused to limp or give in to his pain. Let his opponent see no weakness in him.

He was aware of people speaking to him as he passed...the Clansingers and even others he didn't know, touching him lightly, wishing him well. He thanked them softly, almost totally detached, and focused on White Bull.

He studied his enemy as they both stood before High Sun, noted the strange greenish-white skin, the powerful body it covered. *He's strong and he's fit. I can only hope his weight makes him slow.* He also had some kind of tooth implant, extra canines thrusting up behind his ordinary ones. *Great; he'll probably try to bite me.*

They stood at center-circle, hands on the spear pole. Rampage's yellow eyes glowed with his intensity, trying to intimidate his opponent – *kind of hard to do when he's a head taller than you...*

"Begin" – and White Bull lashed out at once.

He struck air. Rampage had been expecting it and dodged aside. He ducked back in close and brought both hands up, knife-edge, under the foe's armpit.

Churrr, the crowd said. The bigger man yelped with sudden pain. His opponent had moved unbelievably fast...

Rage seized him. He bellowed and rushed the other warrior.

Rampage dodged again, a little slower this time, and his strained muscle throbbed when he shifted his weight onto it.

White Bull was not without skill, for he lashed out sideways and struck Rampage a glancing blow. The Plains warrior moved quickly to restore his balance, just as the big hunter lunged on top of him.

Rampage yielded to the momentum, fell backwards, and with arms and legs braced, directed White Bull on over him in a flying throw.

The albino fell with a thud and a grunt, and Rampage landed on hands and knees beside him. *Finish it. Finish it now.*

Propped on his still-uninjured arms, he pivoted to kick sideways with both feet. *T'churr! Like kicking a rock!* White Bull went down, though, and the crowd went mad.

Rampage lurched up on his knees and swung both arms down in a hard chop to the neck. The other grunted, but his head came right back up. *Not good enough.* Rampage's tired arms were losing strength.

He tried to leap up, to throw himself on the other's back, but a bolt of pain shot through his left thigh and his leg collapsed. He hissed with pain, and as he struggled to stand, White Bull loomed up before him.

"What's the matter, little one?" the giant sneered, "Your leg hurt?" And his huge hands reached for the warrior's throat, while his clan howled in anger at the tactic. *No honor there.* Rampage let himself fall away on his weak leg, and kicked out sharply with his stronger one. He knocked White Bull's leading leg out from under him, then rolled away as his enemy fell forward.

He was clear. Rampage shoved himself to his knees, but his head was yanked back sharply. *What?*

White Bull had seized his long hair-tail, and pulled on it.

The trick was so unexpected that Rampage was pulled backwards without resistance, straight into his enemy's powerful arms. Immediately his breath was crushed from him and he saw flashing lights. He gagged and twisted, helpless.

A tremendous blow fell – on White Bull – and his arms broke away from the warrior's throat. Rampage fell to his knees, gasping.

"IF I TELL YOU AGAIN, YOU FORFEIT!" High Sun stood between them, holding the big albino off the ground and shaking him. The he tossed him ten *kri* away, effortlessly, to the raucous approval of the crowd. Incensed by the hunter's dishonorable tactic, the clan leader had intervened.

Deliberately he turned his back on White Bull, who stood rubbing his own throat, looking humble. Quite normally, even kindly, High Sun asked Rampage, "Can you stand, *vr'*warrior? Can you continue the fight?" Sadly.

He's giving me a track out...but he'll lose his daughter to that beast... and so will I. Rampage nodded. "I...can stand, *vr'*Leader," he croaked. "I will fight."

The crowd burst into a lung-splitting roar. High Sun lifted his chin, once. For a brief moment, his eyes caught Rampage's; and the warrior saw both respect and sympathy there.

The clan leader gave Rampage a moment to struggle to his feet and stand there, swaying, before he moved away.

The two fighters confronted each other again. Rampage had never felt so tired. Every fiber of his being cried out for rest, and his body hurt in a hundred places. But he could not abandon K'orrynia to this beast. He wondered groggily if White Bull had somehow 'arranged' the bone draw in his favor – by palming the long bone, maybe? He decided High Sun would have caught it, though. ...His mind was straying...

Suddenly White Bull rushed him and he had to act. The powerful shoulder met his half-blind retreat, and knocked him down onto his side. One last try – diaphragm jab – White Bull fell on him and the hunter's midsection met the warrior's fist and knees. He yawped and was dislodged.

Rampage squirmed out from under. But that was all he had to give. Exhausted past all endurance and in constant pain, he tried to get a vise-lock on the albino's head, but White Bull threw him off with laughable ease.

On his back now, Rampage tried to roll upright, but got a kick for his trouble and skidded several *kri* in the dirt. Still he tried, got up on both knees, then one – then his world exploded in a blinding flash of pain to his jaw.

He went down again, but he couldn't give up, he must not; he'd come so far and waited so long…

Something twisted his injured leg and sent whitefire agony through the thigh. Rampage screamed and fell back.

Then something landed on his throat like an iron bar, and his world went black…

...In his mind Rampage could see himself writhing out from under the heavy arm, forcing himself free with an uncounted burst of strength – getting up, slamming White Bull down…

"Rampage…brother... can you speak? Can you hear me?" a voice came out of nowhere.

Oh good, they've stopped the fight again and I can get up and-

But when he opened his eyes, he saw Flashing Sky bent over him, and the shaman next in line. A world of pain flooded back into his leg, his throat…

"Fl-Flashing Sky?" he whispered.

The Chief Hunter whipped around to the shaman. "D'asault! He's awake!"

"Thank the Great Spirit. Bring him to my lodge."

The Chief Hunter turned to Rampage and spoke very gently, "Just lie still, my brother, and I'll take you in for healing."

"But – but the fight. I have to" – Rampage began, and stopped.

Flashing Sky's face was etched with sorrow. "No, son. There is no more fight. The fight is over."

Disbelief stabbed the warrior's heart. "No. It can't be…K'orrynia"—*I have come so far for you. I have waited so long...not for this...not for this.*

A wellspring of heart's agony erupted within him: he had lost – and lost *her* – forever. Grief crowded his throat; his vision blurred... *This is how the Dancer felt...now it's come to me....*

"Rampage?" Flashing Sky reached for him, but Rampage dragged himself away. He did not trust himself to speak. He had lost half his soul – first Broken Spear, and now this...

Blinded by tears, he stumbled from the circle. The clan parted for him, but he did not see any of them. Someone called, but he did not hear. His head was down, his mind racing round and round a ring of despair. Why had his life been spared? Why had they not let White Bull simply kill him...better death than emptiness...*I have no life without her...no life...Spirit of sky and water, let me die...*

Halfway across the canyon floor, he heard the one voice that could stop him, and it did:

"Rampage! Rampage, wait!"

He turned slowly, head still low, to see his love, his life, running from the arena after him.

He straightened up. "K'orryn"-- he began, when further tragedy struck.

The great pterodon, 20 *kri* from wing tip to tip, bigger than a Scout ship, swooped down out of the sky and sank its talons into her back.

Her face changed from urgency to shock, to pain. And the huge flying beast, attracted by the horde of other winged scavengers near the camp, cheated of a feast, had swooped down and snatched up the likeliest lone thing. For once Rampage's plainness had saved him, as her bright colors had betrayed her.

As the girl went limp in its claws, it beat its great wings and cleared the timber gate to the canyon.

*Twenty-five....*The Chase

"NO!" Rampage screamed. He looked wildly around – saw a bow, three arrows, and a spear cached nearby when the owners went to see the fight. Beyond them lay four power sleds.

Rampage forgot pain, forgot injury. If K'orrynia had not just died before his eyes, then she was alive, and he had to save her. In a desperate hobble, he picked up the bow and arrows and the spear and flung himself onto the nearest power sled. Reacting faster than any of the clan, he had it revved and running and out of the canyon, chasing the monster in flight.

Power sleds aren't fast, and older models were even slower and had altitude limitations built in. This one could rise only a few hunters' heights above the ground. Rampage's anxiety keened in his throat.

But the great pterodon had its own troubles. The prey was heavier than it was used to, yet succulent, a good meal for itself and its young; and the creature was reluctant to let it go. But the extra weight dragged at it and slowed it down.

Just enough for the power sled to keep pace with as it glided some 13 *kri* below.

Rampage drove, and cursed his lack of weapons. His trusted vai-ators and laser had been left in the Chief Hunter's lodge. All he had now were these more primitive things. And the power sled's speed was at its peak; he could go no higher and no faster.

He guessed that the beast would take her back to its nest for its hatchlings. That must be why it hadn't simply stopped to kill her yet.

Then he saw her move a little in its grip and knew she was alive. Somehow he had to get a steady shot at the beast before it reached its nest – they nested in the mountains and on cliff tops, he recalled.

He remembered the agony of his raptor wounds, and he dared not even think about what K'orrynia must be suffering now.

For the second time that day, he made a prayer: "Please, Great Spirit, you granted me one fight and not another...grant me her life now." A warrior's plea: *get me close enough to land a blow.*

And he continued to twist the sled around the treetops and tall boulders which the pterodon barely skimmed. *Get clear of these; get closer...*his arms still trembled, but his legs had a chance to rest. Would he be fit at the end? He had to be.

Ahead lay a clearing. Large enough. While steering with one hand, Rampage fumbled up the bow with the other, then the arrows.

The pterodon veered. *No—go straight.* It swerved again. Rampage hooked an elbow around the steering stick. His shaking fingers rested the arrow against the bow, notched it to the string.

Before him the great wings fanned. The trees thinned. Ready... He tried to brace the steering rod with his knees. Draw the bow – *Spirit, I'm shaking.* Breathe. Breathe deep. Exhale.

The pterodon was lifting. *Now.* An arrow flew.

"Rot! The wing!" Rampage snarled. The bird-beast screamed. The arrow jerked free, opening a thin stream of blood.

A tree rushed at him, and Rampage hauled on the controls. Branches whipped the blunt bow, but he got away clear.

Rampage's thigh muscle sheared agony through him; he fell onto the small seat. *This is insane; I can't even save myself.* He looked forward again at the body hanging from the thing's claws and thought, *But I'm all she has. I have to make it.*

It struck him as tragically funny that he wanted to save the woman he loved for another man.

No, to live; just for her to live.

His mind cleared enough for him to realize that if he killed the beast in flight, it would drop K'orrynia to her death below. *Idiot! Where are your wits? You could have killed her yourself just then.*

The nest on the mountain. He would have to reach it along with the pterodon, and kill it there – if the sled could climb at any speed. If the sled could climb at all.

Or he could wound the beast often enough to weaken it and slow it down gradually, without its dropping her. He might be able to leap onto its back, then. Very tricky, especially in his present state. He didn't know what reserves he was running on. *"A warrior stands when he would sooner fall..."*

He concentrated on following the winged beast and trying to see beyond it. There: a stone mountain ahead. And the sparse trees were falling behind. Should he try to shoot again?

He squinted at the mountain. His people's unique wide-spectrum vision allowed him to see in-depth in color as well as from the binocular set of his eyes.

And he could see more great winged shapes wheeling above the peaks.

New plan: he had to shoot *now,* before a whole flock of them attacked.

The ground below was rough but relatively open. Rampage nocked another arrow…*try for the other wing.* The ptero jinked; he stayed with it. Steady, steady…

The second arrow sheared into the left wing, between the long fingers. The beast squawked, bounced in flight, then steadied itself and flew on.

This isn't working – what else?

There must be something…and he came to the same solution Renegade had with the Gets-Behind-You: stay close to it. If it rises at the last fraction, then pinpoint it between his sled and the mountain and make the jump. His and K'orrynia's combined weight should bring it down.

The last arrow must have hurt it; he could detect the slightest irregularity in its wingbeats. And it flew lower, barely above his sled's height.

But he could also see the body hanging limp below it, the long golden mane trailing lifelessly, the brilliant streaks of blood coursing over her shoulders. He shuddered, and prepared himself.

From a cloud-tower in the distance, the mountain solidified to become a massive triangle of rock and stone. It glowed red and gold in the late morning light.

The pterodon was trying to rise. It couldn't. Stubbornly it clung to its prey.

The mountain loomed. Rampage held his course, collision aimed.

Then the beast did the unexpected – it dived.

Rampage almost panicked. Was it going to ground? Or was it falling to gain speed for the ascent? In a *ktarn* of agony, he decided. He pushed the sled forward on FULL to intercept it on the way up. A wall of solid stone rushed toward him.

And the beast was *there* – big as a starship, wide as the sky, ascending before his bow.

The last arrow sprang. An arm-long shaft with three-bladed tip, it dwindled to toy-size and vanished into the body of the beast.

A horrible squall cut the air. The ptero, flapping, bobbling, biting with its sharp teeth, snapped at its unseen attacker.

Rampage hauled his sled back and up as it passed close enough to strike a wing. He ground the brake hard and pulled the craft up into a maelstrom of thunderous wings and stabbing beak.

He was almost directly under her! He forced the screeching motor to a hard slide to reach for her, and she opened her eyes and saw him—

As the ptero bucked in midair, saber beak lancing at him, she acted for the first time. A pair of wristknives flashed out and up, ripping into the deadly jaw.

The beast screamed and began flapping madly to climb away as the sled tilted out from under Rampage – and he, immune at last to pain, made a spectacular leap from its deck, spear in hand, and grabbed the beast's other claw.

It was too much of a burden; the wings flipped up as if blown backward and the creature fell.

It and they nearly crashed onto a rocky ledge where it finally, finally, let go of K'orrynia and she dropped, hitting the ledge with a cry.

Rampage let go and dropped after her. He landed on one good and one shaky leg, braced upright on the good one, knee down on the bad. He set his spear for the oncoming monster.

The pterodon impaled itself through the chest. Rampage held until the spear embedded; then a taloned foot knocked him away and he rolled into K'orrynia.

"Rampage – here!" she rasped, offering her knives. Too late to take and change them from her wrist, he threw his body alongside hers, shielding her, and braced her arm with his own. The ptero flopped in front of them, trying to bend against the spear to reach them.

"Come and get it, dead-meat!" Rampage screamed with the fury of the doomed.

It reached, reached – and suddenly its life-heat smoked from its body, its eyes went dead, and it tumbled backward off the ledge to the ground below.

Silence fell.

Rampage waited a long, long time for the pterodon to resurrect itself and come at them over the ledge, during which he heard nothing but their own breaths, gasping…

Finally he lowered K'orrynia's arm, bent it gently back to her side, and told her wide, startled blue eyes, "Wait here; I have to see."

He crawled to the edge and looked over it. A great broken kite lay there, almost the same color as the mountain, its life energy fading to darkness.

Wild squawks and calls above his head confirmed it. Rampage froze to the stone, watching until the flying carrion-eaters swooped down to the feast below.

When he did move, he did so very, very cautiously, with many a glance at the sky. He reached K'orrynia's side after a long retreat, to see that her eyes were closed and she lay slumped.

A little hiss of breath escaped him and he touched first her head, and then, very carefully, her back: two long bleeding grooves ran down most of its length.

"K'orrynia, my lady, we have to move," he murmured, not knowing if she could hear him.

One more time, warrior, he told himself and rocked unsteadily to his feet. He tried to lift her; his leg gave way and he knelt, transferring her to his back and shoulders…and step by step, half-falling on each one, he took her to the shallow niche from which the ledge protruded.

It was nothing more than a bubble burst in the mountainside, a little dish just hidden from hungry eyes. There were some dead leaves in it and some dead and dying moss, which he might use for tinder later.

"Here," he told her as he set her down gently with her head on a pillow of leaves. "Just rest if you can; I'll try to do something about those wounds." What, he had no idea – no antibiotics to cleanse them, no laser to seal them.

He was half-lying down himself, propped on his elbows, trying to assemble his thoughts, when she reached up and touched his face with her hand. He stilled.

"Rampage," speaking with effort, "for the wounds I have – my medicine…pouches…on my belt…junior shaman, remember?" and she even managed a thin smile, which touched him with wonder.

He clasped her hand. "On – on-course, K'orrynia, I'll try;" and replacing her hand on the ground, he brushed her shining hair off her back and shoulders to look at the wounds again.

He flinched inside and carefully removed her medicine belt. *Thank the Great Spirit for a good fall of Chance,* he thought as he opened one pouch after another. He found a coil of sutures and small knife in one, an assortment of powders in the others. Nothing was labeled.

"K'orrynia, which one?" he asked her.

"The yellow powder," she said and sank back. "Directly in…the wounds."

"Yes, I see. On-stat, my lady. Now steady, hold hard…." He sprinkled the powder along the cuts. At least it didn't seem to hurt her. When it was done, he informed her, stroking her shoulder, and found she had one more thing to say:

"Now find – a grayish powder or paste – wet it – put it on your leg muscle, the painful one."

"Dear heart, that can wait," he assured her.

"No, it…can't. Because next…you have to…stitch me up."

Rampage was aghast. "Me? While you're *conscious?* K'orrynia, I can't. I could never hurt you."

And her eyes filled for the first time, and she whispered. "Oh Rampage, if I had only known…I was so stupid."

"No, no; I can't believe that."

"Yes I was. Truly. I couldn't make up my mind between you and Dancer. And then White Bull added his name…his own idea. And when I saw you hurt, and down, in the match – I *knew.* At last."

Rampage stroked her face. "So that's why you came after me, because you really do care for me?" His voice quivered a little.

"Because I – love you."

And Rampage lost his heart all over again. He put her hand to his cheek and rubbed it, murmured words of love in return, until she stopped him…

…and made him do the surgery.

Before he began he asked her pardon: "Please forgive me, my lady;" and he had to force himself to go on. When the sharp bone needles pierced her flesh, he cried out with her. He grew dizzy and faint – Rampage, the fierce hunter, who never balked at a kill…

But she told him he *must* continue; and he did, until she lost consciousness under his hands and the thread was wet with his tears.

Afterward, he must have passed out next to her, for he awoke on the stone, a hand's-width away.

At least she was still asleep. So. He crumbled some leaves together and tried to make a fire, couldn't start it, and ended up carefully removing her wrist gauntlet and putting it on himself. He sat down cross-legged in front of her, intending to guard their little alcove in the mountain; but he was so exhausted that he began dozing off.

Not that way, he thought, and lay tiredly down beside her, his body stretched out closest to the cave front, the last sacrifice he had to give.

Weariness drained his thoughts and he slept.

***

HE WOKE sometime in the night to feel her snuggled against his back, her arm around his chest, and the deliciousness of it made Rampage know what it was the others shared: Renegade and K'leura, Flashing Sky and Dreamspeaker, Sunrise and Broken Spear – lost forever now.

He no sooner thought it than he realized this would be the only night he would ever have with his beloved. He had lost the fight, and she would marry another.

K'orrynia came out of her stupor to the feel of his chest heaving, his body shaking with great silent sobs. Not knowing the cause, she held him more tightly, whispered soothing words to him, and kept him close, until at last he turned to her and enclosed her gently in his own embrace, and let the contact soothe him.

Again exhaustion claimed them, and they slept that way, front to front, until the searchers found them later that evening.

Twenty-six....Where Tradition Begins

"THEY SLEEP, MERELY."

"Thank the Great Spirit! Yet, have they...?"

"*T'chak.* Look at them. They are as innocent as rain. And he tended her, at cost to himself."

"Yes, I see." A sigh. "And now I must decide."

Both the High Shaman and Chief Hunter wheeled on him.

"Direct your gaze some other way! I would rather be exiled myself, than go against clan tradition."

D'asault would not let him go. "Then pray for guidance, High Sun, and decide with your heart. You are the leader: tradition begins and ends with you."

A longer sigh. "So you say, old friend. Very well, I will leave you and them in peace for a time. Flashing Sky--?"

"My hunters stand guard above and below, and I shall remain here, *vr'*Leader."

"Thank you. This other...I must think on it myself."

He took one final look at the youngsters. The shaman was binding Rampage's injured leg now. The young man stirred in response and moaned, but did not wake. K'orrynia, sensing his distress, edged closer in her sleep, till Rampage calmed down.

The clan leader sighed once more. He rubbed the area over his eyes, then walked the few steps to the outside ledge, where he lowered himself to one knee, and balancing his laser rifle against the ground, stared into the night beyond.

Silently the Chief Hunter also moved to the outer ledge, to keep watch. They sat there for a time, the night air breathing soft and warm in their faces; until Flashing Sky quietly ventured an opinion,

"You know, High Sun, she would have been dead to us forever if not for young Rampage."

He saw High Sun stiffen and glance sharply at him, and braced himself for the outburst to follow.

But it did not come. Instead the clan leader turned his head away, to stare once again into the outer darkness.

They remained in their separate vigils till morning.

***

RAMPAGE stirred when the rising sun shone into the shallow cave. High Sun dismissed the others and knelt by the youngster's side.

At first all Rampage saw was the dark form looming over him. He startled half upright, his clenched fist bringing out the knives. Then he saw who it was, and stopped within a hair of the unprotected chest. His arm shook.

"High Sun…" he murmured.

"Only myself, warrior." He decided to test the young man one more time. "Yet we are alone here. If the only way to win my daughter is to go through me…"

Rampage stared at him. "You, her father?"

High Sun put the rifle down. He unsnapped his laser and laid it aside. "Yes. It is a large planet, big enough for two to hide on until they call a starship to take them away." He knelt there, perfectly vulnerable.

Rampage's arm steadied. Then he lowered his eyes, and withdrew the knives. "I—can't. This is madness. Not even for *her.*" He turned his head aside. *"I...feel my life is lost...to lose her,"* he whispered.

The friendly slap on his shoulder nearly knocked him flat again. "O noble heart! I owe you everything. My life is truly yours, Rampage. You will accept my decision then, whatever it is?"

Rampage closed his eyes. He sank back down. "Whatever…it is."

"What? What's going on?" K'orrynia was awake now, straining to see over Rampage. "Oh, Father! Please, I'll do anything; I'll go into exile, take banishment, only I *must* be with Rampage!"

High Sun gave her a look, not a clan leader anymore, but an exasperated parent. "Don't 'oh, father' *me*, young huntress. If you had been able to make up your mind earlier none of this would have happened. You will go into exile, on-path, but you will not be banished."

The two stared at him, big-eyed.

"Unless, that is," he continued blandly, "your husband-to-be wishes to make his home here, with us."

Shock, wonder and joy crossed their faces in a heartbeat. They looked at each other, then at him, and then practically lunged at High Sun, effuse with gratitude, before they clung to each other again.

He explained his reasoning, though he doubted they heard a third of it: "On those rare occasions when a great bird-beast seizes someone, generally a child, the family goes into mourning and weeps and offers prayers for her soul. She is dead to them, because never has anyone been successful in rescuing the victim...alive

"Therefore," heaving a great breath, his eyes twinkling, "Officially you have 'died,' my daughter, and the one who returns to the clan is surely someone else, found along the trail. There will first be weeping and a mournful Leavetaking. And then – there will be a wedding!"

Other than a muffled cry from the young ones, who were still wrapped around each other, he heard no other reply. He sighed and settled back on his haunches, regarding them with a fond but sad expression. *The Leavetaking will be true for me and Golden Bird, for when my youngest goes she will leave her clan and her old father behind. Aaaah...*

"So," he resumed aloud and found a smile for them, "this is how new traditions are born. No, save your thanks, son, and accept mine to you. Now I will have to do something to placate the ungracious challenge winner, I suppose, and for Dancer of Death, because he has earned it: make a few of my oldest hunters retire, and put those two in the ranks."

They heard a rattle of small rocks falling beneath the ledge, and High Sun told them, "Now lie back and rest, both of you. You are about to be carried home – and on an unbroken sled, if I may say so."

Twenty-seven....Hunt Supper, Wedding Feast

THE HUNT SUPPER and wedding feast was held a few days later, as soon as the betrothed couple felt healthy enough to get up and walk around. They had not attended K'orrynia's Leavetaking, the thought of which gave the bride-to-be cold chills. She had one small serving of revenge, however; for her wedding as a "new person" she would at last be known as Dinosaur Rider. Her mother merely closed her eyes at that. She was overjoyed to get her daughter back alive, under whatever name.

Rampage felt concerned about how the clan would react when they saw who had really returned to them. He discovered something interesting: they recognized her, on-stat, but almost everyone was willing to carry on the deception.

White Bull alone took it with a bad grace, even with his new title of Tenth Hunter; and Flashing Sky made sure he had plenty to do outside the walls in the interim. The big albino had lost much favor because of his tactics, and the Chief Hunter guessed he wouldn't have much trouble with him for a while.

"It was a popular decision, any-route; your lady's choice, I mean," Flashing Sky told Rampage afterward, "given your last opponent's *jhak-ree* tactics, and your own courage in slaying the beast. Those are the things that epics grow out of, *vr'*warrior; and while The People respect tradition, they revere justice. On this trail, justice has been found."

The Dancer of Death's appointment to Sixth Hunter won wide-spread approval. Though slower off the mark than Rampage, he had been very much a part of the search for K'orrynia.

"The Dancer is my choice for my own replacement," Flashing Sky confided to Rampage, "once he is seasoned in say, fifty years or so."

"You couldn't have made a better choice," Rampage agreed, "though you seem hardly old enough to retire, even in fifty years."

"Oh, a man of 61 must start thinking about what he wants to do with his second century – which is to be an Esteemed Elder for my share, and enjoy my children and grandchildren.

"I have hunted large and small creatures across the known star systems for nearly a quarter of my life," he went on; "Here I have found a home."

***

THE DAY ARRIVED in splendor. The People, released from tension and care, with a good Hunt *and* a good fight on their game pole, were ready for a celebration. And their clan leader gave them the full panoply.

First he raised Rampage to the rank of Great Warrior, "in our clan at least-path, whatever you may be elsewhere," High Sun told him. The medallion they bestowed on him was unique: a glittering neck-collar made of the pterodon's fingerlet bones, inlaid with gold, while the heavier pendent itself was skillfully carved in the winged dragon's image, a fiery ruby in its eye. The back was inscribed with his title and his deed.

He also became an honorary member of Dinosaur Clan. "You and your children will always be welcome here," High Sun told him.

Next came the marriage festival. The ceremony itself was a simple one, the shaman repeating the Credo to them, reminding them they were a part of all life, part of the same spirit of creation. The only unusual thing was that he read the rites over an un-bonded couple.

The new pair dressed in their finest: Rampage in his golden armor wearing all his honoraria; K'orrynia in her birdfeather cape, her own Hunt medallion, and shaman's robes trimmed with the many-colored furs which Rampage had sent her.

A sauropod skin from the recent hunt lay stretched upon the ground, and the clan filled it with gifts from the great round of its midsection to the points of its head and tail. The gifts made a wonderful collection, from hand-carved dishes and bowls, excellent weapons of bone and of smithed metals, leather skins, armor and sandals of every hue and texture of dinosaur hide, to musical instruments and hand-carved ivory statuettes, not to mention fancier things of precious metals and stones. It made a pile so enormous Rampage wondered if it would fit even inside a starship. He felt sure they would never get it into the Scout.

Then they feasted: brontosaur roast done in a gigantic pit of hot coals; brontosaur steaks tenderized in a hot sauce, and a medley of pine nuts and native fruits – the Hunting People regard fruits as a garnish, not a staple, in their diet.

That came in addition to all the berry juice, wild–plant wine, hot broth and coddled dinosaur eggs they could eat. When clans celebrated, Rampage observed, they did it up proud.

White Bull was absent from the main wedding feast, since the Chief Hunter had posted him on guard duty; but Dancer of Death was there. Rampage had personally sought him out the evening before and talked to him until they became allies and friends.

"I know what you felt, brother," he told his former opponent. "When I lost to White Bull, I felt every *t'mearn* of anguish you must have known…" not an easy speech for Rampage, at all.

"Ah well, yours was an unfair defeat," the Dancer graciously replied. "Rested, you would have beaten him soundly. I at least had the honor of losing a fair fight to a noble opponent. And as for"—he could not say her name yet – "your bride, I would so much rather she be alive, and marrying *you* than *him,* that I hold no harm in my heart toward you. I am proud to be your friend."

And Rampage was satisfied.

During the ceremony and feasting and most of that evening, the new couple had eyes only for each other. They hardly even heard the amended Ballad of Rampage, added to that of "Dinosaur Rider," a most unusual lapse for Rampage.

Watching them, Golden Bird nudged High Sun gently. "You see, my husband, it was a good choice."

And he sighed – he sighed a lot lately – "So we will be losing her after all, gone to form some strange new clan on a far-distant world. Daughters! We have my two grown sons from my previous mate*, you know, but she is the only child of *ours,* Golden Bird. I do not know if we should try again."

She purred at him, "On-path we should. And you love her better than any son…Let tonight change your trail on this, or I shall."

And he laughed, and announced the Wedding Dance.

This dance was as exuberant as any of the spear dances, though without the weapons, of course; and any of the clan's young adults could seek the partner of his or her choice and test their growing pair bond, or forge one. More marriages usually resulted.

---

* High Sun's first wife died in a hunting accident shortly after they came to the planet. He was a long time recovering; and he does not speak her name anymore.

This time the clan leader himself and his wife joined in, and almost every eligible youngster followed, along with a number of adults. Rampage and K'orrynia led the fiery dance, though it was a long one; and after a time, they were nowhere to be seen…

"They have gone to their Wedding Night lodge, my heart; so tonight the hearth is ours," and Golden Bird led her husband firmly away from speculation and into the fervor of the dance – until he could forget them and himself in joy.

***

PARTINGS---The celebration lasted for three days, until every last member of the Dinosaur Clan from elder to warrior to the smallest *chk-kiy* had eaten and drunk their fill. Adults and juveniles danced and sang and played games of risk and skill till they were ready to drop. Three days was just long enough, Rampage thought.

It was just ending on the fourth morning when a messenger came by skycycle from the research station. He informed High Sun that the starship had come to leave the usual equipment and supplies and to take Rampage home.

This time K'orrynia would be going with him.

The father in High Sun suffered a pang of loss. He would rather both of them stay here: they made splendid members of Dinosaur Clan.

"In many ways you have earned your manhood with us," he told Rampage privately; "And we shall miss you. But you go to form your own clan now, Great Warrior. I recognize that your friends are both your family and your clan. But perhaps you will not forget us, after you go."

Rampage made a negative head motion. "I will never forget you; and someday we'll come back if we can, and bring your grandchildren with us."

"A pact, then? "

"A pact, Esteemed Leader and friend."

Her parents' farewell to K'orrynia took longer and was made privately; and it was like farewells all over this galaxy where parents have to let their children go.

Even D'asault, the old shaman, embraced her and said, "I feel like a second father to you, dear one. Take these medicines with you: they may be of some use in a new home until you can find others. Now I suppose I shall have to train one of those unworthy youngsters as shaman in your stead."

She hugged him hard. “Goodbye, Grandfather. Thank you for all you’ve taught me. I wish you many more years to teach those ‘unworthy youngsters,’ too.”

The starship sent down a couple of supply shuttles to deliver things, trade items ordered by the clan. It gave Rampage a chance to send their wedding gifts back up to the main ship and talk to the captain, who jokingly threatened to charge higher shipping rates for all this extra cargo. Rampage planned to pay them a little more anyway. He made a few purchases, too.

When Rampage and K’orrynia made ready to depart the next day, the whole clan turned out to see them off. High Sun and Golden Bird, Flashing Sky and Dreamspeaker and the High Shaman D’asault led the pack.

“Hold a moment,” Rampage said, and took a hide-covered bundle out of his borrowed Scout ship, where he’d hidden it yesterday. He’d bought final gifts with the precious stones and hides Flashing Sky had been saving for him from his fur sales.

“For you, old friend,” and he gave the Chief Hunter a hi-tech newmetal spear, which despite its ornamental engravings was as light as sea foam and as deadly as lightning. “This one isn’t borrowed, I think.”

And the Chief Hunter was overwhelmed, and embraced the son of his heart.

The shaman got a collection of watertight unbreakable vials and pouches and jars to keep his medicines in, and he pronounced himself well pleased.

The biggest present, an armload even for a grown hunter, was a versatile-powered comset with computer, satellite receptors and printout gear attached.

“For you, honorable second-parents,” Rampage said, “so you can receive our messages, or any others, and send your own to us wherever in the galaxy we are – and pictures too.”

“O second-son,” the clan leader said as they accepted it, “you gladden my heart.”

“And mine,” added Golden Bird; and they put the set down long enough to embrace the young couple one last time.

“This is no substitute for a visit, however,” High Sun growled in mock-sternness – and the couple departed with lighter hearts, to many a call of “safe harbor, safe home!”

Twenty-eight....On Arvien 4

RENEGADE WAS interviewing prospective Hunt teachers when the message arrived. He did his interviews outside in the school's amphitheatre, so he could test the applicants' actual skills.

A few of the hunters objected to the skills test, thinking they had nothing to prove. Renegade thanked those and politely dismissed them. He needed people with more tolerance, for the students' sake.

The hunter he was currently interviewing, Trail Leader, did not object. A muscular man of medium height, he had D'varrk Clan's bold markings: a yellow base with a black overlay breaking into spots and half-stripes on his front.

Mature and patient, he answered whatever questions Renegade asked; and he had been one of Burning Spear's recommendations. He ran through the shooting and unarmed combat tests in a superior fashion, and at a mere 73 years of age, said he wasn't ready to retire.

"I became my clan's Second Hunter only after 60 years of age, after many, many successful trophy hunts and a long wait," he told Renegade. "Unfortunately, my clan has scores of young hunters coming up; and the leader and Elders' Council wanted me and several of the other top-ranked to retire this year, to make room."

"Which others were asked to retire besides you?" Renegade asked, interested.

"Third, fifth and sixth – the older ones," Trail Leader said. "The somewhat younger Chief Hunter and all the other ranked will stay." He glanced down briefly. Then he said, "Great Warrior, I have a good run of use in me yet.... I have no wish to sit by the fire and tell old stories. So when, after the Champion's Leavetaking, we heard of his Hunt School seeking new teachers, I came here. This is a good world; and there is still land available. Although I have never lived outside the clan except on trophy hunts, I have traveled alone; and I am willing to try new trails."

And the older hunter looked at the younger forthrightly and with just a trace of yearning.

*He's too proud to beg, and I like him any-route...*Renegade made up his mind. "We would be honored to have you, Trail Leader. There's ample room at the hall for yourself and your family until you can stake out a land hold;" and he extended his hands, palms up.

The older hunter beamed and took his wrists. "You honor *me,* Great Warrior. My wife and I shall move here within the quarter."

Just as the D'varrk hunter left, Renegade's belt-com chimed. "Yes?"

K'leura was calling: "We have good news from the space station, my heart. Rampage is coming home – and he's bringing his bride with him!"

"Good old Rampage." Renegade felt relieved. "It's on the nock: winter's melted into mud puddles and the grass is growing on the mountain. I wonder what kept him...No trouble; I'll be up to the hall in a moment. Dasrylion can take over here." And he signed off to call the Cold Tracker down from his target setup chores to interview the remaining hopefuls.

***

WHEN THE new Arvien Four – Renegade, K'leura, Dasrylion and Sunrise – got to Nine Systems Station, they found that word of their search had raced ahead of them.

"There must be forty or fifty trophy hunters wanting to see us!" Dasryl exclaimed after they saw all the messages at the com-center. "And we only asked around on Homeworld!"

Renegade sighed. "Well, Burning Spear said not to overlook the trophy hunters. Many of them are looking for a stable life and a home. 'Being hybrids doesn't keep them from being very fine hunters, as you should know, warrior,' was how he put it." And he smiled, half to himself. "By good Chance we arrived a few days early."

They had a whole itinerary: Renegade planned to visit the House of Healing, to get their own and their children's immunizations built up against any exotic diseases. They would also order medical and laboratory supplies to take with them to their new world.

His decision to move there as soon as possible this year hinged partly on the children's and partly on K'leura's condition now that she was pregnant. The decision came a little easier since he'd learned that a space station and house of healing were being constructed to serve the Ten Systems' worlds even before the planets were settled; and that self-defense satellites would eventually orbit each colonized world. There were monsters abroad in this galaxy, and the *tautschen* knew it.

The little group decided to get themselves and their children, born and unborn, checked out first; so they stopped at the expanded health facility. If either child needed genetic enhancement, it could be performed more easily on the fetus.

Dasrylion and Sunrise carried the baby, taking turns on the long walk. A husky child, Smalltusk was marked as Broken Spear had been, except that he had no teeth yet and just a few of his mother's gold-ringed black spots on his back. He had strikingly familiar brown eyes; and Renegade felt he would resemble the old warrior even more strongly as he grew.

K'leura's child was barely thirty days in the womb, a tiny little glowing figure in her expanding uterus, with miniscule arms and legs, pinpoint fingers and toes, and two big round black eyes. Renegade found the whole process fascinating; although his wife could see the baby only in a reflecting-sheet as yet. They watched its progress every day.

Sunrise and Dasrylion made an interesting match, Renegade thought. He wondered sometimes if they were drawn together out of a mutual love for Broken Spear and a need to be near his child. *Like the ashe-kvar for Kyva and Stands Fast,* he thought. But as time passed they grew more affectionate with each other. Sunrise kept close to her new husband, as if she feared he would disappear like the others.

They got their initial genetic tests and updated immunizations and left, agreeing to return for the results in about ten *tare'*.

"What about a look at the shops?" Dasrylion suggested, seeing his wife eye them.

"Anything to keep more interviews at bay," Renegade said wryly; and they laughed.

"You'll have to tally them in sometime," said Dasrylion.

Renegade widened his eyes in mock surprise. "Don't you mean *we*? Krr, which reminds me, we have all those trade things to unload. Maybe the huntresses would like to start circling the shops, and we can track them down later."

K'leura laughed. "That sound ominous, coming from a hunter. Come on, Sunrise; let's leave them a nice clear trail!"

Sunrise shot one last reluctant glance at Dasrylion, but allowed K'leura to coax her away. The couples touched lightly at parting; then the two males watched as their mates and children left them.

"Poor lady, she acts as if every time we part, it will be the last," Dasryl remarked. "But I can understand how she feels."

"So can I. I felt that way about Gra – about Broken Spear when I first came to live with him, remember?" Renegade said. A shadow crossed his face. "Let's get on with it. We have a lot of trading to do, especially for the new ship."

That was their major purchase. They had ordered a fully-equipped Hunt Ship – a *Hunt* Ship, not a standard settlement craft – to be outfitted as a combined colony/Hunt ship, including heavy weaponry and powerful field drive. They were paying for it with their collection of furs, hides and handmade items. Renegade's most valuable find had been a series of Broken Spear's personal journals, spanning over 200 years of his life.

Renegade read the journals and had a revelation of what his mentor's early life had been like; and he decided that the originals would stay with the great warrior's school on Arvien 4; and another set of copies would go to the Twin Worlds with him. In exchange for a third set and the permission to print more for the university and Rydderrak Clan, the Nine Systems Hunt Council had agreed to help pay part of the starship's cost.

By the time he and Dasrylion lugged a formidable load of goods into the shipbuilders' office, they had few things left to take to their old friend He-walks-lightly; which was difficult, since they had come to say goodbye.

"Leaving for good? And so soon? I shall miss you," he told them, "and not just for the trade, even though you helped us thrive here, but because I felt…as if I were a part of your lives and adventures."

That wistfulness again – Renegade was touched. "Good trader, old friend, we'll tell the new teachers that we traded here often, and were always treated fairly."

He-walks-lightly chinlifted, real sadness in his eyes. "Are you going right away? And where is your friend Rampage?"

"Not right away," Dasrylion told him, "but when the Hunt ship is finished. We're here to meet Rampage this time."

With that the trader wrested a promise from them to stop by his shop again after Rampage arrived, and to share meat with him.

"We regret we have only these few furs to bring you," Renegade added.

"No, no; don't mistake me," the trader retorted with a touch of injured pride. "To have four of the most famous warriors in Nine Systems patronize *my* little shop has been more than my making. You leave me in glory. I wish to do something for you; and if Chance falls well, you may get to meet my family here. I have two daughters away at University, and my wife star-hops between factories."

At that point the warriors' wives found *them,* and crossed over to see the trader's wares. He-walks-lightly enthused over them and the children, and began to plan what final gifts he could give them. Sunrise's baby startled him; he saw the resemblance at once.

"He will be the Champion's image… Ah, I mourn with you, my friends. I and my Clan Elders were at the Leavetaking, but the crowd pressed us, and we missed you afterward."

"*Your* Clan Elders?" Renegade said, surprised.

K'leura knew what he meant: "You're in the Trader Clan, then; the 'last clan' it's called," she informed her husband. "Traders make up the so-called 17th Clan. They include many hybrids and freeborns, and some regular members from the other clans – everyone who shares an interest in trade and wanderlust. They handle most of the small-goods trade between the starworlds and space bases and factories. They often rode our starliners, though many traders have their own ships and make their own circuits."

"Milady, I see you know us," said He-walks-lightly. "Before history we were the binding force on Homeworld: the restless travelers, the true freeborns, who carried unique items from one clan to another—meats, clothing, hides, artworks, and tools. We are sometimes credited with keeping the peace between the clans, and giving Homeworld one language to speak."

Renegade was astonished. "Then you have a long history, and I knew nothing about it! My old book on clans never mentioned yours."

The trader laughed. "Out of bias, no doubt. We have always been a loose assortment, outsiders looking in, easy for purists to ignore."

That started Renegade on his questions: "But how did you come here, brother? A shop is a rather stationary place, isn't it?"

"Oh, for some," the other man assured him. "We wanted a stable place for our children to grow up in near the learning center. Now that our daughters are nearly grown, and you, my friends, are leaving…well, I feel the urge to wander again Trading is something like hunting, *t'd'faal,* as your mentor used to tell me. There are new people and new things over every horizon. Perhaps I have stayed in one place too long."

His guests had to leave for the other stores; though not before He-walks-lightly presented each of the new mothers with a whole bolt of cloth, ones they had particularly admired. And that was just a trace on the trail to come, he hinted.

"A good Chance you didn't admire the whole store, or he might have made you a present of it," Dasrylion teased the huntresses after they were out of earshot.

Renegade was silent, still amazed that in all the years they had known him, the trader had never even mentioned his clan, even if 'experts' didn't recognize it.

From the cloth shop, they went on to the armory and others. K'leura was impressed with the way everyone seemed to know the two warriors, and what deference they showed them. Most even knew Renegade by ranking as well as by name.

If I'd known Renegade was so famous, she thought, *I never would have been able to approach him.* Her attitude had done a complete reversal since her early notion of hunters as "primitive" and somehow not quite-as-good-as the starborn. She saw that not only did most of the people here know and respect her companions; they seemed to revere the hunters and warriors as noble beings, as their natural defenders and heroes. She felt that the technicians and researchers she had worked with needed to have their opinions reset.

She herself wore a variation of the huntress's normal clothing: soft leather breast protectors and a simple waist wrap, wider and longer than the usual breech and loincloth – she couldn't bring herself to wear *that* little just yet.

Not that it made any difference to the *tautschen's* superior eyesight. The non-spaceborn would look quite frankly at her body to study her feelings and exclaim over her baby, all very courteously, on-course, and couched in ritual speech. But it *was* disconcerting.

Yet she wore her Hunt medallion proudly, set in its jeweled neckchain, and she felt *accepted,* as she never had before.

Later, before sleep, she tried to express this to Renegade, about how she had changed from the timid, terrified girl to the strong and capable huntress she was today, slayer of dragons and bone-beasts; and how, after saving her life, he had *given* her life to her.

But all her sweet-natured hunter did was smile and say, "You give me too much hide-share, my love. You took what was already in you and remade *yourself* into the person you were meant to be. I just struck the spark; you are the fire."

That was another thing she loved him for – his utter unselfishness.

Twenty-nine.....The Masters of the Hunt

OF THE 47 trophy hunters who had originally contacted them, only 18 were able to make the interview on such short notice, much to the four's relief. Renegade and Dasrylion split them into two groups, borrowed two small meeting rooms aboard the station, and spent their second day there interviewing Master Hunters – and some Huntresses. Their only regret was that they could not test skills this way. The rooms were very small. Sunrise and K'leura sat in on the interviews.

"I think we should get a good huntress for the school," Sunrise remarked, "someone who has devoted her life to her craft." The others agreed, Renegade remembering how surprised his own schoolmates had been to meet his mother, a Master Huntress and warrior.

Renegade took a moment between interviews to confide to his wife: "I feel as if this should be put 'on the other talon;' all of these people have so much more experience than I – look at these trophy kills! Yet I wear the title 'Great Warrior' while they are only Esteemed Hunter, or sometimes Warrior. It doesn't seem just."

"I see no one of them with a Gets-Behind-You and only two with a Star Beast," she pointed out. "And none with those bone monsters. And you forget that you saved whole worlds, Renegade;" which made him feel better.

He was surprised and pleased to see Starseeker among the applicants. He called the trophy hunter in immediately and gave him a warm greeting, telling him, "Say no more, brother, the position is yours."

"Aahh, I am honored, but it wasn't the teaching post I've come for," the Shadow Clan warrior confessed. "It's to ask if I may join you on your new world?"

Unexpected but very welcome news…Renegade said, "We would be honored to have you. Can you come with us this quarter in our new Hunt ship?"

"No, regrettably, I cannot. I have to finish a contract on a research ship first. Then I'll be able to join you on-planet. It's time I found a home," he answered.

"On-course," Renegade agreed; and they parted for the present. Quietly he told K'leura, "Starseeker lost the woman he loved, a huntress, to the bone-beasts on Ar'raked'dikan. I hear he's been fighting the creatures in our systems too. He's also something of a philosopher; I'll be glad to have him with us."

They did find a huntress who impressed them. Only 58, she was a Master considered good enough to instruct Marsh Clan students and go out as an elder on their hunts – unofficially, since she was a hybrid. After watching her demonstration of unarmed combat skills (neatly done even in the small room) Renegade could see why her name was Striking Snake. "She's near Rampage's quality," he told his friends later. "And her reason for applying is simple: she just wants a chance to belong."

Sunrise and Dasrylion added an excellent Tracker Clan hybrid to their choices: "Taslon, whose parents are from Tracker and Dappled Grass. Judging from his records, he's never lost a beast to a cold trail, and managed to find several lost children off-world. He's also a pilot. –How many does that give us, Renegade?" Dasryl asked.

"Four: Trail Leader from D'varrk Clan and Swift Runner from Rydderrak; now Striking Snake and Taslon. We should look for one more."

"Will they find enough open land nearby to live on, do you think?"

"Churr, " Renegade answered, "I'm going to deed my parents' home and holdings over to the school, so one family can live there; and the school's territory adjoins the big public hunting grounds down in the swamps."

"Good thought. I don't have a holding yet," Dasrylion said, "and my family is large; but maybe I can put in for one just the other side of the mountain."

"That should help. Now let's go over the lists."

They finally settled on a mature hunter of about 50 years. He had a wife and newborn *chk-kiy*, but no real home. Since they could no longer stay on the trophy ships because of the child, they were looking rather desperately for a home in the frontier worlds. "Space travel has no family and no territory," was how he put it.

His only drawback in Renegade's eyes was that his trophies included a few humans. The species was under a temporary hunting ban until Nine Systems Hunt Council could see how they reacted to Renegade and his friends' visit, and if they could be trusted.

Dasrylion defended the hunter: "He said he dropped down into a kill-or-die situation from the start. He was discovered almost on landing and fought off attacks from whole packs of them, all bearing weapons. He described it as 'less a hunt than instant self-defense,' and said he was barely able to get away with his life. 'A treacherous species,' he calls them."

Renegade could sympathize with that. "On-target then; we'll take him."

They told the hunter Taras-tion that he could join their staff. Their final decision made, both the male warriors felt glad it was over. They posted their choices on the base computer and closed up the rooms. They had interviewed everyone who came.

"Now let's get some water for our throats and take a walk," Renegade proposed. "I'm stiff from sitting so long and I've talked myself dry. What about you two?" –to Dasrylion and Sunrise.

"It's a pact, brother," Dasryl agreed.

***

THE THIRD DAY belonged to Rampage.

His friends collected their genetic testing results early and stood on the observation bridge when the starship made tie.

A number of other passengers disembarked first; then they saw the familiar figure in golden armor and gave a collective sigh of relief. The last hunter was home.

"That's him, but where is…" Renegade began, then stopped as Rampage turned to someone just coming from the entry lock behind him. The hybrid warrior's jaw dropped. So did Dasrylion's. The huntresses drew a single deep breath…

…at the sight of the most beautiful woman they had ever seen.

Dasrylion grabbed Renegade's elbow. "Can you *believe--?"*

While Sunrise exclaimed, "She's incredible!"

"Stunning," K'leura agreed; "I've never seen anyone with colors like that."

Renegade started to grin, then to laugh. "Good old Rampage! The Circle has turned his way at last!" He leaned over the rail and called to him, "*Arah*, Rampage, safe harbor!"

Rampage and K'orrynia looked up, and the Plains warrior glowed with happiness. He took K'orrynia's hand. "Look; my friends are here. Come and meet them;" and he led her over to the ramp and ascended.

To the others' delight, Rampage's "Beautiful Girl" was as unselfconsciously gracious and personable as she was lovely. A bit overwhelmed, she returned their lively greetings in a friendly way, more reserved than her husband's uproarious embrace of his friends, but just as warm.

Greetings and partings tend to be emotional with a people as intense as the Hunters: the spacefarer returns from distant voyages; the hunter comes back alive from perilous planets, the warrior from dangerous battles; and their friends and families rejoice that they have returned to them. So with Rampage and his friends.

When they had simmered down, Renegade asked, "Shall we get your gear now? Did you bring much with you?" and was mystified when the pair burst out laughing.

Until he and the others saw the contents of the cargo hold.

"Great Spirit!" Dasrylion cried. "This will fill the entire school ship and bulge out the sides!"

"Close enough," Rampage said with a satisfied air.

Renegade groaned. "If we're ever going to fit it all in, we'd better find a fleet of power sleds and get started .We rented a sleeping alcove for you, Rampage, milady K'orrynia, if you need to rest a while."

"Rest? No, thanks, Renegade; I've had all the confinement I can stand. But K'orrynia maybe…"

She declined. "So have I. I will help, if I may. Then perhaps later we can share meat and hear each other's stories."

***

THEY worked steadily unloading the haul until Sunrise excused herself to feed the baby. The others took up the excuse and gathered round her.

"He's a good feeder, little Smalltusk," Sunrise said proudly as the baby breastfed.

"And strong, too," Dasryl put in.

"He's going to be big *and* strong," Rampage remarked. "I can't get past it; he looks so *like.* It will be like having *him* with us again."

"'The child is not the father,' remember? " Renegade could hear those words from another time, another place. "Broken Spear had a lifetime of experience to draw on.

"Still," he admitted, "it's good to know some part of him goes with us, isn't it? And your own bloodlines add your special talents, Sunrise."

"I'm honored, *vr'*Renegade. Sometimes I forget that myself."

Rampage looked at K'leura and Renegade next. "And you, too; you're going to be parents, too. What a prime start for a new world!"

Renegade smiled. "Your time will come. Anyroute, let's finish unloading before they start charging us storage fees!"

"*Krr,* ah," Rampage coughed, "we already have an agreement on that..." and he told them how he'd had to cut the captain a hideshare for taking everything aboard – which amused them mightily.

***

AFTERWARD, they had their promised meat-sharing with He-walks-lightly. He took them to his own living quarters behind the storefront. It was private and quiet, away from the crowds outside. A magnificent white sloth-bear hide spread over the center floor; while a variety of furs and cloths decorated the rest of the room. One entire wall was covered with a giant tapestry of a great tree sewn on white cloth. Its branches thrust across the wall so it looked as if you peered out from among them. The coloring and detail were exquisite, down to the last hand-sewn leaf.

"Beautiful!" K'leura said, and the others agreed.

"Oh, pleasant at least," the trader smiled, lighting up an electric hearth. "Complete with mock fire. Sometimes I wonder if I will forget what a true fire and tree and sky look like; and then I become restless again."

He had a conglomeration of chairs and benches arranged in a rough circle, and there he seated his guests*. "My cooking hearth is in another room, by the storerooms, for inconvenience' sake," he said. "Your pardon, honored guests;" and he went off to fetch the meal.

The comfortable setting, along with the trader's gift for putting them at ease, soon had them eating and then talking freely afterward.

For the first time, they heard about Rampage's courtship. And they supported him as a family or a clan would, K'orrynia noticed, reflecting his shock to learn of the other suitors, his exuberance at the dinosaur hunt, his admiration of his first opponent and indignation over White Bull's challenge – and his despair at his defeat...and through the whole cycle again with K'orrynia's abduction by the pterodon.

---

* *Tautschen* are comfortable eating in groups, a reflection of the ancient days when pack or pride ate the kill where it fell. Today they are often served from a long buffet table or the meat is passed around the circle of a cooking fire.

Renegade felt disturbed by how White Bull twisted the rules. "We should change that, about the Challenges—we're still Hunt Council members for a little while yet. We can make a suggestion;" and the others agreed.

The trader himself had sat rapt to the end. "What an incredible adventure! You – all of you, the hunts, the adventures – and you are what? Twenty-three or–four years old? Barely into your third decade; and now you are off to settle an entire planet. What will you do when you're 100? Two?"

They hadn't thought.

"You're right," Renegade said in a preoccupied way. "We--I -- just wanted to make a home for us all, something like a clan, but open to everyone, where we could live together."

Rampage sat up straighter. "You know, that's what High Sun said to me: 'Your friends are your clan now,' and I've been thinking, why not? A clan with the latest technology, yet living close to the land in the old way."

"Not like the freeholders, separate but isolate," Renegade said; "*Krr*, we're already at that trail's head, Rampage; that's how we registered our territory. We just need a name."

"We'll give it *yours* then," Rampage said in a burst of generosity.

"*Chak*! That's it – who else deserves it more? Who else got us through everything?" Dasrylion cut in, annoyed that he had hadn't been the first to think of it.

"No, wait; you can't," Renegade started to protest, but was drowned out by a chorus of agreement from everyone there. The Great Warrior could still blush, the trader noticed with amusement.

"And we could add a hunting school," Sunrise put in, "where the Three could pass on Broken Spear's teachings."

"It's a prime idea," He-walks-lightly added. "The Champion would approve, I think."

Renegade finally accepted the name only after Rampage and Dasrylion threatened to 'secede' from the new clan. The creation of another Hunt school also appealed to him; and he sank back in his seat, embarrassed but resigned.

The trader took him out of the trap by gently changing direction: "And after your families are grown, then what?" he pressed them in a friendly way. "There are more centuries ahead of you…a lifetime…and the universe is vast and wide."

Renegade laughed softly. "One trail at a time I think, brother. The next is hidden from us around the Circle."

"And one wild world to tame is enough for the first hundred, *churr*, my friends?" He-walks-lightly said.

"*Chak;* or perhaps it's your own longing that speaks, honored trader?" Renegade turned the point neatly, a twinkle in his eye.

"Perhaps," the trader admitted. "I miss the days when my wife and I were free roamers, stopping and trading at world after world... Ah, well, we may be again; then we'll come visit you on your fierce new world;" and he smiled.

He saw something respond in Renegade's eyes. Certainly the young man was a husband and new father now, with a worthy goal. But he was also a trained hunter and a great warrior, at the service of his people. After that family had grown, who knew what awaited him?

K'leura had seen it too, for she took her husband's hand. "Renegade has given a great share of himself to our people. Who could ask him to do more?"

Renegade pressed her hand. His gaze made the unthinkable promise: *Don't worry; I'll be here for you,* while his mouth said, "We'll welcome you and your family, brother, if you choose to come. And sometimes I think that's what the Nine Systems Council has in mind by allowing us our out-size claim on Blue One: to stand watch over those systems. As warriors we would be at the spear-point. There is that other world, the wasted one..."

He frowned, his lips lifting slightly to clear the tips of his biting teeth; and he glanced around at his pack, his loyal friends: "I hope I'm not taking you all into danger with me," he said very softly.

Rampage sprang to his defense, "Then it's where we *choose* to go, brother. *Tautschen* don't tuck claw and run from any danger, anytime."

"And besides, that world is long dead, and its combatants gone – to dust, both of them," Dasrylion added.

The huntresses stirred uneasily, torn between their desire to protect their new families and their determination not to be shunted aside.

Look at them, He-walks-lightly thought; *they are worried, yet their heads are high and their eyes burn. What noble tautschen they are! How glad I am to be in this company!*

He regretted where he had chased the talk, though. "Your pardon, honored guests," he began, "I have upset you, and I am truly sorry. Let us talk of other things."

Renegade pounced on that. "Forgiven and forgotten, brother. It's a discussion we'll have among ourselves, no doubt. As for now, why don't you tell us about yourself and your adventures in the Trading Clan?"

And the hybrid warrior proved every *t'mearn* as skillful in redirecting the talk out of murky waters as the trader had in unwittingly taking it there.

Thirty....Endings and Beginnings

THEY HAD to stay at the station a few days longer for Smalltusk to receive minor surgery: a few extra salivary glands and a better gene-proofing against cold weather.

"Now he won't suffer from the cold like Broken Spear did," Renegade comforted Sunrise, when the usually stoic baby fretted and cried.

K'orrynia was a great help in supplying pain relief liquid for the baby:

"He should not be expected to act the warrior yet," she said.

Three days later they went home with a few temporary follow-up medications.

K'orrynia had her first look at the awesome trophy hall; and they all met the Rydderrak hunter who had just arrived from Homeworld to teach at the school.

A leaner, longer-legged version of most of the rainforest clan, Swift Runner had been described by Burning Spear as "one of the best of our young hunters. He is an excellent all-round master of weapons, *tch-won'*, tracking, and most importantly, he is a *strategist:* he can formulate a plan in advance of his prey, and plan a hunt to the last detail.

"Do not believe his self-deprecating manner," the Rydderrak leader went on. "It earned him an unfortunate second name here; so I think the change will be good for him."

When the Arvien hunters asked him just what that 'unfortunate second name' was, he told them a little more about himself:

It seems he had selected a large and dangerous rainforest cat on Homeworld for his Master Hunt. He'd plotted out the hunt with unusual care, tracking the beast for a tenday to learn its habits. At the appropriate time, he'd climbed the cat's favorite tree to wait for it; and when the big animal bounded up, he'd shot it to death and escaped without a scratch.

When his fellow students asked how he managed to come off unscathed, he was unwilling to boast about his effort, so he shrugged and said, "Just lucky, I guess."

"And 'Just Lucky' you became, didn't you?" Renegade asked him.

The young clan hunter grimaced. "I've never been able to leave it behind. Please, honored warriors, if you accept me here, I have an unusual request..."

Renegade said without a hint of humor: "You shall be Swift Runner to us, now and hereafter."

"On our Oaths," Dasrylion vowed.

And Swift Runner regained his name.

The original Three prepared the new spring enrollments. They had to turn away students now, there were so many of them, ending up with 70, both female and male.

They also informed Reads-the-Wind and his top-ranked hunters about the new situation at the school and did some preliminary hunting so the new instructors would not have to do that, too.

Renegade cleaned and aired his parents' old home, its memories dead and dry now. He'd rarely come back over the years; and he left most of the items there.

But K'leura saw the *kreppa-tsrr's* skull and the stag's head mounted on the walls and heard their stories for the first time.

"Renegade, why don't you take these with us? And maybe Swift Runner will want copies of them for the hall. They're yours and your family's. You should have them."

"Don't tell me he's copying our Master Hunt trophies and enthroning them up there?" Renegade said with some annoyance.

"The man still does not believe he is a living legend," Rampage called from the next room. "I hope that's one stupendous starship, brothers, if it has to carry us, our weapons, our supplies and our trophies too."

"Not to mention your wedding presents," Dasrylion put in sarcastically,

"And I *didn't* mention them, did I?" came Rampage's sweet reply.

Renegade bit back a laugh.

In a rare private moment, the Plains warrior had asked his friend if he, Rampage, had "changed" after marriage – as if he expected some physical difference.

"You *have* changed," Renegade told him, "but in a different way. That temper of yours has mellowed; most of your nervous impatience is gone, and I think you act like a happier man, now" – which brought a flush of emotions to Rampage's body as he wavered between pride and embarrassment.

They took the two trophies with them, along with the only holopix Renegade found of his parents together.

***

AT LAST, halfway through spring, they heard that their ship was ready, and would be flown from the factory planetoid to the space station in a fiveday. Final payment was due then – and the Arvien hunters racked their three holdings to get enough hides, furs (poor at this season) and exotic meats to supply the voyage and make the payment.

Rampage asked, "Would a dinosaur hide help?" and they threw in the sauropod skin. Still not enough. His friends refused to let him add any more of the couple's wedding gifts, despite their teasing.

Finally Renegade appealed to the Nine Systems Hunt Council for aid; and their old friend Kreh-t'vyk didn't disappoint them.

"They say they'll help us if we form a new Hunt Council out there," Renegade said.

"You mean *we'll* be the council and make all the decisions?" Rampage sounded triumphant.

"Yes, basically; except its extra work we don't really need. But I suppose we'll be adding new members as the other Ten Systems' planets are settled," Renegade said.

"Can't we do a lot of this through the comset?" Dasrylion asked. "The rest is just overseeing progress and taking game status reports."

"…and attending ceremonies and approving Master Hunts, even acting as Elders on those hunts, if there's no one else," Renegade added. "Though I suppose if we eventually open a school, we can hold the ceremonies there. Meetings too."

"And we can claim separate land for the school," K'leura reminded them. "I think I know just the place: a big mesa in a side branch of the Canyon of the Winds."

"Well, what will you tell him, then?" Rampage demanded, meaning Kreh-t'vyk.

"I'll take the consensus," Renegade said. "Who favors the council idea? …Ah. So be it. I'll tell him right away."

So the Ten Systems Hunt Council and Renegade Clan were formed before their members ever reached the new world

***

FINALLY they were ready to depart. Swift Runner volunteered to pilot them to the space station. After that they would fly the Hunt ship back to Arvien 4 for the first – and last – time. At the station, they would pick up their medicines, new weapons, tools, and lab and surgical equipment, along with all the educational material on building houses and in-home systems they could afford.

K'leura was in her 78th day now, her abdomen noticeably swelling, and Renegade was relieved to be finally underway. Hyperlight travel would slow down the pregnancy somewhat, giving them time to build homes and stock up on food before winter set in. It would be early summer when they arrived on their new world.

Renegade still had qualms about taking her out there; but with her healer and lab training, and K'orrynia's shaman training, they made a good pack, well able to handle a normal birth.

So this visit to Nine Systems Station was a sadder one. He-walks-lightly invited them to share meat again and to meet his family…to say farewell. And while the hunters brought only a few good-quality *kai* and tree-climber hides, plus 30 fresh eggs, to trade this time, he, his wife, and their daughters showered the wayfarers with more gifts: beautifully-made winter coveralls and blankets for the children, more blankets for the adults, and three great wall tapestries – familiar scenes of the land near the great hall on Arvien 4…the mountains, the forests, the waters below…all so exquisitely done that praise flew unbidden from their lips. It was a clan's bequest for a leader's household, and the trader gave it with an open heart.

"Ah, our brother, our friend," Renegade told him, deeply moved, "we hold you in our hearts. If you take to the star-trails again, come see us; you'll always be welcome at our hearth."

He-walks-lightly took each of them by the upper arms in turn: *"T'churr,* great warriors, my good friends, a parting is too much like a Leavetaking for me; so I will only bid you good hunting and safe harbor…till we meet again"

"Till we meet again," chimed softly from their throats – their final farewell.

***

THE HUNT SHIP was too big to land at the hall. It made planetide instead at Arvien 4's spaceport; and they used its two Scouts to load the rest of their things..

Swift Runner, Taslon, and Trail Leader, already installed in their new quarters, helped them load. The others were finding homes of their own, while Trail Leader had accepted Renegade's old home.

Finally they had the Hunt ship loaded. "Now there's a wonder!" Swift Runner remarked. "Everything in and still room to sleep – though hardly any to walk!"

"You should see us on an actual hunt," Rampage said, which made the other man laugh.

They made a last round of the trophy hall; and Renegade secured one last thing: his copy of the holopix taken when Broken Spear had given them their Master Hunt medallions. Pictures of the old warrior were hard to come by. This was the only one he had of them all together. He had promised a copy to He-walks-lightly too, and would send it from here. The only other copy hung in the trophy hall...like their hunts together, like their familiar hearthroom, like the mountain hall itself, soon to be left behind.

Renegade's throat constricted. Silently he joined the others at the waiting Scout ship, feeling loss for his old life; for all that he was leaving here.

And most of it already gone, he thought. *Grandfather, old warrior, old friend, the future includes no one but us now, and the meaning we give to it.*

He joined his equally-silent friends, and as they boarded, K'leura took his hand.

The three new Hunt teachers stood to see them off.

Trail Leader knew how they felt and told the others, "They leave the future in our keeping, honored ones. Let us not fail their trust."

They quietly agreed.

Trail Leader raised his spear to salute those aboard the Scout and bade them, "Good hunting all!"

They did not hear with the canopy closed but the nearest of them lifted a hand, echoing his salute, and in moments, the Scout arose and floated free.

Within the *tare',* the great starship itself lifted from its berth, and they were gone.

***Thirty-one*....Above Blue**

"STILL NEGATIVE, Renegade – this completes the survey *and* the 20th or so orbit. Are you ready to make planetide yet?" Rampage was tired of being aboard ship, looking down at the blue world below. They all were.

"Just a hair's more analysis and we will be," Renegade assured him.

"What are you expecting, the same savages who destroyed that other planet? This ship has enough firepower to blast an asteroid to stardust. A *big* asteroid."

"This was the only untouched system in this sector," his friend replied, "maybe because this sun hadn't wandered into the field a thousand years ago…or maybe…" he let it trail off. "Anyroute, the survey looks clear and the new space station has been monitoring everything in this sector; so I think we're alone here—"

"Spirit knows you've been careful enough, Renegade; let's go down now," Rampage argued, ignoring Dasryl's glare.

"I have everyone to think of, including our families-to-be," his friend reminded him gently…*and I feel responsible for all of you,* he could have added. He was the leader; and that unassumed title weighed him down and made him take extra care. Two huntresses were pregnant now, K'orrynia with twins, to Rampage's delight.

The Plains warrior had the grace to blush and fall silent.

Renegade remained deep in thought, watching the blue arc of the world roll by under them. His main concern became the more realistic worry about whether they could build homes on their new territory before the winter settled in, or whether they should go south to the rainforest for a year?

And how long before the two huntresses became incapacitated by their pregnancies, even though their terms had been slowed by hyperspace travel?

"Renegade?" he heard Dasrylion asking, and he snapped to attention to find his friends staring at him anxiously.

"This is not one of those…*bodings*, is it?" Dasrylion asked.

"*T'churr,* just thinking," he smiled. He glanced around at them. "So; are we ready?"

Rampage's eager *"Chak!"* burst out the loudest.

Renegade nodded toward the screen: "Then let fall Chance!"

Rampage gave a joyous roar and sent them into the blue.

***

K'LEURA AND his two friends had picked out some prime land while he was off investigating the Dead World, Renegade discovered.

If you started at the hot springs Stone Pool where he and K'leura had bonded, the clan holding jogged off in every direction to take in several different habitats, from a thick temperate forest to the north and west to a short jumble of low mountains east and beyond to low rolling wooded hills until you came to the sea. The river running next to the Stone Pool broke into two large divisions just west of the mountains. One angled sharply north and provided their boundary line there; the second submerged beneath the mountains and re-emerged south of the first valley, then rushed to the sea. At one point, it rimmed a huge swath of freshwater swamp, dubbed the Caverns of Gloom, and the clan holdings took a small bite of that, too.

This, the largest continent on Blue One, was shaped roughly like a double diamond, widest just above the equator, and Renegade Clan had claimed a third of it, gathering habitats from dropleaf to needleleaf forest, swampy bogs to rolling plains….a clan leader's bequest, indeed.

Most important to them was the short chunky mountain chain sitting in the rough center of their land: a series of low hills topping out in stone, like someone had dropped a handful of rocks at the edge of the forest and left them where they fell. They looked roughly like a large bird's-foot with three cobbled toes in front, and were named the Bird's-foot Mountains.

The two western-most mountains had a saddleback ridge between them. There Renegade proposed they build their trophy hall and permanent winter home.

"Rather than build small separate houses the first year, why not put our strengths together and make one large one, like a great hall," he reasoned, "with private quarters for each family but a big common hearthroom. And add a training room, bathing chamber, and food storage chambers in the heart of the mountain. Winters here are milder than on Arvien 4, but we'll need the safety of our numbers, especially with young children."

"Like a clan in winter, and freeholders in summer?" Dasrylion mused. "Many clans, like Burning Forest and Shadow, bring everyone closer in for the barren seasons. Some build great lodges for them."

"Plains doesn't," Rampage said, then added hastily; "Any-route, it'll be easier than to build three separate houses, all scattered."

"And it will let us take care of the *chk-kiy-teh* better," Sunrise put in.

That decided, they began their main project in a mixture of innocence and ignorance, as they found out. They would construct a huge hall-type dwelling in the mountain saddleback to house their families and more. It would hold their whole clan as their numbers grew, giving them both private and social living areas.

They would chisel it out of solid rock with the Hunt ship's laser-cannon, fine points being added with smaller tools, and any weak points strengthened. It would be powered by nuclear fusion, sun and wind the first year, until geothermal units could be sunk into the ground next year (their optimistic estimate). The underground river was tapped for running water and electrical needs; and just as carefully re-routed through layers of sand and stone to cleanse it before it rejoined its source.

That gave the male *tautschen* two things to do: build the hall, and hunt almost daily for food. The females insisted on doing some of the hunting too; though Renegade trembled whenever he saw his ever-more-pregnant wife set off with her companions.

Finally they compromised: Two males and a female, or two females and a male, could hunt every third day, K'leura very little. Between times, the men would work on construction, while the women racked the skins to dry, cared for Smalltusk, and collected and tested native plants for medicine and other uses.

After a tenday of this, every one of the three males was aching to get off construction duty and go hunting.

"And I thought *hunters* had to be in good condition!" Dasrylion moaned, sweating and bruised after a day's heavy labor; "but my wrists are open to anyone who does *this* for a living."

"*Churr,*" Renegade agreed; "although most colonies have some heavy machinery to help. I only hope we've been doing this right. We have to finish the water flow system, complete the foundation over it, wire and insulate the inner walls—and plumb them, too; then connect the whole thing to the power source inside the mountain and to the solar panes and wind-caves on the mountain tops."

Rampage pressed a hand to his aching back. "And just maybe water won't flow out of the light-connectors when we're done...*Vascht!* This makes for a lot of small biting pain, brothers. Next I suppose we have to blast the food storage chambers out of the rock, too?"

"We'll able to use the ship's laser cannons on those." Renegade said.

"I'm glad you bought self-charging tools and everything," Rampage said; "Any path to shorten this string..." and he rubbed his back harder.

"Let's break for a rest," Renegade said, and they gratefully complied.

***

THE HIGH POINT of every day came with the communal bath in the Stone Pool at sunset. The heated water relieved aches; and K'leura felt it helped to float her rapidly-expanding abdomen.

"I feel bloated, like some big ball of gas," she mourned to Renegade. "I can hardly carry my swollen self across the ground from the home site to the pool any longer."

"You look beautiful to me," Renegade put his arm around her; "and so does the little one. How lively he is! Look, you can see him yourself now, can't you? And you should ride a power sled to the pool, hereafter."

As he eased her weight back against his arm, K'leura looked at him gratefully. The added weight and its constant strain on lungs, heart and upper body muscles, was beginning to affect even her superior *tautschen* strength. She needed his closeness and support. They could see the child was a boy, Renegade's second son, and the warrior himself could hardly wait to see what he looked like on the 'outside.'

Sunrise and Dasrylion, meanwhile, were teaching Smalltusk to swim, floating him carefully back and forth between them in the pool. The baby had learned to crawl aboard ship and now ate tender solid foods. As Sunrise's natural milk supply dried up, her body would make ready to bear again, rather to her dismay. They had brought heat-suppressing drugs with them; but since the little clan had already begun their families, they might as well have them all at once. And Dasrylion wanted another child, his and hers.

"I'm going to nurse the next one for *years,*" Sunrise said to him. While nursing, she could not get pregnant.

"Let's get a girl, first," he countered.

***

RAMPAGE shared Renegade's anxiety as he watched the two glowing dots in K'orrynia's womb enlarge and grow. Despite K'orrynia's assurance that she was fine, that K'leura was fine, that every manner of thing was fine, Rampage became more protective daily. Soon they would be forced down to four hunters instead of six, and these only part-time.

The hunting didn't go as smoothly as it could, either. They barely kept ahead of their appetites by their some-time schedule; and Renegade worried. True, they had the whole summer to gather in food; but this construction work was taking longer than they'd planned.

They were going to have to hold a drive hunt, and soon. *Let us just finish the storage chambers,* he thought, *and get the refrigeration units in. Then we'll have a place to keep our meat.*

***Thirty-two*....Hunters and Prey**

RENEGADE and Dasrylion were finishing the freezer units one day in mid-summer when they heard a loud clopping noise coming from around the mountain's near shoulder. Exchanging looks, the two quietly slipped into defensive positions, lasers trained on the coming sound…

…as a small group of the hoofed, one-horned grazers came ambling into view, the lead one bearing –

"*K'leura?*" Renegade said in surprise. "You're *riding* them?"

She laughed merrily. "Just *one* of them, dear husband. This one." She bent forward and murmured something to her steed, and her hand moved in its mane. It snorted and paused nearly at the warrior's side.

K'leura swung herself smoothly around on the creature's back, pointed her toes, and dropped gently to the ground as Renegade caught her. Smalltusk was purring from a sling on her back.

"How do you like my *other* project, besides the medicine plants? I can recommend this type of travel for the eldest of Elders, and the most pregnant of women."

"This is amazing." Renegade reached out to touch the steed's long-haired neck, while Dasrylion edged around to the herd's other side. "I know we haven't hunted close to camp, so we would have emergency food when we needed it – but how did you convince them to let you get on?"

She beamed at him. "Time. Time and patience. This group is a family. All of them – there are seven – are related to that lead mare I was riding… one young son, one mate, four daughters. That one's the mate, Dasryl, the stallion." As the big animal stepped toward him, the trapper backstepped hastily. "He's the biggest and most powerful. Would you like to ride, both of you?"

"*Krr*...I think I'll pass," Dasrylion said as he watched that long sharp horn swing in his direction.

"Renegade?"

Renegade's anxiety over K'leura was tinged by his strong sense of curiosity and wonder.

"Well, if you're going to go climbing onto strange animals, I suppose I'd better go with you. Dasrylion, are you sure?"

"Sure as sunlight, brother. You're not getting *me* up onto one of those," the trapper declared. "Go ahead. I'll take a little rest here."

"On-stat, K'leura. Which one?"

"Take the stallion. And don't try to steer him—I don't know how to do that very well yet...hold a moment;" and she swung herself up by balancing on a flat rock, waving off Renegade's move to boost her. "Like this."

"Well and *good,*" Renegade muttered. He went to the even bigger stallion, which was golden with white tail and mane, put one hand on the crest of the neck, the other on the rump, and before the animal could react, gave a little jump and straddled him, facing front.

And a world of muscle and bone shifted under him as the stallion sidled and danced. The horned head lifted sharply, and Renegade jerked backward. What was he supposed to hang on to, here?

As for balance – he tightened his legs around the ribcage involuntarily, and they began to move.

"Uh!" the surprised hunter said.

"No toeclaws or he'll fight!" K'leura called cheerfully after him. He heard the double clip-clop of the mare approaching. "There you go, my love. Let's ride."

And she came alongside him to lead the herd at a fast walk outward.

This sort of thing needed a whole different set of muscles, Renegade discovered. His natural combat balance was superb; and if he "sat" the mount tightly, he found he could reduce the jarring sensation of its movement.

K'leura's mare took them on a slow circuit into the nearby forest, along a game path; and Renegade found he was enjoying himself.

Grandfather would have liked this, he thought, remembering Broken Spear's Master Hunt story...*a steed big enough to carry us*; *this and the dinosaurs. And look how happy it makes K'leura!*

She glanced back at him over her shoulder. "How do you like it?"

"Prime!" he called.

"Good!" she cried. "We'll go back now; they need to forage...I think I can turn her...a little faster, though..." And she managed to turn the mare and did something with her arms and legs, shouting "Hai! Hai!"

The herd seemed to leap forward. "Uhn! Uh!" Renegade grunted, grabbed the mane, the shoulder – anything to hold on.

A few hard jolts and they were *flying* – the gallop so smooth they felt airborne. The ground flowed by a tall Hunter's height below; the cantering hooves thundered; and the wind streamed past his face as the great steed rocked him in the thunder of its passage. Soon he was yelling "Hai! Hai!" to the stallion as they swept up the slope toward Dasryl again.

The animals were named *K'sarians* – Windrunners – from that day forward.

***

HUNTER'S LUCK --- While Renegade and K'leura enjoyed their ride, Rampage and the two other huntresses stood on danger's point in the swamp.

They'd flushed a little bunch of *noot-kai*, or swamp deer*, killed one, and followed the rest into the swamp, hanging the first kill from a tree so it wouldn't slow them down. Rampage wanted to take a few more: one would barely feed them all; and their clan needed meat to store as well.

Camo-suits off because of the water, they set to the trail. They followed it for a little distance in the muck when suddenly an animate mountain reared up out of a heap of fallen timber and bellowed at them.

It was a giant quill-carrier, big as a bull krolf, which they had named the "Ball of Knives." It lurched toward them, and assumed a defensive position humped like a hill, head between its forelegs, its heavy tail lashing and flinging out a hail of man-length spines.

"KKT!" Rampage cried. "Back! Back under cover!" and they retreated before the flying spears.

So here they were, in a rough triangle on the landward side of the formidable beast, uncertain what to do. Meanwhile the swamp kais' padded feet carried them farther and farther away, and the Ball of Knives was blocking the path beyond the deadfall.

"Why don't we just climb those trees around it?" K'orrynia called to her husband.

"Look at them. They're conifers 100 *kri* tall, and at least 20 *kri* apart. It would be too much risk to have you jump them with us, K'orrynia; or Sunrise and I would have to leave you behind with this creature," Rampage called back.

---

* Not "deer" as we know them, of course, but herbivores of about that size, with keen senses and fleetness of foot.

"What about killing *this*?" Sunrise shouted across. "Can we eat it?"

"My thought exactly," Rampage said. "Question is – how?" He peered out from behind the tree bole. A massive hump bristling with red, black and white spines, its tail still twitching, greeted his eyes.

"*T'chrrt!*" he muttered.

Its head was still tightly tucked, its humped body a mass of spines with the vital organs protected everywhere but underneath. That ruled out his favorite weapon, the vai-ator. "Where are those skinny *hstaen* things when you need them?" he grumbled. The so-called landsnakes or *hstaen,* large weasel-like creatures, could burrow underground to get at the Ball of Knives.

"Vai-ator's no good," Rampage called to his hunting pack. "We'll have to try lasers. K'orrynia, Sunrise, can either of you get a neck shot? I'm near the tail end here."

"I can, Rampage," K'orrynia returned.

"On-stat. Just aim and shoot, then take cover again – watch the reflexes!"

And he was flabbergasted to hear her sweetly-sarcastic reply of "Yes, Elder. Whatever you command. *Tschk!"*

She's been learning from me, he grinned, and kept an eye on her, aiming his laser to blanket. Sunrise did the same from her side.

The bolt whooshed home, solid hit between the shoulders. And then everything went mad.

Firelines shot up in every direction as the beat's quills actually *deflected* part of the charge. Blue fire careened through the trees at them, and the Ball of Knives went into a spasm of tail-flogging.

"Down! Get DOWN!" Rampage screamed at his partners as first a laser flash seared the tree above his head and next a hurricane of quill-spears came at him. He dodged behind his tree just as one living spear exploded a rotten log at his feet.

A tremendous crashing and thrashing followed, along with boar-like squeals and grunts of rage. Unable to shout over the noise, Rampage went to his headset and called his pack.

"K'orrynia! Sunrise! Are you hurt? Anyone hit?"

A few agonizing moments passed, then they answered, "No…not I, husband," and, "On-stat, Rampage; nothing here."

He heaved a sigh of relief and started to raise his head again, when he heard a mighty cracking and splitting sound, like whole trees being ripped apart.

He sprang twice his height up the nearest tree and looked around the trunk.

Sunrise's voice confirmed what his eyes saw: "It's on the move, Rampage. It broke through that deadfall as if it was so much paper, and it's charging deeper into the swamp."

"Blast and burn!" he growled. "Your pardon, Sunrise. You two wait till I come out, then follow me." He dropped from the tree and made for the former pile of fallen timbers, snatching up several of the beast's own quills on the way. *Maybe these can stop you,* he thought. *Why didn't I bring Flashing Sky's lucky spear?*

The huntpack re-formed in the clearing and waded through the debris of broken boughs and wood splinters after their prey. It wasn't hard to follow; it was making as much noise as a bull trey-horn and splashing out to open water at a fast waddle. Just beyond the treeline it paused and stood on its hindquarters, snuffling the air.

The creature turned its back to them and shuffled farther out. Rampage slipped forward into the water after it…

…Just as it stepped into a pothole and vanished underwater.

A pause, a swell of water, the tail flipped up once and fell, sodden. Rampage leaped backward to solid wood.

Sunrise screamed, "Rampage! In the water!" as a surge of silver eel-like creatures boiled up from between the sunken tree roots and streamed by the hundreds toward the swirl of blood and spears.

"KKT! Hunters, to land!" he gasped.

They didn't need encouragement. All three fled to the safety of logs and standing trees.

Where they watched their would-be dinner torn to pieces by the huge armored beast that rose from its bolthole where the Ball of Knives had fallen – and those pieces devoured to the last morsel by the ravenous *sr'rk't* eels, with their sharp teeth and instinct for blood.

When it was over, all that was left of the Ball of Knives was an array of spines radiating out from the bolthole, along with rings of blood upon the water.

The three hunters looked at each other in silence.

After a time K'orrynia said, "*Krr,* at least no one was injured."

"It came too near the mark," Rampage grumbled. He motioned them to retreat ahead of him so he could guard the rear.

"Just hunter's luck," Sunrise comforted as she passed him. "We still have the *noot kai.*"

"Yes; and *this,*" And savagely Rampage lunged and speared a fat chameleon-like creature on a tree trunk.

Sunrise leaped straight up, spun and came down facing him, teeth bared, before she realized what had happened.

"*Br-rt*, Sunrise, I'm sorry," Rampage was contrite. "Your pardon, I didn't mean"—

K'orrynia had stopped too, and turned to stare at him in disbelief.

"I crave your pardon," he found himself apologizing to both of them

Kind-hearted Sunrise touched his wrist gently. "I take no offense, brother. Only – a little *warning* would be nice."

"My thanks; and as you say, we have the swamp kai." He slipped the chameleon off his impromptu spine-spear and hung it on his belt.

As it turned out, they didn't have the noot kai. More "hunter's luck" awaited them. They stared incredulous at the tree where the kai had been hanging. Only a pulled loop of rope and a scattering of hide and hair remained. Some enterprising creature had pulled their catch down and carried it away.

"Maybe we can track the other beast," Rampage suggested after a silence. He looked again at their doleful faces, and at the rapidly-sinking sun. "On the other talon," he amended, "whatever took this must have been near the size of our spiny friend. It didn't even have to climb to reach the noot-kai. So why don't we just get onto the power sled and go home – slowly? Maybe we can flush something out as we go."

But their bad fall of Chance held all the way home.

***

THAT NIGHT the little clan dined on a very thin stew of tree-hugger, a few sour berries, and some of their dried meat supplies.*

No one spoke. They finished their meal outside the Hunt ship, threw a few sticks on the fire, and sat watching it and the spangled sky above.

Finally Renegade stated the obvious: "Something has to be done. We can't build *and* hunt; yet we need to do both, somehow. We need to have a game drive or a major hunt, and soon."

Rampage felt morose about their poor luck that day, although nobody blamed him. These things just happened; you had to hunt new territory for a long time before you got to know its animals' habits well enough to make your kills quickly.

K'orrynia spoke up: "What about your traplines, Dasrylion? Can we get our meat out of those?"

---

* On Pets: K'leura's Windrunners now qualify as "pets" or kept animals; and as such are generally exempt from eating, unless the Hunters themselves are starving. To kill and eat something that trusts you is regarded as a grave betrayal.

More gloom. "We could, if I had all my traps out, and *if* I had time to study and learn the game trails well enough to make a good catch every time. As it is, most of my traps are buried beneath a few hundred *mearn* of supplies. I'm working with a limited number of them now; and those take only smaller prey."

"So that leaves us at trail's head where we began," Renegade said. "We have to have fulltime hunters who are *not* at risk, or we have to find a big herd of animals and take a number of them."

"Why don't we go inside and look at some of our survey maps?" K'leura suggested. "It's been scarcely more than two tendays since we made them." She silently hoped that no one would suggest the Windrunners—even those out in the forest. She had come to think of them as *her* Windrunners, and the thought of killing them chilled her...

Renegade already knew that.

But now "Good throw!" came from several throats at once; and the hunters damped down their fire and went to their usual berth, the Hunt ship.

Unfortunately, the maps had been made by photographing the terrain from orbit before they made planetide, and mostly of their present site; so any information they had was dated. They'd caught the edge of the grasslands, but not enough to tell them much about herd movements there.

Until the factory planetoids in Nine Systems sent them their survey satellites, they'd have to update what they had by taking the Hunt ship back into orbit, or use one of the smaller Scouts to make a continent-wide search –which could take days.

"And since we're taking more supplies out of the ship every day," Rampage put in, "we'd have to leave them behind; and scavengers would find them and drag them off..."

"We're bound to find some large herds on the plains," Dasryl began, when Sunrise interrupted:

"Hold; this may be something. See that branch of the river to the north and east of us? The one which goes all the way out to the sea?"

"Churr-urr," said Renegade slowly.

"Look at these concentrations of bird life – here, at the estuary."

"Oh!" K'leura exclaimed. "I see it! The life-patterns increase there, as if it were a huge breeding ground for sea birds."

"It still should be, even now," Rampage was getting excited; "when the young are fledging and the adults molting." He looked up in triumph. "Easy prey, easy kills. We could get there in less than a day with the Scout ships; two, if we took the sleds..."

"…and catch all the fish and birds we could eat," Sunrise finished for him.

Eyes bright again, they looked to their leader.

"Wait," Dasrylion protested; "don't we need nets or something similar?"

"We have capture nets, brother," Renegade said. "All we have to do is rig them to drag …"

"A *boat,* Renegade, we need a boat." Dasrylion rarely disagreed with his friend, but when he did, he could be stubborn. "I don't suppose you can track down one of those, can you?"

Rampage eyed him in disbelief. *He* was usually the group's protestor here.

Renegade grinned at him. "On point I can. We have one; or rather we *brought* one along with the other supplies. It's here on board ship, tucked into its own shelf, within easy reach. And we may be able to use the sleds over water and drag the nets from them."

That settled it. All six of them would leave at first light, flying not the Scouts, but the Hunt ship itself, to inspect the great tidal bay in the northeast. They could carry the boat, the nets, the Scouts, everything aboard ship and put in a day or two of hunting. It should be enough.

As he slept that night with K'leura, his front nestled against her back, Renegade felt the faintest tingle of a doubt, far back in his mind. But he was too tired to remember what it meant…

Thirty-three....Saltwater

Their predawn flight brought them to the bay within a tare'; and they saw sunrise over the ocean.

The river narrowed before it met the sea and ran between stony banks. At the ocean, it widened abruptly, the rocks rising to low cliffs on one side, and dropping into tidal flats on the other.

Seabirds rose in calling clouds above the bay. They nested on the northside cliffs. There were other kinds of animals there too, larger and heavier sea mammals that had come to birth their young.

"I see warmbloods by the ten-score on those rocks," Dasrylion remarked, scoping them through his facemask. "Apparently it's a breeding ground for them, too," Beneath the mask he was smiling. "We may be getting some hunting luck at last."

"There are shoals of fish near the surface, too," Renegade said. "We'll take the two Scouts and rig them with nets and go trolling for birds and fish. First, though, we'll land a Scout on those rocks and take some of the animals – plenty of meat there."

He and Dasrylion took one Scout, Rampage and K'orrynia the other, and swooped toward the rocks. They were able to fly over without alarming the animals much. Sunrise and K'leura, with one small child and one unborn, had to stay near the Hunt ship.

"We'll need help with the cleaning, so please rest now," Renegade tried to mollify them. "K'orrynia can come back with the first load and help you..."

"Don't fret," Sunrise told K'leura sardonically as the Scouts lifted away. "We will get to do the butchering, t'churr!" Concerned, she asked,

"Are you feeling on-stat, K'leura? You look like you're very close; and the baby's shifted to head down."

"I know," K'leura suppressed a groan; "he flopped around in there like some big fish. Now I feel this pressure – and he's very quiet. K'orrynia brought some medicines with us, though; and she's a trained surgeon, on Chance it happens here" She leaned against the ship's hull, trying not to think.

Sunrise patted her arm. "Don't worry. It will be on-path. You look just the way you should. I know." And she stayed close while they watched the hunting pack scour the cliffs.

While K'orrynia's Scout hovered over the rocks at the sea side to head off any animals that tried to break for the water, the second ship set down well behind the herds.. The hunters emerged and began selecting their prey.

In a surprisingly short time, 24 good-size carcasses lay on the rocks, and they were done. The second Scout rose to let the other animals escape to the sea. Some did; but most were so unused to being hunted this way that they milled around in place. All four hunters walked the killing-ground unhampered to remove the quarry.

The Scouts made two trips to bring all the meat and leave it on the sandy side of the estuary near the Hunt ship.

"Just give it a start: try to put the offal onto this sled so it can be dumped in the water," Renegade told the two women. "We're going to set the nets now and go fishing…" and looking directly at K'leura, he promised, "We'll be back to help you."

"I'll help now," K'orrynia decided, much to their relief.

The male hunters went off again, nets extended from a Scout ship's capture jaws and dragged low behind a power sled to harvest the bay, which squirmed with fish.

The three huntresses set to work on the heaps of flesh by the sea.

"Let's do one at a time," Sunrise suggested; "then we can bag the meat and dispose of the insides so nothing's left to attract – no, Smalltusk, stay away from the knives. Go look at these other nice beasts; that's it…"

They had taken two species of animals from the cliff hunt: one had a short, square body with four flippers for limbs, a long slim neck and a small head. The other was longer and slimmer. It had a shorter neck with a rough "mane" of hair, and a head somewhat like the Windrunners'. The orange mane extended to the beast's shoulders; and while the front limbs were flippers, the hind ones had fused into a broad horizontal tail.

Both species were solidly packed with meat; and true to their code, the hunters had taken only the excess males and barren females.

On their fishing foray, the hunters made several passes over the bay, dipping their nets and bringing them up jammed full. They barely had to scoop below the surface; the water was so thronged with life. Soon piles of fish lay heaped beside the sea mammals' bodies, with game bags thrown on top to guard them from scavenging birds. The three men rejoined the women to help with the cleaning.

"We'll have to test the fish for eating quality; we know the mammals are on-stat," Renegade said. He fetched a portable analysis unit from the Hunt ship and brought it over.

"I know one taste we're going to get very tired of this winter," K'leura remarked, rubbing blood, sweat and oil from above her eyes.

"Or even before this winter," Rampage grinned at her.

"Maybe we'll have finished the main chambers by then," Dasrylion said, "and be able to get back to land hunting, for variety."

They had not after all used the boat. A small, lightweight motor craft which included a sail, it lay beside the Hunt ship, almost forgotten. It would be more useful for smaller bodies of water like lakes and ponds; and Rampage had the notion of fitting it with an above-board fan motor, so they could explore the great swamp without being eaten alive by the sr'rk't eels.

The skinning and butchering took much longer than the original hunt. By the time the sun passed the zenith, the huntpack was hot and tired. K'leura in particular looked weary and sick.

Concerned, Renegade touched her shoulder and said, "Why don't you rest for a while, my lady? Perhaps all three of you?" He glanced at the huntresses.

K'orrynia was about to protest she wasn't tired yet when she saw how K'leura looked, and agreed with him. Sunrise needed no urging. Smalltusk was up to his knees in blood and fish guts, and getting cranky for a nap.

"I'd feel better if we could wash off somewhere," K'leura grimaced at her smeared arms and legs.

"So would I," K'orrynia declared. "There are some tide pools on this side of the river-mouth. We might be able to bathe in those."

"That would be a relief," K'leura sighed.

"And I could clean off Smalltusk and even get him to sleep," Sunrise agreed.

"You're going where, now?" Renegade asked them. "Krr, I see. Don't get out of sight or voice range, if you're bathing – and don't forget the alarm sensors..."

"Don't forget to take your weapons!" Rampage shouted after them; "and keep your wristknives on at all times, and don't'—

The three huntresses turned their heads as one, wicked gleams in three pairs of eyes. Simultaneously they chimed, "Yes, Elders!" and sauntered away.

Rampage and Renegade exchanged glances, dumbstruck, while Dasrylion actually bellowed with laughter.

Winding down, the big trapper wiped his eyes and told them, "I'll take the boat over and anchor it in one of those little pools for them. It has depth alarm sensors, so it will be more useful than the standard ones. You great-aunties may stay here and clean more fish!" and he walked off, chuckling, while his two friends stared after him, torn between pique and laughter.

***

THE SMALL POOL they chose was deeper than it looked, and the three huntresses were able to submerge most of their bodies. Sunrise dunked and swam Smalltusk a few times, then placed him on the warm sandy shoreline under a light pelt for cover, with a motion detector for company.

"Good," Sunrise said. "Now for me – t'chrrt! Watch these sharp rocks below, sisters…the pools are sand above, rock beneath." She had stubbed a toe, twisting the toeclaw aside, a painful but minor injury.

"There's a sandy bottom in the middle, covering the stone," K'leura remarked from her post in the pool's center. "And the water's warm."

"It is a nice warm day," K'orrynia agreed, unbinding her long golden mane. "I hope I can get used to winters here – go ahead, Sunrise; I'll watch him."

Daylight glided by. Neither the women, busy with bathing, nor the men, bent on preparing the meat before dark and taking it aboard ship, noticed how a mist seemed to form around the sun, or how a line of deep blue-purple clouds seemed to be massing in the south…

…and everyone had forgotten about the tides.

The day's second tide, the withdrawal, was almost upon them. And tides on this particular bay were spectacular.

The narrow river channel formed a tidal bore: once a day the seawater thundered into the rock-ribbed channel with the speed and force of a powerboat. Returning, it ripped out of there back to sea the same way, aided by the titanic pull from the twin planet, Blue Two. Tides were enormous everywhere on this world, and weather changes frequent and strong; but this tidal bore was an especially powerful one.

It was coming: a dull roar droned from up-river. The air suddenly prickled with electricity, and dark clouds blanketed the sky from the south.

A warm strong wind switched on, scattered a rainbow of fish scales across the beach before it.

The three huntresses looked up. "Something's wrong," K'orrynia said. "A storm is coming. Sunrise, K'leura, we had better leave here, and quickly."

"Coming," Sunrise pulled herself out, slung on a wrap, and picked up the baby.

K'orrynia paused. "K'leura! Hurry!"

K'leura, farthest from shore and nearest the river, called, "I'll get the boat! Go ahead!" And she plowed slowly over to the boat, which bobbed and swayed unaccountably.

Out on the butchering ground, the three warriors stiffened against the sudden wind.

"Storm," Dasrylion said. "We'd better pack and load."

"What about…?" Rampage glanced toward the huntresses. Two were already coming out of the water.

"You load; I'll get them!" Renegade had to shout to be heard against the increasing roar. Was that just the wind? What else? He dumped his cleaned fish into a sack, the sack onto a sled. Rampage and Dasrylion heaved more bags on top of that, nudged the sled forward and headed for the ship.

Renegade began walking toward the tide pool. He had time before the storm. A little rain and wind wouldn't bother them much any-route. And yet, he didn't want anyone left out in it.

He began by walking. He saw two women out of the water, K'leura by the boat.

Then he saw what was coming down the river channel, and he began to run.

K'leura, holding the boat still with one hand and hauling up the small anchor with the other, had the feeling that this would go more smoothly if she got into the boat. She felt it so strongly it was like a command. So, balancing both hands wide apart on the frame, she tugged and grunted and finally slid heavily into its shallow seat.

She heard screaming or shouting, and raised her head over the side to see Renegade running full-force over the ground, shouting, the others waving in place frantically.

And something struck the side of the boat a massive blow, and tore it out of the pool and into the river-race.

"KALOORAH!" Renegade screamed in pure terror as he saw the seaward wave hoist the little boat and spin it away.

Beware of saltwater – now he remembered and now he knew – too late.

His love, his life, his world was being stolen from him.

Without a thought, Renegade made the leap of his life across the surging tide pool, thirty kri into raging water, and was dashed away with it, the boat, and the woman he loved.

Four people stood locked in their tracks as Renegade, K'leura, and the boat disappeared into a swell of the sea. Then Rampage ran for their two remaining mates, shouting to Dasrylion, "Power the ship! We're going after them!"

And the storm struck in all its fury.

***

RENEGADE had one chance for the boat and he lunged for it. He hit the water like a rocket and kicked out to swim.

--when the undertow caught him and pulled him down.

Renegade closed his larynx and fought to go forward. Since he'd taken off his mask while he was cleaning the meat, he would have to depend on his powerful lungs and his strength to keep from drowning.

The current whirled him to the surface, and he saw a flicker of white vanish over a hump of water. The boat. He churned for it. If he could reach it and hold on, the tide would slow in time and he could--

Something struck him on the shoulder and tried to wrap itself around him. He ducked, came up and grabbed—

- The anchor chain as it whipped past. It slipped through his hands, stopped with a jerk at the anchor itself. Then a gale force wind snatched them both and hurled them north. Renegade snapped at the end of the chain like a whip-crack.

He had it; he had it; he just had to hang on and breathe sometimes.

But the air was full of flying water, and he had a hard trail just keeping his mouth clear and his lungs empty. He prayed for strength to the One Spirit; but most of all he prayed for his old mentor to help him in his time of need...forgive my ignorance; please help me to help her. Save her and the child...

The storm spun him closer to the boat. With a mighty kick that shoved his head and shoulders out of the water, he stared across the purple-black sky and jade-dark water.

And saw her there, clinging to the sides of the boat, bowed low from her knees, trying to protect her living burden.

She raised her head and glimpsed him in the water. He could see her mouth form his name before whitewater sprayed between them and whip-snapped the boat away. It flung him in the opposite direction, and his back and shoulders stretched with pain.

Renegade hung on and tried to think. The tide and the storm were bearing them north along the rocky shore. The tidal force was slowly weakening, and the counterbalance of his weight gave the boat some drag. If he hauled himself along the anchor chain, he might reach the boat and be able to steer for a quiet spot on shore.

Grimly, the waves battering him and the wind howling round him like a horde of deadly foes, he began to pull himself toward the boat, a kli at a time.

Once he left the anchor behind and its weight swung loose, it began to whipsaw over him. But he was focused now, no fear and no pain. No surrender…the hunter does not expect honor from the prey.

His plan was dashed away when a huge cliff loomed before them, a stone-slab peninsula thrusting out directly to their north, and the stormwind drove them toward it.

Horror rose in his throat. At this speed they would be smashed into it with killing impact. Muscles bulged and sinew stretched as he tried to backpedal against the wind; and all his strength availed him naught. The cliff grew until it filled the sky.

K'leura saw the look on his face and glanced over her shoulder. The rocks reached out. She gave a despairing cry and hugged the bottom of the boat, her arms and knees over her stomach to protect the child.

At the last instant Renegade saw it – a tiny arch of darkness at the foot of the cliff, water in its mouth. A cave – and if he could push the boat…

He stopped fighting the current and lunged into its heart. He struck the boat's stern with hands and head, jolting it. K'leura felt the shock, looked up, stretched for him…

He felt her touch, gasped out, "K'leura, no! Hold hard!" and threw every sinew and fiber of his being into shoving the boat into the cave.

And he did. He saw it plunge, prow to stern, into the little darkened niche – just before the next wave lifted his body sideways and slammed him into the rock.

"No!" K'leura screamed as she felt his hand wrenched away. Forgetting everything else, she heaved her ungainly self over the backboard, half-fell into the surf, and seized his wrist again.

No, don't let him be hit anymore, she begged, pulling. The boat slid away under her and she fell face first into the water. Her legs kicked out, struck bottom and arose, hauling her Renegade in from the sea.

The storm's force was muted here, and the water only waist deep, but the body she dragged in was limp and unresponsive.

"No, no. no." she sobbed as she caught him under the shoulders and pulled him along – to where? Where could she take him?

She followed the boat bobbing ahead of her with the vague idea of placing him in it; and first her waist, then her knees rose above water, and she was climbing a sandy slope into the cave.

Sand floor met rock roof at a sharp angle; she nearly bumped her head on the cave's low ceiling. She stopped and stretched Renegade on the sand, pulling the clumsy backpack off him so he could lie flat.

She searched his unresponsive body for injuries: there, the left-side ribs. Was he breathing? Water, water in his lungs. Frantically she rolled him onto his stomach and began pushing down on his diaphragm. (Mouth-to-mouth resuscitation is difficult for the Hunters: they cannot make a good seal with anyone older than a child because of the large biting teeth and very thin everted portion of the lips.)

Let him live, let him live, let him live, she prayed in rhythm with the strokes.

A gush of water came from his mouth, then another. And he coughed, gasping for air.

He was alive! She tumbled off his hips, and he spasmed in pain as his broken ribs grated against each other.

"Oh my love, my love, wait. I can fix it," she promised, turning him over once again, more gently this time. He was heavy and she felt a little cramp of strain. No matter; she had to get this done.

His eyelids flickered. She spoke softly to him and he subsided, but seemed to be breathing normally. Better he stay unconscious, though, for what she had to do.

Her people's wide-spectrum vision was a boon in the dark: she could plainly see the extra heat around Renegade's two cracked ribs. The sea's force must have been tremendous to break that strength of bone.

She had nothing of her healing supplies with her, but Renegade had his backpack. She dragged it to her, rummaged through it to get his med-kit. She found a quick-setting gel to hold the fractures together and a small surgical laser, but no large bandages. A small sterile pad and the belts off Renegade's own leathers would have to do.

Quickly and carefully she made the small cut, put the ribs in place and squeezed out the gel. Her warrior was still unconscious, but he breathed evenly and his heartbeat was strong. She had to strain to hold the fractures together a few moments until the gel hardened – and another pain shot through her, deep and bright.

She knew what it meant, but pushed the thought away. She couldn't think about the baby now.

Once the gel hardened, she resealed the opening with the laser and laid the gauze pad in place on top of it. Now she could tighten the leather straps around it.

They kept slipping though; so she un-cinched Renegade's waist-belt and wrapped its wider strap over the rib cast. There. That would hold.

She was breathing hard, as if she'd just run a race. She sat down beside her husband, touched him gently.

His head moved but he did not wake.

"You'll be just fine now, my hunter," she assured them both. "You'll be on stat."

Then, bending her knees up and her head down to rest on them, she prepared to wait.

Something white bobbed at the edge of her vision, on the dark water. Oh. The boat. Better haul it in to shore, or they would have no way out of here after the storm.

Wearily she got to her feet and walked down to the water and into it, ankle-deep. She leaned toward the boat.

And a burning stab of sheer pain racked her almost to her knees.

K'leura gasped, breathless with its fury. Something low down inside her gave way, and a burst of watery fluid washed down around her knees.

"Oh," she panted; "not ...now...oh—uh!" Another fiery bolt: she turned and half-walked, half-crawled back to Renegade.

The baby was coming; her mate was hurt, unaware; they were lost in a storm...and she was alone.

By the time she reached his side, the labor pains were coming in long, tearing waves. Oh little Rebel, she told the baby, I hope you're ready for this. Between the poniards of pain, she hollowed out a place for her hips in the clean sand and pulled Renegade's soft loincloth under her.

Then she lay back and let the rhythm of the pains take her.

***

THE WAILING of the doomed woke him where nothing else could. Dimly and far away K'leura called to him, and he responded.

Because she needed him and he must help her.

Renegade opened his eyes to the darkness in the sea cave, to the lash of waves upon the rock, and the body of his wife straining beside him. Her head was thrown back, her eyes closed when another spasm rippled through her, and she cried out, wail and scream together.

Groggy and fearful, he tried to sit up, nearly fell back as his own pain ground into him, and then did get upright, next to her, one arm encircling her.

"K'leura?' he wavered; "What's wrong? Are you hurt?"

She jumped at his touch, and looked at him. "Renegade! You're alive!"

"On-course I am," he said gently, stroking her face. She doesn't feel normal…drenched with sweat, yet shivering too. "Just tell me what's wrong, my heart, so I can help."

Despite her torment, K'leura gasped out a laugh. "No, my—love, my hunter, this…you cannot help…" then her body stiffened in his arms and she arched against him with the pain. "Aah-ah!" she cried, and his heart raced. What was happening?

"The—baby…" she whispered; "Our baby…is being born."

"Oh Great Spirit!" Renegade almost went numb with shock. All his training, all his skill, and nothing had prepared him for this. "What can I do?" he whispered, knowing even as he spoke that he was almost helpless. "There is something for pain, in my pack."

She pulled both his arms across her chest. Her full breasts pressed into them, but he felt no desire now.

"Too late…for medicine," she murmured, sinking against him in exhaustion. "Just…be with me…and watch…and wait, with me."

And through the long dark night of the storm, that is what he did.

***

IT FELT like an eternity before Renegade finally saw the baby's head push to the end of the birth canal, and then…

"K'leura," he said, "the head, it's coming. It's almost over."

She stirred a little, wet and clammy and tired, and replied, "Yes; if I push…just a little more. Renegade, go down there and catch him. I don't want him…born alone."

"I will," her husband whispered as he set her head and shoulders down very gently on the sand. He crawled over to her legs, which were sprawled and quivering with pain.

And there came the round little head, turned away from him, pushing clear. K'leura gave a last, unbearable heave, and her shriek split the sky.

As the baby shot forward and dropped into his father's outstretched arms.

Renegade lifted him, a tiny, slippery bundle, held the little being up to his eyes, breathed gently upon the scrunched-up unhappy face; then rubbed him with a pelt scrap, rubbed life and warmth and breath into him. The baby shook furiously, his two round dark blue eyes opened, and he inhaled, then exhaled in a high, indignant squall at being forced out into the cold.

Renegade laughed. "There you are! Little Rebel, good journey! Day's-light to you!" He hoisted him overhead, laughed again at the angry little howl, and rocked him against his chest, feeling nearly delirious himself.

"...Renegade?" a very tired whisper now.

"Oh, Rebel," the father smiled, "come and meet your lady mother, whose face you have never seen." And he brought the infant the few steps over and knelt beside his wife.

"Is he--?" K'leura began, and relaxed as Renegade beamed at her and laid the baby in her arms. She tucked the little one close, put her head back and closed her eyes.

"He's fine. You hold him and rest while I take care of some things here," Renegade almost crooned to her. Despite the pain in his side, despite his own fatigue, he was lighthearted with joy.

He returned to the birth area, snagged his pack in passing and got the med-kit out: Already used, I see. But there was enough antibiotic liquid left to fill two syringes; and he had plans for that.

K'leura shed the placenta next; the "second birth" they call it; which Renegade lifted carefully to keep the cord untangled as he set it aside. He would burn it later, after the life fluids had passed to the child...

Next he opened a watertight sac from his own supplies, filled it with some analgesic and water purifier dust, shook it thoroughly, and laved her lower abdomen and inner thighs with it, scrupulously avoiding the vaginal opening. He did that twice, then covered her with the only clean thing he could find – a bit of leather from his pack. He took away the drenched loin and breechcloth under her and slipped some of the antibiotic into her hip with a syringe.

Finally he crawled back alongside her to see how mother and child were doing.

K'leura lay heavy with sleep, but the baby seemed to be active, searching for something with his toothless mouth. Renegade watched him, perplexed, until it struck him, and be berated himself for his ignorance.

"T'chrrt! I'm an idiot, or worse! Here, little one, let me help." And balancing the baby on one strong hand, Renegade eased him over to one of his mother's breast. Gently he pressed the aureole, and milk leaked freely from the nipple, as it did when she was in season. He urged the nipple into the baby's mouth, pressed again, and suddenly the little one's jaws were clamping down in a chewing motion, and the milk was flowing into the hungry mouth.

The baby nursed for a few moments, then sputtered and coughed, drew in a few quick breaths, and nursed again.

"Breathe or eat, it's a hard decision, isn't it?" Renegade murmured, and chuckled at the fierce biting motions. "I can see why mothers stop nursing when the spears* start to show, churr, little Rebel?"

K'leura blinked awake, because of the feeding or the sound of her husband's voice. She struggled and sat up: "What's going on – oh, I see. Is he…is he healthy?"

"He's fine, K'leura. Really fine."

"But we haven't any blankets; what if he gets cold? Newborns do."

"Ah. Covering and warmth. On target, my heart." Renegade sounded remarkably jovial. "Here we all are, naked as newborns ourselves, but we can warm him. Watch and see."

And while she cradled the nursing child, Renegade fetched one more thing – his laser, discarded on the sand.

K'leura's eyes widened. But all Renegade did was switch the infrared aiming device on LOW. Carefully he ran the beam up and down the infant's body; and he and his wife massaged the little one all over with their hands.

And Renegade remembered how, a long time ago, someone had done the same for him, when he was a little boy near death, and brought life back to him again… "You have learned how to take life, now learn how to give it, as well"…and soon, he put the laser away.

He gave the baby the last cleaning-cloth from his pack; and little Rebel responded to food and warmth with contentment. He let the nipple go, balled his little fists, his fingers already armed with sharp nails, curled his toes and let his eyes close – with a tiny burp for emphasis.

His mother and father laughed. Then Renegade ran his right arm under K'leura's shoulders and eased her and the baby back down. He had one more task before he lay down himself. He crawled a short span away and fired the bloody clothes and the afterbirth, so no predators would be attracted to the scent. He scooped sand over the ashes and returned to his wife and child, where he re-inserted his arm under K'leura's shoulders and sank down next to her.

The couple's arms crossed over the baby and sought each other's sides. They cradled him between them. Renegade's cracked ribs still hurt, but the pain was receding with weariness.

---

* Teeth

Mother and father looked at each other over their newborn child, and closed their eyes to sleep, one more time.

***

THE STORM subsided at last. The morning sun rose over the sea, casting the cliff into brilliant copper and sharp shadow. The tide began to roll back in, inexorable and hungry. The peninsula blunted most of it, but its force would not be denied.

The little boat, moored by its anchor chain tangled in the rocks below, tugged at the line, yearning toward the cave-mouth and the sea. Its white shape squeezed out the rapidly-filling aperture…

...far enough so the white glisten caught the eye of the patrolling Scout ship, flying almost at sea level in one last desperate search.

"I've got them! Or the boat, any-route," Rampage called to the other craft. "And there's a cave. Land on the cliff top and follow me down!"

Thirty-four....Reprieve

THE SLEEPERS responded to the quick ministration of comfort and care when K'orrynia went down with Rampage. As the baby appeared between them, Rampage almost dropped his med-kit.

"*T'churr!* There's…there's a *baby*, K'orrynia!"

She didn't even pause in her work, though she smiled. "On-path there is, my warrior. Who runs trail may read. I could see the signs when we arrived. Now hurry. The tide is returning."

Renegade moved under their touch, half-awake, as Rampage and K'orrynia lifted him into the little boat beside his wife and child. "Rampage?" he mumbled. "You found us? How—are they?" With an anxious glance at his family.

"Living and breathing, leader. Or we may just call you 'lucky' after today. We ranged over 200 *kri-veh* in the Hunt ship during the storm and couldn't find a trace of you. So we came back this morning with the Scouts, and saw your boat peeking out of the cave…just on the nock, I might add. Oh, here's Dasryl. On-stat, brother, I'm going to float them out;" and he had to duck his head to push the boat out of the cave.

"Got you!" Dasrylion said triumphantly. "Great Spirit! Who's this?"

"Brothers, sisters, meet Rebel." Renegade smiled through his weariness.

"Takes after his father, in colors and contrariness," Rampage added. "K'orrynia – *now*, please."

Renegade heard, and started to rise.

"Just lay back and rest, brother," Rampage told him. "We'll do the rescuing from here. K'leura? You too."

After the anchor chain was untangled from the rocks, they were winched away up the cliff boat and all to the Scouts waiting above.

Rampage urged K'orrynia out and sent her after the boat. He delayed a bit, re-entering the cave, to his wife's consternation.

His facemask on and breathing lines attached, he swam back a little way to make sure they'd left nothing behind.

The incoming water was already washing away all signs that two people had lain here, that a baby had been born here; but to Rampage's surprise, the cave made a bend just beyond where they had come to ground. He followed it, noticed the rocks were rimed with colorful crusty deposits, and there was a ledge above his head.

Something bulky there…intrigued, he stood and reached up…

"Rampage? Where are you? What's wrong?" his wife called after him.

"Nothing; I'll be right there," he said through his comset. He leaped up level with the rock shelf and peered over it, clinging by his fingertalons. Yes, there was definitely something under these formations – two things. A few punches with his wristknives and he broke through. He freed the items, took them down, and holding them slightly above water, paddled back to the cave mouth and ducked under.

He popped up directly in front of K'orrynia, who nearly jumped out of the water.

"Rampage, you startled me," she began. Then she saw what he was carrying: an odd-shaped skull and some kind of packet, once transparent but now covered with colored salt crystals like the skull, both like some exotic jewels. "What on the rim of the Circle is that?"

"Don't know yet," he answered, rising. "There's something inside the second thing. Let's get back home and find out."

***

AFTER some solicitous care by their friends, Renegade, K'leura and little Rebel came around nicely. The Hunters are a tough breed: the only disadvantage these three sustained from their adventure was that both Rebel's parents would be out of action for building or hunting for a few days.

Renegade had a remedy for that, too. He and K'leura would use one of the Scout ships to search this part of the continent, checking for game, and discovering what their land had to offer. The little clan had saved most of their catch from the sea. It would be some time before they needed to hunt again.

"That's for the short-throw. For the long one, we need to contact the new space station," Renegade said, "and not only tell them about your find, Rampage, but also make sure we get those weather and survey satellites *now,* not in the indefinite future."

"Yes, leader," his friend said quite respectfully and without a trace of sarcasm, astounding him once again, until he begged him not to do it, and saw Rampage's eyes twinkle.

"Yes, *Elder,* then," he grinned, making Renegade laugh. Yet he'd meant it. And Dasryl was acting the same way.

What did you expect, an empty title, Great Warrior? he told himself. His feat of diving into a rough sea had been no more difficult than fighting the bone-beast single-handed, and K'leura deserved the credit for saving his life at the end. Well, he'd have to badger them out of this unwanted honor somehow.

They all speculated over Rampage's discovery. Both objects appeared to be very fragile, the skull's bone completely replaced by crystallization. The heavily-encrusted packet contained a manuscript of some kind, preserved by its vacuum-sealed envelope. They hesitated to open it, and instead sent a message to Advent Station asking for special transport to send it on for study.

Rampage theorized that the skull belonged to one of the two races that had exterminated each other on the Dead World, many lifetimes ago. The others were inclined to agree with him.

"This one creature escaped somehow," Rampage guessed; "and fled to this world, to that cave, as he was dying, carrying the record of what happened with him; and the wrapping and the cave helped preserve it."

"Decipher whatever's in there, and we may find out what happened to the Dead World, and why there are life-gaps on many of the planets here," Renegade agreed.

The station's research team showed up eleven days later to place satellites over the Twin Worlds and to take the sea-cave discoveries back for analysis. The new Hunt Council of Ten Systems was already providing input.

The little clan also dispatched long-overdue messages to Homeworld and the Dinosaur Planet to let their friends and families know they had arrived, and claimed their world.

Thirty-five....The Great Hall

BY THE TIME fall arrived and dry leaves did their goblin dance along the ground, the Great Hall was finished, at least the first two levels and part of the third: the main hearthroom on the ground floor, the food storage coolers below, and several living suites above. A huge bathing chamber lay below-ground. The clean-running furnaces were operating; and the freezer was stocked.

They parked the Hunt ship in the lee of the mountains at their back door, while the two Scouts and the power sleds went into a large landing bay gouged into the mountain at ground level.

The three families walked their new home together on moving-in day. Hand in hand the couples toured the finished rooms. The Great Hall would be unique in having no separate trophy hall (largely because the builders' time had run out) but those trophies would adorn many other parts of their mountain home.

The furniture, made of solid heavy wood and fat stuffed cushions, stood on fur-spread floors to keep them warm in winter; while their trophies and the tapestries from He-walks-lightly hung on the hearthroom walls.

"It all looks so comfortable and well-aged, as if it's been here for a thousand years," K'leura marveled.

"Yes, and could stand for a thousand more," Renegade said. "Look at those two..." Smalltusk and Rebel were rolling round on the big white Sloth-bear fur in room center, playing. Smalltusk was fascinated by the baby, and never hurt him. In a few years they would become fast friends.

"I have to say, Renegade," Dasrylion remarked, coming up beside him with Sunrise, "It looks better than I ever thought it would, for such a scratch-job."

"A nice safe place for babies to be born," K'orrynia smiled, linking her arm with Rampage's. He smiled back at her.

"For your little girl, Dasryl, Sunrise," Renegade said, mentioning the newest member in-utero, "And for your pair, from the Golden Plains," whimsically re-titling Rampage and his bride.

"All Renegade Clan now," the Plains warrior said, serene at last. "And Starseeker sends that he'll be here next spring, bringing a few fellow-settlers with him."

"*One* of whom, High Mountain Song, sounds very feminine indeed," K'leura smiled.

"In truth," Renegade said happily. "And our little clan will prosper and grow."

He walked with her to a window and they looked out in silence on a world darkening for winter, the autumn trees like torch-fires in the dusk, and he thought: *A warrior must always walk the One Path, but sometimes that path takes him to vistas of beauty, and vales of peace.*

They had come through everything together; and together, they could face anything that came.

He was content.

EPILOGUE.....

....And PROLOGUE

SIX YEARS LATER---The boy wandered in from the rear of the mesa-top training hall. He and his fellow students had been dropped on a strange world, in the wrong place, nearly run down by a stampede of one-horned grass eaters *ridden* by *children;* then picked up by a Shadow Clan warrior and his Tracker wife, sledded across the countryside for about 200 *kri-veh*, dropped off *again,* and told that the Hunt school was on top of this huge mesa. No way up but to climb, the warrior said, and left them.

It must be some kind of test, Ever Asking told himself – although the warrior had had a twinkle in his eye when he said it…

Now here they were, or here *he* was, any-route, since he he'd lost his lone friend from P'taal 5 and the other students to admiring the trophies mounted outside the hall, (did they take them in, in bad weather?) especially a full-size display of dragons, four of them posed in mid-flight. He knew that each of the original warriors and the one huntress who explored this world had killed a dragon, and here they stood on display at the school. The Great Warrior's dragon had been taken last, he heard.

But Ever Asking had come a long way to see someone. And he must find him here, before anything. So he could learn the truth.

He continued on past the outdoor trophies, past the low-slung profile of the training hall itself, toward the front and the wide open space before it.

There, in the arena beyond the hall, he found the one he sought.

Four *tautschen* were training there: One pair consisted of a big dark gray warrior with startling red mane, and the jet-skinned, silver-splashed warrior with the golden mane who'd brought them to the mesa. (So he'd just flown up after all!) These two, red hair and golden, moved round each other cautiously, feinting and testing.

But the *other* pair! Ever Asking stopped to watch, his heart in his throat. For these, one medium brown with a long grey hair-tail, the other gold-and-grey, rose in the air like birds in flight. They exchanged an eyeblink series of kicks and blows, spun around and came down facing each other. Then it was step, kick, pivot, engage, and withdraw – another blink. They stopped and smiled at each other, with a chinlift like a mutual salute.

"Well-thrown!" the brown one cried.

Then the gold-and-grey warrior sensed a presence. He turned and saw the youngster watching.

And Ever Asking saw the black stripe partway down his chest, and the round black spots to either side, and his throat tightened up….

His father, his birth father, whom his schoolmates had never believed was his sire, but *he* always had, moved toward him with an easy natural grace and an expression of wonder.

He was much taller than Ever Asking, on-course, though not as tall as the brown one or as massive as the gray Tracker they called Dasrylion. But his every movement spoke of the ineffable prowess gained on the Warrior's Way. At that moment, Ever Asking knew that every legend surrounding him was true.

Renegade stopped before his firstborn son. The boy looked as if he might weep, or laugh. Could this fine ten-year-old be little Blackstripe whom he'd held in his arms, not quite seven years ago? "Son?" came the deep and gentle voice, and his hands outspread.

"...Father?" whispered Ever Asking. He forgot protocol and practice and embraced the Great Warrior as if he had known him all his life; and his father returned the embrace, hugged him long and hard.

The other students, trailing over from the display area, came upon them and stopped in shock.

"So you've come to me at last!" Renegade exclaimed, and held the boy before him, to look at. "And to finish your Hunt training, too. All this distance!"

"Yes, sir, with a friend. I – wanted to – I mean I…needed to see…" the boy fumbled. *To know if you were real, and my father.*

His father exchanged knowing looks with Rampage, his practice opponent, who had come up beside him. "I'm happy you did, son. This is my good friend and First Warrior Rampage, master of the martial arts."

The boy bowed his head. "I am honored, Esteemed First Warrior."

"Good manners for someone so young," Rampage commented; "better than ours were, if I recall."

Ever Asking looked up to see them both smiling.

"Are you still called Blackstripe?" from Renegade now.

The boy's face and chest heated. "No, Great Warrior I – someone renamed me Ever Asking..." – *an impatient teacher, angered by his eternal questions. It was a joke among the others.*

A penetrating stare from Renegade went deep into his soul.

"I see," the great warrior said finally. He laid a hand on the boy's shoulder and proclaimed loud enough for everyone to hear: "Your name is now TRUTHSEEKER, for only one who questions will find a new pathway to the truth."

The boy's eyes lit up. Rampage knew that look. Truthseeker would follow his father through the gates of Doom, and beyond. *As won't we all.*

Renegade looked over the new students, seven in all, two from P'taal 5, one from Taschen 3, the rest from the local systems. The little group had already attracted the attention of other Renegade Clan members: K'leura and Sunrise looked up from throwing the latest batch of Ball of Knives spears; K'orrynia and High Mountain Song approached along with Dasrylion and Starseeker. Even the toddlers bobbled nearer.

They all wanted to meet the new arrivals, Rampage knew. And Starseeker had said that messages came with them: from High Sun of Dinosaur Clan, wanting to reseed the Ten Systems world of T'saine 2 with dinosaurs and the growing numbers of his own clan. And there was word that Nine Systems had sponsored a new Galactic Expedition of five starships, which would plunge straight for the heart of the galaxy itself, to add to the 81 worlds the Hunting People had already colonized with something extra….they would search for other intelligent life; and perhaps discover why so many such species died out – or were helped to do so.

Bad Chance we didn't get to go, Rampage mused; *what a Hunt that will be!* Still, he and his friends were young as the People reckoned time. They had nearly 300 years left to live. Plenty of time to plan your next century…

He halted his thoughts, for Renegade had reduced the students to silence and utter stillness, and now he would speak:

"Come, young hunters!" the leader thundered; "let us go forth and test your mettle on the field." Looks of disbelief, yet not a word uttered – Renegade was being impressive, making sure he had their absolute attention. Rampage kept his face straight as the great warrior turned and began to lead them away. They followed meekly.

At the second stride, Renegade halted, and said without turning around, "Leave your weapons; you will not need them. For once you grow to depend on a weapon, you will never be able to think without one again;" and he resumed the march. Weapons clattered to ground.

But not before Renegade cast a sparkling eye back at Rampage, just as he was turning again, and winked at him over the students' heads.

Rampage almost spoiled the moment with a guffaw, but managed to pivot away and stare out over the canyon just in time. When he recovered, he passed the wink on to Dasrylion and the others, knowing what the students were in for, and how it would go…

For the Circle comes round again, he thought, *and bears us all with it, from what we have been, to where we would go...*

Printed in the United States
56036LVS00003B/55-60

9 781425 917845